THE SILK FACTORY

Judith Allnatt is the acclaimed author of *A Mile of River*, a Radio
Five Live Book of the Month, *The Poet's Wife* and *The Moon
Field*. Her novels have been shortlisted for the Portico Prize for
Literature and the East Midlands Book Award. Her short stories
have featured in the Bridport Prize Anthology, the Commonwealth
Short Story Awards and on BBC Radio 4. She lives with her
family in rural Northamptonshire.

www.judithallnatt.co.uk
 @judithallnatt

THE
SILK FACTORY

JUDITH ALLNATT

THE BOROUGH PRESS

The Borough Press
An imprint of HarperCollins*Publishers*
1 London Bridge Street
London, SE1 9GF

www.harpercollins.co.uk

Published by HarperCollins*Publishers* 2015
1

A catalogue record for this book
is available from the British Library

ISBN: 978-0-00-752299-6

Set in Minion by Palimpsest Book Production Limited,
Falkirk, Stirlingshire

Printed and bound in Great Britain by
Clays Ltd, St Ives plc

MIX
Paper from
responsible sources
FSC™ C007454

For Spencer, with love and appreciation

ONE

It was on their first day at the house that Rosie saw the stranger child. Standing at the sink, her hands deep in suds, Rosie was gazing vaguely at the sunlit, overgrown garden where Sam and Cara were playing. The sash window had old glass that blunted the image, wavering the straightness of fence and washing line, bending the uprights of trees and clothes prop, pulling things out of shape. Sam was kneeling beside the patch of earth that Rosie had cleared for him, making hills and valleys for his matchbox cars and trucks by digging with an old tablespoon, and Cara was toddling from bush to bush with a yellow plastic watering can. Through the antique glass, Rosie watched them stretch and shrink as they moved, as if she were looking through ripples. She closed her eyes, glad of a moment of calm after the trauma of the last few days. Letting go of the plate she was holding, she spread her tense fingers, allowing the warmth of the water to soothe her. When she opened her eyes, another child was there.

A little girl was sitting back on her heels beside a clump of Michaelmas daisies that grew against the fence. She had her back to Rosie and was holding tight to the handle of a large wicker basket that stood on the ground beside her. Cara seemed unfazed by the girl's presence and continued to move, engrossed, along the row of plants. Rosie bent forward to look through the clearest of the panes and peered closer. The child was small, maybe around eight or nine, although something in the tense hunch of her shoulders made her seem older. Her hair hung down her back in a matte, dusty-looking plait and she was wearing dressing-up clothes: an ankle-length dress and pinafore in washed-out greys and tans, like a home-made Cinderella costume.

Where on earth had she come from? She must be a neighbour's child but how had she got in? The wooden fences that separated the gardens between each of the houses in the terrace were high – surely too high for a child to climb.

Rosie had made a cursory check of the unfamiliar garden before letting the children go out to play. The bottom half of the garden was an overgrown mess, a muddle of trees and shrubs. An ancient mulberry tree stood at the centre, its massive twisted branches hanging almost to the ground and its trunk swathed in ivy. Like the lilac and buddleia around it, the tree was snarled with briars and bindweed growing up through broken bricks and chunks of cement. The path that led down towards the fence at the bottom, which marked the garden off from an orchard beyond, disappeared into a mass of nettles and brambles before it reached the padlocked door.

2

The child glanced over her shoulder, back towards the houses, a quick, furtive movement as if she were scanning the upper windows of the row, afraid of being overlooked. Rosie caught a glimpse of her face, pale and drawn with anxiety, before the girl turned back and reached forward to quickly tuck a piece of trailing white cloth into the basket. Almost unconsciously, Rosie registered that the girl was left-handed like herself, and that there was something animal-like in her movements: quick, like the darting of a mouse or the flit of a sparrow, some small dun creature that moves fast to blend into the background. Something wasn't right here. She had seen distress in those eyes.

She turned away, dried her hands hurriedly and slipped on her flip-flops. She would go gently, raise no challenge about her being in their garden but say hello and try to find out what was the matter. Maybe if she pointed out that her mother would be worrying where she was, she could persuade the girl to let her take her home.

But when she stepped outside, the child was gone. Sam and Cara were playing, just as before, but there was no sign of the girl. Sam had appropriated Cara's watering can and was pouring water into a large hole, while Cara squatted beside him watching. They were both safe and showed no interest, at least for the moment, in following the girl, wherever she had gone. Rosie ran her eyes along the overgrown borders once more, looking for any evidence of an exit route: a path beaten through the long clumps of couch grass, or branches of shrubs bent or broken where she had crawled through, but all seemed exactly as it had been. Well, there must be a gap somewhere, Rosie thought, maybe a gap that the children in the row used as a shortcut to get the run of all the gardens. There had to be some thin path through the overgrown tangle at the far end that she had overlooked or loose slats behind one of the border shrubs that spilt unruly on to the tussocky lawn: dark masses of euphorbia, standard roses rambling and tangling, and lavender grown leggy off old wood.

'Who was that girl who came to play?' she asked Sam.

Sam was engrossed in scraping earth from the sides of the hole down into it and chopping at the sludgy mixture with his spoon. 'What girl?' he said without lifting his head.

'The girl . . . who was over there near Cara.' Rosie gestured towards the clump of daisies. 'Didn't she speak to you?'

'No,' Sam said, frowning as he dug.

'No she didn't speak to you or no you didn't see her?'

'No girl,' Sam said emphatically.

Rosie sat back on her heels and watched her son as he dug and mixed, his face set into a bullish expression that suggested she would get no further. Before the events of the last few months he had always been a sociable child, keen to play with other children, and cooperative, chatty even. Now she often found herself uncertain, unable to get through to him as he lost himself in solitary games, or refused to do what he was told or even to answer her. He swung between periods of clingy dependency and periods of blank withdrawal. It was no surprise to Rosie that he either could not or would not tell her about the girl. His little, ordinary world had been jarred and jumbled, caught up in the hurricane of grown-ups' problems. She sighed and scrambled to her feet.

'It's no good asking you, is it, Cara-mara?' she said, patting her on the head. Cara looked up at her with a beaming smile, holding two fistfuls of mud towards her. 'Lovely,' Rosie said. 'Do *not* put it in your mouth, munchkin; we'll get you washed up in a minute.' She set off around the garden to find the gap in the fence that she must have missed on her first brief exploration.

She examined the fence behind the borders first, parting the branches of shrubs and peering through thickets of roses that had turned to brambles. No holes. She worked her way around the huge mulberry tree to the bottom of the garden, trampling a path as far as she could through the nettles and poking the clothes prop through the yards of undergrowth to test the strength of the fence, slat by slat. She could only conclude that it was all intact. The wooden door in the right-hand corner was solid and the padlock sound. There were no holes where the wood had rotted through, no planks that had come loose, no sections or corners with gaps left in between. No way in.

Returning to the clump of Michaelmas daisies, she stood sucking the back of her hand where a briar had caught her and left a scratch dotted with tiny beads of blood. She looked yet again at the fence behind it, stared at the knots in the wood and the runs in the creosote, dropped her eyes to the patch of grass where the child had been, as if she expected her footprints still to be stamped upon the green. She stared blankly at plantains and buttercups in the turf.

There was a squeal of rage from Sam as Cara, finally losing interest in the fascinating squidginess of mud, moved on hands and knees through the hills and valleys of Sam's carefully constructed raceways. Rosie scooped Cara up and moved her to a safe distance before Sam could take a swipe at her. 'She didn't mean to,' she said firmly to Sam who was staring angrily at the disarray of his carefully placed cars and diggers.

'You two mudlarks are going to need a good wash before you come in,' Rosie went on, taking in the state of Sam's shorts and knees and Cara's plastic pinny. Cara had returned to gathering up handfuls of mud and was gazing with a rapt expression as she clenched her chubby fists to see it squeeze out between her fingers. Rosie filled a bucket with water from

5

the outside tap and knelt down on the grass beside them. Her long hair had come loose from its butterfly clip; fine silky strands had escaped and she tutted in irritation.

She plunged Cara's arms up to the elbows in the clean water and began to rub. 'It's TV time anyway,' she said desperately, 'and if you get washed quickly and change those shorts you can have Jammie Dodgers while you watch it.'

As Rosie resumed the washing up, she gazed out once again at the garden, trying to recapture her earlier momentary calm. It eluded her and she found herself thinking instead of how her mother had loved gardening and how it must have pained her to see the garden, which Aunt May had once cared for so beautifully, going to ruin, overgrowth softening the shapes and blurring the structure.

When May had become too confused to cope, six months ago, Mum had arranged for her to move into a nearby retirement home and had taken over the house, giving up her rented cottage in Somerset and moving up to Northamptonshire so that she could be near enough to visit May every day. She had divided her time between May and Rosie, travelling up and down the motorway each week to see Rosie in London, to help with the children for a couple of days and give her moral support through the aftermath of her messy divorce. It had been too much for her, Rosie thought with a pang. She'd suggested many times that she should bring the children here, to save her mother the travelling, but her mum had always put her off, saying that it was easier for her to come to them than to drag the children and all their paraphernalia on a long trip.

Rosie gazed out at the bushes against the fence, bent over by the bindweed clogging stems and branches. She had a vague memory of a letter of her mother's that mentioned the garden was getting beyond her and that she might have to get in some help. Rosie felt the familiar stab of guilt. She should have seen the signs, should have known that her mother had been saying indirectly that she was unwell long before her visit to them in London when things had gone so terribly and suddenly wrong . . . Rosie's mind swerved from the memory of that night: waking to hear strange moans and strangled noises from the spare room, finding her mother slumped on the floor beside the bed, the sound of her own voice – *Mum! Mum!* She shut it out quickly as she had trained herself to do, a door in her mind closed and bolted, a curtain drawn down in an instant: thick as velvet, muffling.

As she forced her mind back to the garden, a treacherous image came before her of her mum pruning roses at the cottage in a battered straw trilby and a baggy summer dress, her hands too big in gardening gloves. Blinking fiercely, she picked up a handful of cutlery and dumped it into the water. This is no good, she said to herself, no good at all, as she scrubbed with unnecessary vigour. Give in to this and the floodgates would open.

She clattered the forks and spoons into the container on the draining board and turned away from the sink, groping for the kitchen roll. Pressing it to her eyes she stood very still to gather herself together. What was it she had been about to do? Ah yes, she had promised the kids Jammie Dodgers.

She leant against the kitchen table; she would get calm first; she couldn't risk Sam noticing again. 'Mummy, your eyes look funny,' he'd said when he'd walked in on her in the bathroom yesterday, and she had told him that it was because she'd been taking off her make-up with stingy stuff. She had sat on the toilet seat and gathered him on to her lap, leaning her cheek on the top of his head. His face in the mirror had her delicate features and colouring, the same hazel eyes and serious expression. His hair was fine and silky like hers although his was blond and curled at the ends and hers, long, brown with fair lights and poker-straight, always seemed to be escaping whatever bands or clips she pinned it up with. She had hugged him tight, breathing in the scent of warm boy and clean washing. He had wriggled and said, 'You're squeezing!' and she had loosened her arms, suddenly realising the ferocity of her hug. 'Sorry,' she'd said and tried a laugh. 'I don't know my own strength!' aware as she said it of the irony of the well-worn phrase when she felt anything but strong.

Rosie stuffed the muddy clothes into the washing machine as the sound of another cartoon's signature tune started up in the living room. As she glanced around at the pile of drying up still left to do and the crumbs and smears of yoghurt on the table, she felt the familiar drain of energy that came over her so easily these days: the feeling that the smallest task, that she would once have done without even thinking, had suddenly grown mountainous. And there was all the mess outside to clear away . . . She leant against the sink, staring blankly through the wavery glass at the bucket full of muddy water, the muddle of toys spread across the lawn and the place where the little girl had been. It was strange that neither of the children had even seemed to notice she was there, and even stranger that it seemed she had simply disappeared. Could she have dreamt her? Was it possible? She had closed her eyes for a moment . . . She was bone tired after the long drive up here from London the evening before, overwrought by coming here, amongst her mother's things, where every object was a reminder of her loss, overwhelmed by the tasks that lay ahead of her with not a soul here to give her some support.

Not that Josh had been much of a support in London anyway,

she thought bitterly. He had even let her down over the funeral. He'd promised to come and back her up, help look after the children, pay his last respects. She'd felt relieved, grateful even, that despite their break-up she'd have him standing solidly beside her, shoulder to shoulder when it still mattered. He hadn't turned up.

She thought about the service she'd arranged at her local church in Streatham, the small number of mourners that she'd been able to muster, her mum having been taken ill so far from her own home. There had been no point trying to fetch Aunt May, she was too confused to have coped. There were a few old school friends of Mum's who lived in the capital, and a cousin or two. Their voices sounded thin and quavery as they sang, disappearing into the vaulted space: 'Abide with Me' and 'Guide Me, O Thou Great Redeemer,' favourites of Mum's that she would have called 'good rousing numbers' floating up to be lost in the immensity of pillars and rafters.

Her friend, Corinne, the French assistant at the school where Rosie had once taught art, took the kids for the day. Corinne's offer was a huge practical help but it meant that Rosie had no one with her at the funeral to whom she felt close. She stood, holding on to the pew in front as if it were the only thing keeping her upright; unable to control her voice enough to sing. She read the hymn numbers on the wooden board over and over to keep herself from breaking down.

At the burial, she gave up the fight and wept, and one of the coffin-bearers passed her a handkerchief and squeezed her shoulder. Afterwards, she gave everyone a meal at a local hotel and then went back to Corinne's and they drank potfuls of tea together.

At length, Corinne asked, 'How are things financially? Will you be able to keep up the bit of supply work you were doing?'

Rosie looked weary. 'Difficult without Mum there to hold the fort.'

'Can you afford a childminder?'

Rosie shook her head. 'Too pricey. Anyway, I don't want a stranger. Sam's a bit stirred up by it all; he can be difficult sometimes.' She frowned. 'I'll just have to pull in my horns.' Rosie's settlement had included the flat when she and Josh split but she had soon found that she couldn't manage the mortgage payments on her own and had been forced to make a quick sale. The buyer's surveyor had found dry rot and pushed her right down on price so that she'd made hardly anything on it. She'd had to move to a cheaper area and now rented a flat in Streatham: a tiny place on the second floor above a coffee shop and the landlord's first-floor flat. The noise of the high street and the lack of a garden meant it was a lot cheaper but she still found herself struggling by the end of each month.

Corinne, as always, took her side. 'I don't suppose bloody Josh could up the maintenance to help out?'

Rosie snorted. 'I could be dressing the kids in the curtains like a regular family von Trapp before he'd even notice.'

Corinne gave her a hug. 'Do you want to stay over tonight?'

'Better not. I'm trying to keep the kids in as much of a routine as I can. Anyway, it would only be putting off the evil hour.'

She had piled the kids into the car, driven home and carted Cara's buggy up two flights. As she turned the key in the door of the flat, she'd gritted her teeth and stepped into quiet emptiness, the children trailing behind her.

Rosie had sunk for a while, hiding away from the world. After moving flats, she gradually fell out of touch with her other friends and colleagues apart from Corinne. She found herself unable to work up enough interest to reply to emails full of staffroom gossip that she no longer felt part of, and felt that they would have no interest in her everyday round of childcare. She couldn't seem to muster any energy and did no more than the bare essentials at the flat. Her doctor prescribed anti-depressants. They made her feel muzzy; they gave her dizzy spells and sometimes blurred her vision or resulted in vicious headaches that left her drowsy and washed out the day after. But when she went back for her review he had shrugged these off as common minor side effects, telling her that it would take a few weeks before she started to feel better and impressing upon her that she was not to come off them without consultation.

She took the children to the park, as her mum used to on her regular visits to help out, pushed swings and spun roundabouts, her arms going through the motions, her mind blank. Corinne came over once a week after work and they ate takeaway and drank a bottle of wine together. Rosie gave vent to her feelings about Josh and Tania – Tania of the impeccably tailored suits and impossibly slim waist, Josh's one-time colleague, one-time mistress and now full-time partner. Corinne told her the latest on her complicated relationship with Luc, who she hoped would come and join her in England but who seemed wedded to Paris and his job. Corinne brought things from the outside world: books and games for the children, stories and laughter, but when she left it felt even lonelier than before.

Sometimes Rosie cried at night, quietly, so that the children wouldn't hear. She visited the cemetery and replaced flowers that had dried brittle-brown in the heat. Standing at the foot of the grave she tried to tell her mother how much she missed her. It was no good; her mother wasn't there.

*

Rosie passed her hands over her face and roused herself. She would make a cup of tea and then go and cuddle up with the children on the sofa. She felt the need of their soft, warm bodies against her. As she ran the water into the kettle, she looked once more at the garden through the old small-paned window. She thought again about the stranger child, still bewildered about how she could have got in. A breeze had risen and was stirring the leaves of the shrubs and the heads of the Michaelmas daisies. She peered at the shapes, blurring and clearing in the old glass.

Daisies . . . Her mind flew back to another garden, another time, when she was a child: her mother sunbathing on a tartan rug; she, Rosie, sitting on a rusty swing, legs dangling. She remembered muttering under her breath while she was stringing daisy chains: one for her, one for her mother and one for her imaginary friend. For a year or two Rosie had taken her imaginary friend everywhere, summoning her to life as an only child's talisman against isolation, picturing her sharing her meals, walking beside her to school, playing hopscotch with her and listening when she read aloud.

Rosie had thought that her mother was asleep but she suddenly opened her eyes and asked her who she was talking to.

'Only Arabella,' Rosie said without thinking, engrossed in splitting a thin green stalk and threading another one through.

'Who's Arabella?' Her mother propped herself up on one elbow, her attention now keenly focused on Rosie, making her stop threading and drop her hands into her lap.

'She's just a girl I talk to sometimes.'

'People will think you're strange if you go round talking to someone who isn't real, Rosie. If you want someone to talk to, why don't I phone one of the girls from your class and invite them round to tea?'

'They'll be at the park. They like playing outside,' Rosie said sulkily. She had been trying for ages to get her mother to let her join in with the other children but it was always 'too near teatime' or 'too late' or 'too rough'.

Her mother wouldn't be drawn.

'I'd rather play with Arabella anyway. She's just like me – the same age and everything,' she said petulantly.

Her mother sat right up and stared at her and something in her look made Rosie feel uncomfortable.

'What does she look like?'

'I told you, she's exactly like me,' Rosie said.

Her mother's face became red and angry. 'That's rude and you shouldn't make up such stories.' She got to her feet and stood over Rosie. 'Don't you know that it's wicked to tell lies?'

Rosie, alarmed by the sudden change in her mother's mood, hadn't known what to say and had shrugged and looked sullen.

'Go indoors,' her mother had said. 'Go and do your home-work.'

Rosie had slipped off the swing, and trailed indoors leaving the daisy chains to wilt and shrink where they had fallen on the scuffed earth.

Remembering the conversation, Rosie felt the familiar tug of regret that she had often found it difficult to understand her mother, who had suffered strange moods and unpredictable changes in temper so that they had often been at cross purposes.

From a very early age, long before the conversation at the swing, she had been a secretive child, her mother's tension making her careful, afraid of setting off her touchiness. If she ever broke anything she would try to hide it rather than tell her mother. The first hazy memory she had of this was when she had broken a garden ornament. She must have been around three years old. She had been playing alone in a garden while the grown-ups talked indoors and she'd found, peeping out from a lavender bush, a china hare, modelled with its ears laid flat against its back, looking up as if to the moon. Attracted by the smoothness of the sandy biscuit ware she had put her chubby hands around its body and lifted it up. Underneath, something dark was moving, a mass of woodlice disturbed and scattering, some breaking off from the heap and moving towards her feet . . . She dropped the china hare on to the hard slabs of the path and its head broke clean from its body and rolled, chipping eye and ear, to the side of the path. Aghast at what she'd done and terrified of the creepy crawlies, she had stuffed the ornament into the bushes, pulling the leaves around it. It made her sad now to think that this guilty concealment was her earliest memory.

Over the years, whenever she had an accident she'd kept it from her mother: a cracked glass pushed to the back of a cupboard, a book with a broken spine wedged back into the shelf, even cuts and grazes from biking disasters hidden under jeans rather than have Mum 'make a fuss' as her father used to put it. She had never doubted her mother's love for her but had been wary about expressing her own, afraid of risking too much openness in the face of responses that were sometimes prickly, sometimes baffling. Now that it was too late she wished that she had been braver and talked it out with her. Now she would never know what lay at the root of it. And she would never be able to take that risk and say the loving words she should have said.

The kettle boiled and she poured the water into a mug. She stood at the window, stirring the teabag round and round, lost in thought. She saw with sudden clarity what a lonely child she had been. She had been blessed with a vivid imagination and had responded as imaginative children do by drawing on her own resources, creating Arabella, the companion that she longed for. She wondered fleetingly whether the awfulness of the last year: the final break-up with Josh, and then losing her mum, had triggered some weird throwback response. Maybe she had simply dreamt up the girl in the garden, experienced some strange vision brought on by the displacement of being in a strange place, by grief for the loss of a parent, by being so truly alone.

TWO

A month after her mother's death, Rosie had made a huge effort and taken a day trip from London to Northampton to visit her mother's solicitor. She had been baffled to learn that she'd inherited the house. 'But it's Aunt May's house!' she'd said to Mr Marriott as he passed a copy of the will across an acre of pale ash desk.

'Well, no. Actually it belonged to your mother and father but they allowed Miss Webster – May – to have occupancy while she had need of it. Of course, now she's accommodated elsewhere.' A slim young man with a pair of black-framed reading glasses on the end of his nose, he looked at her over them with a lugubrious expression that was at odds with his good looks and which she felt sure he affected in order to appear older and wiser than his years.

'I see,' Rosie said, looking at him in blank bewilderment. She settled Cara more comfortably on her lap, who turned sleepily in against her chest and began to suck her thumb.

'Now that your mother has passed away – your father having predeceased her – the property at Weedon Bec passes to you,' he explained again. 'I take it you know the area fairly well?'

Rosie shook her head. 'We never visited. Aunt May occasionally came to us but not often. I remember May and my father used to argue about it. May was always trying to persuade them to come but Dad wouldn't hear of it. I never knew why.'

Mr Marriott nodded sagely, as if nothing about the peculiarities of families could possibly surprise him. 'I understand that your father's work as a conservator at Highcross House meant that the family had a property provided whilst he was living?'

Rosie nodded.

'But your mother had been living at the Weedon address recently, I believe?'

'Yes. After Dad died, Mum rented a cottage in Somerset, but when May got ill and went into the home she wanted to be able to visit regularly so it made sense to move into the house up here.' Rosie hesitated. 'It was more than that though,' she added thoughtfully. 'She told me that she wanted to go back to her roots, that it was the village that her family came from and she didn't . . .' She felt a catch in her throat and paused for a moment. 'She said she didn't want to end up in some anonymous sheltered housing,' she said, all in a rush. 'She said she was going home to her native place.'

Mr Marriott pressed his fingertips together and looked down at them to give her a moment to recover herself.

Rosie took a deep breath. From the secretary's office behind her she could hear Sam asking for another piece of paper for

17

his drawing. She was relieved that he was behaving himself. 'I still can't really take it in,' she said. 'How long have they owned the house?'

Mr Marriott handed across a piece of thick, folded paper. 'These are the title deeds. The house has been in the family since 1930. It was your grandparents' house and apparently they moved there from another house a few streets away that was owned by your great-grandfather so it appears that your mother did indeed have roots there. Her family seems to have lived in the village for several generations.'

Rosie took the wad of paper in her hand. The house was hers! She would be able to sell it and get some financial security for herself and the children at last. She would probably need to do some work on it; Mum had told her that May hadn't had anything done to the place for years. It would take time but if she did it up she would get a better price – and some independence from Josh; that would be priceless. She was sick of chasing him for maintenance money and she hated asking for his help. She stopped. What about Aunt May? It had been her home. Mum had said that May was never coming back, that she would never be able to live independently again, but what about all her things, a lifetime of possessions? She couldn't just clear the house and throw them out. And her mother's things, what was she to do with them? She wouldn't be able to bear to part with them but there was barely room in her flat for the children's toys as it was. She slowed her racing mind right down; she would have to go through everything and maybe store the things that were May's, and Mum's special things. She wouldn't rush. She would do what her father had always told her: take time; take stock.

The solicitor was leaning forward towards her. 'I was saying that there might be other assets, savings or bonds, but also maybe liabilities of your mother's that need attention. I would suggest that you go through your mother's finances to establish the extent of the estate and then we can progress things further.'

'Yes, yes, thank you,' Rosie said.

'And of course you'll take on the power of attorney that your mother had over your aunt's financial affairs. Not much to do there except make sure that the care home gets paid on time.' He passed her an envelope. 'The costs are defrayed from Miss Webster's savings – all the details are there.'

He rose, shook Rosie's hand and walked with her into the secretary's office where Sam was covering a length of computer printout with pictures of aliens and explosions. As if his professional persona evaporated at the threshold of his office, Mr Marriott's whole demeanour changed. He retrieved Cara's buggy for her, unfolded it and clicked on the brake. 'I know all about these; they tip up if you put too many bags on the back,' he said conversationally. He opened the door and helped Rosie lift it down the steps. 'Safe journey; see you soon.'

The house was the middle one of five, in a tall redbrick terrace that wholly overshadowed the dainty Victorian cottages on the other side of the quiet street. Built on three storeys, each floor had a row of casement windows framed by brick arches giving the building as a whole the look of an institution, which was further borne out by a large date stone above Rosie's door that read '1771'. Rosie wondered what the original use of the property had been. There was something austere about its external aspect although the number of windows and the high ceilings inside meant that the rooms were full of light.

The whole village was unusual, Rosie thought. She'd felt it from the moment she'd arrived. It had been late in the evening when she'd turned off the main road on to a lane that squeezed under the narrow arch of first one old bridge then another, one carrying the railway line and the other the canal. Ahead of her, as the road bent left to descend into the village, was the most monumental brick wall she had ever seen, a block of deeper darkness against the greying sky. Stretching away uphill to the right, solid and as high as a house, broken only by a gatehouse and a huge set of iron gates, it reminded her of a prison wall and she had shivered as she rounded the bend and drew away towards the centre of the village. She passed a playing field, and drove carefully over the single-track bridge that crossed the infant River Nene and on past houses and chapel. Reaching the crossroads at the centre she found a pub, shops and the higgledy-piggledy roofline of houses built over centuries: rounded thatch, high angular gables, tall chimneys and finally the bulky height of the terrace of houses, lamps lit in the windows on either side of the central house, which stood dark and empty-eyed.

Leaving the children asleep in the car she had steeled herself and gone in, switched on the hall light, and found herself facing her mum's camel coat hanging on the coat stand, her bike leaning against the banister rail. She gave a little cry, stepped forward and gathered the coat up, burying her face in the rough wool and soft fur collar. *Mum! Mum!* She called for her in her mind, a child's call of distress; no message or thought beyond the expression of longing to draw her mother to her. She breathed in her mother's scent, clenching the fabric in her hands, then let it fall back to hang from the peg, smoothed down its folds and stepped away, standing for a moment with her head bowed. She let out a shuddering sigh and then propped the door wide open with the heavy Chinese jar used for umbrellas and began methodically unpacking the car, looking neither right nor left in case she should be hijacked by some other object redolent of her mother's scent or touch. She brought in food and stocked fridge and cupboards. Upstairs, she switched on only a bedside light. Ignoring the dimmer recesses of the room, she carried the children in, warm and heavy, and laid them in the double bed where they would all sleep.

Locking up the car, she looked back along the street to the pub with its lighted windows and babble of voices and music. She noticed its illuminated sign: 'The Plume of Feathers' and the image of a soldier's helmet stirred something in her mind. As she wearily climbed the stairs she dredged up a memory of her mother telling her, when she first moved in at May's, that the village had a military history. She hadn't really listened at the time; struggling with the aftermath of her break-up with Josh, she'd had no energy left to be interested in the outside world. What was it Mum had spoken of? The barracks and arsenal, that was it, a huge site that had once housed hundreds of soldiers, with a parade ground and a hospital and rows of vast buildings to house stores of cannon and rifles, gunpowder and shot. She took off her clothes and left them where they fell. As she got into bed beside the curled forms of the children and settled to sleep, she wondered whether the building in which she lay, with its uniform dormitory-like windows, had once been something to do with the soldiery.

On the day after seeing the strange child in the garden, their second day in the house, Rosie answered the door to find a woman holding a bunch of flowers. She had short, dyed-blond hair and a round face that was large but nonetheless attractive with a beautiful complexion and big, calm grey eyes. She was what her mother would have tactfully called 'well built' but she wore tight jeans that accentuated her

21

heavy hips, a black vest top that revealed an elaborate tattoo on her shoulder, and a chunky silver pendant that pulled the cotton material of her top tight over her breasts. The overall impression was of a woman who was happy with her size and wasn't about to hide it. Her clothes seemed to say, 'So, I'm big! Deal with it!'

She held the flowers out to Rosie, saying, 'For you. I heard about your mum; I'm so sorry.'

'Thank you.' Rosie took them: cornflowers, poppies and lavender held together by an elastic band. 'They're lovely.'

'I'm Tally – from next door. I saw you arrive the night before last but I thought you might want some time to settle in so I left it till now.'

'Come in, come in,' Rosie said. 'Come and have a coffee. It's really kind of you to bring me these.' She led the way through to the kitchen, filled one of the canalware jugs from the window-sill with water and arranged the flowers, their colours vibrant against the dark green enamelware, the red of the poppies picked up in the simple decoration.

Tally said, 'They look bonny. Your mum bought that jug down at Buckby Wharf.' She shot Rosie a sympathetic glance and took in her drawn look and the dark shadows under her eyes that her tan couldn't disguise.

Rosie said, 'My gran used to collect all that stuff – Roses and Castles – and Mum caught the bug and added to it. They're pretty, aren't they?' She put the flowers on the table, letting her hand rest for a moment on the handle of the jug where her mother's hand must have rested so many times, and then turned away to set a tray with coffee things. She led the way to the living room where Sam and Cara were eating chocolate biscuits and playing house in a tunnel-like den she'd constructed from a clothes horse and some sheets. They edged their way past

22

and sat either side of the fireplace, the grate filled with pine cones, lending the room a resinous scent.

'Tally . . . That's an unusual name,' Rosie said.

'Not as unusual as Tallulah. That's the trouble with having film-buff parents. I promise I'm not nearly as shocking as my namesake: no cocaine-snorting or cartwheeling sans under-wear.' Tally grinned, a wide smile that lit up her face and made Rosie feel instantly comfortable.

'And you have two children . . . two girls?' Rosie said, digging up the fragments that her mother had mentioned about May's neighbour: she was a nurse on ICU, worked part-time on nights, early thirties, kind, had done a lot for May . . .

Tally nodded. 'Nicky and Amy. Nine and six.'

Rosie thought of the child she'd seen. 'Does Nicky have long brown hair?'

'No, they're both redheads. They get it from Rob; he's a proper ginge. Why do you ask?'

'I saw a little girl . . . in the garden here. She had a long plait, right down her back and a kind of dressing-up outfit. When I went out she'd gone.'

Tally looked at her quickly. 'It doesn't sound like anyone from this street,' she said. 'It could be one of the kids from Dole Row; they're a bit wild, would maybe climb over from the orchard.'

Rosie picked up an uneasiness in her manner. 'Dole Row,' she repeated. 'Did Mum or May ever mention seeing any children?'

Tally hesitated. 'Well . . . May did, but then she was getting a bit muddled, you know. She used to swear that things had been stolen: her chequebook or her purse or her keys. She said there was a child who came into the house and took things but we could usually find them if we looked together or they would turn up eventually.'

23

Rosie stiffened. That morning she had been in the bedroom unpacking the remainder of her clothes when she heard feet on the stairs. It was quiet but for the click of the hangers as she moved them along the rail and she distinctly heard the slow creak of each tread, and a pause every few steps. She thought it was Sam playing a game; he was fond of creeping up on her and shouting 'Boo!' as he jumped out and she would pretend to be terrified and then swoop him up and tickle him. Preparing to feign horrified surprise, she hung the last skirt, went to the door and stepped out on to the landing. There was no one there. The sun from the window at the front of the house lay in bright lozenges on the sisal runner and motes of dust hung motionless and undisturbed in its shaft of light. Sam's voice drifted up to her from the living room, saying, 'No, Cara, don't do that!' She'd hurried down, shrugging the incident away as yet another oddity of her imagination.

Tally was still speaking: 'You know how it is with old people; they hide things in a safe place and forget where they put them . . .'

Rosie nodded absently, trying to remember whether the back door had been unlocked. Was it possible that the girl had come in – just walked in uninvited? Surely a child of that age would know not to do that, would understand about privacy. Perhaps she wasn't quite 'all there', as her mother would have put it. How weird! It made her feel uncomfortable, as though the peace of the house had been broken, her territory violated.

'Once she had a roll of money propping up the cooker,' Tally said. 'Tucked under one foot to keep it level – more than two hundred pounds!'

Rosie brought herself back to respond to her guest. 'Poor May,' she said, pouring coffee and then passing a mug to Tally.

'Mum told me you rang her when May couldn't cope any more but I never knew what actually happened.'

'She got very confused: getting up in the middle of the night and doing her hoovering, setting off for town and then forgetting how to get home again, that sort of thing. We used to take her round a dinner but she wouldn't eat it, said she could only manage tiny bits of soup. Then one day she turned the gas on and forgot to light it – bless her. Rob had to have the back door down to get in.'

Rosie was shocked. 'How awful! Mum never said!'

'Once she was in hospital they did an assessment and sent her into care. I reckoned that if I went through May's address book and rang everyone who was mentioned only by their Christian name I'd eventually hit a relative, and that's how I found your mum. Rob was well impressed with my detective work.' She grinned, that wide smile again. 'He's in the Force – Plod not CID but he's working on it.'

'I must visit her,' Rosie said. 'See how she is. That's another thing I really must . . .' She tailed off.

Tally saw how her face clouded at the prospect, as if she felt so battered by events that it was hard to summon the strength to meet one more challenge. She'd noticed the nervous habit that Rosie had of undoing the hairclip that held her long hair in a twist at the back of her head, coiling it around her hand and then clipping and reclipping it back in place – an obsessive movement, patting and tidying an imagined disarray, restoring order. Her heart went out to her. On an impulse she said, 'Look, why don't you go and see her this afternoon and bring the kids round to me? It'd be easier on your own. You might find the visit quite difficult; she might not even recognise you, you know. She didn't know me from Adam when I went.'

Rosie assumed that the offer was made through politeness

and thought that she shouldn't impose. 'Thank you, that's really kind of you but . . .'

Tally leant forward. 'No, really, it'd be no trouble. Mine'll be back at three. They're on a summer play scheme doing football or rounders or somesuch, down at the Jubilee Fields. They'd love someone new to play with when they get back.'

'Are you sure? Cara's only a toddler; she might spoil their games.'

'We'll do play-dough.' Tally smiled. 'No problem.' She finished her coffee. 'That's settled then. I'll see you at three.'

Rosie saw her to the door, Tally waving away her thanks. She felt her spirits lifting as she thought that Tally was someone that she might be able to confide in, someone who just might become a friend.

In the town, Rosie was ushered into Holly Court by a woman in a blue nurse's uniform who introduced herself as the senior carer, Julie Todd. As she led her through the sitting room where two elderly men were playing whist, she told her how May was doing. 'She has good days and bad days, mind. Sometimes she'll be quite chatty; others you can't get a peep out of her. We keep trying though; it's really important to get the patients to interact. Do visit whenever you can.'

At the door of the sunroom, she gestured to Rosie to wait. 'About your mum . . . May won't have any recollection that she's passed on. We find it best not to mention it; it's too upsetting for her – as if she's newly bereaved each time. I'm sorry to have to bring it up but I felt I should let you know.'

Rosie nodded. 'Doesn't she wonder where Mum is? Mum said she was visiting every day when she wasn't staying with me.'

'She asks sometimes. We just say she'll be along tomorrow and five minutes later she's forgotten all about it. I know it seems awful but it's a kindness really.' She peeped round the corner of the door. 'I'll just go and tell her she's got a visitor. We find it helps to give a little warning; it lets them orientate themselves.'

Nurse Todd went over to a group of chairs at the end of the room and Rosie held back in the doorway. The long, bright room had windows all along its length and French doors opening out on to the garden, which reminded Rosie of a park, with its neat edged lawns, formal beds and summer-house. The back wall was lined with groups of empty 'easy-rise' chairs interspersed with coffee tables and jardinières filled with spider plants or mother-in-law's tongue. Nearby, a lady with a paper on her knee, left open at a crossword puzzle, was dozing, her head bent down on to her chest.

Nurse Todd beckoned Rosie over and she approached her aunt with some trepidation, anxious not to say the wrong thing.

Nurse Todd said, in a loud, clear voice. 'Here she is, May, this is your niece, Rosie, come to see you.'

'Yes, yes, I know. You just told me!' May said peremptorily.

Rosie sat down nervously on the high seat opposite her without proffering the kiss she'd intended. May looked so changed! Her hair, which was once coloured a silver ash and softly waved, was now a steely grey and cut in a straight bob, parted severely on the side with a plain metal hair slide girlishly pinning it back out of her eyes. The coarse hair of her eyebrows had grown thick, giving her a fierce look. And where were the slacks and smart fitted jackets that Rosie remembered? Instead May wore a long droopy skirt and blouse and a chunky cardi that was miles too big across the shoulders. Her body seemed to sit inside her clothes, strangely separate from them, as if a creature had set up home in an abandoned shell. 'Hello, Aunty May,' she said. 'How are you?'

'Have you brought biscuits?' May leant forward and stared, her small, intent face and curled hands giving her a simian look. 'You usually bring biscuits,' she said accusingly.

'I haven't been to visit you here before, May. You haven't seen me for a long time; do you remember me? It's Rosie, your niece, Rosie.'

'So you say,' she said, looking her over. Then, as if she had found some familiarity in her face, she asked uncertainly, 'Not Helena?'

Rosie felt a lump in her throat at the mention of her mother's name and at her aunt's expectation of seeing her. She did as the nurse had told her. 'She couldn't come today,' she said gently, 'so I've come to visit you instead.'

May turned her face away and stared out of the window. Rosie followed her gaze. A middle-aged man wearing a lanyard with an identity tag was setting up a game of hoopla. Rosie wondered if he was some kind of therapist or maybe a volunteer. The residents who had been sitting on the veranda of the summerhouse roused themselves and an old lady in a floppy sunhat shuffled forward to make the first throw, her shoulders hunched with arthritis, her head pushed forward like a turtle. She threw awkwardly and stood looking after the hoop as it rolled past the post. May's eyes didn't follow its motion; she stared as if looking straight through the scene as the hoop wobbled and settled flat on the grass.

Rosie tried again. 'Do you remember coming to stay with me in London? I only had Sam then, he was just a toddler – your great-nephew? Well, I have a little girl too now, called Cara. I'll bring them to see you next time.'

May looked back at her and seemed to be listening so Rosie ploughed on. 'Do you remember when we went over to Kew Gardens and had a picnic? Helena and you, and Sam and Josh and I?'

May nodded, at first tentatively and then more vigorously. 'Hothouses,' she said. 'Flowering cacti. Pelargoniums. The child was cutting a tooth.'

Rosie was surprised; she had forgotten that herself. What she remembered was how distracted Josh had been, how he kept getting up from the picnic rug and striding away every time he got a call. She had been annoyed because he was supposed to be taking time off so that they could have a family day, and instead of helping her entertain their guests he was dealing with work queries every five minutes and champing at the bit to go home – to get back to his computer, Rosie had imagined. Now she wondered if he hadn't even then been keen to take the messages because they were from Tania; maybe they had even been seeing each other, arranging to meet, Josh estimating when he could get away . . . Was it possible? Tears came into her eyes. 'That's right,' she said weakly, 'Josh took us in the car.'

As though May read her mind, at the mention of Josh she leant forward and said, as if confiding a secret, 'Why you ever married him I don't know.' Then, looking around the room as if seeking an audience, she announced loudly, 'The man's an absolute arse!'

Rosie, tickled by May's colourful language, began to laugh.

'Arse! Arse! Arse!' May chanted. Rosie could do nothing to quieten her and laughed uncontrollably, finding a release. The lady dozing at the other end of the room stirred and blinked at them like a waking owl and then subsided back into sleep.

'Pain in the arse!' May ended triumphantly, slapping her knee. 'And that is my considered opinion. Where is my bag?' She cast about her and found it under her seat. 'Do you like Maltesers?' she asked, calm again.

Rosie, dabbing her eyes, said that she did.

May pulled a black leather handbag the size of a shopping

29

bag out from under the chair and up on to her knee. She rummaged inside and then lost patience and began to unpack its contents on to the coffee table beside her.

'What on earth have you got in there, May?' Rosie said as the clutter of objects grew: a seed catalogue, several framed photographs, a *Radio Times*, a thriller with a bookmark in the first page, a crude piece of sewing in colourful felts with a needle dangling from it, a tube of indigestion pills . . . Rosie picked up a toothbrush, covered in fluff. 'Why have you got your toothbrush in your bag?'

'I'm not staying,' May said. 'I'm going home soon.' She pulled out a box of Maltesers and offered it to her.

Rosie took one and then, seeing that May was struggling to pick one up, trying to capture it between her fingers and the base of her stiff thumb, picked out another and popped it into May's mouth. 'Isn't it heavy to carry around with you – your bag?'

May shook her head. 'There are thieves,' she said in a matter-of-fact tone. 'They come in your house. They send her to unlock the door and let them in. They hide behind doors and round the bend in the stairs.' She grew more agitated and began pulling things from her bag as if searching for something else.

'Who do they send?' Rosie said.

'The child. The bad child.'

'What child?' Rosie said uneasily, feeling a prickle at the back of her neck.

Suddenly May upended the bag, tipping the remainder of its contents out on to the table: a battered purse, half a packet of Jaffa Cakes and a TV remote control. She began sorting through them, her hands jerking as she searched. Alarmed by her growing agitation, Rosie said, 'What are you looking for, May? Can I help you find it?'

'Keys, keys! Got to find my keys. Must be here somewhere. I have to get back or she'll be getting in again, taking all my precious things. I have to hide them, lock them up!'

'No one can get in, May, I promise you,' Rosie said, thinking uncomfortably of the footsteps on the stairs. 'All of your things are safe; I'll take care of them.'

May looked at her disbelievingly. 'You can't watch them all the time . . . She comes in and out, just as she chooses . . .' She cast about for her keys amongst the objects on the table, knocking things to the floor.

Rosie laid her hand on her arm and quickly picked up one of the silver-framed photos to try to distract her. 'Where was this taken, May?' In front of a caravan with an old-fashioned, round-cornered shape, a family group sat at a camping table spread with the remains of a meal. Rosie's grandparents looked so young she almost didn't recognise them: her grandfather in an open-necked shirt and with a glass of beer in front of him, and her grandmother holding a cigarette. May and Helena sat either side of them, both blonde and clearly sisters; May about eighteen, in a flowered sundress, a spotted hairband holding back her thick, back-combed hair and Helena, ten years younger, still a child in shorts with a pudding-basin haircut and a big smile for the camera.

May stopped sifting through her belongings and took the picture from her. 'Let me see; let me see.' She passed her index finger over the glass as if the past was touchable. 'Durdle Door, 1958, Clifftops Holiday Park,' she rapped out. 'You could walk down to the beach from the cliff path. It was beautiful, clean fine sand and the most amazing rocks standing out in the sea. I can see it in front of me, a huge . . .' She moved her hands as if to describe a shape for which she'd lost the words. 'Bent . . . a hole . . .'

31

'An arch?'

'Yes, that's it. Not smooth, rough-cut, you know – by the waves. Helena and I went swimming every day, further along. We took a picnic. Helena got stung by a wasp by the bins and I put an ice cube on it to stop her crying . . .' She tailed off.

Rosie, amazed by this sudden flood of memory, tried to encourage her to say more. She had heard that dementia patients could often summon up detailed memories of the distant past even though they couldn't remember what they'd had for breakfast that very morning. 'Who took the photo?'

May's face softened. 'He was the campsite owner's son. He was called Stephen. We wrote for a while . . . then the next year Mum and Dad wanted a change and we went to Filey, then Scarborough the year after that.' She put the photograph back on to the heap face down and turned to gaze out into the garden, her eyes sad, thoughts far away.

Rosie took it and wrapped it in the piece of sewing saying, 'It'll save it from scratches.' She imagined the holiday romance, walks along windy cliffs, stolen kisses at the door of the little caravan. How sad that they hadn't gone back. She wondered how many other loves May had had and still regretted losing. She had thrown herself into her civil service career working in the Highways Department. Articulate and practical, she had risen in a man's world. She had never married. Rosie carefully pinned the needle and thread into the fabric so that it wouldn't get loose in the bag and prick May's finger in her rummaging through her belongings. Like Sleeping Beauty, she thought, her brain making a strange connection to thorny thickets of briar enveloping a pinnacled castle where a girl lay dreaming of love; time stopped for her at sweet sixteen. She reached across and took her aunt's hand.

May looked at her as if she was surfacing from a great depth, struggling to comprehend, 'Helena?' she said at last and Rosie, too exhausted to start all over again, just squeezed her hand.

Nurse Todd came in and seeing their joined hands, nodded and smiled as if this was a very satisfactory outcome for a first visit. 'Shall we put your things away safely in your bag, May?' she said but May was once again lost in thought. Nurse Todd started to pack away the mound of objects. Noticing the TV remote she exclaimed, 'Ah! We've been looking everywhere for that!' and surreptitiously slipped it into the pocket of her uniform. 'This happens all the time,' she said to Rosie. 'May likes to watch *Doctors* but some of the men are very vocal about watching the sport.'

Rosie smiled at her aunt's ingenuity despite male vociferousness.

Nurse Todd said cheerily, 'We'll have to keep it under lock and key. They all do it; sometimes it's like hunt the thimble in here.' She put the tidied bag back under May's chair.

'Can I come and have a word?' Rosie asked before explaining to May that she had to go. She kissed her lightly on the cheek; it felt dry, so soft and loose, compared to the feel of hundreds of bedtime kisses on Sam or Cara's plump cheeks, like a peach that's gone over; her smell was a mixture of sweet and musty. As she bent over her, May lifted her hand and touched Rosie's scarf, a filmy material with a William Morris pattern in cream and pale blue.

'Nice,' May murmured.

Rosie unwound the scarf and softly draped it around May's shoulders. May fingered the edge of the fabric, looking down at its lustrous folds against the dull, bobbly cardigan. She looked up at Rosie with eyes as open and delighted as a child's.

'It suits you,' Rosie said. 'I'll come and see you again soon.'

She followed Nurse Todd from the room and asked about

May's health. The nurse gave a recap: sometimes she became very confused and recognised no one, and she was often distressed when she woke at night. She was in better shape physically: arthritis, but still able to walk independently, her sight still good enough with reading glasses for her to attempt a little sewing although she had to use a darning needle and grew frustrated at the size and ungainly shape of her stitches.

Thinking of her pleasure over the scarf, Rosie said, 'Should I bring in some clothes? She used to be so particular about how she looked.'

Nurse Todd flushed a little. 'There are a lot of spillages. It's better if they're in things that you can get them in and out of easily.'

'I'll have a look what there is left at home,' Rosie said mildly. She hadn't meant to sound critical but felt quite determined on the point. The May she knew would be mortified to be dressed in clothes from some communal clothes store that fitted her like a sack. She smiled, 'I'll pick out things without lots of buttons.' She thanked the nurse and shook her hand at the door saying that she would be back in a few days and asking if it was OK to bring the children.

'Of course. It brightens everyone up to have young faces around,' she said.

As Rosie drove home she reflected that the visit had answered her question: May clearly needed care; she was certainly not going to be able to come back to the house. At least the home seemed sound and the staff competent and well intentioned; that was a relief. She would visit as often as she could while they were here, she decided, and, once she was back in London, when Josh had the children for a weekend, she'd try to get up to see May and make sure she had everything she needed. Still, she thought how sad it was for May to have reached the last few years of her life and to be so alone. However kind the nurses were she was still cared for by strangers. It struck a chord with her own loneliness, now that both Josh and Mum were gone. I have two children, she told herself. I still have someone to love, that's all that matters, but a child-like voice at the back of her mind was saying, But now there's no one to love and care for you, is there? Just like May.

Later that evening, when the kids had been collected from next door, bathed and tucked up – Sam now in the spare room next to hers with his toy cars ranged along the windowsill in a nose-to-tail traffic jam and Cara in a collapsible lobster-pot cot at the foot of her bed – Rosie gave Corinne a call.

'Hello, you, how's it going in the wilds of the North?' Corinne said. 'Everything good?'

'Pretty much. The kids are fine. My neighbour's nice. I've been to see May too; she's a bit of a character . . .'

'And? Something's bothering you.'

'Well, it's silly really, but this odd child turned up and it's freaking me out. She was in the garden and then by the time I went out there she'd gone and I couldn't work out how she got in.'

'How old was she?'

'I don't know, maybe eight, nine?'

'Not likely to mean any harm then; maybe she's just curious about who's moved in? Wants to see if there's anyone new to play with.'

'Maybe . . . but today I think she came into the house.'

'How do you mean, you think she did? You didn't see her then?'

'No, just heard footsteps on the stairs, at least I think there were.'

35

There was a pause. 'You probably imagined it. Old houses are always full of funny noises, and you're bound to be all on edge in a new place and with the trial of sorting your mum's stuff out ahead of you. It probably makes you a bit . . . well . . . jumpy. You know how you can get when you're overwrought.'

'I suppose. But May reckons she comes in the house and steals things.'

'Yeah, all the things she finds later under the bed or down the side of the sofa.' Corinne giggled. 'Come on, you're not going to let yourself get spooked by the wanderings of a batty aunt?'

'No – no, I'm fine.' Rosie let it go. Corinne had a point; May was in the home exactly because of such irrational imaginings. 'How about you?'

'Well, I've just heard that the school isn't renewing my contract this year.'

'Oh no! Why not? They can't do that two weeks before the start of term, surely?'

'To be honest, I thought this might happen. They've been wanting to make cuts in the department for ages. Actually, I'm not that bothered.'

'How do you mean? What's going on?'

There was a pause in which Rosie sensed a suppressed excitement. 'I wasn't going to tell anyone until I'd told my parents, but what the hell, they aren't to know if I tell you.'

'What? Tell me!'

'Luc asked me to marry him.'

Rosie let out a squeal. 'Corinne! That's wonderful! I'm so happy for you. When? How?'

'I went over at the weekend and we had one of those deep conversations. We're both hating being apart . . . and he'd been scouting around for a job for me. He'd made a contact who works in an agency placing language teachers in foreign companies whose managers need to improve their business French . . .'

Rosie swallowed hard. 'So you're going back to Paris; he's not coming over here?'

'It makes more sense this way. His job pays more than mine; our families are there—' Corinne broke off. 'Oh God, I'm sorry, that was tactless.'

'No,' Rosie said firmly, although the thought of Streatham without Corinne was bleak. 'It'll be lovely for you to have family nearby. What kind of a friend wouldn't be glad for you? And I am – really.' She stopped herself from saying, 'When do you have to go?' She had no right to sound disappointed; after all, when she'd told Corinne she was upping sticks to Northamptonshire for a while, Corinne had understood that she had to do it and had never once moaned. She reframed the question and put a cheerfulness into her voice. 'How soon will you be able to go?'

'I've already started packing,' Corinne said sheepishly. 'Now we've decided, we just want to be together as soon as we can.'

'Right. Well, that's good then.' Rosie asked her about the wedding. It was to be in the spring and Rosie promised to keep the range of possible dates free in her diary. Corinne's happiness bubbled over as she told Rosie about her engagement ring and spoke of booking the church and of hotels and honeymoon plans.

'As soon as you've done what you have to at your mum's place, come out and visit us in France,' Corinne finished.

'It might take quite a while. As well as going through everything I'm going to have to redecorate at the very least.'

'Well, get on to it as fast as you can. I need you to help me choose a dress.'

They said their goodbyes and Rosie laid her phone down slowly on the kitchen table, her mind distracted. As part of her plans, she'd assumed Corinne would be there to go back to when she finished here. Streatham was her base now; she'd made a home there, however modest, for the kids, a place where there would be no more upset, where they felt secure. She had her contacts at the school and knew that when she came out the other side of all this and Sam had started school, she would probably be able to pick up some hours there again, maybe even get her old job back. In the long term, she planned to send the children to the primary that fed into her secondary school so that when they moved up she would be able to keep an eye on them. It was harder for kids with single parents, with only one person there to root for them, and she was going to make sure she was right there whenever they needed her.

She hadn't really realised how much she had been relying on Corinne. Now it felt as though yet another person was stepping off her map. When she returned to London, the small familiarity of their weekly get-togethers wouldn't be there to look forward to; she would be left in uncharted territory without a landmark to hold fast to. Her mouth felt dry as her anxiety rose. Feeling restless and nervous, she knew she would be unable to sit still.

She set out to make a list of the jobs that needed doing in the house. With notebook and pen in hand, she went from room to room, trying to view each one through the eyes of a prospective buyer. The living room needed decorating but was otherwise in good shape; it looked inviting as the evening dimmed, a lamp glowing through an amber shade on the bureau beside the window, a Persian rug on the oak floor, squashy sofas with cream cotton covers, books lining the chimney alcoves. The kitchen needed reorganising to make room for a dishwasher and the veneer on the cupboards was split and peeling. She would just replace the doors, she decided. She couldn't afford to have the whole thing refitted. The cost of doing the place up was going to have to come out of their everyday budget as her savings had dwindled to almost zero. She would manage on a shoestring and do it all herself.

There were a few marks on the wall in the hallway, where her mum's bike still stood and one of her mum's favourite porcelain plates decorated with butterflies and peonies hung on the wall. The paintwork of skirting boards, banisters and spindles needed redoing. She paused at the door under the stairs that must lead down to the cellar. She'd noticed the tiny windows at ground level at the back of the house and at the front the bricked-up chute at street level that must have once been used for the delivery of logs or coal. She undid the bolt at the top of the rough plank door and laid her hand on the brass doorknob, but something indefinable made her hesitate. A cold draught seeped from under the door, chilling her bare ankles and her feet in their flip-flops.

A sudden noise made her start. Faintly, as if from behind the closed door, came a high-pitched sound, a long keening cry, like a distant lament. Tentatively, she put her ear to the door and listened, straining to hear. It ceased as suddenly as it had begun. A faint smell of soot was borne on the stale air that leached through the joints of the boards of the door but now there was no more than the tiny whistling sound made by the draught as it passed through. She waited, shivering in the draught, but the sound didn't come again. She thought of what Corinne had said, and told herself that what she had heard was just the house creaking as the heat left the day and its timbers cooled and contracted. Surely that was it; Mum's cottage had made sounds as it settled, cracking noises and long sighs as the wooden joists and beams relaxed. She dropped her hand from the doorknob; it would be better to look at the cellar in daylight. Some light would shine through the tiny windows at the back. She would give the panes a wash first: they were streaked with the green dust of algae; yes, that was what she'd do.

Her nerves still jangled, she hurried upstairs to look in on Sam and Cara. They were fine, both sound asleep: Sam on top of a rumpled nest of duvet; Cara, who had been grizzly in the heat, cooler now, stripped down to vest and nappy. She lay flat as a starfish, on her back, her arms stretched out above her head, her knees fallen apart, utterly abandoned to sleep. Rosie watched her for a few moments feeling the vulnerability of her sleeping child, the overwhelming desire to protect her. Cara's eyes moved beneath their closed lids – dreaming.

Rosie carried on and jotted down more household notes: there were water stains on the ceiling here, and the electric switches on this floor were an ancient brown Bakelite suggesting that the house had been only partially rewired.

She'd been so busy settling the children in, food shopping and visiting May, that she'd not got round to exploring the top floor of the house, which was reached by a spiral staircase from the landing. She climbed the stairs, her feet clanging on the black iron treads, and found, instead of another corridor with doors leading from it, that she was in a large room with a high ceiling, lit from both sides by pairs of uncurtained windows, filling the space with dusky evening light. As in the other rooms, the floor was made of wide oak floorboards, but here, completely bare and unadorned by rugs, their huge breadth and thickness was more apparent. Rosie wondered at their solidity and the substantial joists that must underpin them. The wood had the patina of age and across the middle of the room was a shiny path, as if many feet had once passed to and fro. There were black marks left by old nails and fixings on the boards beneath the windows and, in front of the marks, shallow hollows buffed to a fine shine, like a dip in a stone step worn by myriad feet. Rosie remembered her initial impression that the building might have been some kind of barracks, but if so, what was the need for the reinforced floor or the many windows, which would surely have been an unnecessary expense? The room was more like a section of a workshop that had run the length of the building; perhaps heavy machines of some kind had been fixed to the sturdy floor and bright light had been needed for the work: light far brighter than people had been used to for ordinary living.

Whatever the reason, the room had a spare and simple beauty. The walls were painted plain white and were hung with the quilts that her mother used to make. Some were made up of intricate patterns of hexagons, plain and floral, spotted and striped, forming a rich mass of colours; some used appliqué to form pictures: a winter wood embroidered with silver thread; a bed of hollyhocks and foxgloves with jewelled bees. They used to hang in the lounge and hallway of her mum's old home, partly obscured by open doors or the clutter of coats. Here, given white space around them and room to breathe, they glowed like fine paintings, each one a bold statement.

Under the windows that looked out over the garden stood a long dressmaker's table and a tailor's dummy that must belong to May. Both sisters had been keen on sewing but May had preferred a practical end in view and had taken up tailoring. Her mother's magnifying-glass stand and an angle-poise lamp stood on the table now, and in the set of open shelves that ran the length of one wall, piles of neatly folded quilting squares lay alongside May's bolts of cloth and sewing baskets.

Rosie walked slowly to the bench. Spread beneath the lamp was a square piece of pale blue cotton, quilted with billowing clouds on which tiny winged dumper trucks and diggers laboured, their trailers and buckets full of puffy whiteness. The words 'Sam's Castles in the Air' were embroidered along the bottom, the needle still pinned to the fabric at the foot of the letter 'r'. Beside the piece were Mum's spare reading glasses, their arms open as if she had just put them aside for a moment to go to the door or answer the phone. Rosie touched the soft fabric as if she could send a message to her mother through her fingertips. She picked up the glasses and very slowly folded the arms before laying them gently back down.

Her head began to ache with the effort of refusing in to weeping. She put the heels of her hands over her eyes and held them there for a minute, willing the headache not to develop into one of the full-blown migraines that had afflicted her off and on ever since she'd started the tablets from the doctor. It didn't work. When she took her hands away the dull throb behind her eyes was still there and she knew that if she turned on the lamp she would recoil and the pain would flower into a tight clamp around her forehead.

She stood in the darkening room looking out of the window, the row of gardens spread below her in the fading light: swings and a sandpit in Tally's garden; a bower with a seat in the garden on the other side, its pale green paint light against dark foliage; patio furniture and rows of vegetables in others. Most had some kind of fruit trees; two others had the ancient remains of old mulberry trees, like her own.

From amongst plum and apple, mulberry and damson trees

came the repetitive call of pigeons settling to roost. The far end of her garden was in shadow, the bent shape of the buddleia and the big mulberry tree casting deeper pools of shade. Rosie stiffened. A small figure was squatting under the mulberry tree amongst the rubble and briars, her face and bare arms white in the dimness. Her hands were moving quickly amongst the weeds as if she were searching for something, her arms plunged deep into nettles and brambles. Rosie gasped. Her head pounding, she reached across the table to open the window and call out to stop her. The girl was scrabbling desperately, as if trying to recover some precious treasure, oblivious to stings and cuts. Rosie tried the long metal bar of the catch; it wouldn't come undone. She pushed against it; the window was locked.

The girl stopped suddenly, and looked over to her left, as if she had heard something. Keeping her head down as if afraid she would be seen, she glanced from side to side, as though checking her escape route, unsure whether to make a dash for it. Like a sparrow in fear of a hawk, she froze and cocked her head to listen. Quickly she rummaged again; then, startled once more, she half stood, clutching the cloth of her apron, twisting it between her hands, as if in an agony of uncertainty whether to stay or flee.

Rosie felt a strange dizziness coming over her, as if she were being drawn towards the child, the kind of vertiginous pull exerted by a mill pond or a drowned quarry – deep dark water that pulled you in. Unable to tear her eyes away from the white oval of the child's face looking up at her, she felt about her for the key on the windowsill and her hand met its cold shape. She groped for the window catch, her hand trembling. She fumbled with the catch, dropping her eyes to see how to get it undone, and in the moment that she looked away the spell

43

was lifted. She gave a little cry and stepped back into the room, dropping the bar as if it were hot.

Outside, a blackbird flew low across the lawn uttering its chattering alarm call and then the garden was silent. Silent and utterly empty.

THREE

1812

'You're late,' the silk master said to Tobias and Beulah Fiddement as they hurried in, their faces white and pinched by the cold, the girl stumbling with tiredness. From behind the wide expanse of his mahogany desk, strewn with scales, measuring rod, oil lamp and lustrous samples of cloth, he turned and pointed to the wooden clock that hung on the wall above his head. Its dial was the size of a cartwheel and it read three minutes to six. 'I won't tolerate tardiness,' he continued. 'I myself have been abroad since cockcrow and everyone else is in their place.'

He leant back in his seat and surveyed them, tucking his thumbs into the pockets of his waistcoat, which strained over his corpulent middle. Despite the illusion of gentility lent by a brocade waistcoat and a well-cut coat, he had the weather-beaten appearance of a seafaring man and was thickset and square. A bushy set of mutton-chop whiskers made shift to compensate for a lack of hair atop but ever failed to draw Beulah's eyes from the signs of old wounds on his bald head: a strange indentation on one side and a series of thick white scars that exerted a horrified fascination upon her and led her to stare in spite of the dangers of doing so. She moved up close to her brother.

'Well?' the master said to Tobias. 'Cat got your tongue?'

Tobias slipped Beulah's hand into his. Making his voice as deep as he could, he said, 'Begging your pardon, Mr Fowler, sir. We're not early but we're not late neither. The clock still lacks three minutes before the hour.'

Fowler turned round to look again with exaggerated slowness. 'So it does, young Fiddement, so it does. But perhaps you could tell me why you're cutting it so fine, to use a saying of our trade? Why you're playing fast and loose, as it were, with my time when you know the penalty for lateness is a five-penny fine?'

Tobias thought of the long dark tramp from the neighbouring village of Newnham, through fields frozen into stiff clods beneath the snow and along cart tracks slippery with ice, Beulah shaking with the cold, his own teeth chattering, and of carrying Beulah pick-a-back once they reached the road into the village, so that he could, at last, run the final stretch. He said tentatively, 'We were held up by the weather, sir.'

'By the weather, you say? Surely just a little dusting of snow?' He leant forward, his elbows on the desk. 'Eh? Eh?'

'I'm sorry, sir. We both are . . . sorry.' He gave Beulah a nudge. She nodded and then hung her head. *Five pennies*, she was thinking; five pennies was most of his wage. Five pennies was potatoes and broth and coals. Five pennies gone was an empty belly and a cold hearth.

The master leant back with his palms on the desk as if considering the matter. The cherrywood handle of the whip that he always carried at his belt was revealed as his coat fell back and Beulah looked away quickly. A smile played at the corners of his mouth. Beulah didn't like the smile. Over the busy noise of the looms above, the clock ticked with a hollow, wooden sound that seemed to reverberate from every wall of the office.

'It won't happen again, sir,' Tobias said.

The long hand of the clock gave a jerk and achieved the vertical of six o'clock with a loud tock.

'You're quite right, Fiddement,' the master said, fixing him with a keen eye. 'It won't happen again and pleasant though it is to be passing the time of day with you, we all have work to get on with. As you can see, it is six o'clock, you are not in your places and your wage will be docked by five pennies.'

Tobias's face blanched and his fists clenched, squeezing Beulah's hand until it hurt but he held his tongue.

'But we weren't late! You kept us talking!' Beulah blurted out.

Fowler's gaze swivelled to fall on Beulah. His fist came down on the desk with a thump that rattled the brass pan of the scales. 'Wha-a-t!' he roared.

Then Tobias was yanking her arm, pulling her stumbling to the stairs as Fowler leapt to his feet and, finding the first thing to hand, grabbed up a handful of brass weights and flung them after them with a curse. One found its mark and hit Beulah's forearm so that she cried out; the rest thudded into the door-frame and on to the boards, thumping and rolling. Tobias pushed her before him up the steep, boxed stairs and they took

47

the tight turn on the first-floor landing at breakneck speed. They ran on up the second flight and emerged, gasping for breath, into the clattering racket and floating dust of the top-floor workshop, where the black squares of the windows reflected a line of small moons from the glass globes full of water concentrating the light of tallow lamps on to the work. Jervis, the master weaver who was training Tobias, glanced over and gave them a quick nod of acknowledgement but everyone else bent their heads assiduously over their work, sensing something was afoot and wanting no part of it.

Tobias looked back over his shoulder to see if Fowler was coming or if his anger was spent. 'Quick, we could lose our positions!' he hissed to Beulah. 'Get in your place in case he comes.' He gave her a little shove and then took his place beside Jervis's loom, taking over from another lad as drawboy, to raise the warp threads that made the pattern.

Nursing her arm, Beulah blinked back tears and threaded her way between the ranks of wooden looms on either side, their foursquare frames closely packed together, each reaching almost to the ceiling with their hundreds of threads and lingoes hanging close and thick as a curtain. Battens thumping, shuttles flying, each weaver on his bench was in constant motion, a dark shape against the yarn like a busy spider suspended in its web.

The children's overseer, Alice, scowled at her: the weavers must on no account be left without yarn to work with and Beulah was already behindhand. Beulah took her place with the other children at the bobbin winders. Each child must fill and refill their tray with wound bobbins, the conical pirns that fitted into the weavers' shuttles, and each must be perfect, without snarl or hitch. Beulah fixed her spool, held the thread lightly with one hand and began to turn the handle of the wooden wheel. Barely as tall as the wheel, she hauled on the stiff handle, her arm throbbing with every revolution. She worked as fast as she could, trying to wind the thread not too tight and not too loose so that it would run smoothly and evenly off the shuttle without causing the weaver delay, but she couldn't get her usual speed up. The thread seemed to have a mind of its own, looping and snagging, and her tray filled all too slowly as her bruised arm began to stiffen and refused to be forced at the pace she needed.

Every now and then she glanced at Alice to see if she was coming to check the trays. She was ever ready with a shove or a slap for anyone who had fallen behind, though at least, unlike the master, she kept an open hand.

Beulah wished it was evening and she could be at home with Effie, who would give her supper, rub comfrey salve on her bruises and console her as Mother used to. Then she remembered the five pence docked from their wages and worried what Effie would say. She hoped she would be cross. Cross was better than sad; she couldn't bear it if Effie was sad. Effie never cried but sometimes, if Beulah woke in the night, from her bed by the warm ashes of the fire she would see Effie sitting up at the table with her head in her hands. Beulah did what she always did when the master had scared her; she puckered her brow, narrowed her eyes and concentrated on turning her fear into hatred: a deep seam of hate like coal in rock, dark, thick fuel on which she could draw.

Many tales were told about the master. Some said in his youth he had been an adventurer, and had sailed on a voyage to find the Northwest Passage, some that he was nothing but a Spitalfields mercer who had made his money from the labour of families in weaving garrets and had moved north after a brush with the law, leaving them to starve. Others said that he

49

had devised an instrument for discovering new mines and had made his fortune in the Americas. All that was known for sure was that ten years ago he had bought up a bundle of property in the village: a row of cottages, two inns – the Harp and the Bull – the silk manufactory and the High House at the end of the street, where he lived with his wife, Tabitha, and his daughter, Hebe. Beulah had caught sight of the same fear in their eyes that she was determined to check in her own. For all their full bellies, fine clothes and feathered bonnets, she wouldn't want to change places and live under their roof; no, not for one day. Fowler by name and foul-tempered by nature, she thought as she rested her arm for a moment before threading another spool.

In the workshop, muted conversation began again amongst the weavers and drawboys, adding a background hum to the clack of the looms. The room began to lose the worst of its clammy chill with the labour of its inmates, regaining its usual smell of sweat and human breath. The girl next to her, Biddy, said in a low voice, 'What did the master do?'

'Threw one of they weights at my head,' she said, 'but his aim was out of true.' She finished off the pirn she was filling and put it in her tray. She glanced round at Alice and saw her busy with her own winding. 'Do you want to see?' She pulled up her sleeve to reveal a swollen forearm already turning blue and they inspected it together.

'It's a bad 'un,' Biddy said. 'You'd best keep out of his way.'

Alice stood up, placed her palms in the small of her back and stretched. She began to check the trays, working her way along the row of children, picking out any pirns that were badly wound and giving the child the sharp side of her tongue. Jonas, a clumsy boy with big hands more suited to ploughing or building, had clearly spoiled several as Alice fetched him a stinging blow on the side of his head that left him snivelling.

50

Biddy glanced down at Beulah's half-empty tray. Quickly she picked up a few of the pirns from her own full tray and dumped them into Beulah's. She signed to Thomasin, the girl working on the other side of Beulah, to do the same. Thomasin hesitated, frowning, and then grudgingly passed a handful of spools over while Biddy made a great fuss of bending to set up another bobbin so that her body blocked Alice's line of sight.

All three girls were busily winding again by the time Alice reached them; they held their breath as she peered and poked into each tray with her quick eyes and her veiny hands. She hesitated at Beulah's as if puzzled by its contents when Beulah had clearly been struggling along at half-speed. She looked suspiciously at the three of them, her mouth set in a hard line. As she passed on to the rest of the row, Beulah mouthed her thanks to Biddy, who gave a tiny nod, and to Thomasin, who muttered, 'Never mind that. Bread at dinner is what you owe me.'

Jonas was sent round to collect the trays and deliver them to the weavers and the task of filling more began again.

Lieutenant Jack Stamford reined in his horse from a trot to a walk as they left the snow-covered fields and turned out on to a cart track, where ice showed dark and glassy in the ruts. The mare's breath steamed on the air as she snorted and side-stepped, dancing a little at the treacherous feeling of ice beneath her hooves. 'Shh, gently now, Maisie, gently.' He held her firm, leant forward and laid his hand on her neck until he brought her to a standstill, his red tunic bright above the chestnut's glossy flanks.

He looked around to get his bearings. Every morning he inspected the men at reveille at first light before riding out from the barracks to exercise Maisie, taking a different route

51

each time to put the young mare through her paces and school her to meet the unexpected with equanimity. Barking dogs, carts to squeeze past in narrow lanes, marshy ground that sucked at her fetlocks or streams with stones that shifted underfoot all triggered an instinct for flight from a nervous yearling, and patience, firmness and, above all, practice, were needed to build the reciprocity of trust that he required between horse and rider. They must be able to rely on each other completely. After all, she could one day carry him into battle.

Behind him lay the white, open fields through which he had followed the line of the river away from Weedon Royal and out to the west. To the left, the track curved away and narrowed, as though it was petering out; to the right a church tower was visible in the distance and Jack deduced that it belonged to the village of Newnham. He would ride that way and then on to the woods where he could attempt to cajole Maisie in amongst the trees and accustom her to the crack of wood underfoot and the sudden slide of snow from laden branches.

He took a deep breath of the biting air, feeling a sudden joy fill him that was born of the emptiness of the glittering scene, the creak of saddle leather and the feel of the reins, and the freedom to turn wherever he wished. He clicked his tongue to Maisie to walk on, encouraging her to a deliberate pace as she picked her way. Over the tops of the bare hedgerows, the fields spread in pristine white, save for the occasional deep tracks of fox or deer and the lighter patterns of bird prints.

He passed a fine farmhouse with dairy and grain loft, stable yard and carriage house, and a garden with a spreading cedar tree, and rode on past a field of sheep, a dun yellow against the snow. Beyond was a dense acreage of coppiced hazel trees, each nut tree with many thin trunks growing from the stump of last year's cutting to form a bushy growth of dark, damp wood, the branches outlined in snow. Black and white, the scene epitomised the depth of dead winter; the slow and secret sap was frozen and all colour and life had shrunk back to the roots to hide deep below the surface of the earth.

In the stillness, Jack suddenly caught a glimpse of movement, someone bending, moving silently beneath the trees. He drew Maisie to a standstill and watched.

A young woman. A young woman wrapped in a thin dress and a shawl the colour of a wood pigeon's breast. Stooping to gather something from the ground and place it in the shallow basket at her feet, she came out into the light as if born from the shadows. Intent on her task she drew towards him and he sat motionless, watching the soft contours of her body as she moved among the stark, stick-like trees. Looking more closely he saw that snowdrops grew in clumps around the trees, their green leaves choked with snow but their white and drooping heads pushing through. It was these that the girl was gathering, clearing away the snow with her hands to pick each stem delicately until she had a posy and then laying them in the basket and packing the stems with snow. As she drew nearer, the light caught her profile; her face was inclined to the ground, and the curve of her cheek and its delicate colour struck him, the flush of blood strangely moving, speaking to him of Life in the barren scene as strongly as did the snowdrops. He held his breath. Here was life in adverse circumstances, beauty in a wasteland. A gift.

Maisie's flanks quivered beneath him as she shivered. He had kept her standing too long. Automatically he moved her forward and her hooves struck on the track.

Effie looked up and saw a soldier passing, his red coat as bold as the haws in the hedgerows, his dark horse shiny as polish and everything bright as a vision. He looked back over his shoulder and their eyes met as he raised his hat to her. She gazed at him without smiling. Effie knew that men meant Trouble. Nonetheless, even though it was only half-full, she picked up her basket so that she could straighten up and watch his departing back as he clip-clopped on along the lane, smart as paint. As he passed the other women who were working at the far end of the nuttery, she saw him tip his hat to them and felt unaccountably disappointed.

She tutted at herself and bent back to her work. What a fool to let her eyes wander after a man, however handsome, she berated herself, and a soldier at that! Better to concentrate on filling her baskets; the carter would be here within the hour to collect them and then she must get back home to start work on Mrs Millington's washing. She set her mouth in a firm line and returned to her gathering. The rent was due and paying it would mean little left to tide them over until Tobias and Beulah brought their wages home at the end of the week. On top of that she would have to endure Hob Talbot's visit to collect his money, with his constant reminders that they had no right to the tied cottage since her father had passed away and were only living on his farm through his grace and favour. He would invite himself to her fireside and ask for a drop of ale and her 'good company', and watch her as she poured his drink, with the hungry look that made her flesh crawl.

She picked another handful of the tiny flowers. Her fingers were bare for the delicate work, her hands covered only by fingerless gloves that gave little protection. She placed the flowers in the basket, packed more of the stinging snow around to keep them fresh on their journey and then rubbed her palms together in an attempt to restore some life to stiff, numb hands. Despite the arduous work, bent double and aching with cold, Effie had not grown immune to the beauty of the flowers as had the other women, who talked in a businesslike way of 'cropping' and 'packing'. She still found the flowers beautiful and took pleasure in their perfect shape and the thin line of green that traced the edge of their petals. She observed them in all their moods, the way they fluttered in an icy breeze or hung, drooping, when it was still. She marvelled that something so frail could push through the frozen earth and the crust of snow and thought of them as dogged little flowers, each year achieving their reassuring miracle.

Jack rode on through the village and out past the water mill until he came to the woods. He turned off the main track and coaxed Maisie haltingly along a track bounded by the lumpy snow-covered shapes of brambles and dead bracken. A crow landed on a branch a few feet away, showering the path with snow, and Maisie whinnied and shied so that he had to throw himself forward over her neck to avoid hitting his head on a branch above him. Swearing, he gripped on tightly to avoid being thrown and reined her in firmly, turning her in tight circles to stop her bolting, as the crow, disturbed by the noise, flapped away again. Maisie snorted and shook her head. She planted all four hooves firmly on the ground and wouldn't give an inch.

Jack knew this mood of hers and sat tight, giving her time to calm herself. He let the reins go slack so that she could drop her head and investigate the fallen snow that had alarmed her. He patted her neck while she flicked her tail. The wood, muffled in snow, seemed silent at first but as he sat, relaxing in the saddle, small sounds reached him: a stream trickling with meltwater, a robin's high piping song, the sough of branches as a breeze passed through and was gone. He felt a restless happiness he couldn't name. Each sound fell upon his ear with an intense sweetness, as though his senses were suddenly attuned to a new pitch. The very branches cradling the snow seemed charged with light. Beside him, beads of water dripped from the ends of the twigs and it was as though he felt the slow gathering of every drop.

He walked Maisie on towards the sound of water, a strange excitement fizzing in his blood. The path narrowed and meandered until he rounded a tight bend and in front of him lay a stream with three mossy planks laid across it. Plates of ice floated on its surface and on the far bank stood a roe deer, a doe with her spindly legs planted and her head down to drink. Jack stopped Maisie. They were upwind and the creature took a moment to register their presence. It lifted its head, water dripping from its muzzle, its nose twitching as it searched for their scent, and looked straight at him with candid, liquid eyes. For a moment Jack felt the privilege of meeting face-to-face with a wild thing. Then, with a flurry of snow and a flash of its white rump, it was gone.

Jack let out his breath. The restless excitement that had been building in him crystallised. The image of the young woman came before him again; there had been something pure in the moment, almost holy. He had never seen anything so perfect. When she had looked up at him he had felt a shift, a change, a sense of communion. He must see her again. He must go now, while there was a chance that he might catch her before her work there was done.

The path here was too narrow to turn Maisie, the matted bracken making the undergrowth impenetrable on either side. With excruciating slowness he coaxed her over the mossy plank bridge and rewarded her with a piece of apple from his pocket as she reached the path once more, urging her along as best he could until they reached a path that turned left, back towards the edge of the wood. 'Walk on, walk on,' Jack muttered to her as they went, for what if the girl was gone? He knew nothing about her, not even her name. Would she be there if he came another day? The group of women could be itinerant labour, here today and gone tomorrow, disappearing as swiftly as the crop of flowers they picked. The thought that Lieutenant Jack Stamford should not be pursuing a girl who might be no better than a gypsy never entered his head; all he knew was that he must look upon her again.

Emerging at the edge of a field, Jack set his course by the church tower whose bells were now tolling the hour of ten o'clock. Maisie, relieved of the terrors of creaking branches and frozen puddles, was persuaded into a steady walk over the level pasture and Jack urged her on until they reached the lane through the village. He passed a cart rumbling slowly along, drawn by two bays in jingling harness, the carter hunched in a blanket with his hat jammed down over his ears against the cold.

Turning into the lane that ran down to the nuttery he slowed to a sedate pace, gathered the reins in one hand and sat back in the saddle to appear as one casually returning from a ride along a customary route. A gaggle of women, gossiping and laughing, came out of the entrance to the nuttery and turned away from him, down towards the farm. His eyes passed quickly over them: she was not among them. For a desperate moment he considered calling out to them to ask where he could find the girl in grey but he immediately dismissed the idea; at best they would think it odd, at worst he would appear ridiculous. He slowed his pace and looked around in case there was any other route she might have taken.

Ahead, in the gateway to the nuttery, a pile of flat, lidded baskets were now haphazardly stacked. He guessed that they awaited collection by the carter he had passed earlier on the road. As he approached, he saw the girl emerge carrying a last basket and he let out his breath. She reached up on tiptoe and placed it on the top of the stack, but the baskets, roughly stacked on uneven ground, were unstable and the pile teetered, overbalanced and, before she could grab it, fell in a crash and bounce of wickerwork, snow and flowers. She cried out in consternation.

Jack slid from Maisie's back. The girl stood surveying the muddled debris. 'Oh, they will all be bruised!' she said, as much to the air as to Jack, and, pulling a basket from the mess, she began picking over the flowers, discarding those that had been crushed and reassembling new posies from those that were still good.

'Come, let me help you.' Jack hooked Maisie's reins over the gatepost and then lifted a fallen basket that was still closed and intact and put it down to one side of the still teetering pile. 'Shall I set these straight first?' he asked her.

She nodded with tears of vexation in her eyes. 'I'm to wait for the carter. He'll be here directly; the blooms have to reach market before noon.'

'Don't worry; we'll soon set all to rights.' Jack took down some baskets and started to straighten those beneath so that they sat more firmly. 'Who buys all these snowdrops?' he asked, to draw her into further conversation, and then, more daringly, 'I dare say they're posies for sweethearts?'

Effie glanced up at him quickly, thinking him rather forward. 'Certainly not,' she said briskly. 'They go to the big houses and hotels in the town in time to grace their tea tables.' She closed the lid of the basket she'd tidied, even though it wasn't completely full. She would have to share the good flowers between the baskets and hope no one would notice that each basket was a little short. If the load were a whole basket light it would certainly be missed.

Jack took it from her, stacked it and then bent opposite her to help gather up the flowers. 'They're so delicate,' he said. He looked straight at her. 'Very pretty.'

Effie blushed and bent her head low. Her hands moved quickly and efficiently over the snowy ground. Jack saw that her fingerless gloves were sodden and her fingers red and chapped. He found himself wanting to cover them with his own and warm them; he hated seeing her hands so raw with cold. He imagined holding them between his palms, blowing warm breath upon them or kissing them back to life . . .

The sound of hooves and wheels turning into the lane reached them, and Effie worked even more quickly, tucking bunch after wet bunch into the last basket. The slow rumble grew louder and she closed the basket and pushed it towards him, saying, 'Quick! He's here!' She scooped up the remaining squashed flowers, broken stems, snow and all, into the lap of her dress and ran back into the nuttery to hide it behind the nearest tree, while Jack hefted the basket up on to the stack. He took Maisie's reins to steady her as the carter turned the other horses in through the gateway and drew them to a halt with a creaking of leather and a jingling of harness. 'Good morning to you,' Jack said.

'Where's Talbot's girl?' he said gruffly, looking Jack up and down with suspicion. Jack nodded towards her, his heart lifting as he recognised the name of one of the local farmers – not a gypsy then; she must be settled here, maybe living somewhere nearby.

The carter climbed stiffly down and began to load the cart. Effie joined him but when Jack stepped forward to help too, she shook her head behind the carter's back. When the load was on board she stood on the far side, as if to distance herself from him as much as possible. As the carter counted the baskets he looked curiously from one to the other and Effie seemed to shrink further from him, crossing her arms and tucking her hands inside her shawl as if she would fold herself away completely. At length, the carter wrote a receipt and handed it to her. She nodded, tucked it into the pocket of her dress and set off down the lane without a word to Jack.

Feeling foolish, Jack stood waiting as the carter drove further into the nuttery entrance to turn the cart and, with much muttering and cursing at the horses, finally drove away with a backward glance and a scowl in his direction. As soon as the carter looked away and touched the horses with the whip, Jack mounted, turned Maisie's head in the opposite direction and walked her along the track after the girl. He soon caught up with her and she looked round in some agitation.

'Thank you for your help, but you didn't ought to have stayed. People do talk so, you know,' she said. 'Not that I'm not thankful, I wouldn't want you to think that, but I'll bid you good morning . . .' She tailed off in confusion.

Jack said quickly, 'I shall see you safely home. Do you have far to go? Won't you ride?' He halted Maisie, slipped from the saddle and stood with one hand on the pommel ready to steady it as he handed her up.

Effie, still disturbed by the carter's meaningful looks, shook her head emphatically.

'Then I shan't ride either,' Jack said and proceeded alongside her, leading Maisie by the reins.

Effie could think of no answer, feeling rather overcome by all the attention from this young man. He confused her so – he was treating her like a lady. They walked along in step. After a little while, Jack said, 'It seems to me that after sharing such disaster, we should at least be properly introduced. I don't even know your name.'

'Effie . . . Effie Fiddement, sir.'

Effie. Jack turned the name around in his mind. 'Were you christened Effie or is it short for Euphemia?'

''Tis the short version, Euphemia being a bit of a mouthful,' Effie said.

'Jack Stamford, at your service. And this is Maisie who has a mind all of her own and has decided today that she likes neither birds nor bridges.'

'She's a fine horse,' Effie said tentatively and reached over to stroke her muzzle with her fingertips.

'Do you live hereabouts? With your family? Do you work for Hob Talbot?' Jack checked the questions that were forming thick and fast in his mind for he wanted to know all about her but felt that he must tread slowly and softly not to scare her away.

'I live on the farm, and take whatever work is offered on Mr Talbot's land,' Effie said simply, not giving too much away.

'And what do you do out of snowdrop season?'

'Oh, the snowdrops don't last long. Most of the time I have to take in washing but all us maids help outdoors at harvest and when the hazelnuts are ready too.'

'And you have a family?' Jack prompted.

'A younger brother and sister. Our mother passed away three years ago and our father followed soon after.' She looked away.

'I'm so sorry,' Jack said gently. 'It must be very hard for you.'

'We get by,' Effie said stoically. 'You aren't from these parts, are you?' she enquired in return, for his accent was strange to her and folk in these parts were generally reserved to the point of taciturnity, not like this open-faced young man.

'No, I'm from Bedfordshire, the third of five brothers and

the only one to join the military; the others are all clergy like my father. He has a living at Oakley, near Bedford.' As he spoke, a clear picture of the parlour at home came before him: his father's books and sermons filling the shelves that lined the walls, a good fire in the hearth and his parents conversing as his mother sewed and his father worked, with a delicate touch, at the model ships he made. Each one was completed with the masts lying flat so that they would slip through the neck of a bottle, to be raised again like magic, once inside, with tiny threads. On every ship's side was painted the name of a son and they were given as gifts as each one had reached their twelfth birthday, but kept on the mantel for all to enjoy.

He remembered how his brothers had all answered their father's playful question about what they would do if they owned such a ship by saying that they would send her overseas to bring back books, fishing rods, a violin. Only Jack had said he would sail her himself, of course, and see the world from the Americas to Marrakesh. His father had smiled and said he had a vivid imagination. Jack felt the sharp pang of homesickness that always accompanied such recollections. His elder brothers were both married now, with children of their own, and settled near his parents; part of a close family life of visits and tea parties, walks and picnics. Well, he had taken a different path in search of excitement and a more active life, and one couldn't have everything . . .

'You miss your family,' Effie said, seeing a wistful expression pass over his face.

'A little,' he admitted. 'But God knows, I have enough to keep me busy with fifty men to oversee.'

'You are from the barracks at Weedon Bec?'

Jack nodded. 'Though some call it Weedon Royal, since the garrison was built.'

''Tis a monstrous place, is it not? The walls seem to take in an area bigger than the village itself! And the place is quite overrun with soldiers, more than five hundred of 'em, I've heard – all filling the inns with drunkenness and brawling with the locals.'

Jack pulled a face. 'It's true it can be difficult to keep some unruly elements orderly when they're on furlough but I can assure you that on duty all is order and discipline.'

'Well, I dare say we are all glad enough of it keeping us safe from Old Boney,' Effie said as they reached a place where the track forked, the main thoroughfare continuing and a thin path splitting off from it. It was evidently little used, as weeds grew down the middle, dead and brown, sticking out of the snow like rusty wires. The path wound down to a wood where a cheerless chimney without a wisp of smoke could be glimpsed between the trees.

'Can I accompany you to your door?' Jack asked.

'No, no, don't trouble yourself,' Effie said hastily. 'I shall have to get back to work directly. Thank you once more for your assistance.' She bobbed a curtsey and set off down the overgrown track holding her skirts aside from the brambles that grew from the hedges, all clogged with snow.

'I hope we shall meet again,' Jack called boldly after her. 'I'm often out riding in these parts.'

Effie hurried on, telling herself that she must not smile, even though his obvious admiration warmed something in her heart, but as she reached the bend that would take her from his view she found herself turning, quite involuntarily, to look back. He raised a hand in farewell and she inclined her head before walking quickly away.

What foolishness is this? she thought to herself. A soldier – and a lieutenant to boot; he would be collecting girls' hearts like loose change in his pocket. She was not some silly maid to have her head turned by a red coat and a handsome face, she said to herself sternly. And yet . . . he had not seemed glib or practised in his compliments, and he had told her something about himself . . . She was glad that she had stopped him from coming down to the cottage; she would not have liked him to see where she lived. In a rush of confusion, she realised that if she were not at least a little impressed by him she wouldn't have cared about him seeing the place.

As Effie passed through the trees to the deserted clearing beyond, the cottage came into view, if cottage it could be called, and she came face-to-face with the evidence of the difference in their stations. Once two dwellings, the left-hand side of the building was now derelict. Their neighbours were long gone, forced out since the farmer was no longer obliged to provide board and lodging for his hands but merely to pay a wage and 'hang the consequences' if it proved insufficient to feed a family and still cover the rent. Since the enclosures, there was no longer common land left for grazing a beast of one's own or rights to gather firewood or take a rabbit for the pot. The low, thatched roof had fallen in, leaving spars of joists and beams showing like a chair frame through old upholstery. Beneath the patchy snow the reed thatch was grey and mildewed, streaked with vivid green moss and straggling weeds. Sagging and collapsed, the cottage seemed to have become something almost organic, more compost heap than building. Pigeons roosted in it, spattering the earthen floors with droppings. The door hung crookedly from its hinges and the window, with its missing panes, resembled a crossword puzzle with its blacked-out squares, through which small birds hopped and flitted at will.

Although the other side of the roof was still supported, it was worn through in places so that Effie had to place a series of jugs and bowls under the thin places to catch the rain. The one small window and low door were overshadowed by the deep eaves and let in little sunlight even in summer. Dark and damp, with rotting frames and one of the small panes plugged with sacking, the dwelling seemed, each year, to moulder a little further towards the state of its neighbour, which stood as a constant reminder of its likely fate.

Effie picked her way down the path to the door, past the wilderness that had once been next-door's garden on one side, and on the other, the remains of her own vegetable plot which was now visible only as lumpy rows of raised snow. At the side of the house a few hens pecked disconsolately at the ground where Tobias had cleared the path of snow so that the family could reach the well, the wooden privy and the fields beyond.

Once inside, Effie stripped off her wet gloves and set about riddling the cinders and ashes in the grate. It was almost as cold inside as out and her breath steamed before her. She set the ash pan aside and laid kindling in a pyramid, ready to be lit on her return, and then moved the clothes horse with its drapery of yesterday's damp washing close beside it.

As she spread the shifts and shirts out on the wooden rails, the carter's receipt rustled in her pocket and she wished that she need not deliver it to Hob. She shivered as she thought of the slow way he always took it from her hand, as if it were a billet-doux.

She crossed the ends of her shawl in front and tied them tightly behind her so that she might have both hands free. As she carried the ash pan to the pit outside she could feel just the slightest residual warmth from the grey cinders. She spread her aching fingers around the tin and thought again of the smiling soldier in his red coat.

FOUR

Fowler came out from behind his desk to welcome Hinchin, the parish clerk, and said in a rough hearty manner, 'Enoch!'

'Septimus.' Hinchin nodded a greeting. A tall stooping figure, dressed in black with a high white collar and a sober grey stock, Hinchin was in his forties with fine sandy hair and a face as long as a fiddle. His skin had the bluish tinge suggestive of poor circulation and an indoor life, and indeed he felt the cold badly.

The two men knew each other fairly well, through their attendance at church and at social functions in the village. Fowler extended his square, spade-like hand to enclose the limp white hand before him in a vice-like grip. 'Thank you for agreeing to my little tour; I have much to show you,' he said enthusiastically.

'If this is with regard to the purchase of parish land, Septimus, I can tell you now that there's none to be had. The military have their fingers in every pie . . .'

Fowler waved away his words. 'No, no, it's nothing like that. I need your help in a small matter, that is all – a minor representation to the parish vestry, just a word in the ear of your fellow councillors on my behalf.'

'I can make no promises.'

'I understand, I understand, but allow me to show you around and explain my plans at least. Indulge me.' He gave Hinchin a smile so broad and encouraging that it revealed a gold filling and a missing back tooth.

Hinchin inclined his head and Fowler led the way. 'The stores and my office take up the ground floor,' he said as they climbed the stairs, 'and the looms and frames for the main business of weaving are situated on the upper storey. We shall examine them later.' He pushed open the door to the first-floor workshop. 'But here . . . here is Progress. Here all is Experiment, Innovation and Novelty.'

A busy scene met Hinchin's eyes: the long room was full of men, women and children engaged in activity which made very little sense to him and reminded him most of a bedlam. From a wheel at one end, a barefoot boy carrying a rod containing bobbins of silk ran the whole length of the room to a cross, round which he passed the threads and ran, panting, back again. At the wheel, a man stood turning steadily all the while and shouting to the boy to keep up an even pace and tension. Nearby, a red-faced man put his back into turning the handle of a fearsome-looking frame machine, with shafts and cogs the size of dinner plates, which twisted thread from flyers on to a reel. A foreman stood by with a stopwatch, as if the two were in some fiendish race.

Further along, a group of women sat at machines resembling spinning wheels. Four threads passed from reels through metal hooks fixed to a rail on the wall. They were folded together in the women's hands and given a twist as they passed on to the wheel and then on to a spool as a thicker, stronger thread. In the opposite corner, a group worked at feeding and turning a horizontal octagonal frame and heating a set of copper rollers over a charcoal brazier that filled the air with a sooty carbon smell.

Hinchin, interested despite his determination to maintain a distance and detachment, looked expectantly at the silk master. Fowler threw out his hands expansively to take in the flying fingers of the workers, the bales of raw silk that lay here and there, and the creaks and groans of machinery and floorboards. 'Throwing and doubling,' he announced. 'That is – giving the silk its twist and then winding strands together to make a stronger thread.' He indicated the running boy and the cog-wheeled machine. 'The old against the new – 'tis a little experiment of mine. The boy, if he is not too small, can run fourteen miles in a day and breaks no thread, but of course the process requires another hand: the twister; whereas the throwing machine requires only one and does not wear out or fall sick.' He grinned at Hinchin and marched smartly past the group of women, dismissing them with a single word: 'Doubling.'

They came to a halt beside the brazier as a man in an apron and heavy gauntlets lifted off the copper roller. He fitted it into a frame below a wooden roller, and a woman began feeding a myriad of multi-coloured threads between the two.

'Nonpareil,' Fowler announced. 'My latest venture in ribbon production; each has twenty silken strands, every strand composed of sixty threads.'

Hinchin looked on with interest. 'It isn't woven at all! Is it fused by the heat?'

Fowler gave a satisfied nod. 'Rolled and welded like a strip of metal.' A woman knelt beside the machine, holding a large bowl into which she dipped the bright ribbon as it came off the rollers and was wound on to the octagonal drying spool. 'The glue is made from old parchment, to make the union permanent,' he explained. 'This method I discovered in France.'

'What's in the room beyond?' Hinchin asked.

A furtive look crossed Fowler's face. 'We must be quick,' he said. He opened the door and almost pushed Hinchin through it before shutting it firmly behind them. Three men looked up in surprise and then continued their work again. The room was smoky and hot, the men with sleeves and breeches rolled up as far as they would go. In the chimney corner, a drum-sized roll of gold braid hung directly above a fire like a side of bacon being smoked. 'An order for the military, for uniforms,' Fowler said. 'Only the best quality for our soldiery of course.' One of the men glanced up at him with a knowing look and then dropped his eyes once more to the braid he was winding.

'The room must be tightly sealed,' Fowler said, waiting for the smell and eye-stinging smoke to affect Hinchin sufficiently so that he could suggest to him that they withdraw. The brazier was filled with partridge feathers and scarlet dye-stuff that lent a sheen to the gold braid, which Fowler, and all the men present, knew wouldn't last beyond a month.

Hinchin coughed and rubbed his eyes; Fowler ushered him back out into the workroom, giving an unpleasant little smile behind his back. 'Of course, upstairs we produce both plain and patterned ribbon by more traditional means,' he continued as they made their way back, 'for ladies' gowns, hats, lingerie, et cetera, and every kind of folderol and frothy frivolity. Also broadloom silks for shawls and dresses; for this I buy in organzine ready prepared to use.'

69

'And this weaving, you say, is your main business?' Hinchin said as they climbed the stairs. 'Why then, may I ask, do you experiment and diversify so? Surely you could have two floors of productive weavers instead?'

Fowler stopped in his tracks and turned to face him. 'Why, Vertical Integration, man! Vertical Integration: control of the whole process from start to finish. That is the way forward!'

For a moment, to Hinchin, he appeared quite mad, his eyes staring and his collar knocked askew by the agitation of his hands as he sketched out his plans on the air.

'Integration is the key to Expansion,' he pronounced, 'and I intend it to be complete. You shall see – yes, you shall see.' He turned and led the way to the second floor, in a state of barely contained excitement and whistling between his teeth.

In the unheated workshop, the workers' breath misted the rows of windows, as if their spirits were drawn out of them and pressed ghostly against the glass. The hands of the weavers moved quickly with shuttle and batten, each man working to his own rhythm as if dancing to a different tune that only they could hear. The result was a cacophony of wooden thumping and clattering, most discordant to the ear. The floor was strewn with tiny scraps of material and ends of thread, and the atmosphere was thick with fibres and filaments of silk. The clack of looms and winders was punctuated by the coughing of the children, who seemed most sensitive to the irritation.

As they reached the bobbin winders, Fowler and Hinchin stopped and looked back to survey the whole room. The children beside them worked on diligently, only stealing the odd glance at the stranger when stopping to change a pirn. Within moments, Hinchin was clearing his throat and took out a pristine white handkerchief to blow his nose; the effect of the thick air was really quite unpleasant, he thought. 'The dust must be injurious to the health of your factory hands; don't they find the fibres choking?' He held the cloth over his nose and mouth.

Fowler raised his voice over the noise. 'Nonsense! They're used to it,' he said dismissively. As he spoke, he noticed Beulah Fiddement in the row, the girl who had recently been late and had been insolent. 'They're coarse as clods and lack your finer sensibilities,' he continued. He saw Beulah stiffen, angry colour rising to her face. The girl has spirit, Fowler thought with surprise; I shall have to break it.

He turned to Hinchin again and pointed out to him the different tasks of the weavers, some working the broad looms with their drawboys raising the warp threads to make the pattern, and others at the ribbon looms that could weave twelve ribbons at a time. 'We make your galloons and ferrets, as we say in England, and your houppes and crépines, bourrelets and cordons, as the French would have it,' he said with a flourish. 'Anything and everything required by the foolishness of fashion.'

Hinchin, who was feeling the chill, fidgeted from foot to foot and said testily, 'But what has all this to do with the vestry, Septimus? I fail to see how I can be of any assistance with your enterprise, admirable though it is.'

Fowler put his hand on his arm. 'Have patience just a little longer; there's one more thing I'd like to show you.' He took him to the window and they looked out over the snowy yard and orchard behind the manufactory. At one side, a great number of fruit trees were laid flat on the white ground, their roots in the air, slowly falling into decay. In their place stood rows of bare-branched saplings of a type that Hinchin was unable to identify. Each had a wide spreading shape with a great proliferation of shoots and twigs at its extremities, and the bark had a rich orange glow, unfamiliar and exotic in the dead, winter landscape.

'Sericulture! The farming of the worms that spin the silk, *that* is my next venture,' Fowler announced triumphantly. 'You will see that mixed in with the apple and plum, on the far side of the orchard, there are ancient mulberries?' He pointed to large trees, gnarled and twisted, with boughs so low to the ground that some touched the earth itself. 'Those gave me the notion; they will remain and gradually the other fruit trees will be replaced with young mulberries, as you see here.'

'But surely worm rearing is the domain of the Mediterranean countries?' In the face of Fowler's manic enthusiasm, Hinchin chose his words carefully. 'Is our climate wholly . . . suitable?'

'They're growing, aren't they?' Fowler said rudely. He checked himself, remembering that his purpose was to win Hinchin over. 'King James had a similar project,' he said grandiosely. 'In Chelsea – a thousand trees.'

'But it was unsuccessful!' Hinchin remonstrated. 'And to root out productive apple trees . . . Do you really think it wise?'

Fowler placed his hand on Hinchin's shoulder. 'Enterprise, Hinchin. Enterprise! Why, if no one is willing to Experiment, commit Funds, risk Capital, no Progress will be made!'

His tone was so vehement and his gaze so intense that Hinchin felt he could say no more. Fowler led him from the room, explaining, as they returned downstairs, his intention to convert the cellars into rearing houses by installing stoves and tiers of worm beds, and to import the silkworm eggs from a merchant he knew from his travels in Italy.

Back in his office, he beckoned Hinchin over to the desk, took from the top drawer a shallow glass case and laid it carefully before him. Under the glass, displayed on a board padded with dark blue velvet, were rows of moths, their wings spread flat, each body fixed with a glass-beaded pin. Fowler pointed at each male and female pair, reeling off the names of the specimens. 'Here are your Muga and Tusseh silkmoths of the Indian jungle, Syrian, Japanese Oak and Spicebush varieties.' He swept his hand over moths of varied hues, some with wings patterned with bullseyes or delicately marked edges. 'None of these are suitable for our climate, but here' – he tapped the glass – 'we have *Bombyx mori*, the silkmoth of China, the Workhorse of the Genus, being the most prolific producer of Quality Silk.'

Hinchin peered closer. The two moths were the plainest in the case. Their furry bodies and short broad wings were a dull cream colour, against which their dark beady eyes and the arcs of their large feathery antennae stood out in sinister contrast.

Fowler said, 'The female is the larger of the two – also fatter as it is swollen with eggs.' He indicated the abdomen of the larger moth, through which a pin passed at the centre. 'When she emerges from her cocoon her belly sac can hold five hundred eggs. Copulation occurs tail to tail and the eggs are laid on the empty cocoon casing until its white capsule is glued all over with pale yellow dots.'

Hinchin nodded as if he were considering this carefully. He thought them rather ugly and quite unlike the delicate native creatures, with their flimsy wings, that fluttered softly around his night-time window.

'This species has been domesticated for five thousand years and can no longer survive without the intervention of Man. They are quite unable to fly and the caterpillars don't wander.' Fowler jabbed at the glass again as if to underscore his point. 'These are the moths I shall rear, as the quality of their silk rules supreme,' he finished pretentiously.

He put the case away and drew from the drawer below a book of cloth and ribbon samples, which he opened up with a flourish. 'And this is the final product once the cocoons are unwound, thrown and reeled, dyed and woven.' He passed his hand lingeringly over a smooth, pale green silk, patterned with flowers and seedpods in pink and ochre, every leaf, stamen and petal clearly defined. 'See the excellence of the workmanship? This is what I have my men strive for: work that is of superior quality, every piece flawless.' He took a blue ribbon between his thumb and forefinger and rubbed its silken sheen. 'Feel it!' he commanded, and Hinchin duly followed his example and nodded his approval.

Fowler looked up from his samples with his face alight. 'Is it not amazing that something so beautiful can come from something so ugly?' He gently turned the leaves of fabric with his forefinger so that they rippled from gold and royal blue to rich wine and the most delicate ecru and then let them run back sensuously through his hands.

'Indeed,' Hinchin murmured, feeling quite overcome; Fowler's fervour engendered in him a feeling of nervous exhaustion.

'Let's retire to the house and take some refreshment.' Fowler rubbed his hands together in his enthusiasm. They passed out into the street, where horse and foot traffic had turned the snow into a clay-coloured slush. They walked to the crossroads where Fowler's home, the High House, a three-storeyed, white-washed building with a smart black front door and brass knocker, seemed to look down its nose at the low, loaf-shaped thatch of the Plume of Feathers Inn opposite.

Fowler let himself in, barked at the servant girl to bring tea, and showed Hinchin into the parlour. The room was light and pleasant, with deep window seats curtained with hangings of yellow, patterned silk. A group of small occasional chairs, their seats covered with cross-stitch needlework, were set beside a good fire and others stood around a card table. A wool rug of a floral design covered most of the floorboards, and the walls were hung with copperplate engravings of Italian classical scenes with ruins in the foreground.

They sat down before the fire: Fowler stretching out his legs towards the warmth and clasping his hands over his belly; Hinchin with his black clothes and angular frame sitting on the tiny chair as awkwardly as an incorrectly folded umbrella.

'So, have I convinced you of the genius of my scheme?' Fowler said.

'It's certainly a daring enterprise,' Hinchin said cautiously, pinching the material of his trousers just above his knees and giving them a neat tug to loosen them and save making a poke in the fabric.

Fowler nodded fervently. 'I shall have the whole process under one roof eventually and intend to modernise at every stage. My connections on the Continent have proved most productive and my new looms are to be brought out through Lisbon.' He tapped the side of his nose. 'I've ordered Jacquard machines – the most ingenious new inventions.'

Hinchin looked at him enquiringly.

'Machines that use punched cards to weave the pattern.'

Hinchin drew in his breath through his teeth. 'You have a large amount of new machinery in the manufactory already; are you not concerned that you may over-extend yourself? It'll cost a good deal of money.'

'The machines do away with the need for a drawboy. The pattern is replicated automatically and their operation requires far less skill, so wages can be reduced,' he said airily. 'But you're quite correct that I must recoup my investment quickly. I have other plans to reduce my labour bill – and that's where we come to the matter I'd like to discuss. That is where you can help me.'

Hinchin raised his eyebrows.

Fowler continued, 'What I intend is to offer employment to young paupers, both here and also from other parishes.'

Hinchin opened his mouth to object but Fowler raised his hand. 'No, hear me out. It would provide me with a ready supply of young labour: children of an age to be apprenticed. I should supply their food so that would relieve the parishes hereabouts from providing their upkeep.' His eyes gleamed as he thought of the beauty of his plan: boy apprentices indentured for seven years and the workhouse paying him upwards of ten pounds per child – and all he need provide would be some bread and slop twice a day!

'And what of your existing workforce?' Hinchin asked.

Fowler looked impatient. 'Most would go. I should need the master weavers at first of course, to instruct the apprentices.' He shrugged.

Hinchin, though aware of Fowler's laissez-faire beliefs in business, couldn't help but be astounded and was lost for words. Did he really intend to lay them all off en masse? They could barely afford to feed themselves as things were and would be thrown on the mercy of their parishes . . . presumably to be re-employed at no cost as paupers. The thing had an ingenious cunning; he must grant him that.

'It would be a service to the county,' Fowler said soberly. He assessed Hinchin. He didn't think he was the reforming sort, with their talk of coercion and 'white slavery', although some of the vestry such as Parson Hawkins and the parish constable might be harder nuts to crack. 'It's an ambitious plan, I know. Some might say over-ambitious,' he added self-deprecatingly, 'but I hope you've been impressed and can support its *enterprise*. I should dearly love you to champion its merits to the vestry.'

'The vestry would naturally have concerns about any further influx into the village,' Hinchin said diplomatically. 'The population has already grown ten-fold since the military arrived with all their attendant tradesmen, and whilst it's true that business is booming, there's a deal of concern over the number of inns and bawdy houses and the undesirables they attract. I fear that the parish won't want any more outsiders gaining a toehold.' He knew that some of the vestry would be against paupers coming in, even as workers, for fear of difficulties removing them and returning them to their place of settlement. Should they fall ill or be unable to work, there would be a danger of them claiming relief from Weedon Bec parish. Others of the vestry would prick up their ears at the thought of a quick solution to the expense of the upkeep of the local poor and think it worth the risk. But what if Fowler's ship ran aground, with trade affected by Bonaparte's blockade and exports on the wane? The parish could be left footing a much larger bill for poor relief. Hinchin was a man who, in an argument, liked to test the water and make sure he was on the winning side. For the moment, he would err on the side of caution.

Fowler was leaning towards him avidly. 'But you can persuade them? Have a word in the right quarters? Eh? I would, of course, show my appreciation, should the outcome of the vestry's deliberations be favourable.'

'I shall certainly put it to them as an idea,' Hinchin said in a non-committal way.

The servant girl pushed the door open, staggering under the weight of a huge tray laden with tea and fancies. She placed it very carefully on the card table and then bobbed a curtsey.

Fowler, sensing that winning Hinchin over might be a longer game than he'd thought, gave a quick nod, as though he was satisfied. 'Ask the ladies to join us,' he said to the maid and she hurried away. He helped himself to a pastry. 'I find business always gives me an appetite,' he said good-humouredly through a mouthful of crumbs, shoving the plate at Hinchin. 'Please do take one. Accept some hospitality.' He gave Hinchin a meaningful look. 'Plenty more where that came from.'

Hinchin rose to his feet as Tabitha and Hebe, Fowler's wife and daughter, entered, followed by the maid.

'Sit, sit.' Fowler waved him down. 'It's liberty hall here – make yourself comfortable.'

Hinchin exchanged greetings with the two ladies, and they slipped into their places while the maid poured tea into delicate Chinese bowls. Tabitha, her mousy hair parted in the middle with tight ringlets over her ears like two hands of sausages, had a wide, soft face with anxious grey eyes. Hebe was a pretty girl of sixteen. Despite her fine, pale blue morning dress in the latest fashion, with its high waist from which gathers flowed elegantly at the back, she still had the figure of a child, her bosom tiny and her arms thin in their long tight sleeves. Ribbons and bows adorned neckline and hem, as though she were a walking advertisement for the Fowler family's trade. A mass of dark curls were pulled back into a bun by a red velvet band, a few teased out to frame her pale, heart-shaped face.

Hinchin asked politely after the ladies' health, but before Tabitha could answer, Fowler said, 'Tabitha is well. She has a strong constitution. Hebe is not as robust as one could wish.'

Hebe, who was sitting quietly, sipping her tea, flushed as her father piled her plate with cakes and fancies. 'Father, please, I shan't be able to eat them.' She held out her hand to remonstrate.

'Of course you shall,' her mother said quickly.

Fowler put the plate on to her lap. 'You're too thin. You need a bit of meat on you, girl.'

Tabitha enquired after Mrs Hinchin and the children, and the talk continued along domestic lines while Hebe nibbled at the corners of a pastry and cut a cake into tiny squares, the better to convince her father that she was eating – a ploy of which he was well aware. He liked to see his womenfolk well covered. Hebe's thinness was an irritation; it seemed a constant rebuke, undermining his status as a man providing well for his family. He laid it aside for the present; there were more important matters at hand.

'I was telling Enoch of my plans for the manufactory,' he said to Tabitha; then he turned once again to Hinchin and said baldly, 'Perhaps Tabitha here could call on Mrs Hinchin?'

Tabitha glanced at him in surprise. It was hardly proper to invite oneself!

Hinchin stalled. 'I'm sure my wife would find that very pleasant sometime, but now I fear I really must go.' He dusted down his trousers and rose to his feet.

'Say, Tuesday next? In the afternoon?'

'Erm, I'll have to enquire . . .'

'Excellent. You can let me know the precise time, after church on Sunday.' Fowler clapped Hinchin on the back as he saw him to the door. Hebe let out a sigh of relief that her father was not going to stand over her while she ate, as he sometimes did at mealtimes. She took the opportunity to surreptitiously return the cake to its serving plate.

When Fowler returned, he said to Tabitha, 'Get alongside Mrs H., and then stick to her like glue. There's a favour I want from Hinchin and you're going to help me get it – understand?'

Tabitha nodded mutely.

FIVE

On Saturday morning, Rosie sat in the car at the service station with the kids, waiting for Josh to pick them up for the weekend. She had come more than halfway to meet him; he was half an hour late and her irritation was mounting. The day was scorching and she was wasting precious petrol running the engine in order to have the air conditioning going and keep the kids cool. Her head ached from watching out for Josh's blue Peugeot amongst all the cars constantly pulling in and out of the parking bays, the sun glaring off their metalwork. She peered round the obstruction of the streams of people wandering back and forth from McDonald's and M&S Food.

A bang on the roof made her jump and there was Josh,

bending down and pulling a daft face at Sam through the side window. Rosie got out of the car saying, 'You gave me a fright; I didn't see you arrive.'

'New car,' Josh said, pointing out a dark blue Mercedes E-Class parked in the row behind her. Through the smart, tinted windows, Rosie saw Tania sitting in the passenger seat trying to look anywhere but straight ahead of her. Rosie felt her muscles tighten; it was an unspoken agreement between them that Josh picked the children up alone. Rosie was prepared to make an effort to be pleasant to Josh for Sam and Cara's sake but exchanging small talk with the woman who had stolen her husband was a bridge too far. Pointedly, she turned her back on her and began unpacking the children's things from the boot: nappy bag, lunch boxes, Sam's little rucksack.

Josh took Sam over to see the car saying, 'What do you think of this then? It's a bit of a beast, isn't it?'

'It's a monster!' Sam said. 'I want to sit in the boot and go backwards, Daddy!'

Josh opened the tailgate and Sam clambered into a seat without a backward glance. Rosie stifled a pang, reminding herself that it was good that Sam should be so happy to go; she would feel far worse if he were miserable. Josh came back over with a box of stuff that she'd asked him to pick up for her from the flat. 'Where are you going to take them this time?' she asked.

'We're going straight to Legoland – that's why I've got Tania with me. Sorry about that.' He gave the wry, boyish smile she had once found so appealing and which she now ignored. 'And tomorrow we're going to Sunday cinema and then on to Mum and Dad's for a barbecue.'

'Oh, lovely,' Rosie said automatically, registering that, as usual, the children would be entertained anywhere rather than Josh and Tania's immaculate apartment and that they would have no chill-out time and would come back exhausted and grumpy.

Josh took the buggy out of the boot and settled the cardboard box in its place. 'I got all the things you asked for. Are you planning to stay a while then?'

'Thanks. It's a change of scene for the children,' she said, wanting to avoid an argument about it being inconvenient to have to travel to pick up the kids.

Josh looked at her appraisingly for a moment as if trying to decide whether he could push it further.

Rosie turned away and lifted Cara out of the car seat. Her hot, sticky little body clung on like a limpet. 'Mumma, mumma,' she said as she tangled her fist in Rosie's hair.

'Daddy's here,' Rosie said, feeling her throat tighten. 'You're going to have a lovely time at Daddy's and Mummy'll come and get you after two sleeps, OK?' She kissed Cara on the forehead where her baby hair was stuck in damp strands and nodded to Josh to take her.

Josh held up his palms in front of his pristine pale blue shirt, saying, 'Are you joking? Look at the state of her!'

Rosie glanced down at Cara. Her T-shirt, which had been clean on when they came out, was streaked with orange juice stains and soggy pieces of rusk. As if Rosie was in the habit of sending the children out in a state, Josh said, 'Couldn't you have spruced her up a bit?'

'There are clean clothes in the bag,' Rosie said sharply, shoving Sam's rucksack into his hands. 'Kids get messy. Get over it.' She marched over to the Merc and stood waiting while Josh brought the car seat and fixed it in beside Sam. As she bent to put Cara in the seat, Cara hung on tighter and Rosie whispered to her as she undid her fingers from her hair and buckled her in. Cara began to cry. Tania fiddled with the radio rather than look round.

Rosie fished in her handbag for Cara's yellow elephant, an unsavoury-looking piece of blanket that had started life as a glove puppet but was now almost unrecognisable as an animal at all. Refusing to be comforted, Cara cried harder, arching her back and wriggling in her straps. Rosie, feeling more and more upset, tucked the toy into the seat beside her and forced herself to step back. 'Don't forget she likes her elephant to sleep with,' she said to Josh, 'and she likes everything cut up *really* small and she still likes a bottle last thing, instead of a sippy cup . . .'

Tania, apparently unable to bear the noise any longer, finally turned round and said to Josh in a weary voice, 'Can't we just go?'

Josh closed down the tailgate, a glass barrier between Rosie and Cara's red sobbing face. She thought she might burst into tears herself.

'Will you be all right?' Josh said.

For a moment Rosie's guard went down but then she saw the way that he was looking at her as if assessing her in her scruffy shorts and flip-flops, Cara's rusk crumbs stuck to her vest top, her sunglasses pushed back to capture a straggling bird's nest of hair.

He said, 'You are coping, aren't you? Mum and Dad could have the kids for a bit longer if you want. You look terrible.'

Stung, Rosie brushed the crumbs from her front. 'I'm fine,' she said crisply, 'and you'd better go before our daughter becomes apoplectic and Tania's illusion of "child as fashion accessory" is irrevocably shattered.' She pulled her sunglasses down over her eyes, walked back to her car and forced herself to stand there so that she could wave to Sam and Cara while Josh pulled out. Was it so obvious that she was struggling? She *was* feeling the strain: sleeping badly, picking at her food, constantly worrying about money, the children, their future.

She couldn't truthfully say she was coping. The pills were still giving her dizzy spells and some awful headaches and now there was the strange child, too, who appeared and disappeared. If she told anyone of the latest visitation, of how she had witnessed a strange child, searching for something, right in amongst the nettles and briars of her overgrown garden, wouldn't they think it outlandish, even crazy? Wouldn't they say she was imagining things, losing the plot?

The big, shiny car moved sleekly through the car park. Insult to injury, she thought; on two decent salaries, not only could Josh and Tania afford it but they had to go and choose the ultimate family car. She remembered a conversation she and Josh had had when she'd first been pregnant with Cara, about the practicalities of transporting a growing family: trikes, scooters, camping stuff, bikes, maybe more kids someday, a future rolling out before them. Bitterness welled up inside her. The car turned the corner and set off towards the slip road and the motorway, ferrying her children away.

When Rosie got back to the house, she felt that she must fight the lassitude that always came without the children to keep her occupied and engaged. It would be better if she kept busy. She gave herself what her dad would have called 'a stiff talking-to'; instead of brooding, she should take the opportunity of the peace and quiet to tackle the jobs that she'd been putting off. She filled a bucket with soapy water, put on rubber gloves and went outside to wash the cellar windows as she'd planned.

She pulled away the nettles and sticky-weed that grew around them and cleared the sunken airbricks of debris: stones, old leaves and snail shells. As she washed the small panes, the algae smudging and smearing under the cloth, she peered through the thick glass at the bulky shapes of objects in the cellar but could see no more than broad outlines through the dust and cobwebs covering the inside of the panes. Her curiosity piqued, she went indoors and got clean water to tackle the other side of the glass.

At the cellar door, she set down the bucket and paused, listening. All was quiet and the draught at her feet was no more than cool air being drawn up from a room below ground level. In the broad light of day her previous apprehension seemed fanciful, a suggestible misinterpretation of the natural noises of the house. She tutted at herself as she grasped the doorknob, turned and pulled. The door, warped by damp, wouldn't budge. She gripped the doorknob with both hands and tugged hard until suddenly the door gave with a shudder and swung open, revealing a set of stone steps that twisted halfway down, and flaking brick walls, streaked here and there with green. Cobwebs hung everywhere, dotted with dead flies and caked with brick dust. She flicked an old Bakelite switch but no light came on below. Taking care not to brush against anything with her bare arms, Rosie hauled the bucket down the steps, noticing a crack in the brickwork that ran down the wall in a zigzag from top to bottom. She hoped it was just the moving and settling of an old building over time and not something she'd have to get a surveyor in for. If the house needed underpinning before she could sell it, she was sunk.

It was dim at the bottom. The windows, greyed over with dirt, let in two weak shafts of light that barely illuminated the pile of lumber jumbled at one side: an iron bedstead, an old kitchen cupboard with its door hanging open, a stack of boxes, the top one full of glass jars that May, a keen cook, must have meant for jam. As Rosie stepped into the room, she caught a movement ahead of her and gasped, only to realise that, partly obscured by a trestle table, a full-length mirror stood against the wall, its gilt frame chipped and battered, its surface speckled where the silvering had deteriorated. She gathered herself together – what was the matter with her? Frightened of her own reflection! She had let the sight of the odd child in the garden get to her, and now she was jumping at the slightest thing. Ridiculous. Nonetheless, it had given her a jolt and she hurried to fetch the stepladder so that she could reach the high windows and then wiped them over as fast as she could. There was something beyond the chill down here that made her shiver – an atmosphere.

Standing back to view the result, she noticed a rusty iron pipe fixed to the wall in the corner. Its lower end stuck out into the room at a point level with her knees. From there it travelled up in a straight line, fixed to the wall with brackets, to a point level with the windows, where it bent and disappeared into the wall above ground. She deduced that it was a flue, the remains of some ancient stove that must have once discharged its smoke outdoors, although now there was no sign of its egress outside; that must have been bricked up long ago.

With a last quick glance around to assess how much work there would be in clearing the cellar and whether she'd need a skip to do it, she picked up the bucket of filthy water and climbed the steps. The door was shut. Her throat tightened. She had left it wide open when she brought the ladder down, knowing that she'd have her hands full on the way up. Perhaps she'd left the back door open and a breeze had caught it? She put the bucket down on the steps behind her, turned the door-knob and pushed. It wouldn't budge. She broke out in a prickly sweat. Oh God, she was here on her own . . . she could be stuck down here all day, even into the night . . . She thumped on the door in frustration. Think, think, that was no good! She took hold of the doorknob with both hands and kicked the door hard. It shifted a little at the bottom but the top was stuck fast. It would have had to slam with some force to jam this tight, so why hadn't she heard it? She braced herself with her shoulder against the wood and then barged, once . . . twice . . . the third time it gave, juddering open so that she stumbled into the hall.

Rubbing her bruised shoulder, she carted the bucket out to the kitchen. The back door was shut. She felt the hairs rise under her collar. If Sam had been here she would have thought he'd done it as a joke – but Sam wasn't here. Rosie wedged the cellar door open with the handlebars of the bike before she went down to get the stepladder. *Like a trick played by a child* . . . The thought made her shiver.

She bolted the cellar door, swilled out the bucket and cleaned herself up; she must keep busy, not dwell on the fact that she was missing the kids or give in to morbid imaginings. It was her own fault; she should have wedged the door in the first place, been more cautious in a house she'd not yet come to know.

Rosie remembered the box of stuff that Josh had gathered for her from the flat and went to get it from the boot of the car. As she picked it up to carry it into the house, Tally came out of her front door with their spaniel, Polly, on a lead. 'Oh good, you're back,' Tally said. 'How did it go?'

Rosie pulled a face. 'Cara created and the Wicked Witch of the West was there, but apart from that it was fine.'

'Want to come for a walk? Leave it all behind you for half an hour?'

Rosie nodded, jumping at the opportunity of some company. She was glad of the chance to put off the rest of the tasks that she knew she should tackle whilst the kids were away too. Next on the list was to go through the papers in her mother's bureau as the solicitor had suggested. Well, she could deal with bills and bank statements but there would be photos, letters, Mum's handwriting . . .

She shoved the box into the hallway and set off with Tally away from the centre of the village past the old chapel schoolrooms and a row of modern houses, until the street became a lane leading uphill and bounded by hedges. Hereford cattle grazed over a field full of humps and bumps. Slow and sturdy, they turned to watch them pass with huge patient eyes.

'Strip farming,' Tally said, pointing to the broad undulations. 'You got to farm a strip of the good land and a strip of the bad so everyone had a fair share.'

Rosie wondered at the signs of medieval toil still written on the landscape, clear as lines on ruled paper. They walked on and she let the regularity of their footfall soothe her. 'Have you lived here long?' she asked.

'Oh no, only fifteen years – there are families here who go back generations. We're definitely still incomers.'

Rosie remembered the solicitor saying that her grandparents had moved house within the village and that her great-grandparents had lived here too, maybe even ancestors before them. How odd to think of families staying in one place for generations when nowadays most people moved far from their childhood home and often many times in a lifetime, just as she and Josh had done.

If she had roots here, what did that make her? Did that mean she wasn't an incomer? She said, 'Fifteen years seems quite a long time to me. Josh and I never stayed anywhere more than a couple of years. We never had much cash – tried to put everything into bricks and mortar. We'd buy a flat and do it up to sell on. We never got a chance to finish the last one though; it was a mess. I had to sell it as it was, half-gutted.' She sighed.

Tally was looking at her encouragingly, willing her to continue but Rosie fell silent. Maybe moving around was part of the problem; we never really settled, she thought sadly. We didn't give ourselves a chance. Her nerves felt jangled after seeing Josh, her emotions churned into a mixture of bitterness and regret. How could something that had started out with such hope have come to this? She thought of the way he had looked at her, as if she had finally lost it. Perhaps he was right; she had been seeing and hearing some very strange things. She was about to open her mouth to tell Tally about seeing the girl in the garden again, but then hesitated. She couldn't say she'd seen her disappear in a moment: that she was there and then gone. It was too odd. Besides, she had already asked her once about the child; Tally would think she was fixated. She closed her mouth and said nothing.

They carried on up the hill, towards the village of Farthingstone, the sun beating down on them, the quiet of mid-afternoon broken only by the crunch of grit, the click of the dog's claws on the road and the chirruping of hedge sparrows. They gained the top of the slope and the road levelled out to pass along a ridge with open fields on either side. On their left, the fields were pieced in green, brown and yellow: pasture, ploughed fields seeded with winter wheat, and bright oilseed rape, stretching away across a valley to a further ridge beyond, where another village stood, its church tower white in the sunlight.

'That's Stowe Nine Churches,' Tally said.

'But it's only got one,' Rosie said, confused.

Tally laughed. 'True, but it's high so you can see nine from over there, looking back over the countryside. If you walk a mile or so further you come to even higher ground called Castle Dykes. It was an Iron Age hill fort and then later there was a medieval motte and bailey castle. It's surrounded by woodland now but you can still see the earthworks. They must've chosen it so they could keep a good lookout for enemies.'

'What about the other side?' Rosie asked, walking across the road to look back across the valley towards the village. 'Can you see our houses?' They picked their way through thistles and leant on a five-bar gate that gave on to a vast field of standing corn, still green but growing heavy and ripe. Here, the swell of the ground in front of them blocked the view of the village and the water meadows in the valley so that they looked straight across to the huge military arsenal on the lower ridge opposite. Overshadowing the village, it stretched for half a mile. Eight enormous Georgian buildings were arranged in two rows facing them, many-windowed and solidly built in red brick and slate; each was the size of a modern factory. Massive and uniform, they dominated the landscape, their windows gleaming in the sun like ever-watchful eyes. Three hundred yards to the left ran a long row of windowless buildings with their gable ends face on, so that their pitched roofs made a zigzag pattern. The flat face of the perimeter wall bounded all, broken only by the occasional blob of green where a tree grew from a crack in the brickwork, and by the scrawl of graffiti: the chunky letters of some youth's tag sprayed as high as a man but reduced to a pathetic squiggle on the vast acreage of the wall.

'It's Georgian,' Tally said. 'George the Third had it built as an armoury and as a retreat in case Napoleon invaded – or at least, that's how the story goes.'

'It's amazing when you see the whole thing,' Rosie said. 'From down in the village you're only really aware of the wall and the gatehouse.'

Tally pointed to the larger buildings. 'Those were the store-houses. They stowed twenty-five thousand muskets in there.

And you see those big arched doors at the bottom? The blue ones? They were so they could roll the cannons in and out. And there were barracks, a hospital, officers' houses, everything.'

'Why here?'

'We're supposed to be the dead centre of the country, so the furthest point from any coast, I suppose.' She gave a wry smile. 'Apparently even a king needs a bolthole.'

'What about the buildings with no windows?'

'They were the gunpowder stores and blasthouses. Every second one was packed with earth in case of explosion, otherwise I suppose they could've all gone down like dominoes. You can't see it from here but there's a spur off the canal that runs between the storehouses. Thousands of barrels of gunpowder were brought in by boat. Nice and smooth by water – I don't suppose anyone would've wanted to bring it in by cart!'

Rosie gazed at the scene before her, imagining it busy with red-coated soldiers unpacking and storing the barrels and guns, the shouts of men and the whinnying of horses on the parade ground, sentries patrolling the boundaries of the huge arsenal. On this summer Saturday the whole place was still and quiet, the only movement the shimmer of a heat haze above the metalled roads.

'What's the place used for now?' she asked.

'Warehousing mainly, some businesses; some of it just stands empty.'

'Like the statue of Ozymandias, King of Kings, all shattered in the desert,' Rosie said dreamily.

Tally smiled. 'Mmm. Lo how the mighty are fallen.'

Above them a lark poured out its full-throated song and they both looked up to find it, a dark speck in the blue. They watched until it dropped down to its nest, a cup of dead grass somewhere amongst the wheat in the field below.

Rosie sighed. 'It's beautiful up here – so peaceful.' She could feel her shoulders easing, the stress falling away.

Tally said, 'Down by the river's another good place to walk. We could take the kids sometime.'

'Thanks, that would be nice.'

Tally suggested that they make their walk a circular one and they made their way further along the ridge, chatting about the children and Tally's work, until they reached Gayton Lane, a single track road that cut back to the upper end of the village. As they descended the steep hill between high-banked hedges laced with cow parsley, they met a woman coming uphill with a terrier in tow. Polly pulled on her lead and when the two dogs met they sniffed each other, cocking their ears and wagging their tails. The woman, a country type with neatly cut grey hair, a checked seersucker shirt, shorts and proper walking sandals, said with a smile, 'You've got some company today then?'

'Yes, I've been giving Rosie here a bit of a guided tour about the history of the place – our illustrious past.' She introduced them: 'Tricia – Rosie. Helena Milford's daughter,' she added in explanation.

Rosie saw a flash of recognition cross the woman's face followed by a look of sympathy as her brow furrowed. She braced herself to receive condolences but instead Tricia asked solicitously, 'How is your mum? I heard she'd moved back here to look after May. I've been meaning to look her up.'

Rosie, confused, looked helplessly at Tally, and then said, 'I'm afraid she's recently passed away . . .' She stumbled over her words, 'It was very sudden – a heart attack . . .'

Tricia put her hand to her throat. 'I'm so sorry. I had no idea! How awful for you.' She shook her head as if unable to take in the news. 'I can't believe it; I knew her from when she was a girl. We were at school together.'

The sound of a vehicle reached them, grinding through its gears as it tackled the hill, and a mud-smothered Land-Rover approached. They stepped apart, retreating to the tangled verges to let it through, and it disappeared in a haze of exhaust fumes, a panting sheepdog looking over the tailgate, tongue lolling.

'See you soon,' Tally said, taking the opportunity to close the awkward encounter. 'Enjoy the rest of your walk,' and she led the way on down the hill.

Rosie followed her, raising a hand in farewell. When they were out of earshot she said, 'Do you know Tricia well?'

'Not really, we just bump into each other sometimes with the dogs.'

'You don't know her second name or where she lives then?'

'No. Sorry. Why?'

'Nothing. I just wondered. I thought I could ask her about Mum at school,' Rosie said, not sure how to explain what she had seen in the woman's face when they had been introduced. Tricia's look of sympathy had come before she had learnt of her mother's death. It must, then, have been directed at her, as if there were some reason to feel sorry for her or for her family. She felt both curious and unsettled. Why should this stranger pity her? She looked back over her shoulder but Tricia and her little dog had already rounded the bend and the lane was now empty save for a few sparrows flitting between the lacy heads of the cow parsley and the dusty ruts of the road.

She caught up with Tally and they followed the lane back into the village, Tally pointing out other features: Fern Hollow Farm with its medieval stonework, a triangular village green with an oak tree and a fingerpost and, further on, a picturesque house with mullioned windows that was once a priory. They walked through an estate of modern houses and old folks' bungalows and as they turned back into their own street, Rosie asked, 'Do you know anything about our houses? They were workshops of some kind, weren't they?'

'It was all one originally, before it was partitioned off into houses – a silk factory,' Tally said. 'That's about all I know.'

'Ah, that makes sense. The marks on the floors must be where the looms were, then. Have you got those on your floors? And worn patches where the weavers must've stood?'

Tally nodded. 'You can see the polished paths where people walked too. I bet if you looked either side of the walls the paths would join up. They probably ran the whole length of each floor.'

Rosie gave a little shiver. 'Bit strange to think of that: people passing up and down.'

They arrived home and Rosie suggested tea but Tally had relatives coming for supper and said she'd better get on. Rosie said goodbye and let herself in. The house was quiet except for the sound of a tap dripping in the kitchen; too quiet, Rosie thought. It felt empty without the children, empty and purposeless. Instead of going to make herself a drink and tackle the paperwork, she knelt down beside the box in the hall, peeled back the parcel tape and began to unpack the things she'd asked Josh to gather for her from the flat. There were books and extra toys for the children, her coloured inks, pens and brushes, a good supply of sketchpads and watercolour paper stretched on to boards. At the bottom was her 'treasure chest': an old lacquered jewellery box in which she kept tiny objects she'd collected for their colour or shape.

She put the toys away in Sam's bedroom and took her art materials up to the studio room on the top floor, where she sat down at the dressmaker's table and laid them out before her. She opened a creamy pad of paper and flipped forward through pages of watercolour sketches. Her last proper painting had been done on a rare excursion out of London when Mum had looked after the kids so that she could attend an examiners' meeting. Mum had encouraged her to take a break and stay over for a couple of nights in a country hotel and she'd painted a series of views of the house and grounds rendered in soft spring shades. The colours were lovely: golden Cotswold stone and lavender-shadowed wisteria, the sparkle of a fountain against a yew hedge, a walled garden walk bright with foxgloves. She looked at them with pleasure.

She carried on through the pages of rudimentary drawings and notes for lesson plans that followed. The job and the demands of two small children had meant she'd been unable to get any time for serious work of her own. Doodles in the corners of the pages revealed her boredom with the repetitive curriculum that had given no scope for her own imagination.

She stared at the last image, a sketch of boxes of varied shapes surrounded by notes on perspective, and then very deliberately tore the paper from the pad. Its perforations came away from the metal spine with a satisfying popping sound. Taking several pages together she tugged hard, ripped them out and dropped them on the floor, working her way back in time until only the hotel images and clean pages remained. Tiny scraps of paper were left inside the spiral binding; she leant forward and blew them away. They sprinkled the surface of the table like flakes of ash.

She smoothed her hand across the paper. Her mind mirrored its blankness. Nothing. What if nothing would come? She would make marks – any marks. She picked up an ink pen and drew the squat shapes of the ink bottles before her, and then doodled faces on them: a grumpy expression for the Indian ink, with thunderous black clouds emerging from its top, a fat, comic face with rosy cheeks for vermilion – Sam would like these – and a Green Man's face for viridian, tendrils spilling from the pot and twining around each other like mad hair.

A minute later she grabbed up one of her boards with stretched paper, rummaged for a bottle of distilled water and mixed a palette of sunset colours. She had an idea, something that Sam would love that might easily have come from one of his beloved storybooks. She painted on a colour wash: a shady grey foreground, a red horizon fading through orange and yellow into a purple and indigo distance. She opened the black Indian ink, dipped in her pen, hesitated, forming the broad composition in her mind. Tentatively at first, she began to draw the distant turrets of a castle and then, with bolder strokes, the sinuous curves of a dragon guarding its treasure. The ink flowed into the wet surface taking unexpected directions and making dark, star-like blobs, challenging her to interpret and incorporate and giving the work a loose, freehand quality that she loved. Soon she was engrossed, using the deepest red patch as a baleful eye, the clots of dark ink in a scribbled foreground as a thicket of brambles grown up around the dragon's pile of coins. The sounds of children playing next door and the pigeons' never-ending burbling drifted in through the open window, ebbing and flowing around her, unheeded. A rectangular patch of sunshine moved across the table, unnoticed. She hung suspended in the world of the picture: only the connection between her eyes and her moving hand existed, everything else had fallen away.

At last she sat back and sound seeped back into her world, music and voices from Tally's garden, the crackle of the barbecue. She laid down her pen and appraised her work. The picture had a mystical quality – yes, she had definitely captured something. The dragon's coils twined around its hill of gold, like the fingers of a miser's fist. One eye was open, just a slit, full of spite and suspicion, as if the viewer had just awoken him. The dark sky loured above and the impenetrable thicket threatened below, but the reds and golds of the creature's treasure shone through him as though dragon and hoard were becoming in-distinguishable, almost one.

Perhaps it's too disturbing to give to Sam, she thought, it might give him nightmares. Maybe I'll save it until he's a bit older and just give him the inkpot drawing for now. Nonetheless, she was glad she'd done it; it was good, even she could see that. She would frame it and hang it here in the studio.

The smell of barbecue fuel and grilled steak reached her and she realised she was starving. How long was it since she'd eaten? She didn't remember having anything for lunch – breakfast then. That often happened when she was painting: time shrank as her mind expanded.

Filled with the excitement of new creation, she went downstairs and raided the fridge. She'd let it run down as the kids were going to be away but there were eggs, ham and some leftover salad. She made an omelette and, whilst it was cooking, opened the bottle of white that she'd bought 'for emergencies'. She justi-fied the expense to herself: for treats too, she thought defiantly. She would take as her motto: 'celebrate every small victory'. She sloshed some wine into a tumbler, laid a tray and took it into the living room. While she ate, her mind was busy with another idea. The delicate cow parsley, creamy white against the dark green of the hedge . . . perhaps she could use spatters of wax to sketch in the cow parsley and then a colour wash and inks over it, so that the colour of the paper would be retained for the flowers. They would show through with just the right feeling of insubstantiality. She finished her meal feeling buoyant. She would tackle Mum's papers next. She was ready. It would be fine.

*

The bureau was locked. Rosie thought about her mum's habit, at the cottage, of leaving the house key in a flowerpot in the garage. 'Third pot along, top shelf,' she'd always told Rosie. She could hear her voice in her head, 'In case I'm ever out when you come home.' Even when Rosie and Josh had been married for more than five years her mum always referred touchingly to her visits as 'coming home'. On the bureau were the lamp, a photo of Rosie reading a story to the children and a blue and white ginger jar that proved to be empty. Up high on the bookshelf beside her were more knick-knacks. She reached up on tiptoes to run her hand along it. A wave of dizziness hit her as she stretched up and she had to put out a hand to steady herself. I shouldn't have left it so long without eating, or drunk that wine either, she thought. Bowing her head for a moment she waited for the room to stop whirling. Slowly and more carefully, she reached up again. The third ornament in the row was a flowered china vase and as she took it down, something chinked inside it. She upended it over her hand and the key slid out on to her palm, followed by something pale and soft. Ugh! A moth! She tipped her hand over; the key tinkled against the edge of a shelf as it fell but the moth landed upon it. The thing was alive. It righted itself and began to move slowly along. It was the weirdest moth Rosie had ever seen: cream all over, with a huge swollen body, like a maggot but with tiny wings that were thick rather than delicate and covered with ridges, like lumpy veins. The creature's head, thorax, even its legs, were covered in fine silky hair and its dark comb-like antennae and blue-bottle eyes, both so much larger than any other moth she knew, gave its head the sinister look of a praying mantis. It dragged itself along the surface, moving its wings feebly.

Rosie wanted to get rid of it but couldn't bear the thought of touching it again. She picked up the tumbler from the tray

98

and put it down over it, trapping it inside. It crawled around beneath the glass, vibrating its wings and shivering its feathery antennae, making Rosie shudder.

She went to the kitchen and washed her hands. She'd never seen an insect like this before. She pulled her phone from her bag, typed in 'moths' and scrolled through the images. In moments she'd found *Bombycidae,* the genus, and *Bombyx mori,* a species within it – a silk moth, just as she'd guessed at some instinctive level the moment she'd caught sight of it. She looked at more pictures: caterpillars upside down on mulberry leaves, glued there by strands of silk and the tiny hooks around their sucker feet; pale ovoid cocoons stuck all over with shiny lemon-coloured eggs; a male moth, smaller, with a two-inch wingspan, the female larger, fat with her swollen egg sack. She read that neither were able to fly although they could crawl and climb. The worms lived on mulberry leaves. Was it possible that it had come from the tree in the garden? It didn't seem so; the article said that they could no longer survive in the wild but needed specific temperature and humidity levels and could only live when farmed by Man. She shook her head and picked up a piece of card from the junk mail piled on the table to slip under the glass. Whatever the case, as far as she was concerned, the moth was going outside.

But when she returned to the upended glass she saw straight-away that it was empty. Stupefied, she lifted it off the shelf, unable to believe her eyes. There was a mere smudge against the wood, a silt of the finest pale powder as though the decay of weeks had taken place in minutes, as if the thing had decomposed in a whisper. She sat down hard on the upright chair at the desk. It had been trapped; it couldn't have just disappeared! Unless . . . unless she had imagined the whole thing.

She rubbed her brow. There had been the dizziness again

beforehand, just like the time she'd seen the girl under the tree
. . . and today she'd been about to tackle looking through Mum's
things. Perhaps she wasn't as ready for this as she'd thought
and her subconscious fear had surfaced in this strange way. Yet
she had felt the creature in her hand! She picked up the key
from the carpet and placed it on her palm – she thought she
could recall the sensation of the moth in her hand: the solid
body pupa-like, the softer wings. Tally had mentioned that the
place used to be a silk factory of course . . . and she'd mixed
wine with tablets again – perhaps that made the side effects
worse. Yet it had felt so real!

Feeling unsettled, she fitted the key into the lock of the
bureau but then stopped. She told herself to stop being so
suggestible, to be adult about this and get on with the job in
hand. She turned the key in the stiff lock with a click, and then
paused again. It felt strange to be opening the bureau. She
remembered how, as a child, seeing her mother writing letters
at the desk, she had wanted to climb up on her knee to see
into the little cubbyholes or even be allowed to play at tidying
it. Mum had told her no, saying that it was her private place
for keeping important papers and had bought her a toy Post
Office with tiny envelopes and ink stamps to keep her happy.
She had been thrilled and accepted that the desk was off limits.
After all, growing up, she'd had her own privacies: first the
imaginary Arabella and then journals full of teenage crushes
and cigarettes cached in a shoebox at the back of her wardrobe.
Everyone had secrets. She hesitated again. Surely this sense of
the forbidden was just another trick of her mind, a delaying
tactic to protect her against going through things so intimately
connected with her mother. It had to be done. With a new
briskness she pulled out the supports for the fall-front and
opened it.

On either side of three small central drawers were pigeon-holes stuffed with papers. In front of them stood a clutter of office paraphernalia: rolls of sellotape, scissors, boxes of drawing pins and elastic bands and a clumsy terracotta clay pot that Rosie remembered making at school and had thought long gone. She cleared the objects to one side and started method-ically from the left, taking out each piece of paper and placing aside, in piles, those that needed some action: bills to pay and magazine subscriptions to cancel. She worked on steadily, undisturbed by the occasional shadow as someone went by the window on the way to the pub or by the noise of passing cars. After an hour she had thrown out old receipts and bank state-ments and reduced the paper to a manageable minimum. So far, so good, she thought as she moved on to look at the contents of the little drawers.

The first two drawers held mainly photographs: snapshots of their family holidays; a nice picture of her father before he got ill, looking up from hammering in a tent peg with a broad grin on his face; Rosie in a ballet tutu, Rosie sitting in a rowing boat, Rosie as Aladdin in the school play. She paused over a picture of her parents on their wedding day – so young, younger than she was now, her father's hair curling fashionably over his collar, her mother dark-haired then and with a complicated 'do', her eyes kohl-lined and her lipstick pale. Rosie felt sad and thought that she would buy a good album and mount them properly so that she could look at them more easily. She would write down what she could remember of the where and the when and would show them to the children as they got older so that they had an image of their grandparents, so that they wouldn't be forgotten.

The next drawer stuck and she had to pull and jiggle it. The reason soon became clear; it contained one large manila envelope, the end of which had got caught at the back of the drawer. She almost gave up and left it for another time but she was intrigued by the fact that it was both bulky and sealed. At last she tugged it free, tearing one corner in the process, and the drawer fell out with a rattle. Written on the front, in her mother's elegant hand, was the word *Keepsakes*.

Rosie picked at the edge of the gummed flap of the envelope and peeled it back. She slipped out a sheaf of papers with the bold coloured frames and distinctive print of official documents. The first was her parents' marriage certificate, the next her birth certificate:

> When and where born: *Fifteenth January 1984,*
>   *Northampton General Infirmary*
> Name: *Rose Angela Milford*
> Sex: *Female*
> Father's name: *Michael Milford*
> Mother's name: *Helena Milford, née Webster*
> Occupation of Father: *Curator and conservator*

Underneath was what she first thought was a copy. But the name was wrong. *Lily Clarissa Milford*, it read, born on the same day, to the same parents.

She felt as if a kaleidoscope had been turned, shaking her world into a new and dizzying pattern. She placed the two sheets side by side as if by careful comparison she could make sense of the impossible. There had been a sister. No, more than that – a twin. She had had a twin sister. Understanding came upon her like a slow revelation. Beyond the shock, beyond the Rosie who sat pale and still, another Rosie viewed images from her past: lying curled under a patchwork blanket with a cold space beside her where once there had been a solid, matching warmth, a feeling of asymmetry as she walked with her mother holding her hand, playing noughts and crosses with Arabella. She remembered her mother's migraines after childhood parties, tired eyes behind birthday candles . . . *click* went the shutter as each picture came before her. *Click*: the sound of something falling into place.

With trembling hands she lifted the papers to see what lay beneath. There was a white folded card with a decorated border of gold flowers and a gold cross in the centre.

Lily Clarissa Milford
15th January 1984 ~ 4th August 1987

Only three years old. 'No . . . Oh no,' she said to the empty room.

She opened the Order of Service and words jumbled before her eyes: *Opening Prayer, 'The Lord's my Shepherd', Corinthians Chapter 13, 'For Those in Peril on the Sea', 'O God our Help in Ages Past', Commendation and Farewell . . .*

How had this awful thing happened? She had had a twin; she wasn't meant to be alone; she had always somehow known it. She had had a twin who had been taken; gone from her so long ago that she had no conscious memory of her, just an awareness of something not right, an absence, as if part of herself was missing. Anger rose up in her against her parents. How could they have kept this from her? What she felt was rage! Not to tell her, to keep it secret and shut her out, as if the loss was all theirs and she had no right to grieve! Was it to protect her? Did they think they could save her from missing her twin? You might as well expect someone not to miss their shadow. She had always thought that there was something wrong with her; she hadn't understood the deep abiding loneliness that seemed to go far beyond her situation as an only child. Why had they not told her? It was a betrayal.

The envelope underneath the papers still had some things in it. She fished out a photo: her mother holding two bundles, babies wrapped in soft white blankets, her face open in a way that Rosie had never seen it, her smile full of confidence and fulfilment. The first part of the words 'Maternity Wing' showed on the sign in the background. Rosie imagined her father taking the snap outside the hospital – a family about to drive away towards their life together.

She upended the envelope over the pile of papers and two tiny circlets of plastic fell out. These were pink, not transparent like the identity bracelets that Sam and Cara had worn, but each had the same fastener, the same slip of paper with faded writing. She picked them up and held them, barely as big as the circle made by her finger and thumb: *Rose Milford 5.30 a.m. 15/1, Lily Milford 5.40 a.m. 15/1*, she read. She was the eldest then.

She imagined the cold January morning on which they had been born. Had her parents known that they were to have twins? She would never know that now. She imagined them giving the tiny infants names: Rose and Lily, names chosen to differentiate them, the red and the white, yet to treat them fairly as if to say, to us you are both flowers of equal perfection. A pair.

Every day since she had lost her mum there'd been some ordinary, tiny thing she'd wanted to tell her or to ask her: that Cara had cut another tooth, that she'd read a novel her mother would have liked, how to make the banana muffins that the kids loved, what was the name of the piano teacher she'd had in primary school? Each time it happened, in the instant she remembered her loss, her heart lurched and righted itself, she pulled herself together and carried on. But now, here were huge questions that desperately needed answers; they could not be put aside and she was left like a child calling into a tunnel, receiving only echoes in reply.

However long it took, however difficult the search, she was going to find out what had happened. She would start by searching the house for letters, diaries, anything that might hold a clue, even though her instinct told her that the envelope in front of her, which had been so carefully sealed and hidden, was likely to be all there was to find. If there was nothing else amongst her mother's belongings, she would talk to May, try to lead her back to the distant past in the hope that some vestige of memory might remain that would shed light on the tragedy and the reasons for her parents' silence.

She closed the bands together in her hand and held them tight, her knuckles pressed to her mouth as the sense of loss overwhelmed her.

SIX

Rosie was standing in Tally's kitchen, having brought round a broken dining chair that Rob had offered to glue and clamp for her.

'Let's have a look at the damage then.' Rob bent to examine the crack where the back had come away from the seat.

Tally said, 'What happened to it?'

'Sam jumped up and down on it last night,' Rosie said ruefully. 'He got into a complete strop because Cara knocked the table and his Lego model fell off.' With a pang, she thought of her sharp words when Sam had started shouting. She had lost her temper and yelled back at him: 'Don't be such a baby! Cara's supposed to be the toddler, not you!' He had thrown a huge tantrum; red-faced and bawling, with his eyes screwed up, he had jumped up and down on the chair as if there was no room left for the feelings inside him and they had to come out in violent motion. Rosie, shocked at her irritability and at his reaction, had stood frozen for a moment, completely at a loss. 'Honestly, I didn't know what to do with him. He was beside himself. In the end, I just picked him up and held on tight until he subsided.'

Tally glanced outside, where the children were playing in the garden, the spaniel, Polly, wandering between them. 'He seems all right today. It's probably just all part of dealing with some big changes. I'm sure he'll settle down.'

Rosie turned to the window. Tally's girls had taken their guinea pigs out of the hutch and were showing Cara how to stroke them. Sam was sitting in the sandpit with his back to them, flattening an area in which to line up his trucks. Amy brought her guinea pig over to him, a ginger and black one with a white patch over one eye. She squatted down beside him and held the creature out to him. Rosie willed him to take it, to say something, to *join in*. He glanced up for a moment as if annoyed by the interruption and then returned to his task, Amy's friendly gesture barely ruffling the surface of his consciousness. Amy took her pet back again, cradled it in her arms and wandered off to the border in search of couch grass to feed it. Rosie sighed.

Rob rummaged in his tool box and fished out a series of clamps to see which one would fit. He was a big, cheerful man. Rosie had got to know him too over the last couple of weeks, as she and Tally popped in and out of each other's houses to chat or get the kids together to play. He seemed to be always busy building or mending something, whenever he was off duty, and said it kept him sane after shifts attending RTAs and nightclub fights and hanging around at A&E or court. He liked to work with his hands, doing something simple and productive so that he could see an outcome for his labours at the end of it.

Rosie, looking out at the borders bursting with late summer colour, said, 'The garden's looking nice; the hydrangeas are gorgeous.'

'It's full of weeds,' Rob said. 'Don't look too closely.'

'You're joking, aren't you? Weeds R Us next door.'

Despite Rosie's attempt at a light-hearted tone, Tally detected weariness in her voice. She took in Rosie's frayed jeans and old hoody, her lack of make-up, or her usual earrings, or even a watch. 'Do you want a hand clearing it?' she asked, worried that Rosie was struggling.

'No, you two are helping me no end already. No, I'm going to concentrate on getting the house straight first and let the garden die back. It'll be easier to clear it in winter.' She hoped that she sounded plausibly enthusiastic and that it wouldn't be apparent how completely overwhelmed she felt.

Since finding out about Lily, a fortnight ago, she'd been too down to get on with much. The tins of filler and pale azure paint that she'd bought for the living room were still stacked in the hall. She'd searched the house thoroughly for clues about her twin but had found only a pair of first shoes, white T-bars, wrapped in tissue paper in a drawer. The leather was decorated with punched star-shaped holes and was scuffed grey at the toes. They could have been Lily's, but they might just as well have been her own. There were a few birthday cards and Mother's Day cards, together with a handful of childish drawings that she recognised as her own, and an exercise book with her first English essays on subjects like 'My Pet' and 'My Best Day Out' – but no letters. There were photo albums, one a wedding album and the other a family one with pictures of birthdays and Christmases, high days and holidays. There were no pictures of Lily and the earliest birthday picture was at Rosie's fourth birthday party, showing her blowing out four striped candles on a cake.

She'd been to see May several times but had got nowhere. The weather had turned heavy and thunderous, presaging the end of summer, and May was cranky, fed up with the humid heat and the flare-up in her arthritis. She had talked a little about the distant past, remembering her childhood and teenage days with Helena clear and bright as the park where they had played, moving from swings and seesaws to tennis and boys. Questions about her later life: work, friends, becoming an aunty, met with blankness, then a faltering return to the early days with her sister, so that her memories only made Rosie feel her own loss more keenly.

Rob squeezed a generous line of wood glue into the cracked frame of the chair. 'Can you hold it tight together while I put the clamps on?' he said to Rosie. She obliged while he positioned them.

Tally said, 'Do you want to come to the Country Park with us tomorrow? Feed the ducks?'

'I can't; it's Josh's weekend again and I've got to get the kids to the services by ten. We'd love to do it another time though.'

'Well, drop round when you get back. Have some lunch with us.' Tally knew how flat Rosie felt without the kids' routine to keep her busy; she would need something to get her through the weekend. 'How are you getting on with your art? Are you getting a portfolio together? Have you sent anything out yet?'

Rosie brightened for a moment. 'I have actually. I've put them on my website and I've sent out good copies of the dragon one and some others to a few children's publishers, as print samples.'

'That's great,' Tally said warmly. 'More power to your elbow!'

Rosie managed a smile.

Rob finished winding the last clamp. 'There we are. If we leave it overnight that should do the trick.'

'Thanks, Rob. You're a star. I'd better press on; I'm taking the kids to meet May this afternoon.' She pulled a face. 'Just a quick visit, I reckon. I'm not sure how the energy levels of the under-fives and the over-seventies will mix.'

'Hmm, good luck with that,' Tally said.

Rosie went to tell Sam to bring Cara in but hesitated in the doorway. Nicky was busy holding Cara's hand so that she could feed carrot sticks to the guinea pigs, but Amy, in her quiet way, had persevered with Sam and was kneeling next to him using a little dumper truck to build a pile of sand, while he used a digger to shovel it up and move it elsewhere. They both pushed the tiny toys with slow deliberation, reversing and manoeuvring them, raising and lowering trailer and bucket. Amy asked Sam something and he frowned and failed to answer but she simply returned to her role without further comment. Both seemed engrossed in Sam's game, and Rosie felt a rush of relief to see Sam interacting, however slightly, with another child.

Mindful not to risk another of Sam's tantrums, she went and squatted beside them to admire the roadways and building site they'd made. After a minute, she explained that they had to go. She asked Sam if he'd like to leave his trucks there so that they could pick up their game another time, thinking that he would say no and then consent to pack them away in the ice-cream carton that served as their container. To her amazement, he glanced at Amy and then agreed to leave them.

Amy said, 'Let's put the lid on the sandpit so Polly doesn't mess everything up.' They solemnly lifted the lid on together, and Sam came away without a fuss.

*

110

At Holly Court, Nurse Todd suggested that the children might prefer to be outdoors and led the way through to the gardens, where the lawn was dotted with croquet hoops. Sam ran on ahead and Rosie, with May on one arm leaning on a stick and Cara holding her other hand, teetered gently down the path towards the summerhouse.

'He's very . . . *bouncy*,' May said, looking after Sam as he raced over and yanked open the glazed summerhouse doors.

'That's one way of putting it,' Rosie muttered to herself. 'Careful, Sam!' she called out.

Sam emerged, dragging a croquet mallet behind him. 'Look, Mum! I've got a hammer.'

'No, sweetheart; you're not allowed that.'

Sam pulled it down the steps, looking mutinous.

'No,' Rosie said firmly. 'Put it back nicely.'

As they reached the summerhouse, she saw the box of wooden balls and told him that he could take just one and roll it through each hoop in turn. 'See how many goes it takes you and we'll clap if you do any in one go,' she finished. She helped May into one of the generously upholstered bamboo chairs and subsided into another with Cara on her lap.

'How are you, Aunty?' she said. 'This is Cara.'

May took no notice. 'My bones ache,' she said petulantly, rubbing her knees and then her elbows. She laid her head back on the cushion and closed her eyes.

Cara wriggled down off Rosie's knee and she lifted her back on again. Thinking that May was going to take a catnap, Rosie fished in her bag for a nursery rhyme book to entertain Cara. She began turning the pages, singing first 'Pop goes the Weasel' and then 'The Grand Old Duke of York' while she jigged Cara up and down on her knee. When she began to sing 'Hey Diddle Diddle', she was aware of May's wavery voice joining in.

111

'"... and the dish ran away with the spoon,"' they finished together.

'Do you remember singing that to me when I was a little girl?' Rosie asked softly, trying to lead her back to a time that might include memories of Lily.

May opened her eyes and looked at her in an unfocused way. 'Mother used to sing it to us,' she said dreamily. 'She used to play it on the piano.'

Rosie sighed. It was hopeless. The summerhouse was warm, with a sweet, slightly sickly smell of wood and creosote. Squares of light from the small-paned windows lay across her lap and she cuddled Cara in, as the child began to relax into sleep, her mouth half-open, her head lolling against Rosie's breast.

Suddenly, May leant across and touched Cara gently on the cheek. 'Which one is this? Where's the other one?'

Rosie stiffened. 'Who do you mean, May? Does she remind you of Rosie? Is that it? Do you mean, where's Lily?'

'Lily's gone,' May said sadly.

Rosie hardly dared breathe. 'What happened to Lily?' she asked, trying to keep her voice light.

'It was an accident, a terrible accident.' She shook her head, frowning. 'It was Maria's fault. Helena was never the same after.' She passed her hand in front of her face as if to flap away a pestering insect. 'We don't speak of it.'

'I don't remember Maria,' Rosie said casually, afraid to break the spell of May's remembering.

'The Spanish girl. The one that Michael got to look after the twins so Helena could work ...' She faltered and tutted at herself in frustration. 'Like a nanny. What d'you call them?'

'An au pair?' Rosie hazarded.

'That's it.'

Something stirred in Rosie's memory. A dark-haired girl with a long ponytail and freckled skin. A park playground. Being held under the arms and spun round, legs flying out, socks wrinkled round ankles, squealing with delight. Taking turns on a slide: Maria waiting at the bottom to catch them, first Rosie flying down to the bottom and jumping off, yes, then Lily . . . Lily in cotton dungarees and with pigtails and a chubby face, pushing herself off at the top and coming zooming down towards her . . .

'And what happened? What went wrong?' Rosie asked with a lump in her throat.

'I'm not to talk about the accident. That's what Michael said.'

Rosie tried another tack. 'Why not, May? Why should you not talk about it?'

May gripped on to the arms of the chair, looking fierce. 'He thought it would make Helena ill again. That she'd have to go away to that place; that she might never come out. But he was wrong. I said we *should* talk about it, that she needed to grieve for Lily. We argued and argued but he wouldn't change his mind, and he took her away.' Her eyes filled with tears and Rosie put her hand over her aunt's bony fingers. 'I didn't want them to go. Michael said it would be best – a new start for them. He said there were too many reminders in the village, too many people who knew and might bring it up.'

'You mean they moved from Weedon Bec to Highcross?'

May nodded.

Something was beginning to make sense. She thought of her mother's periods of acute anxiety, when she would become restless and unable to sleep. She would watch TV late into the night or see the doctor for sleeping tablets. She remembered her father's efforts to keep Helena from withdrawing: weekends away for 'a change of scene', hobbies taken up together that lasted only weeks before being laid aside, references to things Rosie hadn't understood at the time – 'counselling', 'the talking cure'; the move had not been enough. She remembered herself at the centre of their arguments, how torn it had made her feel: endless disagreements over what she could be allowed to do, her mother's appeals that horse-riding or gym or even school trips were dangerous, and her father's brisk replies about 'mollycoddling' or 'cotton wool'. 'Life *is* dangerous,' he'd said once in exasperation, and her mother had looked at him as if he'd slapped her.

May said, 'I took their house on but they didn't come back, not even for Christmas. They didn't want to face it, kept it all under the carpet, didn't want you . . . I mean Rose, to know . . .' She looked from Rosie to Cara as if suddenly confused and stopped short.

'How did the accident happen, Aunty?' Rosie tried to keep the urgency she felt from her voice. 'You can tell me now, can't you? I'm all grown up.'

May made her mouth a firm, straight line.

'May, please! I really need to know!'

May put her hand over her eyes. 'Swept away,' she murmured, 'just swept away.' She began to weep.

'I'm sorry. I'm so sorry, May. I didn't mean to upset you.' She felt her own throat tighten and squeezed May's hand. 'We won't talk about it any more.' She gave her a tissue but May just held it in her hand, so she took it back and dabbed her cheeks and then, as she would for one of the children, held it to May's nose and said, 'Blow.'

From the corner of her eye she saw Sam kick the croquet ball into the border. He mooched over to the summerhouse. 'You said you would clap, Mummy,' he said. 'You said you were going to watch.'

Her heart still thumping, she said, as cheerily as she could manage, 'I'm sorry, love. I can watch you now.'

Sam glanced uncertainly at May with her weepy-looking eyes and back to his mother. Make everything as normal as you can, Rosie told herself in an effort to steer through the current of emotion that her scraps of memory had brought whirling behind them. 'Can you find the ball and have another go?' She longed to get away on her own to have a chance to think, but first she must calm everything down for the others. She nodded encouragingly to Sam and he trailed off to retrieve the ball. She touched May's hand and said, 'Look, May; let's see if Sam can get a hole-in-one. Remember when you and Helena used to play golf on the links course at Clifftops? Why don't you tell me about those days?'

That evening, despite all her efforts, the children seemed to pick up on her disturbed state and were difficult to settle. It was nine o'clock by the time she had read to Sam from his current favourite, *The Little Prince*, and no sooner had she got him down than Cara woke with a wail. She knelt by the lobster-pot cot and put a hand on Cara's tummy while she soothed her and sang her back to sleep. The evening was humid, sticky and uncomfortable; she smoothed Cara's hair away from her face and folded back the blanket. She turned on the Cinderella nightlight that stood on a stool beside the cot and from the windows of the blue and silver pumpkin coach a faint, cool light glowed.

Rosie tiptoed from the room with the strains of 'Lullaby and Goodnight' still echoing in her head. She went slowly downstairs, thinking that all the songs she sang to Cara were ones her mother had sung to her. It made her feel sad. Even though there was continuity about it, tonight it felt too poignant. She started picking up toys in the living room and returning them to the wicker toy box. Suddenly she stopped, a ragdoll dangling from her hand. Something was moving in her brain . . . something to do with songs and the leggy, sprawling shape of the doll . . . suddenly, it was there, fully formed, a voice singing that was not her mother's:

La araña chiquitita trepó por la pared,
Vino la lluvia y al suelo la tiró ¡plof!

Chiquitita spider climbed up the wall,
Down came the rain and threw it down, plop!

Maria's incey-wincey spider song. She groped for more: brown fingers walking up the pale inside of her arm and then tickling, laughter . . . it faded away.

She tried to picture Maria's face as she sang but nothing would come. May had said that Lily's death had been an accident and that it was Maria's fault. Rosie's mind flicked over myriad possibilities: Lily pulling away and running into the road; or climbing up to a window left open, or a lake, a river, a slip, a fall, a moment's inattention; all nightmare scenarios that she and probably all mothers had hovering at the back of their minds. Maria had been young, just a girl really, too young to have had experience bringing up kids of her own.

She tipped the last of the toys into the box. There had been other games, she was sure. Lions and tigers – that had involved crawling around under the furniture, Lily and her being chased on all fours, and hide-and-seek, *one elephant, two elephants . . . ten elephants . . . COMING!* Who was it coming to find them? Mum or Dad? There was a big tree you could hide behind. You could get right in amongst the branches. It had smelt strange – musty – and there was something squashy underfoot. She shut down the lid of the toy box and went out into the garden to carry on tidying away the debris of the day.

Twilight was falling, the grass felt cool and damp beneath her feet and the honeyed scent of buddleia hung in the air. Automatically, she began filling a plastic crate with balls and bubble bottles, Cara's stacking cups and Sam's dumper truck. She bent to pick up Sam's cars from his diggings: a big patch now with beaten mud racetracks lined with little pale stones gleaned from the soil. Flashes of sandy colour in amongst them caught her eye and she picked one out between her finger and thumb: a shard of biscuit-ware pottery. She found others and laid them out on the slab path, turning them over and over.

Surely it couldn't be . . . May had said that Rosie had lived at this house as a child but she had no recollection of it. She picked up Sam's red metal spade and scraped a long furrow in the soil until she hit something hard; then she dug around it to loosen the earth's grasp on it. She lifted out a rounded object to see the sketched eyes and the unmistakable shape of the long ear of the hare she'd broken long ago. Her body prickled with sweat as if she were again the child full of fear at what she'd done . . .

Slowly, she straightened up and turned towards the overgrown part of the garden. As if in a dream, she walked towards the mulberry tree and stood at the edge of the nettle bed surrounding it, peering between its drooping, twisted branches, some bent to the ground creating a shady hiding place within, deep and cavernous to a tiny child. A sharp, musty smell caught her nostrils and she leant forward to look in under the branches where the undergrowth was spattered with mouldering fallen fruits, dark juice staining the broad bramble leaves and serrated nettle leaves beneath.

In here, Rosie! Quick! Get under!

117

Coming . . . ready or not . . .

She backed away and subsided on to one of the patio chairs. With a sharp sense of loss, the memory of being gathered in under the tree suddenly became clearer in her mind, Maria's arms around her and Lily, staying very still and not making a sound.

She closed her eyes. What else? What else did they do together? She remembered sitting on a hard bench seat, being strapped into some kind of square truck with Maria between her and Lily. Maria had put her arms around them both then too, and Rosie had felt both happy and sick with excitement at the same time. Then the cart had sped along a track, up and down, mountains and dips, at the apex of each slope a glimpse of something sparkling; there had been a rattle and a clatter and the smell of sweat and patchouli . . . she felt uneasy. There was something here, something important. She remembered that her legs had felt wobbly when they got off the little rollercoaster. Had they been at a fairground? The wind had been blowing; she remembered her hair in her face and the noise of its buffeting. There had been fish and chips and, later, ice cream. She shook her head. Perhaps that had been on a different day.

Where could they have been when they went on the rollercoaster? She thought again of the way the horizon seemed to glitter from the top of the peaks – the seaside. They had been at the seaside. But why did she feel dread grip her when she thought of the way the wind blew and blew?

She squeezed her eyes tight shut in concentration . . . Collecting pebbles and long, blue razor shells. Damp sand gritty between her toes, a wet swimming costume that rolled into a tight band and stuck to her when she tried to get it off, her mother's voice saying 'skin a rabbit'; all of these could have been from any number of holidays, she thought; there was no memory of Lily beside her. Then, suddenly, the sound of the wind again, boisterous, blustery, windbreaks flapping somewhere down below her, something yellow in front of her, flicking round and round, flickering with the sun so bright behind it she could hardly see. Then a horrible sound, someone gripping her hand so tight it hurt – that sound – someone screaming . . .

Rosie sat bolt upright in the chair, gasping for breath. *Tick-tick-tick*, the sound of the whirring yellow object was still in her ears, although the pictures had gone. She put her hand to her throat, feeling sick and exhausted, her pulse beating fast in her neck. The garden had grown dim and she had the strangest impression that the darkness was spreading out from her, a miasma of fear and sadness. She stared at the grass at her feet where dew had formed, unwilling to raise her eyes. She dared not look towards the mulberry tree where she sensed that the darkness concentrated and thickened as though in answer to her own black thoughts. She felt, rather than saw, a girl's shadowy shape beneath the branches, a pale face peeping between them, its expression pleading, calling for her. *Come and find me . . . come and find me . . .*

Keeping her eyes downcast, she stumbled across the uneven slabs of the patio and hurried indoors, shutting and locking the door behind her. As she turned on the kitchen light it seemed to her that the darkness leapt at the glass pane of the door, pressing up against it, a flat square of impenetrable blackness. She turned her back on it and made her way upstairs. Undressing in the dim glow from Cara's nightlight, she let her clothes lie where they fell, and crawled into bed.

Some hours later, she was woken not by a sound but by a sensation. Something light, like hair or feathers, had touched her cheek. She lay still on her back with her eyes closed. There

119

it was again, this time on her forehead and then her lips. She passed her hand over her face and blearily opened her eyes. In the dim glow of the nightlight, between her and the ceiling was a haze of falling whiteness, which, as her eyes found their focus, resolved itself into its constituent parts: hundreds . . . thousands of tiny threads. The air was thick with them. Half dreaming, half waking, she watched for a moment, as one might watch snow through a window, coming down thick and silent, mesmerised by its steady, continuous falling.

The room was cold and she shivered, rising to awareness through the muzziness of sleep. What was this . . . *stuff?* She felt it on her eyelashes as she blinked, dusting her bare arms and shoulders, slippery under her fingers on the surface of the duvet – strands of silk.

At the foot of her bed, beside Cara's cot, a figure was standing, looking down at the sleeping child. Through the thick air, Rosie saw her shape silhouetted against the blue-white light of the nightlight: a small figure wrapped in a shawl and with a long plait hanging down her back. A scream formed in Rosie's throat but couldn't issue from her mouth; her body felt heavy; she was pinned to the bed like a butterfly to a card. She saw the girl's serious face, intent on her daughter; in frozen immobility she saw her white hands reaching over the rail as the child bent towards her . . .

With a huge, trembling effort, as if pushing her way through quicksand, Rosie raised one hand, groped through the thickening mist of filaments for the bedside lamp and snapped on the light.

Nothing. Yellow light flooded the room, returning the pastel colours of the floral duvet and curtains, the clumsy shape of the lobster-pot cot, the air as clear as glass. Rosie leapt out of bed and in two strides was lifting Cara, warm and heavy with sleep, and clutching her to her breast. Cara, rudely awakened, let out a long bewildered wail. 'There now, there now; it's all right.' Cara began to cry in earnest. Rosie rocked her to and fro, comforting herself as much as Cara. 'It's all right. It's all right,' she said.

There was a thump from Sam's room as his feet hit the board floor and then running footsteps. He appeared in the doorway in just his pyjama bottoms, his hair all tousled, and stood there blinking. 'Cara woke me up,' he said grumpily. 'Why's she crying?'

'I . . . Silly Mummy woke her up,' Rosie said. 'I must've been having a nightmare.' She looked around at the room: its ordinary debris of clothes and books, hairbrushes and cosmetics. No intruders. No floating silk or dusty film of threads. But it had seemed so real! The ticking noise and the flashing yellow brightness came to her again like a sickness. What was happening to her? She sat down suddenly on the edge of the bed and Cara's subsiding sobs gained strength again. 'Shh, shh,' she said, rocking and rubbing Cara's back. 'Come on,' she said to Sam, 'Let's get in all together.' She didn't want either of them out of her sight. Rosie got in and sat up in bed with Cara snuggled down beside her.

Sam climbed in on the other side, burrowing down under the duvet. 'Can we have the light off?'

'Not just yet. Mummy's going to read for a bit,' Rosie said. She picked up her novel and made a show of finding her place.

Once the children were asleep, she put the book down and simply sat, watching the room. The clock on the bedside table ticked away the minutes as if nothing whatsoever had happened; the children's breathing grew regular and light; far away a train rattled through the night and then the ordinary, everyday quiet returned.

*

Rosie woke with a start; someone was hammering on the door and leaning on the doorbell at the same time. The noise stopped, as if whoever was down there was listening to see if anyone was coming to open up. Bright light edged the curtains; she must have slept in. Cara was still asleep beside her but the duvet was pushed back on Sam's side and the bed was empty. Her heart turned over as she remembered the night's events but then subsided as she heard the familiar strains of loud cartoon music from the TV downstairs. Of course, it was all right; Sam had got himself up, that was all.

She struggled from the bed as the row downstairs started again. 'OK, OK, I'm coming!' she called out as she hurried down, barefoot and in her pyjamas. She opened the door a crack, thinking that it would be some deliveryman with the wrong address. Instead, Josh was standing on the doorstep. Behind him, his car was parked nose-to-tail with hers. Scowling, he slowly took his finger from the doorbell. 'Are you up at last? Can I come in?'

'Yes, yes, of course. Come in.' Automatically, she stood back and opened the door to let Josh into the narrow hall. Still coming round from heavy sleep, her mind seemed fixed on her strange night-time experience, as if the floaty, cottony stuff were filling her skull, making normal connections impossible. She turned on her heel and squeezed past her mum's bike to get to the kitchen. 'What are you doing here? Do you want tea?' she said.

Josh followed her, making a meal out of getting past the bike. 'You can't be serious!' he said. 'You were supposed to meet me at the service station.' He turned his wrist over to stare at his watch with exaggerated concentration. 'Oh, two hours ago at least.'

Rosie stopped, the box of tea bags in her hands. 'Oh God! I forgot.'

'You *forgot?*' Josh raised his eyebrows.

'I mean, I knew yesterday – I had it all planned, only I had the most awful night. I must have gone off really heavy when I finally did get to sleep.' She rubbed her forehead as if smoothing lines away.

'Have you been drinking?' Josh asked, his voice deepening.

'No!'

'Or taking sleeping pills?'

'No I haven't,' Rosie said sharply.

Josh folded his arms and surveyed her. 'Because I sat there for ages wondering where you were, thinking you might have had an accident; that something might have happened to the kids.'

'Well, why didn't you call me?'

'I did,' Josh said drily.

Rosie's eyes flew to her bag on the table beside them, where she knew her phone was – right at the bottom. 'Well, I'm sorry,' she said. 'I'm not usually like this.' She plonked the tea bags down and took some bread from the bread bin for toast.

'Haven't the kids even had breakfast?' Josh said. 'For God's sake, Rosie, we're supposed to be going to Monkey World. Remember, I told you – Sam wanted to do the junior zip wire through the trees? I booked for two o'clock. It cost the earth!'

'Look, I said sorry. I was up in the night with a horrible nightmare – really weird . . .' Josh was looking at her with a strange, wary expression. She pushed her hand through her tangled hair. 'Things haven't been easy, right?' She felt her voice tremble a little and was furious with herself.

Josh went to the living-room door and Rosie heard him telling Sam to turn the TV off *right now* and go and get dressed. 'We're going in ten minutes,' he finished.

She pushed the button of the toaster down; she would do

toast and marmite and they could eat it in the car. She heard the thump of Sam's feet as he stomped up the stairs and Josh returned.

'He doesn't want to do what he's told, does he?'

'He's fine, just a bit unsettled by all the changes,' she said defensively.

'Why don't you go back to the flat then? It's a bloody nuisance having to hare up and down the motorway to pick them up.'

'I didn't mean that kind of change.' *As you well know*, she thought. 'Anyway, it's not as if I've taken them off to Aberdeen, it's only forty miles apiece.'

'Or a damn sight further today. Sleeping in until midday! What's the matter with you?'

They glared at each other.

'There's nothing the matter with me, I just had a bad night, that's all.'

He looked sceptical. 'Are you sure? Because if you're depressed, it would be better to get something for it. It's not really fair on the kids.'

Rosie said stiffly, 'I'm not depressed.' There was no way she'd tell Josh that she was taking pills.

Josh let the silence lengthen. Pointedly, he looked around at the messy kitchen: a pile of dirty clothes on the floor beside the washing machine, last night's dishes still in the sink, a litter of crisps and a smear of jam on the table. Upstairs, from Sam's bedroom, the sound of a computer game began. 'You know what your mum was like.'

'I'm not.'

'All I'm saying is there's a history.'

'I'm fine.'

'Because my first concern has to be the children.'

'I said I'm fine.' Rosie raised her voice and pushed past him.

She ran upstairs, a mixture of anxiety and anger coursing through her, a pressure in her chest.

She picked Cara up, changed her nappy, dressed her and cleaned her teeth, telling her that she was going to have a lovely trip to some woods with her daddy. She took her into Sam's room and told them both that they could have toast in the car. 'It'll be like having a picnic on the way,' she said brightly.

'But I want Sugar Puffs,' Sam said.

'Toast will be nicer.'

'Toas . . . toas . . .' Cara repeated.

'I don't want toast!' He clenched his fists, on the verge of working himself up.

'Plee-ease, Sam,' Rosie said, at the end of her tether.

The unfamiliar tone in his mum's voice made him pause.

'That's my good boy,' Rosie said and shepherded him downstairs, carrying Cara on her hip.

Josh was already at the door and, without speaking to him, she put Cara into his arms and went to wrap up the toast in tin foil and fetch the children's bags.

Josh strapped the kids in and took the bags from Rosie. 'Three o'clock tomorrow at the service station then,' he said. 'You won't forget?'

'I'm tired, not mentally deficient,' she snapped.

After they'd gone, Rosie made tea and took it up to the bathroom. She stood under the shower with her eyes closed, letting the warm water run over her hair and skin, trying to focus on the sensation and let it soothe her uneasiness. Although she'd never admit it to Josh, she was really worried about the things that were happening to her: the strange memories that were surfacing, the waking dream, the appearance of the girl . . . Well, *seeing* things: that wasn't normal, was it?

125

She opened her eyes and the white steam filling the bathroom took her back with a lurch to the night before and the heavy, choking sensation that had felt so real, not like a dream. She wondered if the anti-depressants might be behind it all, whether the muzziness she often felt was only part of a far worse side-effect, but she quailed at the thought of cutting back on her pills. She knew she wouldn't cope without them. If she could just get back on top of things Josh wouldn't be able to needle her so. She didn't like the way he had said 'my first concern has to be the children.' What did he mean? He seemed to imply that she wasn't in a fit state to look after them properly. He needn't know she was taking anything; nobody need know. The phrase 'mother's little helper' drifted through her mind, making her feel anxious once again. She wondered if this was how her mum had sometimes felt: as though what was demanded of her was just too much, as if she were crawling through the days with her secrets a crushing weight on her back. The steam was horrible; it made it hard to breathe . . .

She turned the shower off, stepped out and wrapped herself in a towel. The shower dripped for a few moments and then stopped. Silence. She dried herself slowly, listening to it. She would put the radio on when she went downstairs; get some voices in the house. She thought about the night to come. Perhaps she would leave the radio and the light on through the night.

SEVEN

1812

Effie sat next to the fire in the shepherd's cottage, a newborn lamb wrapped in a sack upon her knee. She dripped some beestings, the ewe's first milk, from the pen filler on to her fingers and tried again to get the animal to open its mouth, holding her wet fingers to its muzzle so that it should get the scent of the milk. 'Come, come, won't you give suck, little one?' she murmured to it, but it lay inert, its damp body smeared with streaks of blood and blue-white matter.

The shepherd, old Martin Eben, had found it caught in a drift against a hedgerow with its dead mother. The snow had come down fast and the north-easterly was whipping it into drifts before he could gather all the flock in from the lower pasture; the worst snow he'd seen in twenty years. Even though

Hob Talbot had set the other men on to help gather the sheep into the fold and had stridden out himself in overcoat and gaiters, there were still ewes unaccounted for. Seeking shelter in the lee of the hedges, deep in between the gnarled roots of cob and hawthorn, a few might not be found until the spring thaws and the gatherings of crows. This lamb had only a slim chance, for it must have the beestings in the first twenty-four hours of its life or it would not survive. The shepherd had brought it back over his shoulder to one of the pens made of hurdles and thatch within the fold, and tried to introduce it to another ewe. He had rubbed it with the afterbirth of her single lamb to make it smell like her own and put it to the teat but the ewe had repeatedly rejected it. The lamb's strength had begun to wane; it would not suckle and he had been forced to bring it indoors to try feeding it by hand.

Once again, Effie rubbed the lamb's body briskly with the sacking to try to stimulate the coursing of its blood. This time, it struggled weakly, its bony knees digging into her thighs as it tried to rise to its feet. Quickly she dipped again, held her dripping fingers to its mouth and exclaimed, 'There, now we have it!' as the lamb's rough tongue rasped her fingers. She picked up the pen filler and skilfully substituted it for her fingers, smiling as the lamb coughed and then swallowed as she squeezed the dribbles of liquid on to its tongue.

The wind whistled in the chinks between stones and lintels. The dwelling was crudely built and the circle of warmth around the scant fire was a small one. She felt the cold against her back and the draughts around her ankles and was glad that she had worn all the layers she owned. Snow blew in below the door in gritty puffs of vicious cold. She was glad, too, that Beulah and Tobias would have been safely at the manufactory before this blizzard started and hoped that it would blow itself out long before they made their way home. She hoped that Jack had not been fool enough to set out in such weather and re-assured herself that it was certainly too poor to ride.

After their meeting on the day that the boxes of snowdrops had toppled, he had returned each day at the same time, as if his ride always took him along the same route and coincided with the departure of the carter, so that they might walk together from the nuttery. She had been shy and cautious at first but he had asked her many questions. He said that he knew nothing about these parts and had enquired about the countryside around them and the history of the villages, to draw her into conversation. She found herself telling him where the source of the river was to be found, bubbling up from underground beneath a path near the woods, and the stories of the lords and ladies entombed in the churches, their sleeping alabaster effigies carved so fine you could trace the strands of the lords' beards or the embroidered flowers on the ladies' bodices. He had spoken of his family and his boyhood in Oakley, until her reserve broke down and she told him of her father's work as carpenter for Hob Talbot's estate, for which he needed to read, write and figure, for measuring and the drawing up of plans. He had taught her mother, who in turn had taught Effie, for her father believed that learning was a way out of poverty for the common man and that it should be the birth-right of all, for all were equal in the eyes of the Lord. He had written, in the front of their family Bible, the words of the old radical, John Ball: *When Adam delved and Eve span, Who was then the gentleman?* Effie had smiled as she told him this; partly at the memory of how readily her father used to quote it and partly in recognition of how she could bandy words with Jack quite happily on subjects that others would assume beyond her station both as a woman and as a common farmhand. His

129

interest and his easy conversation made her forget the difference in their stations.

She had told him Tobias and Beulah's names and ages, proudly, as if she were their mother, and a little of their natures and accomplishments: Beulah swift to smile or anger and quick to learn her letters; Tobias, less interested in book-learning than craft and skill and, at fourteen, leaving boyish things behind, determined to become a master weaver and raise their lot. Here she had stopped though, as she wished to say nothing of the family's money troubles.

Then one day Jack had not come and she had walked home alone, realising for the first time how much she had come to look forward to their exchanges and berating herself for letting her heart soften over a soldier. An hour later, as she struggled from the well behind the house with a pail whose handle almost froze to her skin, she had heard a knocking at the door and, rounding the corner, had come upon Maisie tied to the gatepost and Jack at her door, raising his hand hesitantly to knock again. 'Maisie threw a shoe,' he said ruefully. 'So it was Shanks's pony for me.' He looked perished.

Effie had stood there at a loss, blushing that he should see the state of the cottage in which they lived, clutching the bucket before her as if she could hide behind it and her shame be swallowed up.

'Forgive me for calling on you without an invitation,' he said, 'but I was so disappointed not to see you.' He looked at her with his hopeful, open expression. 'I thought you might wonder where I was.' He stepped forward. 'Please – let me carry that for you,' and she relinquished the bucket and found herself opening the door so that he could take it to the fireside for her.

Remembering her manners, she offered him refreshment,

apologising that she only had small beer and oat bread in the house and he said that he would only take it if she let him 'earn his keep' by replenishing the woodpile for her. He led Maisie into the neighbouring derelict cottage, drew water for the horse and rubbed her down before setting to work splitting logs, while Effie took the chance to set the room a little straighter and cheer the fire.

As they sat together at the deal table, breaking bread and talking, Effie put from her mind all thought of the piles of washing yet to do, of the tin in which too few coins rattled, of the pantry cupboard empty save for some carrots and a few potatoes that would barely make a soup. For a short, glorious hour she was neither labourer nor tenant, nor washerwoman nor stand-in mother, but simply a woman talking and laughing with a man. His attention warmed her as thoroughly as the fire, a prickle of excitement on her skin as sudden and unexpected as the rising sparks thrown by the crackling logs.

At length he apologised that he must leave as he had a duty that afternoon to oversee a delivery of a thousand muskets from Birmingham, to replace those sent recently to London. 'I must make haste, as I shall have to lead Maisie,' he said, 'although I had much rather stay.' At the door, he had taken her hand and, as their eyes met, he had raised it to his lips, holding her gaze. Although she knew that this was the gentry's farewell to a lady, she had felt that his eyes and his touch were more ardent than form required. She returned to her work all of a dither: sorting the washing all wrong so that wool and worsted got in with the cottons and letting the copper boil over, nearly putting out the fire.

Since then he had visited almost every day, staying for as long as his duties would allow. Each time he helped her with whatever task she had on hand, until Tobias noticed the growing woodpile and the mended chicken coop and commented that she need not take over his chores and, rather haughtily, that it was a man's work. After that, she only allowed Jack to draw water for her, so that no trace should be left of his presence.

He began to bring gifts. First he brought a pair of gloves that he said were to protect her hands when she was working at the nuttery but, although they were soft, pliable leather, she knew that, wearing them, she would not be able to feel the slender stems of the snowdrops, thin as grass, and so had not been able to use them. If she had come by them any other way she could have sold them and the family could have eaten well on the proceeds, but instead she had laid them away at the bottom of the clothes chest: guilty treasures. Yesterday, as he was about to leave, he had brought out a parcel wrapped in crackling paper: a shawl of pale mauve wool woven so fine that when she held it up the light shone through, revealing a delicate cobweb pattern. 'It's the loveliest thing!' she'd exclaimed. 'But I couldn't wear it. Everyone would know I had a follower. It's far too good for me, anyway.'

He had placed it around her shoulders and taken her by the hands, holding her at arm's length the better to look at her. 'Never say that. Nothing is too good for you, dearest Effie,' he'd said, looking gravely into her eyes. Then he had drawn her towards him and they had kissed; a long kiss that had left her breathless and quivering when they drew apart. He had touched her hair, laying a shining strand against the pale wool before kissing her again on the forehead, like a blessing, and taking his leave.

She had said nothing to Tobias or Beulah of Jack's visits. She had been concerned when he had been calling at the nuttery to find her, in case any of the other women should be lingering or the carter with his suspicious looks should still be there.

132

There were plenty in the village who gossiped and some who envied her the cottage, however humble, and said that her family had no right to it after her father died. They said that it should have been given to one of the other labourers, usually citing their own kin in particular, and that orphans belonged in the workhouse. Effie feared that a rumour reaching Hob suggesting anything less than blameless behaviour on her part could bring that state about all too quickly.

She lived from day to day, longing to see Jack. She was glad that now he visited her at home, where the track led nowhere other than her house and no one had any reason to come, but at the same time she knew that should he be discovered there it would be near impossible to pass his visit off as chance. The risk of discovery was less but the circumstances more damning. Far better that Tobias and Beulah knew nothing, for what they didn't know, they couldn't let slip.

For the umpteenth time, Effie bent to replenish the tiny pen filler ready to dribble a little more on to the back of the lamb's tongue and rub its throat to encourage it to swallow. There was a scuffling with the latch and Martin, the shepherd, came in with a gust of freezing air that almost blew out the tiny fire. He pulled the door closed behind him, making the flames bend and dance, and strode over to hold his broad hands out over its meagre warmth. 'Oh, 'tis bitter cold, m'duck – colder'n a dog's nose, a woman's knees or a man's behind.' The snow dripping from his sleeves made the fire hiss and sputter. He nodded at the lamb. 'There's still life in 'er then?'

Effie nodded. 'She's thawed out and taken a fair bit.' She stroked the lamb's ears.

'You'm the same patience as your father, God rest 'im. We worked alongside each other twenty year and he'd allus stick at a job 'til it were done.' The shepherd squatted down and lifted the animal's chin. 'Eyes're bright enough,' he said. The lamb stretched out its neck and let out a long bleating cry. He stood again. 'Bring 'er along. There's summat I want to try.'

Effie gathered the sacking around the lamb and followed him from the cottage into the whirling whiteness. The wind took her breath away so that she must put her head down and gasp, and the snow stung her cheeks and eyes: gritty particles of ice rather than soft flakes. The shepherd's heavy boots sank in, leaving holes in the snow that Effie stepped into, in a vain attempt not to overtop her own button boots. Ice water seeped in at the eyelets and through the holes in one sole and her teeth began to chatter.

They reached the fold; Martin called to one of the men to open the gate and they sidled quickly through and got in amongst the wet press of sheep. Hob and one of the labourers were busy examining the ewes and dividing them into two separate pens: one for those whose udders had dropped, showing that their time was close, and the other for those that still had some way to go. When Hob caught sight of Effie, he paused and straightened up to get a better look at her.

A well-built man in his mid-forties, his thick dark hair was still only a little grey and good food and comfortable living had kept him in rude health; he cut a fine bulky figure, swathed in his great coat. He was known in the village as a man of appetites: a big drinker, a hard hunter who had an eye for the women; last year a dairymaid, Susannah Cleave, had been sent packing by the mistress, setting tongues clacking. He turned to give an order to the labourer, as if he were about to come over, and Effie's heart sank. She wanted neither his attention nor the gossip that would attend it and she bent her head over the lamb, trying to avoid meeting his eye. Martin dropped back beside her and made some show of checking on the lamb.

134

'You mind the maister,' he said. 'He's one o' they men as acts like the wife at home has her head up the chimney. You come along o' me.' He took her elbow and steered her over towards the lambing pens. Hob stayed where he was, his gaze following their progress around the edge of the flock.

'This un's the ewe we tried before.' Martin pointed into one of the rough thatched shelters where a black-faced ewe stood ruminating, another lamb asleep in the straw at her feet. 'Put the lamb in with 'er,' he said, 'I'll be back presently.' Effie did as she was bid and the lamb tottered a few steps and sank to its knees. She righted it and gave it a little push towards the ewe but the ewe showed no interest. She pushed the lamb closer but each time she tried it the ewe walked away.

Martin returned with one of the dogs. 'This un's a good quiet un,' he said. He put the collie into a pen two down from the ewe, with an empty pen between them. 'He won't bark or scare 'er something dreadful but having 'im there should make 'er feel a bit more motherly, like.'

The ewe, sensing the threat, walked fast up and down the pen and then stood in front of her sleeping lamb, her nostrils flaring as she took in the scent of the dog. Effie found a patch of straw where the ewe had urinated and rubbed it over the orphan lamb's back. Slowly she approached the ewe, set the lamb down on the straw in front of her and backed away. The ewe sniffed the new lamb, sniffed again and began to lick until the lamb struggled awkwardly to its feet. It swayed for a moment and then took a halting step forward. The ewe, its eyes still fixed upon the crouching dog, stood still and let it find the udder. The lamb found the teat and began to suck, weakly at first and then with eyes closed, ears laid back, its whole being concentrated on its awakening struggle for life.

Effie and Martin exchanged a smile, Effie feeling the triumphant elation that a new life always brought. They leant on the hurdle watching for a few moments. 'I reckon she's taken to 'er now,' Martin said. 'I'd best get on and you'd best not stand about.' He looked around to locate a farmhand working at a distance from the master and said, 'Go on down and help Jones.'

Effie made her way down the line of pens, tying her old worsted shawl tightly in front of her to leave her hands free for lambing. Beneath her clothes, her body was warm, wrapped in pale mauve wool. She could feel it as she moved, soft against her skin.

Beulah stood at the long table in the kitchen at the back of the silk factory, peeling potatoes. Mrs Gundy, under whose supervision Beulah had been placed three weeks ago, was poking at a ham bone in a huge pot of boiling water, scraping off the scraps of meat that still adhered to it in order to make a thin stock in which the potatoes would be boiled and served to the workers as 'broth'.

Beulah's legs ached from long standing and her fingers ached from long peeling but neither pain was as bad as the ache for the company of the other children still working upstairs. She had no understanding of why she had been singled out for this punishment, for punishment she was sure it was; she had seen the gleam in Fowler's eye when he had told her that she was relieved of her bobbin-winding duties and would now be maid-of-all-work and like it. She had bitten back the urge to question why she must leave the others and he had stood over her as if waiting for her to speak, watching her like a cat with a mouse between its paws. She had cast her eyes down so that he shouldn't see her dismay. 'You are a sullen, ungrateful child,' he'd said and, taking her by the arm, he'd pulled her roughly from the line and the frightened glances of the others and clattered down the stairs, hauling her behind him so that she stumbled and bumped her way down the steps and arrived in the kitchen close to tears. She had blinked them away. She would not cry in front of him. He peered into her face giving a sneering kind of smile and pushed her towards Mrs Gundy, saying, 'Help in the kitchen and general errands, Mrs G. May be required for deliveries from time to time. To be kept busy fetching and carrying. Any idleness, send her directly to me.'

Beulah peeled the last potato, dropped it into the bucket and added the peelings to the overflowing pail of pigswill beside her. Without turning round, Mrs Gundy said in her flat voice, 'Take the slops out and then collect the eggs.' Beulah hefted the pail up in front of her with the handle at her chest and struggled outside. The snow had stopped and the wind had dropped, leaving a blue sky and clear air sharp as spring water. The trees in the orchard were shapes outlined in white: the felled apple trees softly rounded, the new saplings straight and twiggy and the older trees sculptural in their twisted shapes, trunks patterned by peeling bark and patches of green and yellow lichen. The chicken house at the back of the orchard was topped with an eight-inch layer of snow, as if it had been crowned with a hat. The hens pecked around the dungheap for grubs and worms, tan feathers and red wattles bright glimpses of colour between the trees.

Beulah gave good day to the carpenter as he passed her on his way in with a long length of timber; he was building shelves in the cellar in readiness for the trays that would eventually hold the silk worms, at Mr Fowler's request. She tramped over a stretch of virgin snow, with its frozen crust that gave under her feet with a crunch into softer powder beneath. It pinched her toes in her holey boots and soaked her dress so that it clung to her ankles.

137

The pig was a brute: a lumbering, snorting, stinking beast, and Beulah dared not go into the sty. The first time she'd done so, she'd almost been caught between its huge bulk and the wall and had been afraid she'd be crushed, for the hardest of pokes and shoves made no odds to the creature; its thick, sparse-haired hide seemed to have no feeling. Next time, she had searched around until she'd found an old barrel and upended it beside the sty wall as a makeshift step.

She rested the bucket on top of the wall, clambered up on to the barrel and tipped the slops over into the trough below, calling, 'Pig-ho! Pig-ho!' The pig emerged from the makeshift lean-to shelter, which consisted of an old door propped on its side against the wall. Its ears flopped over its eyes and its legs were covered in filth, giving it a comical look, Beulah thought, like a fat pink lady with long stockings. She stole a few moments to amuse herself by scratching its back with a stick, and watched it rub itself against the brick wall in an ecstasy of relief from itching. 'You wicked creature!' she said to it. 'You greedy hog!' becoming bold now that she was relieved of the need to get too near it.

She perched herself on the wall and took a handful of straw from the grey pile beside the sty, to wipe out the bucket and then line it in preparation for egg collecting.

Out of the corner of her eye, she caught a movement among the trees of the orchard, but, turning to look, saw nothing but a blackbird hopping from branch to branch. She clambered down from the wall and made her way past the rows of sapling mulberry trees towards the hen house. She climbed the shallow ladder and ducked her head in through the low door. Once her eyes had grown accustomed to the dimness, she slipped her hand into each nesting place in turn to feel amongst the straw for the solid smoothness of an egg. She soon had a dozen or so and climbed back down, intending to search the other laying places she knew: in the hollows of the roots of certain apple trees and the sheltered nooks under the blackcurrant bushes.

As she rounded the corner of the hen house, she came face-to-face with an olive-skinned boy, a little older and bigger than she, squatting down with his hand stretched beneath the wooden shed, in the act of reaching for an egg that had rolled underneath; he had two others cushioned in his upturned hat. His coat was tattered and so threadbare that it had a greasy look. His breeches barely reached down to his knees; he wore no stockings and his feet were bound in sacking.

'Sorry, missus, to have frighted you,' he said, glancing quickly around to see if she had anyone with her.

'You're one of the gypsies from up Castle Dykes,' Beulah said. 'You shouldn't take anything from here. The master is a *bad* man.'

Keeping his eyes on her face all the time, he curled his fingers around the egg and brought it out from under the shed. 'We has to eat, see?' Slowly, he placed it next to the others in his hat, not caring for the smudges of hen dirt and feathers.

'Oh, please don't! He'd beat you if he caught you! I've seen him bang a boy's head against the wall until he didn't know which way was up! He'd beat you and then fetch the constable as well.'

'But he'll not catch me. You'll not tell on Hanzi, missus, will you? You'll not turn Hanzi in?'

Beulah looked at the thin figure before her, his skin goose-bumped and his footcloths a waterlogged mess. She shook her head. In an instant he sprang up and was running, bent low, using the hedge at the back of the orchard as cover until he reached a gap and squeezed through, disappearing as quickly as a rabbit down a hole.

Beulah leant against the side of the hen house, her heart still hammering. She waited there for a while, to make sure that anyone watching from the windows of the factory who might have glimpsed the running figure shouldn't connect her with it. At length, she emerged casually and began working her way around the laying places. She found no more eggs, which, she thought, was hardly surprising, as other fingers had clearly been there before hers and she wondered, crossly, whether Mrs Gundy would scold her for not finding sufficient. Nonetheless, she had been hungry herself often enough to recognise the boy's starving look and to pity it.

In the event, she didn't have to worry, as when she returned with the eggs she was summoned upstairs to the first floor where the overseer told her that she was to take a basket of bindings for retrimming uniforms and deliver them to the military depot. She was to take them to the East Lodge, and say that the delivery was meant for the clothing stores, and she was to wait for a receipt.

Beulah laboured up the hill towards the garrison. The basket was large, awkward and heavily laden with many stacked rolls of tapes, and the cart traffic had turned the snow to muddy, slippery slush. As she reached the bastion at the corner of the huge walled enclosure, she was conscious of a pair of eyes upon her and dared not glance up at the lookout slit, behind which a sentry must be posted. She drew in tighter against the great wall, as if she could scuttle along, unobserved in its shadow, like a little spider hugging a wainscot.

The East Lodge was a rectangular gatehouse topped by a cupola and wind vane, and built of yellow brick, in contrast to the vast expanse of redbrick wall either side. It gained its intimidating stature not only because of its solid, foursquare shape, but by the fact that it was built over an arm of the canal and the semi-circular tunnel that gave the water entrance beneath the building was equipped with a heavy iron portcullis, which was raised to let barges in and out and lowered to secure the entrance, descending to touch the bottom of the Cut. Beulah didn't like the building's face. Its blind window openings, bricked in for security, were like blank eyes above the down-turned mouth of the tunnel opening and the barred portcullis was like a prison gate.

Today, however, as she approached the swing bridge that was used to cross the canal, the portcullis was slowly opening and a long black barge was waiting to gain entrance through the building. She stood aside to wait. Boy and horse passed in front of her, followed by the rounded shape of the boat's load, hidden under a grey and greasy oilcloth, like the humped back of a leviathan. The boat was steered by a man dressed in a rough smock coat with a cloth tied around his head against the cold. He hawked and spat into the murky green water. As the port-cullis creaked and groaned and the boat moved forward, another boat hove into view, whilst down the road ahead came six sweating horses drawing a huge limber on which sat a fat driver and a sturdy nine-pounder gun. Beulah, overcome by the noise and the scale of all around her, wished that she could turn tail. She stayed, poised uncertainly beside the canal, wondering how she was to make herself noticed amongst all the busyness.

She was soon glad that she had waited as she observed the driver stop at an iron gate in the wall, at which he appeared to speak. Just like the story in the chapbook that Effie had read to her, the gate opened as if he had said 'Open Sesame' and the horses and limber passed through. Now she at least knew how to gain entry and once the traffic had dissipated and the bridge swung back into place, she hurried forwards. No sooner had she reached the gate than an iron grille slid back and a pockmarked face appeared and demanded she state her business. Beulah repeated what she'd been told to say and once more the gate swung open; she entered and the gatekeeper closed and barred it behind her with a sonorous clang.

Beulah stared wide-eyed at the huge storehouses that towered on either side of the canal and at the boats drawn up against the wharves, where crowds of boatmen and soldiers unpacked barrel after wooden barrel in an unending stream. Each was covered in hides to prevent sparks struck from the wheels of the barrows from igniting the gunpowder. In the distance was a wide basin where further barges were turning, and beyond them row upon row of magazines. Near at hand were workshops from which hammering and hissing issued, and the whole was so busy with men, horses, carts and so forth that there was barely a path to be followed between them. The gatekeeper gave her a push towards the footbridge that was constructed against the gatehouse and spanned the canal. 'Up there,' he said abruptly. 'Go in that door and someone from the Public Offices will attend to you.' He turned back to his duties at the gate.

Beulah climbed the steps and entered. She found herself in an empty hallway with three doors. She hesitated. There was no one to whom she could tell her errand so what should she do? Strange grinding noises came from behind the central door, which, she guessed, must house the winding mechanism and windlass for the portcullis. The door on the left was firmly closed but the one on the right was open and voices came from within. In the hall, opposite the open door, was a settle. The master had a similar bench outside his office where merchants, agents and deliverymen sat waiting to be called in to see him. She sat down on the settle, placed the basket beside her and waited, swinging her feet, for someone to notice that she was there.

Through the open door, she saw a group of soldiers with their backs to her, sitting at a table, deep in conversation. Muskets hung in racks along one wall and a flag was pinned above the fireplace where a good coal fire glowed. The table was strewn with papers and account books and the remains of a meal had been pushed to one side: pewter tankards, earthenware bottles with marbles in their throats, plates with hunks of bread and pools of gravy. The smell of a rich stew hung in the air and Beulah felt her mouth filling with saliva at the thought of cramming it with bread doused in sauce . . . of licking the plate until it shone . . .

She paid little attention to the men's conversation at first. They talked of shipments of ammunition, of artillery bound for Lord Wellington's forces in Portugal and mentioned places she had never heard of: Ciudad Rodrigo and Badajoz where things were 'hotting up' against the French. Beulah, used to the adults' talk at the factory of 'Old Boney' as eternal enemy and bogeyman, paid little heed. 'Our gallant lads' had gone to the aid of the Spanish and Portuguese and were keeping the French occupied, and jolly good too, Beulah thought; there was less chance of the Monster invading and the Prince Regent coming to Weedon Royal and drawing danger after him. Everybody knew that the grand pavilions, the officers' buildings faced in stone and shining white on the hill, were meant for a retreat for His Royal Highness, should the need arise.

The talk moved on to speculation about the build-up of arms at the arsenal, with much grumbling about the extra duties it entailed.

'No sooner do we ship out powder than more is ordered in, tenfold,' one said. 'The men labour like Sisyphus with his boulder.'

'And what need, I'd like to know, for two hundred stand of arms to be in readiness at all times?' another asked. 'Be there ever so many thousand passed on to London, always a thousand must be kept oiled and polished in reserve.'

Then, one word made Beulah sit up straight and listen, and that word was 'weavers'. The small, stocky sergeant, whom the others called Clay, was speaking. He lolled with one arm over the back of his chair and had listened to the others with a disdainful smile. ''Tis for the weavers and stocking knitters, of course,' he said. 'For the containment of unrest.' He looked at them as though they were dullards. 'They used to work in their own homes and set their own prices. Now they have to either hire frames at exorbitant prices or work for a master on the new wide frames for a pittance. They strain against their yoke and go beyond the law. Did you not hear how, in Arnold, the knaves broke into the workshops and cut the jackwires from the frames? It cannot be allowed.' He leant forward and tapped the side of his nose to say *keep this to yourselves*. 'Some say that foreign agency is behind it as the support and mover of the whole: French arms and men ready and waiting in Ireland, spies fomenting trouble between men and their masters as the spark for a general uprising. And we are at the heart of it, within reach of Nottingham, Leicestershire, the ribbon weavers in Coventry, any pocket of disturbance where dragoons and arms are needed.'

The third man snorted. 'Let them riot, I say! It would be a diversion. I'm for a chance to use all that cavalry drill – better than sitting here ticking off tally sheets like a set of draper's clerks! Not exactly what we trained for, eh? Eh?'

While the three men laughed, Beulah heard the sound of boots trotting sprightly up the steps outside; and the tall figure of a young lieutenant entered the hall. He closed the door behind him, returning the hall to dimness and lending the scene through the open door the brightness of a tableau. Faced

144

with the picture of some of his men so clearly taking their ease, Jack paused, cursing under his breath.

The sergeant was holding forth again. ''Tis not merely the stockingers and weavers,' he said. 'There is some solidarity among the masses, who all want bread. Despite rewards offered, not one blackguard in Arnold has been turned in. Not one arrest has been made!' He glowered at them.

Jack's eyes grew used to the dimness and he discerned a very large basket on the settle next to a small girl leaning forward, her eyes and mouth wide open.

The sergeant brought his fist down on the table, making the plates rattle. 'We must teach them a lesson they'll not forget,' he said. 'We're equipped to do it; we're well placed to do it and 'tis our duty to the King and the rule of law to do it!'

Jack put out his hand to Beulah to instruct her to remain where she was and strode into the room. The two lower ranks scrambled to their feet and saluted. The sergeant removed his arm from its resting place on the back of the chair and got up slowly, with studied insolence.

'Wilmore! Aiken!' Jack rapped out. 'I believe you are to relieve the sentries on the west wall.'

The two men muttered, 'Yessir,' and gathered up their hats and gloves. Clay made a move to do the same. 'You will do me the courtesy of remaining, sergeant,' Jack said. 'I would like a word.'

The two men filed past with sideways looks at their sergeant. Clay's colour rose at their obvious awareness that he was about to be chastised. Jack closed the door behind them and they trooped past Beulah without even noticing her. Beyond the closed door Beulah heard the young man raising his voice. She picked out a word here and there: *disgraceful, breach of security, not to be repeated.* At length Clay emerged. He shut the door softly behind him but, as he turned, Beulah saw that his face was red with fury. Once outside, he ran smartly down the steps, escaping from the scene of his humiliation.

A minute passed in which Beulah became more and more anxious about what she had overheard. For two pins she would slip away herself but the thought of her reception if she were to return to the manufactory without making her delivery was enough to keep her glued to her seat. The door opened and the lieutenant called her in.

The papers on the table had been set in neat piles and the plates stacked on a wooden tray. The lieutenant stood before the fire with his hands behind his back. He asked her quietly what business had brought her to the garrison and she explained and passed over the paper she'd been given. 'I see,' he said. 'And were you kept waiting long?'

'No, sir,' Beulah said quickly, 'not long at all.' She looked down at her basket, practising all the skills she'd learnt in the workshop to keep out of trouble and make herself seem insignificant and slow-witted.

Jack looked at the child before him: her slight build, the heavy basket she'd been sent with, her thin clothes and pale, chilled face. He nodded as if satisfied she told the truth. Indicating a three-legged stool beside the hearth, he said, 'Sit here and set down your basket. I'll write a receipt for you to take back to your employer.'

Beulah sat down and surreptitiously stretched out her feet towards the coals, feeling the heat at first sting her toes as sharply as chilblains and then the spread of the glorious warmth over her damp boots, stockings and sodden petticoat hem.

Jack sat at the table and carefully wrote out a receipt and a note for the quartermaster at the clothing stores. He would take up the matter of the reception of civilians with his captain but without mentioning specifics. He trusted that Clay had taken note of what he'd said. It had clearly discomfited him to be caught out in front of the lower ranks he seemed so desirous to impress. Jack would leave it at that; he was not vindictive.

He gave the receipt to the child, who kept her eyes downcast as she mumbled her thanks. Remembering her expression of alert attention when Clay was speaking, Jack was not convinced of her naivety. He gave her a farthing for her trouble, saying casually as he dismissed her, 'Too much ale makes men full of strange fancies. My apologies to your employer for keeping you.'

After the child had gone, Jack settled himself at the table to check through the requisitions and stores reports that Sergeant Clay and his assistants had compiled. Despite his best intentions, he found his mind wandering, taking off across the countryside to find its way to Effie, like a homing pigeon flying through the snow. How he wished he could be with her instead of being cooped up by his duties and this damnable weather!

He had been in a state of agitation ever since he had reached a momentous decision. Effie was in his thoughts every waking hour. When he was soon to see her, his spirits rose to a pitch of excitement and as he rode out he felt as though he could take on the world on her behalf. When he was away from her his anxiety mounted that the hardships under which she lived would prove too much for her and make her ill. He couldn't bear to think of her labouring on the farm in this bitter cold. Nor could he stand to see her with dark rings under her eyes from rising early to haul pails of water to and fro for other people's washing, in an effort to make ends meet. She was proud; it was no good offering money. She would be offended and wouldn't take it. He brought food on the pretext of bringing a luncheon they could share, each time ensuring that there were provisions left over that he insisted she keep. He brought gifts to see her smile. It was not enough. He wanted to take care of her, smooth away the worry lines, and see her blossom. The night before, he had dreamt that she was in his arms, warm and safe, but as their lips met she had melted away like sand beneath his touch and he had woken, cold in his narrow bed, with the moonlight lacing the frosty window beside him. He had known then what he must do. He could not do without her and must make her his wife.

Laying the requisitions aside, he sat, absentmindedly rolling the pen under his forefinger on the table. He must think calmly and logically about how this was to be achieved. He wanted to go to her with a plan, to impress her with his seriousness. He was afraid she would think it too soon, too bold, but he could *not* wait! There were obstacles, but if he had devised ways to overcome them, surely she would say yes? She must say yes!

He would have to see Captain Harris to apprise him of his plan and ask about the waiting list for married quarters in Ordnance Row, although he feared that he might be refused point-blank because of Effie having dependants. He would also need to request permission to take leave so that he and Effie could visit his parents, and to write to his father to let him know he would be visiting with an important matter to discuss. Jack knew that Effie wouldn't be considered an ideal match for him by society at large: a carpenter's daughter with an un-supported family in tow, but he trusted that his father's calling would make him charitable and that Effie's sweet, open nature would win him over so he would give his blessing. To be real-istic, Jack thought, we might need more than his blessing. If there was no hope of married quarters within the barracks, he would have to look for a cottage to rent in the village that was

148

big enough for all and he feared his pay wouldn't stretch to it, given that his board and lodging at the barracks were part of his remuneration. If he could gain his father's approval, perhaps he would settle a little money upon them as a wedding gift, as he had for his brothers.

But first he must propose. Here his heart made a strange kind of struggling leap, as if hope and fear were equally matched and warring within his chest. Later, he would need to ask the captain's permission formally and see the parson about the reading of the banns. All that could wait. First he must frame the words that would convince Effie to be his.

EIGHT

At the end of the working day, Tobias told Beulah that he was going to a public house with some of the men, and that she would either have to walk home on her own or come too. Beulah trailed behind them feeling angry. She hated it when this happened. She wanted to go home for she ached all over, but it was dark and cold, and she knew that on the way there were places in the hedgerows that seemed to shift in moonlight: stumps that looked like crouching, hump-backed dwarfs and branches that seemed to grope towards you like grasping boggarts. On the other hand, she didn't like the Blood Tub either. The place had a sign that read 'The Admiral' and a picture to match but everyone knew it as the Blood Tub.

Many new drinking dens had sprung up around the village

to service the soldiery: houses pressing parlours into service and blocking off their private quarters with a bar at which they served ale and rum. The locals avoided those frequented by the soldiers: the Horseshoe Inn, the Plume of Feathers and twenty more. However, lately a new influx of Bedfordshire Militia men were packing out these hostelries and some, losing patience with waiting for their drink and the sweaty press of men, spilt rowdy out into the street and made incursions into the locals' territory. Both soldiers and villagers now frequented the Admiral and drink was often the spark that lit the tinderbox of aggression between the two.

Beulah followed Tobias and the group of weavers through the streets. Jervis, Tobias's mentor, led the way, followed by Jim Baggott and three other craft weavers of the old school, men who once worked for themselves, at home with their families. Behind them came Ellis Coulishaw and Griffith Hood, both veterans who had become weavers by reason of their injuries. Tobias and Saul Culley, another drawboy, brought up the rear. Beulah slipped in behind them as they filed into the inn. Jervis nodded to the landlord and, as they took up their accustomed places round an oak board, Beulah crept between the settle and the table to sit in the sawdust at Tobias's feet, out of the way of any trouble. She hunched her knees up under the tent of her dress and wrapped her arms around them to warm herself. A few old men were sitting around the fire, talking and nodding. They sucked on their clay pipes and paid no mind to the weavers. The candles burning in sconces on the walls made grey smoke marks, greasy streaks on the pale stone; the flames of those on the tables guttered and danced in the draughts from the ill-fitting window sashes.

Jervis put a coin down on the table and the rest of the men followed suit. A skinny girl, hardly older than Beulah, brought

151

tankards and a jug of ale-and-water. Tobias took a long draught before passing his down to Beulah with a quick 'All well?' She drank greedily, clearing the clagging dust and fibres from her throat, until he took the tankard back and leant in, elbows on the table, to listen to the conversation of the men.

Jervis was talking to Ellis Coulishaw, a tall bony man who had once been a sailor with an upright bearing. Now, he walked with a limp, his shin bone shattered by a musket ball, and had taken up weaving, like many other veterans, as his meagre pension was insufficient to feed his large family.

'So, you say the master is investigating yet another newfangled mechanical contraption, down on the first floor?' Jervis asked.

Ellis nodded and the men and boys craned in to hear him reply, his voice kept low against listening ears. ''Tis a loom he's shipped in from abroad, unlike anything we have here. Taller. Bigger. It has a chain of punched cards that hang atop, folded like . . .' He sketched a square shape in the air. '. . . like an accordion, in pleats. There's a treadle, and as you work the cards move through. Where there is no hole, those threads are blocked and where there is a hole, the threads pass through, so that the pattern is formed.'

'So there is no drawboy to pull the harness and draw the threads?'

'None is needed. The skill lies in the initial threading up of the frame; after that 'tis child's play. It produces more cloth, more complicated patterns. And it is *fast*.'

Jervis frowned. 'And the master?'

'Strode around, viewing it from all angles as if it were a very statue of Venus, rubbing his hands and muttering, "As I thought, as I thought." I swear he'll be ordering them in by the dozen, has probably already done so. I tell you, they'll put half of us

152

out of work straightaway and the other half will lose most of their wages . . .' His voice became higher and louder so that Jervis patted the air to say he should speak more softly.

Ellis continued, 'I'm telling you, we need to act and act fast.' A mumble of 'hear, hear' came from some of the men and was taken up by Tobias and Saul.

Griffith Hood, the oldest of the men, with sparse white hair and a high colour, asked drily, 'What have you in mind? If we refuse to work these new machines and they no longer need great skill, Fowler will simply put apprentices or even women in our places.'

'So we are all to become automatons on half-wages!' Ellis exclaimed, shoving his tankard away from him so that ale slopped over its lip and on to the table. 'Today my wife kept two of the children at home for lack of shoes and abed for lack of coals. And I'm to tell her now that soon we must feed the children on half of not enough!'

The door swung open and Jervis put a restraining hand upon his arm. A group of infantrymen entered in high spirits, jostling at the door and talking loudly. The weavers fell silent, all aware that it was unlawful for them to gather and converse on such matters. 'Look more jolly, lads,' Jervis hissed. 'We needs must talk but we don't want to swing for it!'

The soldiers gathered at the bar, one of them beating on it with his fist for the landlord. Another, who swayed on his feet, staggered towards them shouting, 'Where is our drink! How's about you give us a welcome?' He made to reach for the jug on the table. Ellis, scowling, half rose and put his hand on the jug's handle. Jervis leant between them and said pleasantly, ''Tis all but empty, soldier. Better to order afresh,' and one of the soldier's companions pulled the man away.

The landlord arrived with ale and gave the soldiers a cheery good evening but he exchanged a glance with Jervis and led them to a free table on the other side of the room. There, they started a noisy game of cards, disagreeing loudly at every hand and occasionally breaking into snatches of song. Beulah, who had shrunk herself into a ball, like a hedgepig, when the drunken soldier had reeled towards them, peeped out between her fingers to see the weavers huddling close to talk once more in lowered voices.

'Tis true that this state of affairs cannot continue,' Griffith said in his slow, measured tone. 'We can barely afford to put bread in our mouths. But the common folk have no say. If we petition, the government ignores us and the masters have it all their own way.'

Ellis drank the remainder of his beer in one draught and set down his tankard hard. 'We are nothing to them – a mere commodity,' he said bitterly. 'If we gather to express our grievances, they set the cavalry upon us.' He raised his voice in the direction of the soldiers. 'They come down on us with the full weight of the law, yet they turn a blind eye to those who injure us and throw us on the streets! 'Tis no good appealing to the impartiality of a law that forbids both rich and poor to sleep in doorways!'

'Shh! Shh!' Jervis quieted the chorus of agreement. 'We must keep to the problem in hand.'

'It is the same problem writ small,' Ellis said. 'The master grows fat off us, in his High House. He rides in his carriage and pair while he treads us into the dirt. He and his kind must have more and ever more; they cannot be satisfied but must build an empire founded on our misery!'

'There must be something can be done,' Jervis said. 'But we must be circumspect and not put ourselves or our families in jeopardy.'

'We could destroy the frames.' Jim Baggott, a dour man, who had listened without comment until now, voiced what several were thinking.

There was a moment's silence.

'Others have done it,' he said. 'I met a drover told me the weavers in Rochdale wrecked their frames and burned down the House of Correction. They made their mill owner sign a wage agreement, on his knees in the street.'

Beulah, alarmed by the turn the conversation was taking, looked up at Tobias. He sat hunched forward with the other men; his face, lit from beneath by the candlelight, was flushed with excitement, his jaw set hard. She reached up and tugged at his sleeve but he pushed her hand away.

'I would dearly love to see the master on his knees,' Tobias said and Saul muttered his agreement. Again the men fell quiet, for all remembered Fowler whipping Tobias for falling asleep and Saul still bore the scar where, the year before, Fowler had dragged him by the ear until it was almost off, pulled out of its socket and the bottom of it torn from his head.

Beulah nudged Tobias's arm harder and this time he ducked his head and listened to her. His face grew sombre. 'My sister has overheard something at the garrison,' he said to Jervis.

Jervis looked over to see Beulah's face peeping above the table. 'Let's have her out then,' he said and Tobias helped her scramble up on to the seat beside him.

'Some soldiers were talking,' Beulah said in a whisper, looking sidelong at the infantrymen in the opposite corner who were now playing a rowdy game of dice. 'They spoke of the arms and men stationed here, not in readiness for battle against Old Boney but to put down any disturbance in the counties hereabouts.'

155

'There you have it,' Griffith said. 'They would have the dragoons on us for sure if we protest openly.'

'Then it must be in secret,' Ellis said, 'as with the stockingers in Nottingham. A man I met on the London road said they cut the jackwires from the new wide frames and ne'er a one of them was caught. 'Tis true the constable dragged three of 'em from their beds and told them they'd been informed upon but 'twas naught but lies. They kept their counsel and the authorities had no proof and had to let them go.'

'Nonetheless, it is a risk we should not take lightly,' Jervis said. 'Think of those in Spitalfields who broke frames and paid dearly; they were hanged outside their workshops.'

'What choice do we have?' Ellis slapped both hands upon the table. 'We must nip this in the bud or face penury. Would you see your children begging in the street? That's what it'll come to. Drive men into a corner and their only defence is attack!'

The mutter of agreement from the men was a low growl, like a dog woken from its slumber.

'Very well,' Jervis said. 'Frame breaking it shall be.'

'But won't the master know we've done it?' Tobias said in confusion.

'He will know that some of us have done it but he will not know who. There will be no proof and he cannot turn us all out; he has orders for cloth to fulfil. He cannot find out the culprits, not if we make our pledge to stand together and all are strong enough not to break it.' He looked around at each man's face in turn and each gave the slightest of nods, Griffith holding up his hands and giving in. When Jervis came to Tobias and Saul, he said, 'Are you youngsters in or out? Be aware that a crime against property is treated harsher than a crime against persons and the new law against

156

frame breaking makes it a capital offence. There's no shame in withdrawing.'

Tobias and Saul glanced at each other and said with one voice, 'In.'

'What about the child?' Baggott said. He glowered at Beulah. 'You must hold your tongue, or you'll regret the day . . .'

Jervis stopped him and turned to her, his face serious. 'You'll have no further part in this, Beulah, but what you've heard tonight must not be breathed abroad. Do you understand? We must have your word on your silence.'

Beulah nodded vehemently.

Jervis released her from his gaze and turned back to the men. 'Then it is settled. Whenever the machines arrive, be it weeks or months, Ellis will inform us. Meanwhile, each one of you must equip yourself with hammer or pick, for all men present will be required to strike the blows. They must be got in absolute secrecy for 'tis a hanging matter to go about armed.' He paused, to make sure that all understood the weight of his words. 'It will be done at dead of night and each will return to their houses where their families must swear they have been all night, and must arrive for work in the morning as if all is as usual.'

'How will he know our demands?' Ellis asked.

'We must write them down in an unsigned note,' Jervis said. 'But who has learning enough to do it?'

The men shuffled their feet and looked down at their hands for, truth to tell, not one of them could write more than his name and some knew only how to make their mark.

Beulah, who could write a clear hand thanks to Effie's teaching, shrank into her shawl. She wanted nothing to do with it. She had told them what she knew, that would have to be enough. It made her tremble inside when she thought of the constable, of soldiers, and, worst of all, of the master's wrath to come.

'I can do it,' Tobias said, with a lift of his chin. 'I can write the note.'

The countryside was ice-bound for three days but when the weather turned milder the thaw was fast. As Jack rode over to see Effie, the sound of running water was everywhere: gurgling in the ditches beneath the last crusts of snow, running in rivulets in the roads leaving sticks and pebbles in its wake and grit washed into patterns like sea-shore sand combed by the tide.

Jack stabled Maisie in the derelict cottage and knocked on the door. There was no answer but he could hear Effie singing inside. He thought to look through the window but the panes were misted so he knocked again more loudly and then let himself in. The dim room was foggy with steam and full of washing. Piles of clothes ready for ironing lay on the straw pallets that served as beds for Effie and Beulah; wet sheets and shirts were draped over clothes horses in every corner and, above the fire, petticoats and stockings hung down from the wooden dryer like pale stalactites in a dark cave. Effie was standing at the table applying a flat iron to a cotton dress spread over a blanket. Her face was flushed with the heat, her sleeves rolled up and her dress loosened at the neck. A strand of hair stuck to her temple and as she pushed it away with the back of her wrist, she looked up. Her face lit up as she caught sight of him. Jack had never seen her looking more beautiful. She set down the iron and came to him, saying, 'I'm so glad to see you at last! How long have you been there? I'm not much of a singer!' She laughed and they embraced.

'Oh, how I've hated being apart from you,' Jack murmured

as he held her, the softness of her bare arms around his neck making his heart speed and his mouth dry. He wanted desperately to kiss her but made himself stop. He must say his piece. He took her hands in his and stepped back. Effie felt that he looked on her like a man dying of thirst finding a cold, clear stream. She smiled at him, meeting his eyes with an open gaze.

'Effie, I want us to be together always. I want to look after you and care for you and never have to be apart.' Jack spoke quickly, the words he longed to say spilling from him in a rush. 'It will take some time. I must get my father's blessing and will have to save to get us lodgings, so you must keep your place here and your work at the farm until I have a home for us.' His eyes searched her face. 'I would dress you in silks and satins if I could but our beginnings will be more humble . . .'

'What are you saying? I don't understand,' Effie said, overwhelmed by the intensity of Jack's expression and the flood of words.

Jack pulled up short. What was he thinking of? He hadn't said the most important thing. He took a deep breath. 'I love you,' he said. 'Will you be my wife?'

Effie felt a huge joy lift her; then, as if she rode a wave that broke against a shore, a great relief washed over her. No more worry. No more striving. No more loneliness. She sank down on to the piles of washing strewn across the straw bed and began to cry.

'What is it? My dearest girl!' Jack put his arms around her and she clung to him. He looked into her grey eyes, flecked with gold and shining with tears and saw himself reflected there. I am yours, he thought, you have captured me as surely as a mirror and I will never want to be let go. For a moment

159

he rested his forehead against hers and then he kissed her face, her closed eyelids, her warm mouth.

They sank back against the soft piles of clothes, their hands searching and finding, fumbling with buttons and ties until at last their bodies could touch skin to naked skin.

As they moved together, the smell of lye and cotton rose from the clothes. Through the wall, they could hear the sounds of Maisie shifting and pulling at the hay. When Effie cried out, the horse gave a soft whicker and then settled again.

Jack woke first. The room was dark; the only light the faint glow from the embers of the fire that had died right down to red jewels within grey ash. Effie lay on her side against him, her head on his shoulder, her dark hair loose across her cheek and breast, her breath light and steady. Jack was filled with tenderness and guilt in equal measure. What had he been thinking? He'd not intended this to happen. He had been weak, had let himself be carried away by the intensity of the moment instead of waiting, as he should, for their wedding night. Would Effie regret it? He touched her hair, drew his finger along its length, to the tiny curl at its end. He couldn't bear it if she regretted it. He would make it right as soon as he could; now that he knew how she felt he would see Captain Harris at the earliest opportunity and begin to put his plan into action. Filled with a sense of purpose he whispered, 'Effie? Effie, my love?' She stirred and opened her eyes. 'We've been sleeping and it's grown late.'

Effie struggled awake and sat up, rubbing her eyes. 'Oh mercy,' she said. 'Tobias and Beulah will be home directly. You must go.' She bent and kissed him before searching for her clothes among the muddle on the bed. She lit a taper at the fire and the room sprang back to life as she lit candles on

160

the mantel. They stood in front of shards of broken mirror, placed there to make the most of the light, and with a kind of wonderment Jack watched himself dressing and Effie moving quietly around the room and setting things straight. Will it be like this? he thought. Let it only be like this.

He helped her by building up the fire and setting the iron back to heat and then caught her in his arms again. 'You are not sorry?' he said. 'We shall put all to rights as soon as we can.'

'I am not sorry.' Effie squeezed his hand. 'Will you be able to come to me tomorrow?'

Jack nodded. 'We shall make plans then.'

They kissed again and then she walked with him to the doorway and watched him lead Maisie out to the track. He raised his hand to her before riding away, his heart too full for words.

He regained the lane that led to the nuttery and spurred Maisie into a trot. The sky was deepening to indigo with low streaks of grey cloud and a full, white moon rising. The wintry trees still dripped meltwater from their dark twigs. As he rounded a bend in the lane, two figures stepped back against the hedge to let him pass. One was a boy, a gangly adolescent who held out his arm protectively in front of the other, a smaller child, a girl with a long plait. Both looked up as he passed and he saw their faces plainly.

As he rode on, a flash of recognition came: the girl with the basket of ribbons who had been at the gatehouse a few days ago. Jack twisted in the saddle to look back at her. She had turned to walk on down the middle of the lane, her feet dragging and her shoulders hunched in weariness. The boy, though, stood looking after him, his hands in his pockets and with an expression that Jack couldn't read. Beulah and Tobias,

161

Jack thought as he rode on. Soon he would be able to visit openly, once he and Effie were properly betrothed, and he would get to know them, draw them into his family.

Tobias spat at the soldier's departing back and turned for home.

NINE

October rain pattered against the windows as Rosie sat at the kitchen table, jotting down figures at the bottom of her bank statement, taking the chance to look over her finances while Cara took her afternoon nap. She was already overdrawn and she could see things were only going to get worse. Paying the bills and the rent for the flat took up almost all of the money coming in from Josh and now she had to pay council tax on the house here as well. As if that wasn't bad enough, the cost of repairing and decorating was proving twice what she'd expected. She added up her likely expenses for the remainder of the month again, in the forlorn hope that she might have made a mistake. With a sigh, she added a further figure to the list. Sam would soon need new shoes.

She had mentioned it to Josh, on the phone, hoping that he would take the hint and offer a bit extra to tide her over. When he didn't respond, she'd brought the conversation round to Christmas and suggested that he could perhaps get them as a present. 'High tops, maybe? Those Spiderman ones that he likes. That way he'd be pleased and it would solve a problem too.' She felt embarrassed asking about something as basic as shoes, as if she'd somehow fouled up and couldn't even provide for her own kids.

'We already know what we're getting for the kids for Christmas,' Josh said. 'A trampoline. Sam'll love it when he wakes up and looks out of the window at Mum's on Christmas morning.'

'Whoa, whoa! Who said they'd be with you guys for Christmas? We haven't even discussed this.'

'It's my weekend. Check the calendar,' Josh said abruptly.

'Hang on a minute, Josh, Christmas is different. Surely we'll share the time between us?' The thought of being on her own over Christmas gave her a horrible hollow feeling.

'We're joining Mum and Dad and the rest of the family; everyone's invited. They'll see their cousins – have other kids to play with. Got to go, the other phone's going,' Josh said, although Rosie could hear no ringing in the background.

He hung up, leaving Rosie fuming. How did he always manage to make it seem that she was in the wrong? Now he was guilt-tripping her, implying that the Christmas she could give the children would be dull, with no playmates, too quiet, boring. Not a proper family Christmas. She had imagined opening presents together, eating toast and jam in their pyjamas, playing Lego with Sam and play-dough with Cara, maybe a walk once the chicken was in the oven and later watching *The Snow Queen* over a big bowl of popcorn. That would've been fun, wouldn't it? She looked at the calendar; maybe Josh was wrong. No – he was right, but at least Christmas Day fell on a Sunday this year. She'd felt a little mollified. She would hate being on her own on Christmas Day but they would still do everything just as she'd planned only on Boxing Day instead, that was all. For the kids, it would be like having two Christmases, one after the other.

She brought herself back to the job in hand, added in the money for the shoes and recalculated. Like Mr Micawber, she was aware that a shortfall meant misery but she had no idea what she should do about it. She sat staring at the column of figures, letting them blur to meaningless squiggles on the paper. Unfocused, she thought; that's how I feel.

Ever since she'd been taking anti-depressants, she'd been coping with this strange sense of detachment. She couldn't risk stopping them: she was doing far more than she had at the flat and was less acutely anxious, but she felt spaced out, as if she were looking at the world through glass, her senses dulled, her reactions slowed up. The dizzy spells and migraines, far from abating as the doctor had implied, were a regular feature. She wondered about the strange perceptions she experienced too. Although she'd had no more night visions, she still sensed a presence in the house: a shadow out of the corner of her eye that she wasn't quick enough to catch, a movement at the turn of the stairs that she tried to convince herself was just the swing of headlights from the road. She was conscious of her thoughts and feelings developing slowly, as if she were watching from outside herself as they rose to the surface. She tried hard to bring her mind to bear on the problem and wrote herself a list:

Ask bank for extra overdraft?
Save petrol
See if leftover paint's enough for bathroom

Send portfolio to more publishers
Sam needs new shoes!!

She could feel one of her headaches coming on.

Sam came in to show her the letter book he'd been given at nursery school. Rosie dragged herself away from her worries and took it from him saying, 'How have you got on then, chump-chop?'

'OK, I think. I've done lots.' He climbed up on a chair beside her while she turned over the pages she'd started off for him: wiggly snakes to copy for the letter S, bouncing balls for Os and Red Indian arrows for Vs.

'Brilliant!' she said. 'Look how many you've done! This is such good work I think I'm going to need you to autograph it.' She pointed to a space under a wobbly line of letters. Sam painstakingly wrote his name and she kissed him on the top of the head. 'What would you like to do to celebrate?' she asked.

'Painting,' he said straightaway.

Rosie hesitated. 'Hmm. Let me think . . .' In the flat, when she'd needed to work, she had sometimes put together a palette of poster paints for Sam and set him up with a big sheet of sugar paper at his own little table alongside her. However, she'd not managed to paint here since the afternoon when she'd had the idea for the dragon picture. Trying to empty her mind sufficiently to let ideas come had resulted only in opening the way for disturbing thoughts to return. A groping after memories of Lily that always turned to fear, as though something horrible lurked just behind the disjointed fragments she could bring to mind. Thoughts of her parents, and their silence. Their secret grief and the fact that they were lost to her made her feel both cheated and bereft.

She had visited May many times now without extracting a

166

single new fact from her, and had no one else to ask about the tragedy. For a while she had hoped she might see Trisha again and had often walked the same looping route with the children. She had never come across her and when she finally asked Tally she learnt that Trisha had moved away to Kent, to live nearer her daughter. She was left in limbo, unable to join together the little firm knowledge she had and the fragments of remembered impressions she could dredge up to make any sense. The past remained a wound that had not been closed and could not heal.

She hadn't the heart to go up to the studio, unpack the artist's materials and then stare at a blank sheet. Sam was bound to notice and ask her what was wrong. Even now he was looking at her curiously, as though the question was on the tip of his tongue.

With a momentous effort, she mustered a smile. 'I've got an idea,' she said, 'but you'll have to help me, OK?' She went to the cupboard under the stairs and extracted a big pile of dustsheets, which she loaded into Sam's arms until only the top of his head was visible, and then squashed them down a bit so that he could see where he was going. 'We're going to make a start on the living room,' she said, picking up brushes and a tin of paint from the stack in the hall.

Sam's face lit up. 'On the walls? Can I have one of the big brushes?'

'Sure can do, deputy,' she said.

They moved the sofa and chairs into the centre of the room, Sam helping to push, so that two walls were clear, and then spread sheets over the furniture and carpet, taping the edges to the skirting boards in case of drips. She opened the tin and Sam peered in at the smooth lake of pale blue. 'It's like the sky,' he said.

'Yep. Sky in a tin.' Rosie was beginning to feel a little better. Here was something she could do that would move things along; she would be one step nearer to selling the house and maybe even solvency again. She dipped the brush in and showed Sam how to take off the excess by scraping it on the side of the tin. 'Now, before we start, there's just one rule,' she said. She drew a big square on the wall, encompassing an expanse of tired magnolia. 'You can paint whatever you like, as long as you stay inside the lines.' She handed him the brush. 'OK? And then at the end you have to fill in the whole square with no gaps.'

Sam made a series of dabs on the wall and then joined them up with a wiggly line. He looked at Rosie.

'Is it a river?' she said.

'No, it's a moustache!'

Rosie drew a square for herself on the adjoining wall. She dabbed two squiggly rectangles, one large, one small, joined at one corner. Sam shook his head. She added legs to the big rectangle and dabbed ears and a nose on the smaller.

'No idea,' Sam said with his hands on his hips.

'It's a dog. A Yorkshire terrier.'

Sam looked at it with his head on one side. 'Funny dog,' he said. 'It looks more like a hairbrush.'

Rosie grinned. 'Well, they do a bit.' She painted the dog over with wide sweeping strokes. She carried on, working the paint in to get a good coverage, concentrating her mind gratefully on the movement and the simple task, whilst Sam made circles and dots, swirls and noughts and crosses in his square.

When she next looked across, she saw that he had a smudge of paint on his jeans. 'Oh, drat. Sam, I forgot to tell you to put your scruffs on. They're drying on the radiator in the kitchen.' He went off to get changed and Rosie painted on, drawing a careful line where the wall met the skirting board, letting all other thought fall away. She started a new patch of wall, losing herself in the regular slap of the brush, letting her shoulders relax.

When she turned again she burst out laughing. There was Sam, painting away in only his underpants, his skinny body speckled here and there with blue. 'They weren't dry,' he said. 'So I just took the other stuff off.'

'Very logical,' Rosie said. 'The boy genius!'

They continued, Rosie chuckling to herself as she glanced across from time to time at the small, half-naked boy wielding an oversized paintbrush. An hour later, with Sam filling in more big squares and Rosie on a stepladder doing the top edges, they had finished both walls and stood back to admire them. Rosie gave Sam a hug and felt happy for the first time in weeks. 'You've got blue hair,' she said, fingering the crispy ends of Sam's short haircut. 'Better get cleaned up.'

While Sam splashed around in the bath, doing more painting with the bubbles on the tiled wall beside it, Rosie got Cara up. Tally had invited the kids round to play with Nicky and Amy after school and Rosie wondered what she should do with the free time. She must go to the supermarket at some point; they were nearly out of food. If she felt dizzy or started a migraine she would just have to pull over and wait for it to abate. Whilst she was in town maybe she could also go and get her hair trimmed – she was aware that it was the first time in ages that she'd given a thought to her appearance – and she could go to the library and choose some new books for herself, for the kids . . .

It was then that the brainwave hit her. The library. The library would have archives with the local newspapers. She knew the date of Lily's death. It must've been reported and there might be some detail about the circumstances – all she had to do was look it up! She felt scared but newly purposeful. It would be better to know what had happened and face whatever it was full on. She put Cara into the highchair, set her lunch in front of her, called Sam and then started cleaning the paintbrushes. She *could* do this. Of course she could.

In the local studies room in the basement of the library, a young woman wearing a baggy homespun dress and with her hair in cornrows told her that the newspapers were all available on microfiche and led her over to the machine.

Rosie sat in the dim corner, her eyes on the brightly lit screen as she turned the dial, scrolling back through time. Letters merged into grey streaks punctuated by the darker splodges of photos as she speeded through decades and then slowed: 1988, 1987, December . . . November . . . October . . . September . . . August . . . 4 August 1987. The front page told of a heat wave and had a picture of the town carnival, banners and floats and a Carnival Queen; the next page had reports of plans for a new school and money raised for a hospice – ordinary things. Then she saw it: a picture of bunches of flowers, still in their cellophane with tiny cards attached, leaning against a green-painted post, and in the background open sky dotted with a few seagulls. She turned the dial a fraction; the article beneath came into view. She caught her breath at the headline and then read on.

Twin swept out to sea by Cornish rip current
Northamptonshire-born Lily Milford (3½) fell from a jetty at Whitesands, Cornwall, on 4 August, whilst she and her twin, Rose Milford, were in the care of their au pair, Maria Salvas. The child's parents, Helena and Michael Milford,

who were on the beach, ran into the water to try to save her but she was swept out to sea and the parents themselves got into difficulties. They were assisted by lifeguards and treated by paramedics for shock and minor injuries.

Emergency services quickly launched a search-and-rescue operation but the child's body was not found. The child's sandal was found by a member of the public two days later, four miles away from the site of the original accident.

The Coroner, Andrew Harcourt, recorded a verdict of accidental death and said that there was nothing that Lily's parents could have done to prevent the tragedy. The child had pulled away from the au pair and had slipped and fallen from the jetty.

Julie Birch from the RNLI said that the tragedy highlights the need for parents to be vigilant around water at all times. 'Unfortunately these tragic incidents that involve young children around water happen in a matter of seconds where supervision by an adult or carer may be lacking or when they are distracted by other things,' she said. A few weeks earlier, an older child was caught in a rip current when body-boarding at the bay but managed to climb on to rocks and was subsequently rescued by the emergency services. Last year, five people lost their lives in similar accidents along the North Cornish coast.

A cold horror came over her as if the water was taking *her*, a freezing shock to her skin and then up over her head, rushing in her ears, closing her eyes, filling her nose, her mouth . . . She gripped the edge of the desk and made herself breathe slowly and deeply. Her instinct about her seaside memories had been right then, that somewhere amongst them lay the awful thing that she couldn't recall. Even now she knew that she was imagining what had happened rather than remembering; the memory was buried deep, deep as a shipwreck on the seabed. The images she had – the rollercoaster, the yellow whirring object and the blustering wind – were tiny, random echoes, faint as the tolling of a shipwreck's bell when a storm stirs the depths.

She thought about her parents then. They had run into the sea even though they must have known that it was useless – a tiny child, taken down in an instant. It must have been something too awful to take in; shock numbing their minds against the insupportable. Afterwards, how long had they waited on the quay, watching the lifeboats quartering the bay, still hoping for a miracle? When had they started to wait instead for the sight that would break them? She imagined them standing together, watching the summer evening begin to darken and the lights from the boats sweeping the waves – the boats finally turning and making for dock – the hopelessness.

Had she been with them, she wondered, between them, hands held firmly on either side? Or in her mother's arms, squeezed tight as though she'd never be let go? And what had happened to Maria? Had they blamed her, railed at her, sent her away? She had no recollection of it. And in the days that followed, had anyone come to support them – maybe May? She vaguely recalled a car journey by the sea with Aunty May sitting beside her in the back seat, while her mother sat in the front, her head resting against the window as if she were sleeping. May had given her a stick of rock and she remembered its sticky sweetness as she sucked it, the car full of silence save for the thrum of the engine. She remembered looking out at the long line of the glittering sea. She put her head in her hands.

'Everything all right?' The librarian looked over at her curiously. 'Did you find what you wanted?'

'Yes. Yes, thank you.' Rosie fumbled with the dial, moving quickly away from the story, obliterating it in a blur of words. She picked up her jacket and bag.

'You sure you're all right? You know you called out? And you've gone very pale . . .'

'I'm fine, honestly. Thanks for your help.' Rosie hurried from the room, out of the library and into the stream of shoppers, slipping gratefully into the indifferent crowd.

At the supermarket she wandered up and down the aisles as if on automatic pilot, scanning the shelves for the things they needed: spaghetti, Dairylea cheese, fromage frais, a mountain of nappies, toothbrushes, porridge oats . . . The fluorescent lights and the beeping from the checkouts made her headache worse. She saw several people she knew from the village: the Saturday girl from the grocer's shop, the old boy who put boxes of runner beans outside his door for anyone who left a pound in the tin, other young mums from the reading group that Tally had persuaded Rosie to join with her. At any other time she would have stopped to chat, enjoying the fact that she knew so many people now, relishing the knowledge that she couldn't go ten yards without bumping into someone from the village and that she was becoming part of that community. On this day though, she nodded and smiled or exchanged a few words, excused herself quickly and pressed on. The sooner she got this done the sooner she could go home.

She passed the deli counter with its pungent smell of smoked cheeses. The assistant, a woman in a pristine white apron and cap, was serving a young man in a Barbour jacket with his back to Rosie. Fleetingly, she registered that he was

173

familiar – something about the way he moved and the set of his shoulders . . . then she was past and turning down the aisle for household goods, hurrying down the home straight, dumping bleach and furniture polish into the trolley without caring about brands or 3 for 2s.

As she made her way towards the tills she reached the flower section and her feet slowed. Bunches of sweet williams, mixed bouquets of gerbera and carnations, hothouse roses and orchids were arranged in a bank of colour before her. She trailed to a stop. Living up here meant that she hadn't been to Mum's grave for months and she pictured the gaudy silk flowers she'd left as a poor substitute for fresh ones in the marble pot at its foot. The photograph from the newspaper floated in front of her eyes. Cut flowers drying and shrivelling in the sun, long ago and far away, a small pile of bouquets left near the water's edge for want of a grave or a stone to mark a final resting place. I could buy some flowers, she thought, but where would I put them? She reached out to touch the waxy petals of a bunch of lilies and found that her hand was shaking. Bleak, bleak, the graves stretched away in their ordered rows; bleak, bleak, the sea stretched away to the horizon, wholly implacable. She drew her hand back. Pointless. Anything she could do was pointless now.

Slowly, she wheeled her trolley over to the checkout and began piling the shopping on to the belt. The cashier at the next till went off on her break and the queue shuffled across to wait behind Rosie. The checkout girl, who had dyed black hair and thickly pencilled eyebrows, passed the stuff over the scanner. 'You want bags?' she said, without looking at Rosie, and shoved a handful towards her. Rosie packed as quickly as she could, conscious of the queue behind her, but her hands didn't want to do what she told them; she fumbled with a packet of biscuits and dropped it and then stuffed one of the bags too full so that the handles broke as she lifted it. She got her hands underneath it, picked it up and dumped it on top of the rest. The woman immediately behind her pointedly looked at her watch.

'Eighty-seven pounds fifty,' the girl said, staring at her screen.

Rosie put her card into the machine and went to key in her PIN. Blank. What the hell was it? It had completely gone from her mind. She tried really hard. It started with a three, didn't it? The woman behind her was getting out her purse and shunting her trolley forward. Why couldn't she remember it? For God's sake, she used it almost every day!

'Eighty-seven pounds fifty,' the girl said again in her flat monotone.

Rosie punched in a wild guess at four numbers. *Card Rejected* came up on the screen. The girl's head jerked up then and turned towards her. She reached across Rosie, yanked the card out and shoved it in again.

'No, no, it's all right. I'll pay by cash.' Rosie rifled through her purse, pulling out all the notes she had. There was an audible sigh from the woman behind her and a subtle shifting of feet from the rest of the queue. Rosie counted: she only had seventy-five pounds in notes. She picked out the pound coins – she could only make it to eighty. 'I'm sorry,' she said in a small voice, 'I can't quite . . .'

The girl stared at her. 'I'll have to get a supervisor to void it,' she said loudly. She reached down under the counter and rang a bell. A mutter ran down the line and the woman at the front tutted and scowled.

'Hello, maybe I can help?' a voice said beside her and Rosie turned to find her solicitor, Mr Marriott, in the unfamiliar outfit of jeans and Barbour jacket, taking a ten-pound note from his wallet.

'Oh, I couldn't possibly,' Rosie said.

'Of course you can; we can sort it out later. There's a cash machine just round the corner,' and he passed the note to the girl, pocketed the change and put the receipt into the trolley before she could say any more about it. He picked up his own carrier bags. 'How nice to see you. How are things?' he asked as if he knew her well, steering the trolley away from the till so that the glowering woman could at last move forwards. 'Are you all right?' he said in a quieter voice. 'What about a coffee?'

Rosie glanced at the clock. She was due to take over from Tally at six and babysit until Rob got in from his shift so that Tally could get to her yoga class. She had half an hour . . . and she felt she was almost on her knees.

Amidst the chatter of voices and the clatter of cutlery echoing in the barn-like space of the supermarket café, they carried their cappuccinos to a table. Mr Marriott slung his Barbour over the back of an orange plastic chair. In place of the office wear of jacket and tie were a checked shirt and chunky sweater in which he looked more comfortable and somehow solid, Rosie thought. The bags he'd dumped on the chair beside him gaped open, revealing a joint of lamb, a bottle of Merlot, two packs of newborn nappies and a tin of first milk formula. Two children then, she thought, remembering his adept manoeu-vring of the buggy at his office: a toddler and a new baby. She imagined him cooking dinner while his wife fed the baby . . . chat in a warm kitchen . . . a proper family. 'Thanks for helping me out back there. I was so embarrassed! Lucky for me you were taking time off today,' she said.

'Mmm, I'm helping out at home for a bit. Just for a few days to give Viv a break. Mum helps a lot but she's not as young as she likes to think.'

Rosie nodded, remembering the early days when she first brought Cara home. Her mum had been struggling with a frozen shoulder and couldn't lift the baby so she'd done all the cooking instead. Even so, Cara had been a wakeful baby and they still could have done with an extra pair of hands.

He spooned sugar into his coffee. 'How are things going with the house sale?' he asked.

'I haven't got that far yet,' she said ruefully. 'I thought if I spruced it up a bit I'd get a better price but there's more to spruce than I thought.'

'There always seem to be unforeseen expenses when a relative passes on, don't there? People often get into a temporary difficulty.' He looked at her sympathetically.

'Oh – no, I hadn't run out of money completely at the till!' She laughed. 'I forgot my PIN. Silly really. Mind you, if I don't get the house done up quickly and sold, it soon might be a different matter.'

He waited, stirring his coffee.

'Before Mum died I was doing some supply teaching in London but I had to give that up.' She found herself telling him about Sam taking things badly, the expense of keeping up the rent on the flat and her DIY efforts that were breaking the bank.

'I'm guessing you're not allowed to sub-let so you can't rent the flat out to someone else short-term?' he said when she'd finished.

'No, the contract prohibits it – and the landlord lives underneath me so no wiggle room to do anything on the QT.'

'Hmm.' He sipped his coffee and gave the problem some

thought. At length, he said, 'Excuse me for asking, but do you feel your solicitor got you a fair settlement in the divorce? Do stop me if I'm intruding but I'm just wondering if we, the firm that is, could help in any way?'

'Well, actually, I didn't have a solicitor.' Rosie flushed. 'It all happened when I was pregnant with Cara, you see. When Josh moved out he based the maintenance payment on us splitting all the bills fifty-fifty.'

'Fifty-fifty, I see.' Mr Marriott rubbed his chin. 'But there are three of you in your household, aren't there? You retain responsibility for the domicile and all the household expenses, because of the children.'

'Well, I suppose you could look at it that way,' Rosie said uncertainly.

He tapped his fingertips together. 'So there was a transfer order for the property and periodical payments agreed from your spouse, based on figures provided by him,' he said, sounding all at once back in his professional persona.

'I suppose so; I can't really remember the details,' Rosie said, looking down into her coffee cup. 'I was in a bit of a state. Josh and I weren't speaking and work was so hectic and there was Sam's childcare to arrange; it all went a bit pear-shaped for a while.' What an idiot I sound, she thought to herself, as though she hadn't paid proper attention to something really important, as though she'd been so busy fire-fighting she'd ignored the earthquake happening right under her feet. She glanced up, expecting to see a look of professional horror at her lack of savvy but his brow was furrowed in concern, wrinkled in the same way that his eyes crinkled at the corners when he smiled. He's nice, she thought; he's really rather nice.

He leant his chin on his fingertips, thinking. 'So, you were working at the time of the settlement but you're not working now?'

'Not until I've sorted everything out here, I'm afraid. In fact it's not really viable until Sam starts school.'

'Might be worth going back to the court. Once you sell the house it'll all change again of course but meanwhile you're providing for your household on a diminished income; there should be grounds for an adjustment.' He got out his diary. 'Why don't we make a date for you to come in to the office again?'

'If you really think . . .' Rosie felt flustered. Josh would be livid and she wasn't sure if she felt up to taking him on.

'Say, next Friday?' Mr Marriott said. 'Two o'clock? Bring your financial information, bank statements and so on.'

'OK.' Rosie nodded slowly. There was no harm in looking into it, was there? She didn't have to take it up with Josh unless she wanted to. Unless you get up the nerve, you mean, said a voice in her head. She glanced at her watch and finished her coffee. 'I'm afraid I have to go,' she said. 'I'll just nip to the cash machine and get what I owe you.'

They retrieved Rosie's shopping from the trolley store and made their way outside. She took out fifty pounds and gave him a ten-pound note.

'It wasn't that much,' he said.

'Yes, but I owe you for the coffee.'

'That was all my pleasure though,' he said and smiled that crinkly smile again so that just for a second she thought: He's flirting with me!

She turned away and began to push the trolley towards the car, feeling a moment's frisson of interest, followed by the realisation that she was a little shocked. He was married! With two tiny children! And surely . . . he was taking advantage . . .

179

she'd let her guard down, let him see she was feeling vulnerable. What was the matter with men? Must they always play the field, married or not? She felt irritated. He had fallen in her estimation.

He helped her pack her bags into the boot and offered to return the trolley for her. 'Well,' he said, lingering, 'I look forward to seeing you next Friday. What with this and then your conveyancing, this could be a long and fruitful relationship.'

He was doing it again! 'Thank you for all your help, Mr Marriott,' she said stiffly, realising that she was even more annoyed with herself for her own treacherous moment of response to his charm. What had she been thinking of?

'Oh, Tom – please.'

She gave a weak smile as she pulled the car door shut and raised her hand only briefly in reply to his cheery wave as she pulled away.

Tally got back before Rob and found Rosie at the kitchen table surrounded by bits and bobs from Halloween costumes she'd been making with the kids. She picked up a makeshift mask, painted a fluorescent green, its broken elastic dangling. 'Whoooo! Ghosts, spooks and spectres!' she said, holding it up in front of her face. Bumps and squeals came from upstairs, where Nicky had made a tunnel out of cushions from the sofa bed in the spare room and, in a black leotard painted with skeletal white bones, was chasing Sam and Amy through the 'ghost train'. Cara wandered around the kitchen putting play food into a plastic cauldron intended for a trick or treat collection on Monday. She brought it to Rosie, who pretended to eat the plastic hamburger and cup cakes and then put them aside so that Cara would set off again to collect new objects.

Tally fished out a bottle of white wine from the fridge and held it up to Rosie.

'Mmm. Yes please. How did the yoga go?'

Tally poured the wine. 'Good, but glasses reach the places classes can't.' She passed one to Rosie, who she thought looked decidedly peaky. 'You look tired,' she said. 'Did you try to pack too much into the afternoon?'

Rosie shrugged, not wanting to talk about what she'd been doing in case it led to what she'd found out at the library. She didn't want to go there. 'I bumped into the solicitor at the supermarket,' she said instead. 'He thinks I should go back to court for a better maintenance settlement.'

'So you should,' Tally said. 'Josh is getting away with murder there.'

Rosie sighed. 'I don't feel as though I've got the fight for it somehow.'

'That's exactly what Josh is relying on,' Tally said drily. 'Any luck with the publishers?'

'I did have one indie publisher come back with some nice comments; they liked the work but had already commissioned other artists for this year's books. I've had three standard rejection letters since then though.'

'Well, I think your stuff's brilliant. You've just got to persevere until it gets on to the right desk at the right time. Yes?'

Rosie shrugged and gave a weak smile. 'I suppose.'

'Come on, what's up?'

'I haven't been sleeping too well, that's all.'

Tally cleared a chair so she could sit down, gathering up a half-made witch's hat – a cone of black card fixed with staples – and an old sheet with eye holes cut in it.

Rosie picked up the green mask and threaded the elastic through the eye of a darning needle, ready to mend it. 'Do you

181

believe in them – ghosts?' she asked. It simply popped out unexpectedly. There, she'd said it.

'No, not really,' Tally said. 'Why?'

'Oh I don't know: odd sounds in the house, things moved from where you left them, the things May used to say went on,' she said cautiously.

'There are always plenty of patients seeing things at work,' Tally said, settling herself comfortably with her arms resting on the table, 'drunks and pot-heads, people with concussion. It's all in the mind, isn't it? Your brain can play funny tricks.'

'But May still talks about seeing a person . . . a . . . a little girl. It still seems to disturb her even now. She seems to find her quite frightening. She doesn't *want* to see her,' Rosie said vehemently.

Tally looked more serious. 'Well, it could be the Alzheimer's or even the meds they're using to treat her. We're just a bunch of chemicals, you know, and things can easily get out of balance; lots of drugs have hallucinogenic side effects.'

'Anti-depressants?'

Tally nodded. 'I didn't know May was on those.'

Rosie, feeling herself blushing, bent to put Cara's toy food under the table for her to find all over again.

'Interesting,' Tally said, resting her chin on a plump fist.

'What is?'

'That it's a little girl May sees and that it started as she began to get ill.'

'How do you mean?'

'Well, sometimes it's deep-seated fears that surface. Perhaps May was aware that her mind was starting to deteriorate and felt afraid of losing her independence. The child could represent her fear of not coping, of being returned to a dependent state.'

Rosie sipped her wine, thinking of the strange child, and of her discovery of Lily too. She had come to the house *in extremis*, raw with grief over Mum, to a house full of echoes of the past that resonated just beyond memory. Perhaps at some deep subconscious level she'd always known about her twin. No wonder her mind was playing tricks on her; she was popping pills that made you imagine things and her desperate need for her lost family was taking those echoes and forming them into a shape, peopling the house . . . calling up a presence . . . The image of the girl bending over Cara's cot came back to her, the remembered touch of the strands of silk making her shiver. She pushed the needle through the tough plastic of the mask, making strong even stitches.

Tally topped up their glasses. 'It's all about perception and belief being affected by our needs,' she said, warming to her theme. 'It happens in ICU all the time. You wouldn't believe the number of relatives who open the windows when loved ones pass on.'

Rosie looked blank.

'To let their spirits go.' Tally said. 'Even people who aren't at all religious do it when they're faced with the finality of death. That's what I mean: folk believe what they need to because the alternative's unbearable.'

Rosie nodded slowly. *Unbearable.* It was true that sometimes she found her loneliness was too much to bear. Even though these haunting visions of the child were disturbing, maybe her psyche dreamt them up as being better than the alternative: the loss of all of her original family.

Tally drained her glass. 'Have a word with the nursing staff about May. It's most likely the meds making this worse. Get them to review what's been prescribed.' She stifled a yawn. 'I'd better get some supper on ready for Rob coming in. Can you stay?' She levered herself up out of the chair.

'No, you're all right,' Rosie said, getting up and lifting Cara into her arms. 'Bath time,' she said, hugging her tight.

Back home, Rosie comforted herself with the normality of the children's evening routine, shutting herself off from thoughts about the revelations of the day by joining in the splashing, bubble-blowing, water-pouring games of bath time. At the end of it she was almost as wet as the children were and changed into her own pyjamas and dressing gown after helping Cara into her sleep suit. 'You're delicious,' she said to Cara as she carried her downstairs for milk and a biscuit before bed. She nuzzled her face against the softness of her hair and breathed in the smell of baby shampoo. 'I could eat you up!'

She snapped on the light switch in the kitchen and the fluorescent strips flickered and hummed into life, pressing back the dark to black rectangles in the panes of window and door. She sat at the table, Cara on her lap drinking from her sippy cup, while she and Sam played the Memory game. They each turned over two cards, looking for matches among the brightly coloured pictures: beach balls, cars, flowers, trains, animals and faces. Sam was good at it, he had a sharp eye, and where once she would have deliberately picked up a mismatch to let him win, she found herself being drawn into the game, both of them avid to find the next pair. She hardly noticed when Cara suddenly stopped her drowsy sucking at the beaker, pushed the cup away and got down from her knee as if someone had called her.

Rosie took her turn, adding three pairs of cards to her pile before turning up a star and a feather and placing them back face down again. 'Drat, you can get both of those now,' she said.

'Mum, Cara's trying to get out,' Sam said, looking past Rosie to where Cara was reaching up and pulling on the handle of the glazed back door. 'What's she want out there?'

Rosie glanced round. 'It's all locked. Come on, Cara, come and sit on Mummy's knee.'

With one chubby hand still on the handle, Cara pressed the other against the thick, frosted glass.

'It's your go,' Rosie said. The glass was already covered with finger smears and, besides, Cara would get bored in a minute.

Cara pulled the handle down and let go, pulled down and let go; each time the handle made a grating noise.

'Cara!' Rosie said without turning round.

'Dirl!' Cara shouted.

Rosie, busy trying to memorise Sam's last go, which had revealed the elephant she needed to match the one she'd spotted on the far left of the table, finally glanced round. Cara had her nose and hands pressed flat against the glass, and she was gazing out into the darkness of the garden.

'What's she doing?' Sam said as Cara took her head back, away from the glass, and then slowly leant her forehead against it once again. He got down from the table and peered through the pane above Cara's head. 'There's nothing out there,' he said, at a loss.

'Boo!' Cara called out and began banging her hands on the glass. 'Boo! Boo!'

'I think she's playing peekaboo,' Sam said. 'Like in a mirror.' He put his arms around her middle to lift her away.

'You mustn't bang on the glass, Cara,' Rosie said. She knew it was toughened, shatterproof stuff but still, it could loosen a whole panel.

Sam picked her up like a sack of spuds and began to walk backwards away from the door. Cara reached towards it and began to cry, squirming in his arms. Sam said, 'Cara! Stop it! You're spoiling our game!'

Rosie took her from him. 'She's tired,' she said. Cara struggled to get down, pushing herself away from Rosie's chest. 'I'll take her up. Back in a minute.'

As she carted her away, Cara started up in earnest. 'Boo-la!' she wailed between her sobs.

'You are one tired girl,' Rosie said, holding her tight and stroking her hair. Once they were climbing the stairs she felt her begin to subside, her body slackening, sobs turning to snuffles.

'Wan' Boo-la,' she muttered pettishly but then she found her thumb and gave in.

TEN

1812

Beulah stood on the barrel scratching the pig's back with a stick, stealing a few moments to enjoy the feeling of watery March sunshine on her shoulders. The sound of hammering came from the rough lean-to next to the scullery door, where the village carpenter, Mr Guilfoyle, had been set to work. Ellis Coulishaw and Nathan Trim, another hand from the first floor, were further along, leaning against the wall beside the main door, where the master had ordered them to wait, as he was expecting what he mysteriously referred to only as 'goods inwards'. They chatted in a desultory fashion and sucked on their clay pipes.

The hammering stopped and was replaced by the sound of tuneful whistling. Beulah jumped down from the barrel and ran around the back of the sty so that she could approach the carpenter's shed without passing the scullery door and being spotted by Mrs Gundy. She peeped round the end of the lean-to. Mr Guilfoyle was sanding the edges of a long, shallow, wooden tray that sat across a broad trestle. Fifteen or twenty more trays were stacked at an angle against the wall of the factory, next to piles of chestnut planks and a wicker basket of tools. Beulah breathed in the peppery smell of cut wood mixed in with the strong tobacco that Mr Guilfoyle chewed in the side of his cheek.

The carpenter was grey and bearded. His rolled-up sleeves revealed veins and sinews standing out in his thick forearms and his fingers and nails were stained a yellowish brown by the oils he used. He glanced at Beulah from under fearsome beetling eyebrows that she noticed had a fine sprinkling of sawdust caught up in them. Keeping one hand on the post of the lean-to, as if she might bolt at any minute, curiosity got the better of her and she said, 'What are you making?'

'Beds for the worms,' Mr Guilfoyle said.

Beulah's eyes grew large. Worms, horrid, wriggly, clammy things, lived in the earth. What would you want to put them in trays for? She hated creeping, crawling things. When Tobias was younger, he used to think it was funny to catch spiders in his closed hands and then let them go beside her. He would dangle an earthworm over her head or collect clockers from under a stone and put a cold handful down her back. She imagined all those trays full of earthworms, tangles of pinkish brown, crawling over each other. 'Why would you want to keep worms?' she said.

'To spin silk, of course,' he said, without missing a beat in the constant rubbing to and fro of the sanding block. 'Your master will get the silk moth's eggs from abroad and when they hatch, the worms – that is, caterpillars – will come out. Hundreds . . . thousands of them.'

'Euuch.' Beulah's skin crawled. Caterpillars were even worse. 'Where's he going to keep them?'

'In the cellar, where he's had the stove put in. They need to be kept warm to hatch out.' He stopped sanding, ran his thumb along the edge of the tray and then stood it up on its side with the others. 'The beds'll be in stacks, one above the other.' He made a slicing movement in the air with his hand. 'Tiers of them, right up from the floor to the ceiling.' He grinned. 'I'm keeping the job of fixing these to the supports in case we get bad weather and I want to get indoors.' He winked at her.

'Silk comes from caterpillars? How?' she asked incredulously.

'Now, that I don't know.' He rubbed his chin. 'Maybe like gossamer comes from a spider? We shall have to wait and see.'

Beulah shuddered. 'Not me.' The thought of a room full of thousands of caterpillars all writhing around together was enough to turn her stomach.

From the far end of the building came the clop and rumble of a cart drawing to a halt and a carter's call of 'Ahoy!'

Through the open lean-to, Beulah saw Nathan rush off to find the master. Ellis knocked out his pipe and stepped forward. A dray horse pulling a cart carrying a huge, angular object with a large sheet of oilcloth tied over it was driven past them and into the yard. The carter jumped down and looped the reins through one of the rings set in the wall. Nathan and the master emerged together, Fowler's face full of excited anticipation. Beulah whipped into the lean-to, shrinking into the space between the planks and the wall, where no one could see her but she could peep out at the proceedings. She hoped she wouldn't be stuck there too long and began to worry that Mrs Gundy might come looking for her, or, worse still, that Hanzi, the gypsy boy, might turn up while the master was about. She hadn't seen him this morning and had left three eggs for him to find, as she always did if they missed their chance for a few hurried words behind the hen house.

Fowler directed the carter and his two men to uncover and unload the cart. Huge wooden frames were taken down, along with several leather boxes. 'Take them up but make no attempt at assembly or threading until I come,' Fowler said curtly to Ellis and Nathan. He turned away to sign the docket that the carter produced and didn't see Ellis hawk and spit on the ground beside the machinery before taking hold of one end while Nathan took the other. Ellis counted them in, as if they were about to sing: 'One . . . two . . . three . . .' The two men heaved, and, red in the face and straining, inched the weighty contraption towards the door and then on up the stairs.

'I take it the others are not far behind?' Fowler was saying to the carter.

'We travelled in tandem. They'll be here directly,' the man said and even as he spoke, the sound of hooves on the cobbles rang out and one cart after another turned smartly into the yard.

Beulah crawled through the triangular space left between wall and trays towards the scullery door, seeing her chance while all were distracted by the hullabaloo. So, they're here, she thought. Two on each cart, that's six in all. She stored it up to tell Tobias in case Ellis had no chance to get upstairs and see Jervis. Her heart, already racing at the danger of being discovered away from her work by Fowler, seemed to jump into her throat at the thought of the weavers' plans. She couldn't imagine that, come Saturday night, rough hands would be laid upon the master's property. The frames had a grand sort of beauty: solid, foursquare and with the sheen of polished mahogany.

Fashioned by some other workman's hands, they were not rough work like the plain wooden trays but precise craftsmanship: carved and jointed, each piece ready to be intricately connected, oiled and smooth.

Mr Guilfoyle had downed tools and stood at the scullery end of the lean-to with his arms folded, surveying the scene. Beulah reached the end of the triangular tunnel and sat back on her heels, waiting. The horses were being tethered like the first and she began to panic that her moment might pass. She edged forward, her boots making a scuffling noise on the ground, and Mr Guilfoyle glanced round and took in her plight. Casually, as if to clear a space in his makeshift workshop, he lifted one of the long trays from the stack and nodded at her to follow. He set off for the scullery door and the stairs to the cellar beyond, so that Beulah could scurry along, hidden on the far side of him, back into the factory. He carried on down to the cellar without a glance at her and Beulah, quick as a mouse, disappeared into the shadowy alcove where the brooms were kept and emerged carrying a pail and scrubbing brush just as Mrs Gundy came scowling through the kitchen door.

Effie and Jack were working together in the garden at the side of the cottage. Jack's red coat hung on a nail sticking out from the privy door; bright in the spring sunshine it swung a little in the March breeze. His shirtsleeves rolled up, he was scraping away the top layer of earth and straw from the potato clamp with a spade, while Effie, on her knees, worked on the section he'd already opened, picking out the potatoes from further layers. The weather was warming and the clamp must be unpacked before the last of the crop began to rot. A burlap sack was tied around Effie's middle to protect her skirt but her hands and nails were ingrained with dirt as she scrabbled the earth aside and felt for the hard knobbly shapes. They worked companionably together. Jack dug in too hard and sliced into a potato by accident so that Effie teased him a little, asking him in a strict voice if he wouldn't mind keeping bayonet practice out of her vegetable garden and then laughing at him when he pulled a face at her and tossed the potato over his shoulder into the hedge. They returned to the task, Jack humming a military air while he scraped and shovelled.

As Effie bent once again over the clamp, the pungent smell of clods and potatoes made her feel a little nauseous and she swallowed hard and tried not to breathe too deeply. She didn't want Jack to guess what she had begun to suspect. She had no appetite until late in the afternoon, and had counted thirty-five days since her last show of blood, anxiously marking them on a paper, crossing through the line of marks on the seventh day, a tally for every week that passed. Part of her wanted to tell him. In her dreams, when she told him, his face softened with love and pride; he took her in his arms and whispered to her that all would be well, that they would soon be wed and safe in their own little house, that he would *make* it well. He stroked her hair and told her that she was strong and fit and had nothing to fear. But in her waking, worrying hours she felt fearful and ashamed. Memories of the lambing were still fresh in her mind: the distressed bleating of the ewes, lambs turned the wrong way, the struggle and blood involved in bringing new life – sometimes a struggle to the death. And they were not yet wed. *Fallen* for a child people called it, and those who were not wed were fallen women. If anyone in the village were to find out, she would be forced by the parish to name the father; he would be fetched in front of the parish vestry and the two of them publicly disgraced. If she refused to name him she would be taken to the workhouse.

If only Captain Harris had agreed to grant them married quarters! They could have been having the banns read by now, only weeks away from making their vows. Jack had told her that the captain couldn't bend the rules to allow Tobias and Beulah a place and had made it sound as though it was all a case of military regulations, but the captain had also failed to grant Jack special dispensation to take leave to visit his father and in this Effie saw not goodwill thwarted by discipline but dissuasion, if not definite obstruction. She could well imagine what would have been said: not a good idea to fraternise with the locals . . . far too quick and impulsive . . . marrying out of your class . . . *foolhardy, ruining your prospects, a chain around your neck.* Jack had been far too sensitive to tell her any of it, but the look of anger on his face when he had told her that he'd been ordered to apply for leave through the normal channels and wait his turn had spoken volumes.

If only his turn could come soon, she thought. She couldn't tell him her fear that she was with child, not before they visited his parents; she just could not. Jack would be bound to act differently; he hadn't a dissembling bone in his body. And his father a reverend! Jack might feel duty-bound to tell the truth and then she would be shamed. Even if they decided to say nothing, his mother would surely notice his reticence and her blushes, and spy it out. No, far better to carry her secret on her own a little longer and hope that the visit would be soon, and that Jack's parents would see how much they cared for each other and be persuaded to bless their union.

She sorted through the potatoes as she picked, putting the good ones straight into a sack. The diseased ones or those that Jack had sliced into by accident she rejected. Those that had started to sprout she put aside in a basket for seed. Moving on along the clamp, she started once more with the top layer, reaching into the dark earth and straw, her hand finding the first cool oval shape. It fitted her palm perfectly, heavy and solid with pale waxy skin, making her think of the white curled shape that must be inside her, growing, getting bigger every day. She put her hand out to steady herself against the mound of earth.

'What is it, Effie dear?' She heard Jack's voice as if it were coming from a long way away. 'Are you unwell?' She felt his hand under her elbow.

'It's nothing,' she said. 'I rose too quickly from kneeling, that's all.' She looked up at him.

'You look a little pale,' he said uncertainly. 'Are you sure you're not sickening for something?'

She shook her head.

He put his arm around her and she leant her head against him. 'When will we go and meet your family?' she asked. 'Can it be soon?'

'It can indeed,' he said. 'I've got three days' leave for this Monday fortnight. I just need to write to check that there'll be room to receive us: that is, that John and the family won't be staying at that time and occupying all the bedchambers. I was going to tell you as soon as I had sent and had an answer.'

Effie hugged him tight, her face turned in to his shoulder so that he shouldn't see her relief and wonder at it.

'So you're pleased then.'

Effie nodded, unable to trust herself to speak.

He slipped his other arm around her waist and nuzzled her neck. 'Is it worth a kiss?' he said.

She tipped her face up to him and they stood kissing among the tumbled potatoes, so still and intent upon each other that thrush and robin flitted to and fro beside them, foraging for worms in the freshly turned earth.

*

Moonlight fell upon the village, on slopes of pale thatch and grey slate and on chimney pots grown cold. It picked out the gleam of the weathervane on the church tower, the shine of the brass knockers on the doors of the Rectory and the High House, the silver of the puddles in the street and the glint of hatchet's edge and lump hammer. The nine men walked silently through the quiet streets towards the silk factory, their faces blackened with coal dust and their hats and caps pulled low. Jervis went in front, carrying a heavy staff, closely followed by Ellis Coulishaw with a long-handled axe over his shoulder, and Jim Baggott with a length of lead pipe under his arm. 'Every man-jack of you must be armed,' Jervis had told them and even Tobias and Saul had come equipped with shovel handle and pick.

They reached the centre of the village and slipped into single file to disappear into the deep shadows below the eaves. Although it was four hours after midnight, a time chosen so that all revellers would be abed but well before first light when ploughboys and milkmaids would be making their way to the fields, the night watchman would be somewhere about, padding his solitary rounds. With no sound save for the rustle of a coat or the creak of a boot, they took their way along West Street and emerged on to New Street at the far end from the High House. Jervis signalled for them to stop and they stood for a moment surveying the empty street, the darkened windows of the master's house with its half-closed shutters, and the lines of blank factory windows on which the moon shone directly, revealing the dark humped shapes of the machines inside.

Tobias's heart thumped in his chest as he followed Jervis and the other men out into the street and down towards the factory. As they passed into the entryway between the factory and Mrs Oliphant's bawdy-house, Saul was posted to wait at the corner as a lookout, to watch the street and make the call of a screech owl if anyone should appear. Tobias felt more anxious still as he parted from Saul and was left to take his place with the older men.

A candle bobbed in a window and Mrs Oliphant's large pasty face, framed by her night bonnet, appeared above it and then disappeared again. All stood stock-still. The scullery door opened with a creak and the lady of the house stood in the doorway, holding up the candle and clutching together the edges of her nightgown at the neck. She didn't scream at the sight of the group of men, as Tobias had felt sure she would, but raised her eyebrows and stepped forward, pulling the door half-shut behind her. 'Jim Baggott, is that you? What's amiss?' she hissed.

Baggott looked down and shuffled his feet.

From inside, a slurred voice called out, 'What're you at, woman? Come back to bed!'

Jervis stepped forward into the patch of light cast by the stump of candle. He gestured towards the factory and held his finger to his lips.

Mrs Oliphant gave a quick glance behind her as bed springs creaked. 'A soldier wants a warm body for his money, not a cold bed,' came the voice again.

'Oh, hold your blab, I'm coming d'rectly,' she said. She inclined her head to Jervis and, shielding the candle in her cupped hand against the draught from the door, went back inside, closing it gently behind her.

Tobias let out a long shaking breath and followed the others round the corner of the factory. Now it was time to do his part. The coal chutes were too small even for his slight frame but each cellar had a window to let in a little murky light. Ellis counted along to the fifth window, a small aperture glazed with tiny panes of bottle-bottom glass. He wrapped a sack around the head of his axe to muffle the sound. The first swing stove in the middle with a crash of glass on to the brick floor below. The next blows splintered the remaining wood, sending shards of glass tinkling from the edges of the frame.

'Boots first,' Ellis whispered. ''Tis too high to risk landing on your pate. We'll lower you.'

Jervis and Ellis took a hand each; Tobias climbed through the hole and they lowered him down, his feet kicking unsuccessfully in search of the floor. 'Let me drop,' he hissed. As they let go he felt a searing pain under his arm; his feet hit the floor and he stumbled backwards and sat down hard on a pile of coal. In the pitch-dark corner, he put his hand to his armpit and found the cloth of his jacket and shirt ripped open and a warm, wet patch where a jagged edge of glass must have remained in the frame and cut him as he fell. He felt as if he might be sick.

A huddle of heads were blocking off the moonlight from the window. 'Are you safely landed?' came Jervis's voice.

'For the Lord's sake, get the scullery door open and let's proceed with the business,' Ellis said.

Tobias pulled his shirt free from his trousers, balled up the material in the hollow of his armpit and clamped his arm down at his side. He felt his way to the stone steps and climbed them with one hand held out before him, until he touched the wood of the cellar door. He pushed and it swung open as Ellis had said it would, for the bolt had been hanging by one screw for a fortnight and the master had been too busy with his grand schemes to notice. As he hurried through the scullery, there was a scurry of movement and a gleam of eyes that made him jump and bark his shin on a stack of buckets as rats disappeared behind the mounded sacks of turnips, flour and potatoes piled in the corner.

He felt for the bolts on the scullery door. He could just reach the top one, which slid across smoothly, but the bottom one was stiff and he had to work the catch up and down to ease it across. Outside, he could hear Ellis grumbling and Jervis shushing him. At last he got it clear, opened the door and everyone piled in.

'Right,' Jervis said. 'Lanterns.' Jim Baggott and Griffith lit them and held them aloft, revealing the eight of them, with faces black as chimbley-sweeps, a deal table, baskets, pails, brooms and mops spilling from an alcove, piles of provisions in sacks and a long shelf ranged with leather fire-buckets. 'Before we start, let me just remind you that afterwards you must get quickly home, stow your tools, wash away every trace of black, get into your nightshirts and into your beds, as if you've been there all night, tight as ticks with your missus. Understand?' There was a mumble of agreement. Jervis nodded, satisfied. 'When we get up there, keep the light well covered,' he continued. 'Jim, you go in front. Griffith, bring up the rear.' They shuffled on through the kitchen and along the corridor to the stairs. The door to the master's office stood open, weights, scale and yardstick laid neatly on the desk and the white face of the clock looking back at the moon like a great, wide-open eye. Tobias hurried past.

On the first floor, moonlight lay in skewed rectangles across the wooden boards but it reached no further than the doubling wheels, which cast strange elongated shadows as if their spoked wheels had been squashed to ovals and their spindles stretched out like spears. The new machines were in darkness, ranged in a row on the other side of the room, their canopies reaching almost to the ceiling. Jim and Griffith put the lanterns on the floor at either end of the row so that a dim light was cast upwards and glowed on the sturdy frames of polished wood

198

and the white loops of card hanging from the Jacquard heads in accordion pleats, all punched with holes as if inscribed with strange hieroglyphic writing.

'Right, lads,' Jervis said. 'Line up at the ready.' The men shuffled along until all were stationed in front of a frame. Jervis stepped forward and rammed his heavy staff between the main frame and the Jacquard head of one of the machines, preparing to lever the two apart. He raised one hand ready to signal. 'For hand-fashioned work at the old-fashioned price, eh, lads?'

'Aye!' came the rumbling response and, as he brought down his hand, all struck together. Ellis swung his axe at an upright as if he were coppicing a tree and the frame lurched forward, the heavy head collapsing into the machine's innards where Jim smashed the end of the lead pipe down upon it, pounding it to a flattened mass. Tobias, gritting his teeth against the pain under his arm, brought the pick down upon the batten of the machine nearest him and pulled it away from the frame with a sickening sound of splitting wood. All around him, shafts and heads crashed against one another, warps were rent side to side and the thick chains of folded card fell to the floor in unruly heaps like crumpled washing. The men's faces were red, their eyes fierce and intent as the room filled with the pungent smell of the sweat of labour and fear.

Above the uproar, Jervis signed to Tobias to use his pick to rip the piles of card chains and Tobias, despite his wound, was carried along in the fervour and set to, pitching the sharp point into a heap and bracing his foot against it as he pulled to tear it apart.

Ellis and Jim had worked themselves into a fury and had hit on a method. With grim-set faces they got either side of a machine and began to rock it, making use of the play in the

199

structure that was fixed together with wooden pegs and wedges, aiming to tip it forwards.

'Mind it don't go through the floor!' Griffith called out to them above the din, but it had already reached its tipping point and the weight of the head pulled it out of their hands. Both men leapt back as it hit the boards and smashed like a dropped egg, shafts and treadles flying outwards. The noise reverberated like a thunderclap, the very floor beneath their feet seemed to dip and ripple under the impact. Ellis began to laugh and Jim dusted off his hands as if to say it was a job well done.

'You are too passionate!' Jervis shouted above the din of banging and chopping.

''Tis quicker and more thorough,' Jim said, moving along to the sixth frame, the last in the row still standing intact.

Over in the High House, Fowler awoke from troubled dreams and lay wondering what had crept into his sleep to make him toss and turn until his nightshirt was a sweaty tangle twisted round him. Tabitha, too, seemed disturbed in her sleep; she rolled on her side and then flopped back again on to her back. Fowler got out of bed to take a piss. The candle was out and he felt around under the bed for the chamber pot. He took it over to the window, where the shutters were half-open to let in a little moonlight, and relieved himself, looking out blearily into the street. A small movement at the corner of the factory caught his eye; a dog or a cat, he thought, or maybe some randy soldier slipping away from Mrs Oliphant's.

Inside the factory, despite Jervis's remonstrations, Jim and Ellis heaved at the last loom and two other men left off what they were doing and joined them. Griffith came behind Ellis and tugged at his sleeve. 'It's too risky! The noise is too great!' he was saying but amidst the din his mouth appeared to open and close soundlessly.

As it tipped, the men sprang back. The frame cracked and snapped, crumpling sideways as it hit the floor so that debris flew out and a shaft caught the lamp and sent it rolling across the floor. Griffith hobbled forward and swept up the lantern before the scraps of silk and thread strewn over the boards could catch alight. He held it aloft, swinging crazily above the wreckage of beater and reed, delicate warp and weft, mails and lingoes smashed into a tangled mess beneath the broken wood.

Fowler, at the window, standing over the steaming pot, suddenly came wide-awake. A light. A light was moving in his factory. The hairs on the back of his neck stood up. The light disappeared as if it had been quickly doused.

'Thieves!' he shouted, causing Tabitha to sit bolt upright in fright. 'The knaves are after my silk!' Even as the words left his lips his sleep-befuddled brain recognised that the light had not been in the windows of the storerooms downstairs, where the bolts of fabric and drums of ribbon were kept, but on the first floor where all his new enterprises and experiments were housed. 'Damned villains!' he roared. 'They're after breaking the frames or burning the place down!' He threw open the door and bellowed downstairs for his manservant, Samuel, who slept beside the range, and then pulled on his breeches and boots, gathered up his coat and clattered down the stairs.

Samuel emerged from the kitchen, pale, yawning and struggling into his jacket. Fowler clipped him for his slowness. 'Go straightaway to the guardhouse. Knock up the soldiery and tell them the silk factory's being put to the torch. Tell them it's an insurrection. That'll get 'em moving.' He unlocked the door. 'I shall go for the constable. Be quick and quiet and we shall catch the rogues red-handed.' He pushed the boy outside as Tabitha, holding a candle before her, came to the top of the stairs asking if her silver was safe, Hebe peered out curiously behind her and the maid locked herself into her room and hooked a chair under the handle.

The dust of silk threads fell slowly around the weavers as they stood panting, looking at the wreckage, their ardour spent. 'You have the note?' Jervis said. Tobias fumbled in his pocket and drew out the folded paper.

As Samuel stumbled into the street, the sound of a screech owl split the night, not once but twice, and he turned and ran as fast as he could towards the barracks. The sound fell eerily into the silence in the factory. There was a moment's pause, in which a pile of debris settled, raising a sigh of dust, and then Jervis shouted, 'We're discovered, lads! Make haste! Out the back, quick as you can!'

Tobias dropped the note, grabbed up the pickaxe and ran. The men pushed and scrambled their way down the stairs, Jervis bringing up the rear and urging them to be swift and secret and remember their vow. Out in the yard, Tobias hesitated, looking for Saul. The sky was no longer black but fading to an inky blue against which the brightness of the moon began to diminish, telling Tobias that beyond the buildings, over the fields' horizon, the sun must be drawing its crack of yellow light. He leant against the scullery wall for a moment, his head swimming. The air struck cool against his front and he realised that the whole side of his shirt was soaked with blood where the action of wrecking the machines had opened the wound further.

Saul appeared, looking terrified. 'Hasten away! The master's out of his house!'

'Follow me,' Jervis ordered, leading them into the deep shadow of the orchard. Bending double under the low branches of mulberry and apple trees they made their way to the back hedge and found a thin place to push through. 'Now, scatter and don't look back!' Jervis said as he counted them through and each took their different ways, melting into the shadows.

Fowler stood in the factory with the parish constable, Mr Boddington, a big-boned man in his middle age, whose dark eyebrows were drawn together in a constant frown of concentration. They held their lanterns above the piles of broken timber. From outside, the sound of marching feet and barked orders reached them, as a group of men were detailed to scour the fields and others to go post-haste to the houses of those weavers whose addresses were known and bring them out for questioning.

'You say these are all new machines; the older items were left untouched?' Boddington asked, as if committing to memory all the salient facts.

Fowler didn't answer, but put his boot beneath a piece of shattered wood and toed it away as if to see if anything under it was salvageable. Still unable to take in the absolute destruction before his eyes, he picked up the end of one of the chains of cards, barely hanging together for the gashes across its width: the thread of its strange language cut, its neat rows of punched messages torn in jagged pieces. He let it drop.

Boddington tried again. 'This scourge of frame breaking is becoming so widespread I'll warrant there's organisation behind it. 'Tis prudent to involve the military; for all we know it could be the start of a wider uprising. Come daylight, we should comb over the remains in search of clues to their identities.'

'No need for that. I know who's behind this,' Fowler said through clenched teeth. ''Tis Jervis.'

203

'That's as may be, and he will be questioned, as will they all, but we shall still need proof.' Boddington moved along the wreckage, poking it with his nightstick and pushing pieces aside.

Fowler said, 'Give me Jervis to myself for an hour and I shall get it out of him.'

Boddington looked up sharply. 'All shall be done through due process of law, Mr Fowler,' he said with iron in his voice.

Fowler strode to the window and put his fists against the frame and his head against the glass. Hundreds of pounds! Hundreds of pounds' worth of machinery reduced to nothing more than kindling. By God, he would make them pay! He watched foot soldiers move off in twos and threes, funnelling away down the side streets and alleyways of the village, whilst pairs of cavalrymen set off along each of the four main streets leading from the crossroads beside the High House. One set clattered over the cobbles beneath him along New Street and out to the Farthingstone Road.

Behind him, he heard Boddington draw in his breath and turned to see him bending to pick up something white from the floor. Before Boddington could inspect it further, Fowler had taken it from him and was unfolding the paper. A small vein pulsed beside his eye and his scowl deepened as he read:

Wee Hear in Form you that wee will not stand for the new Mee Sheens as they will put the gratest part of us Out of Work and into Starvashun. Bee Fore Almyty God wee sware wee will pull down any new Mee Sheens, you Dammd Villannus Roag.

Fowler crumpled the note in his fist and then dashed it to the floor, muttering profanities under his breath. Boddington picked it up, smoothed it out and read it for himself. 'Do you recognise this hand?' he asked.

Fowler shook his head. 'Most cannot write.'

'Then that is good and we shall find out those that can,' Boddington said with satisfaction.

ELEVEN

Tobias couldn't risk making his way directly through the village to the west side where the track to Newnham lay. As he had slipped along the alley at the back of the orchard that led down behind Mrs Oliphant's, he'd heard the sound of horses and the shouts of men massing in the street outside the factory. The village would be crawling with soldiers and more would fan out around it to search the fields, like red ants on a green cloth. He would have to outrun them by giving the village a wide berth, skirting it in a loop. He thought quickly. If he could cut across the fields to the south, he could reach Castle Dykes and the woods of Everdon Stubbs and travel west under their cover to reach the road to Newnham and home. A favourite poaching spot, he knew every badger path and bolthole in the undergrowth and could move silent as a shadow between the trees. They would not find him there.

He stole into the field that bordered the Farthingstone road leading south out of the village. In the dawning light, cows grazed peacefully around a grassy tumulus built by ancient hands for worship or burial, its purpose long forgotten. The beasts' breath steamed as they pulled at the dew-laden grass. Crouching low and holding his arm folded across his chest to staunch the bleeding of his wound, Tobias left the safer shadows of the hedgerow and crept across the open ground towards the far side of the mound, where he would be out of view of the road and could make better progress. He cursed under his breath as the cows raised their heads to stare at him curiously and he hurried on, though the faster he went, the weaker he felt, his legs refusing to go where he intended so that he staggered a little like a drunken man. Just as he regained the hedge at the far side of the pasture, he heard the creak of the field gate.

He pushed quickly through the hedgerow and out of sight. Beyond the upward slope of the field in front of him, the road swept round in a great westerly curve along a ridge; he must get across it in front of the soldiers and cut through the valley on the far side to reach the cover of the Stubbs. He squatted and peered back through a gap in the twisted branches. A soldier was riding slowly along the margin of the field looking into the hedge and ditch bottom, stopping every now and then to scan the field. He held the reins in one hand; the other rested on his pistol. Shivering, Tobias stayed motionless until the soldier moved on. Then he worked his way up the incline, bent double behind the hedge. His breath came heavily, the extra effort of the climb slowing him down further. He half ran, half stumbled until he reached the road.

From the vantage point of the ridge he looked back towards the village and, in the growing light, saw another splash of red quartering the field on the other side of the road. So, two men working methodically to check every ditch and hiding place on either side of the road. He looked out over the valley on the other side of the ridge and the dark line of the woods at its westerly end. There were five fields lying between him and escape. He would need to creep along two sides of the square of each field, whereas they were checking all four, but then they were mounted . . . Could he outpace them? He would have to carry on, working his way in the lee of the hedges, taking a zigzag route towards the Stubbs and always keeping a field in front. But oh, how heavy every muscle felt and how his arm throbbed and his pulse beat in his ears! And soon the sun would be fully up. He stumbled on.

Jack paused for a moment as he reached the top of the ridge and surveyed the scene. The sun had cleared the curve of the earth and its pale disc shone upon the land and glinted on the sails of a distant windmill. Long shadows streamed across the fields from ash, elm and elder rising from the ancient hedgerows. Jack narrowed his eyes. If he were a fugitive, he would use those shadows. And if he had to hide, he would crawl deep into the hedge itself. In places the beech and black-thorn hedges grew six feet thick, a tangled mass of interlacing branches smothered in ivy, rooted in sandy banks. Yes, he would squeeze in between those roots, where the growth was thickest, like a rabbit gone to ground. He stared into the shadows, trying to accustom his eyes to the gloom, but all seemed still. Behind him, down in the cow pasture, he heard the sound of girlish voices, Clay's voice joining them, laughter. The milkmaids were come into the field with their buckets and stools, no doubt, and Clay had stopped to dally with them. Jack let out an irritated sigh. He would have to have words with him yet again, but for now he would press ahead and cover the land between ridge and woods, hoping to cut off any miscreants from reaching them. If they made the trees he'd have lost them.

Tobias reached the foot of the valley and began to climb the other side but his legs felt like lead. He knew the soldier was gaining on him. Dropping to his hands and knees, he crawled a little way but he could feel a warm trickle down the inside of his arm and knew he couldn't go much further. He glanced back. The soldier was unhitching the chain at the gate; he must hide now while he still had the chance. Ahead, an elm growing in the beech hedge cast black shade. He reached its sprawling roots and, just beyond it, found a badger run. Forcing himself through the narrow gap and into the centre of the hedge, he pulled branches down over the hole as best he could, curled himself up into a ball and silently prayed.

Jack almost missed the broken branches beside the old elm. He lost concentration for a moment, when the cawing of crows rising from the wood in a clatter of wings rung out over the valley. He walked Maisie on, watching the birds circling and wondering if a human interloper had disturbed them. As they settled again in the trees he realised that his thoughts had been distracted and he turned Maisie around to retrace his steps.

Tobias, shivering uncontrollably, his arms clutched around his knees, stared at the litter of dead beech leaves at his feet. Wisps of sheep's wool were caught on the lichen-covered twigs around him and they shook in the easterly breeze. He had heard the soldier pass. He could smell his own blood and thought that if the soldiers had used dogs he wouldn't have stood a chance. As he let his breath go, he heard the jangle of the horse's bit and knew that the rider had stopped. Terror prickled his skin and turned over his stomach. The soldier was coming back. A sob rose in his throat and he held it there.

Jack slowly approached to look more closely at a place where a branch was broken – recently broken, by the pale colour of the wood. He drew his pistol. He leant from the saddle, parted the branches of the hedge and found himself looking down upon the slight figure of a boy, dressed in dun-coloured clothing that melted into the colours of woody trunk and old leaves. The boy's face looked up at him: a startlingly pale face streaked with black marks, the eyes dark with fear. With a shock of recognition, Jack realised that he knew that face. He had seen him in the lane at Effie's. The boy cowered back as if expecting a blow.

Jack said, 'Tobias? Tobias Fiddement?'

Tobias nodded, speechless with fear.

Jack glanced around quickly to see if they were observed. A flash of red further back along the ridge told him that Clay had regained the road. He spoke urgently. 'You must wait. Wait here until I send my sergeant out of the way. As soon as it's safe, and my back is towards you, make for the woods. We'll be searching no further than the fields.' He glanced towards the road again, quickly sat straight in the saddle and turned Maisie to walk on up the hill once more. Without looking back, he said, 'Tell Effie I sent you home,' and resumed his even pace along the hedge.

As he went, he had the strong sensation that Clay's eyes were on his back. Sure enough, as he turned the corner so that his path ran parallel with the road, Clay's mounted figure was silhouetted darkly against the sky, waiting. Jack forced himself not to rush though he longed to spur Maisie into a trot. He chose a point to pause again and appear to inspect the ground and then carried on along the far edge of the field and back to the road, where Clay came to meet him and get further orders.

'Any sign?' Jack said.

'Not a footprint, sir. Yourself?'

'Nothing.' Jack's nerves made him brusque.

A strange expression flickered across Clay's face. 'But you found something to give you pause?'

'Nothing of import: an old sack in one place and a cast horseshoe in another,' Jack said quickly. He pointed to the far side of the road. 'You continue down that side and we'll meet at the edge of the woods. And if you happen upon any other maids from the village, no philandering along the way,' he said over his shoulder as he rode away, nodding a curt dismissal.

Clay curled his lip but did as he was bid. He trotted his horse along to the gate on the village side and rode through. This field, full of sheep, had the new hawthorn hedges of enclosure, low and dense, and he worked his way around it and the next quickly. Instead of carrying on, he returned to the road and shaded his eyes to see where Jack had got to. Then he turned tail and trotted back to where they had spoken. He rode straight down to the tall elm on the left-hand side where he had marked Stamford turn back and stand so long. When he reached the spot he frowned. Branches were broken on both sides as though something large had pushed through. He slid from his horse and squatted beside the hole. In the middle of the hedge, leaves were squashed into the mud as if someone had been there for some time. He peered at them, reached in and picked up a handful of copper beech leaves. He smiled as he held them in his palm; their faded russet gold was spotted with a reddish brown that was still wet under his thumb as he passed it across.

He looked up quickly and scanned the fields. Nothing moved save for a few crows and a dot of red up towards the woods:

Stamford quartering the last field. Clay looked thoughtfully at the handful of leaves and put them in his pocket.

When at length they met again on the ridge, Clay asked Jack if they were to attempt a search of the woods.

'Insufficient manpower,' Jack said. 'We'd have no chance of success with only two men. I've ridden there before and the whole place is a tangle of fallen trees, briar and bracken, fit to hide an army. We'd be on a fool's errand.'

'As you wish, sir.' Clay gave an unpleasant smile.

In the distance, from the direction of the village, a shot rang out. Clay turned his mount smartly towards it. ''Tis no matter. Once we have one we shall have all,' he said grimly.

Effie and Beulah had woken to find Tobias gone.

'Off rabbiting again with Saul Culley, I'll be bound,' Effie said crossly. Although his catch had often made the difference between dinner and a wakeful night with an empty belly, she had spoken to Tobias repeatedly about the dangers of poaching and forbidden him to go. There were gins and snares in the woods, designed to trap a man, keepers who would shoot first and ask questions later and justices who would string a man up for taking no more than a brace of pheasant.

Beulah, who would normally moan about her brother making her late, said nothing. She dragged her feet over getting dressed and appeared so quiet and peaky-looking that Effie asked her if anything was wrong. She shook her head. 'Then you'd better eat up and set off without Tobias,' Effie said.

Beulah glanced anxiously out of the window. Where was he? He was supposed to have been back before morning so that if there were a pursuit he, and all of them, would be found at their homes, abed as normal. He was supposed to be back so that they could walk to work together as they always did and arrive clear of suspicion. Something bad must have happened. She wanted to tell Effie but they had made her promise to tell no one. Jim Baggott had taken her aside only yesterday to glare into her face and tell her she must be silent as the grave. She returned to trailing her spoon through her porridge, making runnels of thin blue milk between lumpy greyish islands. 'I don't want to go without Tobias,' she said in a small voice.

Effie, on her knees riddling the grate ready to re-lay the fire, said, 'Best make a start, dearest. I'll make him a piece to eat on the way and then he'll soon catch you up.'

'But what if he doesn't?'

'If he doesn't, that's his own fault. At least you won't be late and get into trouble.' She rattled the poker hard in the fire-basket.

Beulah slipped down from her stool at the table, lingered over wrapping her shawl around her and was finally shooed out of the door with a kiss.

An hour later, Effie was mixing soap and lye for the day's wash when she heard the door latch squeak open. She turned, ready to berate Tobias once more about poaching, only to see him pulling the bar across the door. He tugged at it with one hand, the other arm held awkwardly across a shirt stained with blood.

'Whatever's happened?' She dropped the whole packet of lye into the bowl and hurried over as Tobias leant his back against the door, his face grey and drained. She sat him down at the table and plied him with questions while she removed his jacket and shirt, poured a bowl of water and cut a bandage. The wound was a deep gash from his armpit to the underside of his upper arm, where the glass had sliced into the muscle. She washed it with muslin, padded it with cotton cloth and bound it tight to stop the bleeding, her face growing more and more anxious as he spoke.

'. . . so, we're to go to work as usual and hold our tongues so that the master will not know which of us had a part in it,' he finished.

'You can't work like this – you'll not keep that injury hid!' Effie said in disbelief. 'And there'll be blood on the glass . . . in the cellar . . . Oh, Tobias! How could you be so foolish!' She threw down the remains of the strips of cloth and paced to and fro in front of the hearth. 'Even without that mishap, surely you must've seen how dangerous it was to do this and to write such a note? How many are there who know their letters? I'll wager not more than two or three!' She hurried to the window and peered out. 'They'll come for you. You mustn't stay here.' She went to the cupboard beside the mantel, took out bread and cheese, put half in front of him and wrapped the rest in a cloth.

Tobias looked at her with the face of a frightened child, unable to take in what she was saying. 'Jervis said to do everything as usual,' he said, 'and none of us would come to any harm.'

She took his hands and looked searchingly into his face. 'Think, Tobias,' she urged. 'Men have been hanged on slighter evidence than this and with less cause. Why, a boy your age was hanged for the stealing of a spoon! Jack's given you a chance – you must take it.'

'But where will I go?' he said helplessly.

'Head over the fields towards the locks at Braunston,' Effie said. She reached up for the tin hidden on top of the cupboard, where she kept the money she'd been saving towards the family's new home once she and Jack were married. 'See if you can pick up work on the canals. Here . . .' She shoved the tin towards him. 'Use this to pay for your passage until your arm is healed.'

Tobias opened it and wondered at the weight of coin inside. Where had Effie got such money from and what was she saving it for? The soldier, he thought, and instantly felt distrust rise in him and a curse for all the agents of government. Yet the soldier had spared him, had saved his life. Confused, he emptied out the coins and thrust them deep into his pocket.

'Head west on the canals and get as far away as you can. Make haste! They could be here at any minute.'

She helped him put on his jacket, easing the sleeve over his injured arm. 'Travel light and fast. Send a message as soon as you can to let me know you've found a place and that you're safe and well.' She went to the door and looked outside. 'Don't say where you are, though, in case the message is discovered.' She beckoned him forward and hugged him close. 'Now, hurry,' she said, 'and go secretly and safely.'

She watched him cross the track and turn to raise his hand before slipping through the gate into the field beyond. Then he was gone from view.

She hurried up the ladder stair to the loft room where Tobias slept and quickly gathered his few belongings. She stuffed them into a pillowcase and straightened the bedcovers so that it would look an orderly, planned departure and not that of a runaway, leaving in haste. She took the pillowcase outside and hid it under an upturned bucket inside the chicken house, in fear all the while, listening for the sound of men in the lane. She must go about the business of washing as usual so that all looked innocent when they came. She must think of exactly what to tell them: that Tobias had been talking for a while of trying his fortunes as a weaver in Spitalfields and had left very early to be at the Watling Street in time for the cart traffic at first light.

As she re-entered the cottage, bandage, bowl and bloody

cloth met her eyes, lying on the table in full view, and her heart leapt in her chest. What was she thinking! She threw the rags on the fire and took the bowl outside. She tipped it over a patch of nettles in the garden, the sun catching the pink stain in the water as it fell.

'I don't know where he is, sir,' Beulah answered the master for the umpteenth time. He had made her stand on a chair in the middle of his office and had told her she would stand there until she told him the truth. Her legs and back ached as she stood, twisting her apron in her hands. Fowler walked around to the back of the chair and Beulah craned round to see.

'Stand straight!' Fowler roared at her and she snapped her head round again. He rested his hands on the back of the chair and spoke over her shoulder, his head level with her ear, his breath on her cheek. 'Do you know what it is that's burning in my yard?' he asked her. 'Do you know what that smell is?'

Beulah, barely perceptibly, shook her head.

'It's . . . my . . . money,' Fowler said slowly. 'My new frames that *someone* has seen fit to chop to matchwood.'

Beulah could feel the warmth of his body close to her, could smell the trace of snuff adhering to his bushy whiskers.

'I will ask you again,' he said softly, 'and it will go better with you if you give me a truthful answer. Where is your brother and what was his part in this?'

Beulah held herself very still, fighting the urge to leap down from the chair and attempt to flee. She blinked. Effie had always taught her that lying was wrong and she'd also made a promise to the weavers to tell nothing. She repeated the only thing she could say that broke neither rule. 'I don't know where he is. God's honest truth, sir.'

Fowler shoved the chair, making it rock, so that Beulah

gasped and reached backwards to grasp the rail and steady herself. The master grabbed her arm in a grip that fingerprinted it with bruises and twisted it up behind her back. 'I said stand still!' he shouted, twisting harder so that she yelped in pain.

The door swung open and the constable entered. '*Mr* Fowler! What is this!' he exclaimed. 'Our investigations do *not* include laying hands upon minors!'

Fowler let go of Beulah's arm and, seeing her chance, she scrambled down on shaky legs and sat down with a bump on the chair.

'What news?' Fowler demanded. 'Have any of them talked?'

'Not yet.'

'And the captive, Saul Culley?'

'A ball caught him in the thigh. He'll need a doctor before he's fit for questioning.'

A gleam came into Fowler's eye. 'Shot, you say? He may be persuadable. I shall have my own surgeon look at him.' Seeing Boddington's uncertain expression, he added: 'To give an opinion on whether the limb can be saved, you understand.'

Boddington glanced down at Beulah, who was bent over, nursing her arm. 'Send the child back to her work, Mr Fowler,' he said. 'These things are not for her ears.'

'In just a moment,' Fowler said amiably. 'First she must tell us where her family lives. You must be able to do that, surely?' he said to Beulah, leaning his hands on his knees in the attitude of a kind uncle, bending down to her level.

Beulah looked from him to Mr Boddington and back again.

'Newnham, is it? Or Everdon?' Fowler had seen the Fiddement children drenched through enough times to know that they walked a long way and clearly weren't from the village.

Beulah looked at the door, willing Tobias to come through it. Why did he not come? He was supposed to do everything

217

as usual, not leave her all alone to face the master! 'Newnham, sir,' she muttered.

'There, that's better,' Fowler said in a jovial tone. 'Now, where in Newnham?'

'Down the track, off the lane.'

'Which lane? What's it called?'

Beulah shrugged. 'It hasn't got a name. It's just the lane.'

'Don't fool with me, girl . . .' Fowler's hands itched to take hold of her and shake it out of her.

Beulah shrank back in the chair.

Mr Boddington said, 'Who's your landlord, child? Who does your house belong to?'

Close to tears, Beulah said, 'Hob Talbot.'

Boddington nodded, satisfied. 'Now let her go, sir,' he said to Fowler.

Ignoring his words, Fowler asked him, 'What of the enquiries made house to house?'

Boddington shook his head. 'Nothing. The villagers would have us believe they sleep sounder than hedgepigs in winter. Not one will admit to seeing or hearing anything.'

'I shall post bills offering a reward,' Fowler said decisively. 'We'll see whether that will loosen any tongues.'

'The girl, sir?' Boddington insisted quietly.

Fowler went to the door by the stairs and called for Mrs Gundy, who came puffing from the kitchen. 'Set the Fiddement girl to some useful employment,' he said loudly for Boddington's benefit but as Beulah passed him he said, under his breath, 'Don't think I've finished with you. I'll have the truth if it takes 'til Michaelmas to get it.'

'You understand my dilemma.' Captain Harris sat at his desk, behind the pool of light cast by the oil lamp, with Jack standing

218

before him. 'Sergeant Clay has placed certain evidence before me, suggesting that you failed to apprehend a felon and yet you refuse to explain yourself.'

'Sergeant Clay must be mistaken, sir.' The colour rose to Jack's face.

'One man's word against another's is not sufficient in this case, lieutenant,' the captain said drily. Stamford was clearly hiding something. He had no time for Clay, whom he knew to be hot-headed, undisciplined and lazy, but, nonetheless, he couldn't ignore an allegation that Stamford was some kind of revolutionary – an insurrectionist sympathiser – however unlikely it seemed. 'Come now, you must be able to give a more satisfactory account of your actions?' He fixed Jack with a keen eye.

Jack remained at attention, staring ahead and refusing to meet his gaze. It pained him to be unable to answer, for he valued his spotless record and Harris's good opinion, and felt dishonoured by his silence, even if it were only to protect himself against the malice of a blackguard like Clay.

Harris sighed. He prided himself on running an orderly company and had no wish for an investigation that would suggest fraternisation with rebellious elements in the community and would undermine the authority of the military in the area. *Fraternisation.* The word stirred a memory, somewhere in the back of his mind, of a previous conversation with Stamford. Ah – it was Stamford who had asked about married quarters a month or so ago. He'd had to refuse because the woman in question had a younger brother and sister in her care . . . both working at the silk manufactory . . . It all began to fall into place. Now he could make some sense of it. He rolled his pen to and fro across the leather top of the desk. If this came out it could all go very badly for Stamford. Neither would it reflect well upon the army.

He pulled the inkpot and a sheet of paper towards him, dipped his pen and began to write. Jack stood with his arms ramrod straight by his sides and heels pressed smartly together. Behind his deadpan expression he cursed Clay as his enemy and himself as a fool for not realising sooner the extent of the man's spite. What if he were court-martialled? What would become of Effie then? He had tried to do the right thing by her but in solving one problem had only succeeded in creating a greater one.

Captain Harris shook the sand from his letter back into the dish, folded the paper and took a stick of sealing wax from the drawer. 'You will leave within the hour and take this letter to Captain Quilter, who will be embarking troops at Southampton in three days' time, for the Iberian Peninsula. You will be on that ship.'

'Thank you, sir,' Jack managed. It was a reprieve – for that he must be grateful – but his thoughts flew immediately to Effie. 'May I have one day's leave, so that I can put my affairs in order before I go, sir?' he asked. 'There's someone I must visit . . . I mean I have obligations I feel I must fulfil.'

Harris sealed the envelope and pushed it across the desk to him. 'You may not,' he said abruptly. 'The connection with the person, and family, in question is best forgotten – do you not think?'

Jack opened his mouth to speak further but Harris had a dangerous look in his eye.

'Dismissed, lieutenant,' he said firmly.

Jack sat at the rickety table in his room, beneath the small window through which he had stared so often at the stars, thinking of Effie. Quickly he penned a note.

My dearest Effie,

I hope that all is well with the <u>whole family</u>. I write in haste as I am posted overseas and ordered to go tonight. My darling, I cannot tell you how I shall miss you and worry for you but I have no choice. I know that you have a little money saved but before this is gone you must visit Father and Mother, as we planned, and ask for their help, as I do not know how long I shall be away. I shall write of you to them in glowing terms. I realise that you will be anxious about such a visit without me by your side but, my dear, you must do this for my sake as I shall not rest unless I know that in my absence you are under their protection.

God alone knows how long this posting may last but keep faith with me, dearest love, and be assured I intend to survive it and <u>I shall return</u>. I hope that our parting will be for only a short while and the current trouble will die down and soon be forgotten. I shall write again at greater length as soon as I have opportunity but for now am ordered to leave within the hour for Southampton. I fear incarceration would be my fate if I do not comply.

I love you so, dear Effie, and shall long every day to hold you in my arms again.

Yours, with all my heart,

Jack

He sealed it quickly. He would get one of the drummer boys to take it. Yates was trustworthy and he would pay him thruppence for his discretion. He gathered his few belongings and packed them into his knapsack. He stood for a moment in the middle of the room, wondering at how his life had been shaken upside down in the space of just one day. Could it have been only last night that he had sat here planning their trip to

Bedford, anticipating with pleasure introducing Effie proudly to his family? He had imagined showing her the river in which he'd fished as a boy, his father's books and his mother's flower garden.

How strange that an action taken with the best intentions, to protect his beloved Effie from hurt, could lead to such disastrous consequences. When he thought of Tobias's terrified face looking up at him from behind its prison of thorns he knew he could not have acted any differently. Tobias too would be journeying tonight and he hoped he had found food and somewhere safe to lay his head.

He heaved the knapsack on to his shoulder and softly closed the door behind him.

TWELVE

In the baking July heat, Beulah moved along the rows of mulberry trees quickly picking the leaves from the low, wide-spread branches and dropping them into a wicker basket. The worms must be fed continuously: thousands of voracious mouths that never stopped chomping and nibbling; they repulsed her.

She was deeply unhappy. She still missed Tobias dreadfully, even if he used to annoy her by walking on ahead and making her run to catch up with him, or by wanting to go to the Blood Tub at the end of the day. At least she'd known he was in the manufactory somewhere if she needed him and, in dire straits, would have protected her from the master. He had written once to Effie, a few months ago, saying that he'd found work with the canal folk, leading the horses and loading and unloading the barges, knowledge which Beulah tried to forget, repeating in her mind whenever the master looked her way, 'Tobias is gone to London to look for work. We have no word of him.' The last part was true at least: after the first letter they'd had no further contact and Beulah felt sure that he was making a new life away from danger and wouldn't be coming back.

As for Effie, Beulah thought that she must be ill. She was all at once like an old person. She seemed always to be tired and crabby and she moved around so slowly, as if dragging a great weight after her. Sometimes, when she thought Beulah wasn't looking, she rubbed her back as if she was in pain and when she sat down at the table she lowered herself so carefully into the chair that you'd think she was afraid her bones would break. Beulah tried to help her, taking the other end of the heavy washing basket, drawing water or hoeing the vegetable patch. Beneath her love and concern for Effie lurked fear too. She had seen first her mother and then her father taken off, within a year of each other, with the illness that made them cough blood. What if Effie were to be taken too? What would become of her then?

She moved on along the row, picking first from the lower branches and then standing the fruit ladder against the trunk to reach the higher ones and fill her apron. The heart-shaped leaves rustled softly around her, dappling her dress with shade. She wondered, as she did every day, what had become of Hanzi. She always left three eggs for him to find but for weeks now they'd not been taken. Nonetheless, each day she collected them and left new ones in case he returned. Once she had picked up an egg she must have missed, an egg so old that when the cook at the High House broke it, the kitchen was filled with a rotten stink and Beulah had got a slap from Mrs Gundy for her care-lessness.

At the back of the plantation of young trees, before you reached what was left of the old orchard – apple, mulberry and pear trees – a new set of holes were being dug. They were meant for the planting of yet more saplings. Beulah watched as a blackbird pulled a worm from the newly turned soil and hopped away, taking the opportunity whilst the labourers were absent to pick up what food it could. A moment's anxiety assailed her. Had she closed the cellar door securely? Every day the master reminded her that the worms must be protected against vermin: mice, rats, birds; the worms in their open beds would be easy pickings for any climbing or flying creature and all his work and expense on the grand scheme would come to naught. She breathed out a long sigh. Yes, of course she had secured the door; she remembered pushing against it to check it was firm.

The master's enthusiasm for his new endeavour was abso-lute. The worms must be fed through both day and night and he had allowed Alice frequent respite from her usual duties in the bobbin-winding shop to instruct and oversee Beulah in the daytime. At night, ever since the breaking of the frames, he had employed a night watchman, whose other duties through the lonely hours were to keep the worms warm and fed. From midsummer's day, when the small, yellow eggs, stuck to twigs and old cocoons, began to hatch tiny wiggling threads, Beulah had hated them. Now that they had grown to fat, pale caterpillars, the size of her finger, she hated them even more. By August they would be bigger still: the size of the master's thumb.

It was lonely work. Some days she stole a few words with Biddy and the other children when she helped serve the midday meal, but sometimes she saw no one all day, bar Alice and Mrs Gundy: sour faces and hands ever ready to pinch and shove.

Biddy had told her that the master was more tyrannical than ever in the workshops; that his temper blew at the slightest provocation and that he constantly picked fault with the work of the weavers, rejecting their cloth and docking their pay, demanding they weave the pattern anew although everyone knew he took the cloth nonetheless and sold it with the rest. He came down hard on Walter and Jonas who had taken the place of Tobias and Saul as drawboys and went around muttering about some scheme to get in new apprentices instead and sack the lot of them. He had not, however, replaced the Jacquard machines.

Saul Culley had died from his wound. A sullen hatred for the master filled the factory. As he passed along the lines of workers, the evil eye followed him as soon as his back was turned. Ellis barely hid his hostility but Jervis was a broken man, blaming himself for involving the youngsters in the plot.

No one really knew for sure what had happened to Saul. Some said he had contracted gangrene from the wound, some that he had died from loss of blood during the amputation. The woman who came to lay him out said that the surgeon had ordered her to incinerate the sheets Saul had lain in and that she'd seen they were all burned to holes, as if acid had dripped on to them. There were rumours that Mr Boddington had interviewed both the master and his surgeon for several hours before letting them go and had asked for the sheets in vain. Whatever the truth of the matter, Saul had not talked and on the day of his burial a great gathering of men had followed the coffin to the graveyard and not a dragoon had been seen.

Even despite the frightening rumours and all the tension, Beulah still wished she were back in her old job with the company of the others so that she wouldn't have to be near the horrible worms, nor be alone with the master.

She climbed down the ladder and tipped the green contents of her apron into the basket. As she pressed the leaves down to make room for more, she heard a noise. 'Pssst!' It came again from the direction of the hen house and she left the basket, walked to the end of the row of trees and peered out to see Hanzi peeping round the corner of the shed and beckoning her over.

Beulah hurried across the yard, as if busy on some urgent errand, and found him sitting with his back to the warm planks of the hen house, his legs stretched out before him and wearing a pair of boots that were clearly too big. 'Where have you been?' she asked. 'I thought you'd gone for good.'

Hanzi grinned. 'We went off to Appleby for the horse fair. Best part of the year!'

'Appleby? Where's that?' The main market for horses in the county was Marefair in Northampton; she'd never heard of this other place.

''Tis right up north in Westmorland. All the Romanichal gather at Gallows Hill, outside the town, for the buying and selling of the horses. Almost everyone's related to everyone else one way or another so 'tis a chance, once a year, to get reacquainted.'

'How many folk go there then?' Beulah, with her own small family of Effie and Tobias, couldn't imagine the size of such a gathering.

'Hundreds! 'Tis quite a sight to see the celebrations, with the tilted carts and tents covering the hillside and the horses all gleaming from being washed in the river and braided up with ribbons. We sold two cobs and a mule and I got these thrown in.' He looked admiringly at his boots and gave them a little shine with his sleeve. 'You look awful thin,' Hanzi said, casting his eye over her. 'Have you been ill?'

'No, but my sister's not well and the master's making me look after worms and my brother had to run from the soldiery on account of frame breaking, and without his wage there's not enough food in the house . . .' It all spilt out.

'Why don't you take some eggs yourself?'

'Too fragile to hide on my person,' she said, 'and nowhere else to put them.'

He laughed. 'I'm in the same quandary,' he said. 'Having lost my hat.' He pulled a comic, mournful expression. 'When I get back with a pocketful of yolk and eggshells, I shall be in bad trouble.'

Beulah thought for a moment and then took her red flannel kerchief from her pocket. 'Here, you can use this to tie them in,' she said, 'but be careful to carry it under your coat; the colour's bright and could draw eyes to you.'

Hanzi took it from her with a smile and a nod. He dug deep into his own pocket and brought out a handful of mushrooms. 'Here.' He shoved them into her hands.

Beulah's mouth watered at the thought of them fried up in dripping. Quickly, she pushed them inside her dress until they sat above the waistband, squashy against her skin, and retied her apron. She turned to thank him but he held his finger to his lips and signalled that she should go. Only then did she hear Alice's voice asking Mrs Gundy whereabouts the pest of a child had got to. She ran quickly and slipped back into the trees, emerging near the factory carrying her basket.

Alice scolded her, carefully closing the cellar door behind them and chivvying Beulah down the steps. It was hot down there; the stove was kept constantly alight, for, despite the July day outside, the thick walls let none of the warmth in. Without a fire, it would become cold and damp as a cave and the precious worms would sicken and die. The master had schooled both of them in the signs of pebrine and muscardine fungus, and the dire results for them if they failed to keep the air warm and dry. The pungent aromas of lavender, rosemary and pennyroyal rose to meet them: the floor was strewn with herbs and vinegar to keep the atmosphere of the magnanery smelling sweet. The sound of the roomful of caterpillars eating was that of torrential rain playing on leaves: unceasing, deafening and overwhelming.

Alice, her dress open at the neck and her corset loosened beneath, fed the stove with coal and mopped her brow with the back of a red, chapped hand. 'Well, what are you standing there for? Get on and feed them!' she snapped at Beulah, who took up a handful of leaves and began to poke them into the first worm bed at intervals along its length. The tiers of beds were only inches apart, so that her hand hovered horribly close to the worms as she tentatively fed the leaves in. In the murky light from the small high windows, she peered into the trays at the fat oyster-white worms, taking care not to brush against them. If your hand came too near the worms they telescoped their heads and their first few segments back into their bodies so that they swelled out, and rose up menacingly towards your fingers as if they would bite you. Beulah didn't know if they would bite. They might even be poisonous. She didn't want to find out.

For the third time that week, she noticed a foul smell coming from one or two of the beds and, looking carefully, found a scattering of worms in each that were black and inert. She beckoned Alice over.

'Not more! Are you sure you've never let the stove out, not even once?' Alice said in a low voice.

'I swear.'

'Nor let them run low on fodder, nor disturbed them with banging the door, or singing, or jangling the fire-irons?'

Beulah shook her head vigorously.

Alice tutted and muttered as she picked out all the dead worms. She added a few more sickly-looking worms to the handful and threw them into the stove, saying, 'This must be kept from the master. Do you understand?'

Beulah pressed her lips together tight to show she did. They both returned to work, Alice sweeping up the ash around the stove and stacking a new delivery of sacks of coal and kindling beside it, while Beulah went back to feeding the worms.

Moving from tray to tray, engrossed in her careful task, she didn't hear the master enter and jumped at his voice behind her.

'Has the girl been silent?' he asked Alice, for the worms, he had told them, hated noise and she was neither allowed to sing as she carried in the baskets, nor to speak to Alice unless she was spoken to.

'Yes, and the worms thrive.'

'The air's heavy outside and a storm can stop them from eating. If it becomes thunderous later you must take a live piece of coal from the stove with tongs and carry it near to each bed. 'Tis said it calms them and can ward off contagion.'

He walked along the rows of beds, looking into each to check the health of his prized worms and see that Beulah had spread sufficient leaves, until he came level with her and looked over her shoulder. He marked her cautious approach. 'Would you like to go back to your friends?' he said in a conversational tone. 'Do you miss the bobbin shop, Beulah?'

Beulah, slowly and carefully spreading the leaves beneath his gaze, nodded almost imperceptibly.

'Of course you do. Who wouldn't rather be with their friends in the light than alone down here in this wormhole? You know, only your own stubbornness keeps you here.'

Beulah's hand shook a little as she took another handful of leaves but she said nothing.

'Still naught to tell me, eh? Not a thing brought back to mind that your vandalous brother told you? Nor any word of him?' He leant closer as if he expected her to whisper a secret to him, his cheek next to hers. Suddenly he reached into the space above the worm bed and took her hand, forcing it to the back and her bare arm down upon the worms so that she cried out at the touch of their cool yielding bodies. He held her arm there and she felt the sickening sensation of the worms moving on her. As they contracted and stretched in their foraging quest, the tickle of their hooks and suckers rippled over her skin. 'What would you like to tell me?' he asked again, his breath sour with the smell of old tobacco.

A moan escaped Beulah. 'Don't! Let me go!' She squirmed in an effort to get away.

Fowler gripped her hand harder, pushing it down so that the worms on either side reared up and Beulah yelped.

'*Tell me.*'

Between great gulping breaths Beulah said, 'Gone . . . to . . . London.'

Fowler let go suddenly and pushed her roughly aside. Beulah stood with her head bowed, her arm held stiffly away from her side. She longed to wipe the crawling sensation from her skin, to run outside to the water barrel and plunge her arm inside. She would not let him see it. She stayed absolutely still, feeling Fowler's stare.

'Work her hard,' he said to Alice. 'Give no quarter.' Just a week or two longer, he thought, and she will break.

*

Beulah lay fast asleep, curled on her truckle bed, worn out by work at the week's end. Effie picked up her sister's boots, lying on their sides where they'd been kicked off, and placed them at the end of the bed. She folded Beulah's clothes and pulled the quilt up over her bare arms; it was late in the evening and becoming chilly. She hoped Beulah would sleep through peacefully and not wake with nightmares. She had tried to discover the cause, questioning her to find out whether Fowler had been pressing her about Tobias, but Beulah insisted it was the worms that she feared and however much Effie said they were just big caterpillars and all God's creatures, there was no reasoning with her. Tonight though, Beulah slept the deep sleep of exhaustion and didn't move, not even when Effie bent to kiss her, touching her lips gently to the curve of her cheek and resting her hand lightly on her head.

She took out a folded paper from the cupboard by the mantel – the last letter she'd received from Jack, dated months ago, sat down at the table and unfolded its worn creases. The light from the panes of the tiny casement window was fading to a soft, summer twilight but the dimness made no odds for she knew the letter almost word for word.

My dearest Effie,

I think of you every hour of every day, my dear one, and cannot tell you how much I long to see you and with what keen anticipation I receive your letters, which I read many times and keep always in my breast pocket, close to my heart.

I write to you from outside Badajoz. I am well, although greatly saddened by the loss or wounding of thirty of our men when a shell from the town fell amongst us and exploded as we were working to throw up breastworks and

*batteries. In the morning the scene was terrible: mangled
corpses and comrades with legs or arms severed from their
bodies. We have subsequently taken Fort Picarina, a
detached bastion that lies a little outside the town. It had
been mined but our engineers searched for a train (that is,
a line of gunpowder) at dead of night and, finding that the
earth had been disturbed, dug down and cut it off. Despite
heavy fire, we got our ladders up and our hay bags strewn
to soften falls but when the French sentry received no
answer to his cry of 'Who comes there?' such a hail of trees
and boulders, shot and fire-balls rained down upon us that
even as I cried, 'Come on, lads!' many fell or were shot and
hung from the ladders with their feet caught in the rounds.
I shall never forget that awful sight. I could not believe
that any of us would escape and yet I, and around half my
party, reached the ramparts unscathed. My father would no
doubt say that I was watched over and see the hand of the
Almighty in my good fortune. Eventually, at great cost, we
succeeded in gaining the fort only to find most of the
garrison escaped to the town, which is walled and strongly
fortified.*

*We are to move closer now with the intention of
forming batteries in order to make breaches in the walls
with our twenty-four pounders and, ultimately, to storm
the town. I shall lead one of the storming-parties; I trust I
shall not draw the short straw and have to join the
'forlorn hope'.*

*War is, indeed, a most terrible business and perhaps I
should not write of it to you, Effie, by reason of your youth
and womanhood but I know the Troubles of your family
have made you wise beyond your years. We have always had
frankness between us and I hope you will forgive me for*

*unburdening myself thus, and that you will always feel able
to do the same.*

*I hope and trust that you are well, Effie, and that all is
well for Tobias? And Beulah too? This may not reach you for
some time as it must travel overland and then by packet
boat before it reaches England and the mail. I hope by the
time you receive it you will have met with my parents and
be under their protection. I know that you are anxious in
this respect but they will love you, not just for my sake, but
for your own dear self. Write to me soon. I long to see you.
Wait for me.*

Ever yours,
Jack

Effie finished reading and laid one hand on her swelling
belly and the other flat upon the paper, as if by touching the
letters formed by his hand she could touch the hand itself,
across time, across oceans. The paper felt soft, worn to the
floppy texture of cloth by constant folding and unfolding, as
she had read and reread it ever more desperately as weeks
turned to months and no more letters had come. She ran
through all the scenarios she had imagined many times: letters
had been lost and he was at this moment on his way back to
her (this was the scene she dwelt on as an attempt to comfort
herself); for some reason letters could not get through; he
was unable to write because he was ill, or perhaps captured;
he was not . . . She could not, would not, contemplate that
possibility. She had written and written, sending message after
message full of love and care. They disappeared into a void
and every morning, whilst hanging out the washing, though
she stared along the track until her eyes ached, no messenger
ever came.

Jack's words about the frankness between them pricked her conscience as sharply as a bee-sting. She had still not told him she was with child. Her reasons were a tangle even to herself. Partly, even now, with the roundness beneath her hand and the movement of life inside her, as long as she didn't write the words, she could pretend it wasn't happening, hiding it from herself in the same way that she covered it so success-fully from the view of the world under layers of loose clothes. And how could she speak of it? If Jack knew, he would insist that she go to his parents and would brook no disagreement even though she would be bringing shame on the family, shame on him. She would not do it. She had her pride. If only he would come home so that they could face it together! He did not come . . . and every day she grew heavier.

Unbidden, a memory came to her of her mother pacing from one end of the tiny room to the other, like an animal in a cage, lumbering and weighed down, pausing to lean on the back of a chair in pain as her time approached. Effie had been young and scared and when her mother asked her to go for a neighbour she had dawdled over putting on her shoes and shawl, afraid to leave her mother, afraid of what was to come. 'It will happen whether you will or no,' her mother had said, seeing her fear. 'The infant's time in my belly is done and 'tis beyond me or any man to stop it now, so you must hurry and get help.' Effie had heard the resignation in her voice and had run pell-mell along the track to fetch the woman. She remembered the sound of her feet on the dry, packed earth, time ticking in her steps.

As if in answer to the rhythm in her memory, she heard the sound of a horse in the lane and for a moment felt that she had wished Jack into existence. She rose to her feet. The hooves were louder and heavier than Maisie's though, and as

Effie peered out it was Hob's broad-brimmed hat and wide shoulders that she saw above the hedge. She hurried over to the cupboard and stowed the letter away. The rent wasn't due for another two weeks but she pulled out the tin and took it with her to the door, hoping to circumvent his pretext for entering.

As she opened the door, Hob swept off his hat in an exaggerated greeting and leant against the doorjamb. His face had a soft, jowly look and a smell of whisky clung about him. He was clearly dressed for the town, in tight corduroy breeches, brass-buttoned weskit and a swallowtail coat of blue frieze.

'Mr Talbot, you are early; I . . . I cannot pay you the month's rent as yet,' Effie said. 'I can pay two weeks on account and have the other fortnight by the due date, I promise you.'

Hob waved her words away. 'Aren't you going to invite your landlord in?' he said, pressing his hat to his heart with a great show.

Unwillingly, Effie stepped aside. He levered himself from the doorframe, righting himself with some effort and led the way inside. Sitting down heavily at the table, he pushed his hat aside. 'What do you think of my market day finery then, Effie?'

'Very smart, I'm sure, Mr Talbot.' She stood well back, drawing herself up tall and holding the tin in front of her, glad of her work smock and loose pinafore.

Talbot looked her up and down; appraising her appearance with such obvious admiration that Effie was forced to look away.

'A fine day's work, though I say it myself,' he said. 'We sold all the beasts we took and got a good price, so there's cause for a little celebration. What do you say, Effie? Do you have ale in the house?'

'I have small beer, sir.' She fetched a tankard and set it before him.

'You'll drink with me?' He leant back in his chair, his eyes following her as she poured herself a smaller measure. 'Sit.'

She sat down opposite him, the rent tin on the table between them.

'Are you well, Effie? You look unconscionably pretty tonight,' he said.

'I'm well, thank you, sir,' she conceded, lowering her eyes.

He took a long draught. 'Northampton is a fine town, Effie. Perhaps you would care to come with me next market day? There are sideshows and entertainments – 'tis not all beasts and bidding – and there'd be a good square meal with as much as you can drink and a comfortable ride home after. Show you a little of the world, eh? You must tire of always biding in the same spot.'

'That would hardly be proper, sir,' Effie said quickly. 'People would talk.'

'Pff for their talk!' He snapped his fingers. 'What business is it of theirs if I choose to take one of my farmhands?' He leant forward. 'I would pay you' – he looked directly at her as if to measure her response – '*for your company.*'

Effie drew in her breath, blood rushing to her cheeks. 'I would rather have more work here – honest farm work, sir.' She rose from the table but he reached forward and took her hand, holding her back. He turned her hand within his.

'I'm loath to see this hand roughened further; 'twas never meant for hard labour.' He pressed it to his lips and Effie snatched it away with a cry.

He staggered to his feet, saying, 'Come now, Effie, I can make your life easier. Make the sensible choice or there'll not be hard work either.'

Effie stepped back and he lurched towards her, knocking the table so that the tin tipped over, rolled to the edge and fell to the brick floor with a clang.

'Effie?' Beulah stood in her nightgown beside the bed, her hair tousled, rubbing her eyes with her knuckles. 'What is it? What was that noise?'

Talbot steadied himself with one hand on the table and let the other fall to his side, while Effie bent to recover the tin. She placed it deliberately back upon the table. 'I shall expect you Friday week, when I shall pay the rent as due, sir,' she said with dignity.

Talbot scowled at Beulah and swept up his hat. 'Friday week,' he said to Effie. 'Be sure to have the full amount.' He pushed past her and yanked the door open, leaving it swinging on its hinges as he departed. Damp evening air flowed in with the scent of lavender and stocks upon its breath.

Jack, his body slick with sweat, lay on his back under a coarse blanket. Sometimes he muttered to himself and one of the nuns would pause in their pacing along the rows of rough pallets that served for beds and tend the dressing of the suppurating wound in his side or try to feed him water or gruel. He would choke a little down and then turn his head away, wanting only to rest, exhausted by the fever that burned and shivered through him and turned his muscles to straw.

He inhabited a strange nightmare world in which the sights and sounds of battle returned to him in horrifying hallucinatory detail: the climb to the ramparts, drawing himself up over a ladder quite smothered in dead bodies, men falling on the blades of the cheval-de-frise that lay before a deep entrenchment, the slaughter as they gained the advantage and turned the guns around upon the French. He dreamt of entering the town amidst the clamour of the rabble as it was plundered and then, from a window, the sound of a shot and the hot blood pouring from his side . . .

Racked by fever, faces moved in and out of his vision. He saw again the Portuguese convicts carrying away the naked dead, slung over their shoulders like pigs, held by their legs, heads dangling down behind, to be carted away and interred in a narrow hole, so small that they needs must be packed together with great nicety. The face of one of the corpses changed before his eyes, becoming that of a young boy, someone familiar, staring up at him in terror with pleading eyes, but although he shouted out that the boy was alive and must be saved, the convict kept up his steady plodding pace away from him. He tipped the boy into the cart with the others as if he were a log of wood.

Men marched on a square parade ground, a drummer boy beating out a rhythm, red tunics and brass buttons bright in the sun. A voice – his voice – shouted a command and the men halted and stood to attention. He walked along the lines and as he passed, each crumbled as if turned instantly to dust.

A soldier knelt in the gutter drinking like a beast, lapping at the wine that flowed from the barrels broken in the road, the liquid mixing with the foul detritus of the street. Beside one of the barrels, the body of a French soldier lay bleeding into the pools and runnels from the barrel. In the dream, Jack tried to crawl away but the pain in his side pinned him down so that he too fell sprawling, his face against the wet cobbles.

Then a woman's face was before him, framed by a cornered headdress, her hands lifting him up, her voice imploring him in words he was unable to understand. There was something he must remember. He stared at her, looking for something familiar in her face, something he should

239

know. This woman was not the one. She was hidden some-where at the back of his mind: a softness, their two voices whispering, something yielding beneath their nakedness, a candle guttering and her dark hair falling around him. The stranger placed cool cloths upon his brow, her voice murmuring what sounded like a prayer.

THIRTEEN

On the Friday that the rent was due, Effie was hanging washing out on the line strung over the patch of ground behind the cottage. Although it was only mid-morning, the sun was already hot and being outside offered little respite from the discomfort of standing over a steaming tub. Effie had tied her hair up in a kerchief and pinned up the hem of her dress at the front, revealing her petticoat beneath, the better to move unhampered and to catch a breath of air at her ankles. Her sleeves were rolled up above the elbows and, with strings untied, her apron hung loosely in front, weighted by a pocketful of long split pegs. She paused as she felt a tightening under her ribs, across the top of the bowl of her belly. It gripped her for a few seconds and she stood quite still, knowing it would pass: 'false labour' the other women called it, or 'early pangs'. Sometimes the tightenings would come three or four in a row, hot on each other's heels, but then the ripples would die away leaving her calm again. There, it had passed and she could carry on.

The rope washing line, which ran from a thorn tree in the hedge to a hook under the eaves of the cottage, was already half full and she hummed to herself as she pegged out a set of the Rectory's pillow cases, smoothing out their fine broderie anglaise trim. Then, unexpectedly, for he was not due until evening, Hob came around the corner of the cottage, saying, 'Good morrow! I thought I should find you here.'

Effie wheeled round to face him, the wicker basket of washing abandoned at her feet. 'Mr Talbot.' She inclined her head. 'I shall fetch the rent directly.' She turned a little pink, annoyed by his intrusion on her privacy and the awareness that with neither Tobias nor Beulah at home they were alone, the lane as always being quite deserted.

Hob, however, waving the matter of the rent away, leant his back against the warm stone wall of the cottage and said, ''Tis a beautiful day and I'm in no hurry.' His gaze travelled over her and lingered at her petticoat so that she longed to unpin her skirts and put them straight again. His eyes flicked back to her face. 'Pray – continue,' he said. 'Don't let me inconvenience you.' He tucked his thumbs into his weskit pockets as if settling down to watch her. 'I trust you bear no grudge over our conversation the other week?' he said pleasantly. 'Ale loosens the tongue and perhaps makes a man more ardent than a young maid like yourself is used to.'

Effie bent to her basket rather than meet his gaze, picking out the corner of a sheet and searching for its opposite among the tangle of shirts and underclothes. She put the corners together, picked up a peg, hauled the folded side of the sheet out and turned, side-on, back to the line. Hob's voice deepened as he carried on: '. . . but they say *in vino veritas*, Effie, which means a man speaks the truth when he's in his cups . . .' She lifted her arms high to peg the sheet to the line and Hob stopped dead as the sun behind her showed her form in silhouette, turning her cotton apron to flimsy and outlining clearly the bulge of her belly. Effie, aware of the sudden silence, froze with her arms still outstretched, the hairs on the back of her neck prickling and a blush rising like a tide to flush her chest and face. She turned her head slowly towards him and froze as she saw his changed expression.

'Whose is it?' he said stonily, drawing himself up from his lounge against the wall.

Warily, Effie pulled the sheet taut against the rope and pushed the next peg over it. 'I'll not say.'

'Then the parish will get it out of you.' He gave a strange laugh. 'So . . . not so demure after all. For all your posturing, your downcast eyes, your holier than thou . . .' He took a step towards her.

'We are to be married,' Effie said hurriedly.

He caught her forearm and gripped it hard. Effie gave a gasp as he pulled the sheet from her hand and straightened out her fingers. 'I see no ring,' he said quietly. 'So whatever randy lad has had you has tupped and gone.' He dropped her hand and she placed it quickly upon her belly.

'You're out,' he said abruptly. 'There's no room for your sort here.'

'But I have the rent! You can't just turn us out! What of Beulah? She's just a child!'

He raised his palm to stop the flow of words. 'I'll send my bailiff at midday. Leave the rent on the table. Be sure to be gone by then.' He turned and began to walk away.

Effie took a few steps after him. 'But where will we go? Hob! I will not have my child born in the workhouse! I cannot!'

'That's a matter you should have considered before you started your whoring,' he said over his shoulder as he walked away.

Effie stood trembling as the slam of the garden gate died away. Half of the sheet trailed on the path. She lifted it and pegged it, beating at the streaks of reddish dust absentmindedly, and then continued automatically along the line, pegging out smocks and petticoats any old how, drips leaving dark dots on the baked earth. Surely Hob didn't mean it? Surely he would change his mind? But she knew he was bull-headed and proud, used to getting his own way. Susannah Cleave, the dairymaid, had been sent away, cast out from the household, even though the child had been his own. Why would he care that she and Beulah had nowhere else to go and no one to take them in? He would not change his mind. She left the basket still half-full where it lay and went into the house.

In a daze, she spread a grey blanket on the table and laid upon it their few belongings: clothes, an old chap book that had been her mother's, the leather gloves, Beulah's slate and chalks. She counted out the rent into a pile on the table, tipped the few remaining coins into a drawstring purse and tucked it into her pocket. She went to the mantel and lifted down the old wooden clock; she must take anything that could be sold. In the shard of mirror propped beside it, her face looked drawn, her skin with a wan, yellowish cast. She stared at herself. Homeless. Destitute. Pauper. The words sailed through her mind. Oh, where was Jack? His return was their only hope.

She gripped the oak mantel with both hands and bowed her head. She had worked so hard to make a home. How was she to tell Beulah that they no longer had one? The mirror reflected the familiar room behind her: the green light from the garden in the casement window; the battered chairs with their rush seats that she'd mended over and over; the ladder to Tobias's loft, the rungs polished by their feet and hands over years of use. She couldn't bear to think of Beulah coming home work-weary to find her sitting on the step with their belongings at her feet. No, she would walk over to Weedon Royal and find her at the factory; they would set out together and she would try to explain the trouble she was in and endeavour to calm Beulah's fears. She laid the broken mirror face down upon the mantel and then began, resolutely, to tie the ends of the blanket to make a bundle. A plan was forming in her mind. She draped the shawl that Jack had given her over her shoulders, thinking that not only would it help hide her condition but that the fine garment might help gain her an audience. There was something she must do at Weedon Royal before she went to find Beulah. It filled her with dread but she must steel herself to go to the barracks and enquire after Jack.

Effie was directed to the barracks, which stood on the northern slope of the valley directly above the arsenal and near the turnpike road, in readiness for the speedy departure of the Artillery Brigade's horses and guns. A huge parade ground was enclosed on all four sides by a brick boundary wall and buildings: quarters for men and officers, cook-houses, stable blocks for three hundred horses, an exercise shed and gun-carriage buildings. Smaller sheds and buildings housed the shops of collar makers, wheelwrights and smiths, from which the noise of hammering issued, to mingle with the clop of hooves and the shouts of men.

Effie, having been told where to go by the gatekeeper at the arsenal, stood bareheaded in the midday sun, her bundle at her

245

feet, the heat pouring back from the high redbrick wall and shimmering over the flagstones of the parade ground. At length the guard took pity on her, thinking that the girl looked fair exhausted, pale and with sweat on her upper lip. He had no wish to be dealing with a swooning woman and arranged for her to be escorted inside and told to wait. There, she sat in an anteroom waiting her turn to see Captain Harris. His hours for dealing with civilian business were between two and three and she had been at the barracks since noon. Others gradually joined her and sat on the rough wooden forms against the walls, discussing their grievances: a publican suing for recompense for drunken soldiers damaging his premises; a stone sawyer whose tools had been stolen; tradesmen claiming that they had not been paid. When a clerk arrived and opened up a ledger to record the business of the day, Effie had boldly stated hers as a complaint regarding the trampling of corn by cavalry horses and the clerk had merely inclined his head and passed on to the next complainant.

At length, having collected all the pleas, the clerk took the book into the office beyond and then emerged and called Effie's name. Effie, still feeling light-headed and a little nauseous, despite the relative coolness of the interior, surmised that she had a touch of the sun and steadied herself against the wall as she rose, feeling again the hardening of her belly as the muscles clenched and tightened. Glad to have found a way to gain an audience but still not knowing quite what she would say, she entered a wholly wood-panelled room, decorated with sporting prints and battle scenes. The sounds of soldiers drilling in the parade ground outside drifted through the half-open sash: the clump of many feet and the staccato commands of the drill sergeant.

Behind a wide leather-topped desk, a man with a grave face

and grizzled hair and whiskers sat with the ledger open in front of him. 'You have a complaint against the army?' He glanced down at the book. 'Miss . . . Fiddement?'

Effie took a deep breath. 'Only in so far as it has taken Lieutenant Jack Stamford away, sir, and left me in a most difficult situation.'

Captain Harris looked up sharply at Stamford's name. The young woman before him had a delicate beauty, for all that her face was a little thin and her eyes shadowed with fatigue. And she was so young – maybe eighteen or nineteen – little older than his own daughter.

Effie rushed on before he could object. 'I apologise for my misrepresentation of the case to the clerk,' she said urgently, 'but I had to see you, sir. Jack . . . Lieutenant Stamford and I are betrothed yet I've received no letter from him for months. Since his posting abroad I've found myself in difficulties with insufficient funds to pay my rent and with a sister to support.' Effie felt her cheeks colour at her careful omission of Tobias.

'I can give you no money,' Captain Harris broke in sternly.

Effie was affronted. 'I didn't come for *money* but to ask for your good offices in enquiring after Jack! And though 'tis true there's nothing now for us but the poorhouse, I'm from a respectable family, a carpenter's daughter, and I would have you know that anyone can fall upon hard times!'

Captain Harris sighed and placed his fingertips together as if giving the case his consideration. He knew the pattern too well by now; every month some girl arrived, sickening for her army sweetheart, loitering anxiously at the gates, hoping to catch their errant lover unawares. Mostly a case of 'love 'em and leave 'em', sometimes with a child on the way. He looked more closely at the girl, the transparent appearance of her skin, the shawl, worn even in this heat, its long triangular folds worn draped down in front . . . He hadn't realised that matters had progressed so far. 'You understand that even if he could be returned to duty here it would take some weeks – that you would have to make your own arrangements meanwhile.'

The girl stood before him, her eyes downcast. He felt a pang of conscience that he had told Stamford to forget her. The girl had said that Stamford had written at first so he had been keen enough on her to ignore his superior's advice. Leaving aside Stamford's error of judgement that had forced him to send the lieutenant abroad, Harris thought highly of him and did not believe he was the type to shirk his responsibilities. His heart misgave; of course there was one obvious reason why his letters might have stopped: Badajoz, a sizeable action with terrible losses. 'I will enquire,' he said more softly.

'Thank you, sir.'

'I make no promises.'

She nodded quickly.

'That will be all.'

The girl bobbed a curtsey and left. He took paper from the drawer and wrote a note to remind himself to make enquiries of his friend Captain Quilter. The more he considered the matter the more he felt convinced that Stamford would not act in an unprincipled manner. Unlike that shifty blackguard, Clay. He remembered Clay's unpleasant expression when he had told him that Stamford had been accorded the honour of serving in the Peninsula. The same night Clay had picked a fight at the Bull with a local whip maker. A drunken brawl had ensued and after a period cooling his heels in a darkened cell, he had had Clay transferred to duties in the stores. Showing no gratitude for his second chance, there he'd been caught running a nice little sideline selling provisions to a local publican, and was currently in a military prison in Warwickshire. Harris felt well shot of him.

No, Stamford was of quite a different ilk. This sudden silence made him fear the worst. With a sigh, he picked up the brass hand bell from his desk and rang for the clerk to bring in the next complainant.

FOURTEEN

Effie made her way down the hill in the glaring heat, feeling dizzy and sick. The tightenings in her belly, which had started while she waited in the anteroom, had not gone away and as another came she stopped and put out her hand to lean against the wall. Beulah would not be free for many hours: in the summer months the factory didn't turn out until the light began to fail. She thought of going down to the centre of the village to seek peace and coolness in the church but was prevented by her awareness of her graceless state. If the parson found her there she would not be able to lie to him about her trouble and he would surely say that she was not fit for the House of God.

She crossed the swing bridge over the canal, walked on past

the corner of the arsenal and turned into the water meadows that divided it from the village, to find shade by the river. The pasture was full of cowpats and thistles, the infant river meandering through it in a channel that cut deep into the sandy banks in places but widened at the bends, where shallower water ran trickling over weed and stones, and muddy flats were churned by hoof prints where cattle had gathered to drink.

She took shelter in a copse beside the stream, the trees dwarfed by the massive arsenal wall on the slope above them, which stretched westward, unbroken as far as the eye could see. She spread her shawl on the bank, at the roots of a crooked wild cherry tree that overhung the stream. She sat down and watched the pale midges dancing in the shade beside her. It had been a long time since she'd eaten so she unwrapped her bundle to find the bread she'd packed, but when she looked upon it she found she had no appetite and left it where it was. How pitiful the jumble of objects seemed, spread out on the blanket: the clock face out of place as it looked up into the branches of the tree; the tangle of clothes a paltry covering against the strength of the elements; the beautiful gloves with their slim fingers and leather-covered buttons a ridiculous vanity.

She folded the shawl carefully, and put it behind her against the tree so that she could lean back and maybe doze. There was a dull ache in her back and pelvis, like the cramps she used to get each month when she bled, and she couldn't get comfortable. The tightening came again, this time all around her middle, front to back, making her draw in her breath. She tried sitting up straight and then subsided again, leaning back on her elbows, but it made no difference; the pain gripped her until it was ready to let go and then melted away regardless of the position she adopted. Letting out a long breath, she scrambled to her feet, no longer wanting to be still. She paced restlessly along the thin beaten path that ran alongside the river, only stopping when she reached the cattle ford with its mud and mess, then fast back again, not knowing what to do with herself or which way to turn. She stood stock still as another pain engulfed her, holding her belly with her arms folded across it; this time the pain encircled her like a girdle pulled too tight and it left her dizzy and breathless as it faded away. She shook her head as if to free herself from it and knelt beside the blanket, refolding the clothes, pairing the gloves and setting all back neatly to rights. The clock, which had read three o'clock, read only ten minutes past the hour. Yet she had suffered two pains in that time, two deep, cramping pains. She felt faint and put her hands down on to the grassy bank and her head down, a sweaty chill coming over her. She crawled to the edge and vomited into the flowing water. Frightened now, she made a whimpering sound. She wanted to go home. She would get Beulah to take her. Passing her forearm over her mouth, she sat back upon her heels. Tears stung her eyes as she remembered she could not go home; the cottage would be barred against her.

She gathered up her shawl and bundle and stood slowly, pushing herself upright with one hand on her thigh. She must make her way to the silk factory, getting along as best she could between the pains. Beulah would have to help her find a carter to take her to Newnham. The workhouse would have to take them in. There was nowhere else left to go.

Beulah was coming out of the scullery with her empty basket, ready to fetch more mulberry leaves, when her sister came round the corner of the building, bent over like an old woman and with one hand grasping at the wall as if it were the only thing keeping her upright. Beulah ran. 'Effie! Effie, what is it?

What ails you?' she said as she reached her and pulled Effie's arm over her shoulder. Effie shook her head, unable to speak, her face the colour of uncooked dough, and Beulah knew that she had been right; Effie was sick – terribly sick. 'Quick, down here.' With a rapid glance to check for Mrs Gundy, she helped her sister inside and down the cellar steps. There she froze, for at the worm beds, with her back to them, stood Alice, counting the number of cocoons in the fanned twigs of broom and the number of new worms that had started to spin. Effie put her hand to her mouth, overcome by the close heat from the stove, the torrential sound of the feeding worms and the fusty, unpleasant smell of sweet herbs overlaying decay.

'You've been dawdling again, Beulah,' Alice said, without looking up. 'Get on and feed them quickly; they're running short of fodder.' When there was neither answer nor movement she turned and her jaw dropped.

'My sister's sick. I think she's really sick,' Beulah babbled. 'I don't know what to do!'

'Well, she can't stop here. The master's not paid his visit yet,' Alice said. 'Get her out.'

Effie, squeezing Beulah's shoulder so hard that it hurt, looked pleadingly at Alice. 'My time's come,' she said.

Alice stared at her stonily for a moment. She stepped forward, pulled Effie's arm away from her stomach, spread her hand flat and pressed it against her belly.

'I'm barely six months gone. 'Tis too early, surely?' Effie said desperately.

Alice looked grim.

'Can you stop it?'

Alice gave the slightest shake of her head. ''Tis too late for that.'

As a new wave of pain took her, Effie gasped, dropped her

bundle and bent forward with her hands upon her knees. Alice cast around the cellar and pulled together a heap of empty kindling sacks to cover the cold brick floor. Between them, Alice and Beulah lowered Effie down. Alice pulled up Effie's skirts and Beulah saw that her petticoat and underclothes were wet. Alice began to strip them off. 'Go to the kitchen,' she ordered. 'Fetch scissors and string and as many cloths as will not be missed.'

Beulah hesitated. Effie was moaning, 'I can't! I can't!' her head turning from side to side and her hand gripping Alice's arm.

'What's wrong with her?' Beulah whispered.

Alice snorted. 'Nothing that won't be righted shortly. Now, run!'

Beulah hurried to the kitchen door and hid behind it, peeping through the crack. Mrs Gundy was sweeping the floor, stopping now and then to spread tea leaves before her to collect the dust and stop it from rising. Beulah waited in an agony of anxiety, willing Mrs Gundy to be done and go. She wanted to fulfil her task if it would help Effie but why had Alice asked her to fetch these things? What possible use could they be? What was Alice going to do to her? Effie needed a doctor – medicine! Mrs Gundy bent down, groaning, to brush the sweepings into a pan. Beulah danced from foot to foot in frustration as the woman moved heavily over to the table and began to sprinkle it with soda. Halfway through scrubbing it, the master's bell, high on the wall, rang and she stopped working and wiped her hands on her apron. It rang again, harder and more insistently, and, grumbling, she left the room. Beulah darted from her hiding place and gathered the items she'd been sent for from table and dresser drawers.

When she returned to the cellar, it took a moment for her

254

eyes to adjust to the dim light that filtered in through the barred windows. Effie was squatting on the pile of sacks, tangled drawers and petticoat, her arm around Alice's shoulders. Her skirts were bunched up around her waist, her pale legs exposed to the thigh. Not knowing what else to do, Beulah laid the haul from the kitchen down beside Alice, who said, 'Get the other side of her. Let her lean on you.'

As she took her place, Beulah asked Effie how she fared but she didn't reply, didn't even seem aware that it was Beulah by her side. Effie was making strange noises, sometimes panting, sometimes giving a long, deep, animal moan so that Alice told her to hush up and hold her noise and Effie pressed her lips together hard and clenched her teeth to trap the sound inside. Her face turned red and sweaty and she began to make *grunting* noises that reminded Beulah of the sow in the yard. Whenever she groaned and grunted, Alice said, 'Bear down,' and put her hand down between Effie's legs so that Beulah looked away, embarrassed.

Alice, now on her knees, shuffled round to be in front of Effie, who still leant on Beulah's shoulder. She reached between Effie's legs, bunching up the folds of the petticoat beneath her as something dark and wet came out of her, retreated and appeared again. As it emerged once more, Beulah saw Alice pull gently on it until she got it free, and then again on an angular shape so that, as Effie gave a long, low cry, the whole came slithering out, with a great deal of blood, into the cotton petticoat, partly covered in a shiny membrane thinner than muslin. Alice opened the remains of the birth sac with her fingers and Beulah stared at what looked at first like a skinned rabbit ready for the pot, with a pale grey slippery rope attached. Alice wrapped a cloth around it. Effie lay back, leaning on her elbows and Alice pressed one hand at the

255

bottom of her abdomen and pulled gently on the cord so that something dark, bloody and horrible slid out. The grey-white cord pulsated as if a heart were beating within it but there was no movement from the creature curled in the cloth. Beulah, thinking of the things that Effie said to comfort her, murmured, 'There, 'tis all done now. 'Tis all over with.' She pushed the damp strands of hair that were stuck to Effie's forehead back off her face.

'Is it safely delivered? Let me see it!' Effie said.

Alice worked deftly with string and scissors to separate the infant from the afterbirth, her lips pressed together in a thin line of concentration, saying never a word to Effie.

'Give it to me,' Effie said, her voice loud and hoarse. She strained forward to see.

Alice put it into Effie's arms, saying, 'It's a boy.' She bundled the mess up in a sack and went to the stove. She pushed it in on top of the dying embers of coals, and flames began to lick the sacking, which twisted and shrivelled, its contents hissing. A sickening, meaty smell filled the cellar.

Beulah looked down at the newborn. It didn't look like any of the babies she'd seen. The babies that the women carried in shawls tied around them at harvest time were pink and rounded. This one was half the size, with thin, stick-like arms and legs, and its skin was mottled and translucent so that you could see the veins beneath. She gazed into its face. Its eyes were tight shut, the eyelids huge and swollen; its nose was squashed to one side and its lips were wide. The head was pointy with a swollen area on top, squeezed and elongated in the birth. She thought it quite ugly.

Effie cupped the infant's swollen head in one hand, passing the other hand all over its body, stroking and murmuring over it. She opened its fist, no bigger than a walnut, and touched its palm. Its fingers curled but did not grip. Beulah thought that she wouldn't choose to touch it. Its body was all smeared with blood and was greasy-looking, with white stuff in the folds of its skin – skin that seemed somehow too big for its bones.

Effie cradled it in the crook of her arm and then bent and blew gently into its face. Its eyes remained shut. Its brow didn't wrinkle. She began rubbing its limbs again, harder this time, lifting each arm and chafing it between her palms, but when she let them go they fell back, floppy as a rag doll's. She hugged it to her breast and rocked back and forth, looking up at Alice in appeal.

Alice took the baby from her, lifting it from its wrappings. She held it up by the heels. It dangled from her hands. 'There's no life in it,' she said.

Beulah saw the last vestige of hope pass from her sister's eyes. Effie's face crumpled and a high, keening cry escaped her lips.

Alice took the cloth from Effie's slack fingers, wrapped it around the still form and pushed it into Beulah's arms. 'We need to get rid of it,' she said under her breath. Her eyes flicked to the stove.

Aghast, Beulah held the warm bundle tightly against her and shrank back.

'Take it then, 'tis not my kin and no business of mine,' Alice hissed. 'I don't care how you do it but go and get rid of it. Do you want the whole village to know your sister's shame?' Alice knelt beside Effie and rested a hand awkwardly on her shoulder. 'Shush, shush,' she said; then more urgently, 'Don't take on so; you'll have the master down here. Do you want us to lose our positions?'

As Beulah moved away with the baby in her arms, Effie called out, 'Jack! Jack!' and tried to rise. Alice caught hold of her arm; she fell back weakly against the sacks and sobbed hopelessly with her head in her hands.

Beulah laid the bundle in her basket. Her hands would not stop shaking but she forced herself to grasp the handle and lift it. She must carry it as if it were empty, as if this were any normal trip to replenish the worms' food, on any normal afternoon. She went quietly up the cellar steps, listening at the door before venturing into the scullery. Behind her, she heard Alice saying grimly to Effie, 'This is how we'll proceed. As soon as I've cleaned you up and you've rested a little, I shall catch one of the carters and you can pay him to take you home. You have money?'

Beulah peeped out, saw that the scullery was empty, slipped out and quickly pulled the door shut fast behind her, as she'd been schooled. A whiff of the horrible smell of sooty burnt meat hung in the air and she prayed it would not travel and bring curious noses.

Outside, she forced herself to walk, not run, although she was longing to. In the open expanse of yard, under the harsh light, she felt horribly exposed, as if the windows behind her were rows of unblinking eyes and the master standing at any one of them. There was tightness in her chest so that it was hard to catch her breath. She sought the shadow of the pigsty wall and squatted down, sitting back on her heels for a moment and trying to calm herself. She glanced back over her shoulder, furtively, to check that no one had emerged. The windows stared blankly back. As she turned, she saw with horror that an end of white cloth trailed from the basket and hastily tucked it in, looking quickly away from the bundle inside.

Her mind raced. There was only one place she could think of to hide the little body so that it would not be found. She set off once again, entering the rows of mulberry trees at the same point from which she'd emerged earlier in the day, as if picking up her work exactly where she had left off. Once within the cover of the trees she ducked under their low branches, making a beeline for the back of the plantation. She paused within the margin of the trees and peeped cautiously through the newly planted saplings to the latest line of holes dug by the workmen, where the last of the new saplings lay on the ground in a row, their root balls wrapped in wet sacking. The diggings were deserted; a spade stood upright in the earth and a shovel lay propped against a tree where the men had downed tools for their afternoon break. Beulah drew forward to the very edge and looked around for any clue to their whereabouts, wondering if they had withdrawn into the shade of the orchard to smoke a pipe, but there was no sign and she concluded that they had gone to the well for water or to Mrs Gundy, who would sometimes spare them some small beer. Unsure how long it would be before their return, she hurried forward to the first hole in the line, the next to be filled, and knelt down upon the spoil heap, the basket by her side. The hole was wide, to give plenty of room for roots to grow. Deep and straight-sided, flat spade marks sliced through the dry, sandy topsoil and the darker damp soil beneath.

She glanced all around and then stayed still for a moment, listening. The only sounds were the fluting song of a blackbird calling for its mate and the rustle of hedge sparrows flitting here and there. Quickly, she picked up the bundle. She could feel the pliable solidity of the infant's body within the slippery folds of the cloth. She thought that she should say a prayer but shock had numbed her mind and no words would come. Holding it in the crook of her arm, she lay flat on her stomach at the edge of the hole so that she could reach, and lowered it down into the bottom of the pit. The white cloth that had covered its crown slipped away and the head, lolling sideways, was exposed. Beulah stared at the baby's tiny, perfect ear, the whorl inside, its curled edge and delicate lobe. Its skin was pale and waxy, the veins beneath giving it a blueish tinge. With a whimper, she pulled the material over to cover it, only to reveal instead its tiny hand and wrist.

The first spade of earth that she scraped from the spoil heap fell upon the white cloth and trickled away down the sides of the humped shape; the second began to cover it. In the distance, Beulah heard shouts and laughter, male voices, and desperately dragged the unwieldy spade through the spoil heap, scraping earth into the hole until there was a thin covering of soil and stones and all of the white had disappeared. Only the little hand remained uncovered.

As she looked down, there was a movement, a shifting beneath the soil. The baby's fingers, which had been open and loose, curled as she had seen them do when Effie touched its palm. She gasped and bent closer. A pebble, dislodged by her change of position, fell from the side of the hole, a trickle of sandy soil following it. She peered in, listening for the faintest sound. The movement . . . it could have been just the crumbly soil settling; it must have been . . . mustn't it?

Nearby, the chattering noise of the blackbird's alarm call rang out and she panicked. Desperately, she scrabbled more earth over with her hands. The voices were getting nearer, the men making their way along the path beside the mulberry trees. She hesitated, wringing the cloth of her apron between her hands, scraped more earth into the hole, and then, overwhelmed by fear, grabbed up the basket and ran for the trees. She ducked under the branches, hiding in their green shadow. Glancing back she saw that she had thrown the spade down in her haste, forgetting to return it to its upright position in the ground. Hardly breathing, she watched as a man and two boys, in their rough smocks and breeches, returned carrying pails of water to moisten the newly planted saplings. The boys' hair was wet, their smocks darkened with splashes of water and they carried on their banter, pushing and jostling each other to try to make the water spill while the older man laughed at them. They picked up their tools without heeding.

The boys began digging at the end of the row. The man took up the next sapling to plant it and Beulah felt sure he would notice that the spoil heap was spread wide or see her smaller footprints among his own. He slit open the sacking and removed it, teased out the roots and placed the sapling in the hole. As he began to shovel earth in, Beulah had to close her eyes: the weight of it on those tiny bones, the air crushed out of its lungs, its little face against the stony earth . . . Every slice of the spade and slide and drop of the soil into the hole was a torment that made her scrunch her eyes tighter. Still, behind her closed eyelids, she saw the tiny fingers close and the spasm of movement that could have been the earth settling or could have been the small body curling against the weight pattering down on it: a near dead creature shuddering to consciousness as blows rained down. Oh, what had she done! She saw pale shiny roots, like long fingers, growing and grasping, pushing their way down and through . . . She opened her eyes to find the workman beating the earth down with the flat of his spade. It was too late.

Thump! Thump! Thump! The dull sound of tamping and packing the earth followed her as she crept away; it echoed in her head even as her flight took pace, pushing her way through the branches, heedless of scratches and breaking twigs, wanting only to get back to Effie and be comforted. It was still there

– *Thump! Thump! Thump!* – as she broke from the cover of the trees and ran with her empty basket bumping at her knees straight across the open yard and headlong into the scullery, where she came face-to-face with the master.

'And where are you going in such haste?' he said, catching hold of her arm above the elbow. He glanced at her apron, smeared with dirt, and at the empty basket. 'What's afoot?' he demanded.

Beulah kept her head down, her eyes level with the brass buttons and watch chain on his waistcoat. In his hand was the whip he carried; he tapped its polished, cherrywood handle against his thigh. 'Nothing, master,' she muttered. She pulled against his grip. 'I need to be about my business feeding the worms.'

'We'll go together,' he said. 'I was just about to pay my visit.' Moving his grip from her arm to the back of her neck, he pushed her in front of him.

The door to the cellar stood ajar. 'What's this?' the master said, his temper rising. 'How many times have I impressed on you the need to keep the room secure at *all times*? Where is Alice?' And he racketed her down the steps so fast that her feet barely touched the ground.

Alice and Effie were gone. Beulah's stomach turned over in fear. The scissors and string lay on the floor beside the stove. The bloody sacks had been stuffed inside it and had stifled the fire; the door hung open, revealing that it was out. The room was already noticeably cooler and without the masking smell of warm herbs the place smelt like a butcher's shop: a mixture of the iron tang of blood and under it a smell like rotten meat. And it was quiet. The noise of the worms feeding, like thousands of raindrops falling on leaves, all day, all night, had all but stopped.

262

'What the blazes . . . ?' He pulled her with him to the worm beds.

In place of the usual mat of green, the worms squirmed on bare boards, scattered only with tiny scraps of leaves. The living worms, a roiling mass of oyster-grey, clambered over a sticky blackened mess of dead ones, from which the foul smell rose.

Fowler gave a roar of indignation. He moved quickly along the beds checking each one; in each the same pattern was repeated. He yanked Beulah by the arm and pushed her back against the wall beside the stove, jarring her shoulder blades and thumping her head. She slid to the ground and cowered there, shrinking back. Her hands travelled behind her over the flaking brick floor, fingers spread, feeling for the metallic scrape of the scissors. He stood over her, breathing heavily, his face livid, eyes narrowed in fury. As he turned the whip around to use not the rope but the butt end, Beulah opened her mouth to scream and Fowler bent and clamped his hand over it.

FIFTEEN

On Christmas Day, which fell on a Sunday, Rosie drove over to Holly Court to visit May. She had refused Tally's invitation to join them, not wanting to impose on their family Christmas, but the morning had seemed endless and she was glad of the distraction and the chance of some company. The house had seemed horribly quiet since she'd passed the kids over to Josh and being alone only gave her the chance to brood on the bitterness of their meeting.

Ever since she'd emailed to let him know that she was going back to court to renegotiate the maintenance payment, things between them had gone from bad to worse. In his initial furious phone call he'd ranted at her about the things he and Tania would now have to give up: the skiing holiday they'd planned, the chance of moving up the property ladder. Did she *know* how expensive it was paying in to *two* households? Rosie, outraged that he should whinge about missing a trip to Chamonix when she had been saving every Tesco voucher towards Sam's first school uniform, had shouted back, until, with comic timing, they had both rung off simultaneously. Since then they had barely managed to be civil to each other.

They'd met at the service station early on the morning of Christmas Eve and transferred kids and baggage between the two cars in a stony silence. When Rosie bent into the car and said to the children that their presents would be waiting for them at home on Boxing Day, Josh had broken in, 'You mean Tuesday. They're staying with us over Boxing Day.' He stowed Sam's bag in the front passenger seat and shut the door.

Rosie looked at him in disbelief. 'Hang on a minute! That's not what we discussed!'

'Well, I don't remember us discussing what I could afford as child support. *Discussion* doesn't seem to be your strong point,' he said.

'Only because we never manage to do it in a civilised way. I thought it would be better doing it through solicitors. It would stop us getting steamed up,' she said pointedly. 'That's what it's there for, isn't it – the law?'

He walked away from her and round to the driver's side, the kids in the car between them. 'Yeah, and possession's nine-tenths of it. I'll bring them back Boxing Day evening.' She opened her mouth to remonstrate but he drowned her out. 'It's all arranged; the cousins will be coming round to Mum's too and anyway I don't want to drive on Christmas Day. I'm not missing out on having a drink.' He opened the driver's door.

'But Tuesday's too late! What about *my* Christmas? It's all over by then!' Rosie felt her voice rising. A family passing them, on the way to the services building, gave them a wide berth, the parents exchanging glances, the teenage children gawping.

Josh stared at her over the roof of the car. 'You're making an exhibition of yourself again,' he said. 'Have you got no self-control at all?' He glowered at her. 'Here. Nine thirty, Monday evening, and don't forget this time.' He got into the car, slammed the door and left Rosie fuming as he drove away.

Now, as she turned into the car park at the home, Rosie made a little calculation in her head: thirty-three hours to go until she got them back, thirty-three more hours to fill. She'd best keep busy and concentrate on cheering May up. She picked up May's present and put a smile on her face.

There was no one in the office; everyone was probably tied up with preparations for the Christmas lunch, Rosie thought. Quite at home now as one of their 'regulars', she signed the visitors' book in the tinsel-decked hall and went straight to find May in her favourite place in the sunroom. She plonked a smacking kiss on her cheek and wished her a Happy Christmas.

'Is it?' May said incredulously.

'Yep, and I've brought you a present.' She put the flat, rectangular package down gently on May's thin knees.

May just sat and looked at it. 'What is it?'

'You have to open it and see.'

'Is it chocolates?'

'No,' Rosie said, 'but there are Maltesers in my bag and you can have them after you've had dinner, OK?'

May picked ineffectually at the sellotape until Rosie, seeing that she'd never get it undone, ran her nail underneath it so that she could unfold the paper. Inside was a beautiful white leather photo album. May passed her hand across the cover, feeling its padded smoothness.

'You can open it up,' Rosie said.

May turned to the first page. 'Oh!' she said. 'It's me!' A child in a hand-knitted cardi, and with her hair in pigtails, smiled up at the camera with the gappy teeth of a seven-year-old.

Rosie nodded, smiling, and turned the next page. 'And Helena,' she said as they looked at a picture of May sitting in a fireside chair with her baby sister held awkwardly on her lap. They carried on turning the pages that told the life story Rosie had carefully constructed, year by year, from photos found in her mother's albums or loose in drawers at May's house.

May pored over them, every now and then commenting about where a picture was taken. Her responsiveness and recaptured memories made Rosie feel glad; the gift was a success. 'I thought next time I come we could put some more pictures in,' Rosie said, 'maybe the ones in your bedside table here?'

May nodded.

'And maybe the ones in the frames? Then you could put the album in your bag and have all your pictures together in one place and it would save them getting smudged or the glass getting broken and hurting your fingers.'

May turned another page. 'Well I never, my graduation!' She moved on through pictures of the family at Helena's wedding and holiday shots with friends in France and then paused at a photo that had been casually snapped, rather than posed: May laughing, kneeling on a hearthrug, holding out a toy to a baby who reached for it, behind them a sofa and the legs of another woman sitting on it. 'Look – it's you!' May pointed with her claw-like hand.

Rosie leant over, suddenly excited. Her baby self was dressed in a blue flower-printed dress, with smocking across the chest and a Peter Pan collar. One sock was off, revealing toes spread, like her fingers, in delight. She had chubby cheeks and arms and a cowlick of blond hair. The toy was a puppet on a wooden stick: Punch. She remembered playing with it as an older child: you pulled the stick down and Punch's hook-nosed face and outstretched hands disappeared into a cup; pushed it up and the grinning clown popped out again.

She peered closer. On the rug beside May's knees lay another puppet: Judy with her mobcap and red cheeks. Two toys, a matching pair. Her heart began to beat faster. 'Do you remember when that was taken?' she asked May gently.

May smiled. 'It was on your first birthday. You loved that puppet. *I* got it for you,' she said proudly.

'And the other one? Was Judy for Lily?'

May nodded. 'You had a cake too. You two sucked the icing and Helena and I ate the cake.'

Rosie touched the edge of the photo, where, on her mother's lap, just out of reach of the camera, Lily must have been sitting.

May went on, 'Helena saved a piece from each cake for Michael and kept the candles for you to see him blow them out again. That was before they moved away, of course . . .' Her face fell and Rosie broke in quickly before there could be tears.

'Let's see what came next.'

'Was that my car?' May asked, looking at a picture of herself leaning against a green VW Beetle.

'I think it must have been,' Rosie said absently, still thinking of Lily – of the two of them together – with sticky mouths and fingers grasping their stick puppets, entranced by the game of peep-bo as their mum and aunty popped Punch and Judy up and down. Here was something she could shape into a memory. 'Yes, yes, I'm sure it was,' she said, seeing May's expression, still uncertain, writing May's memories for her too.

'It's nice,' May said.

A gong sounded and May stuffed the album into her bag. 'Supper time,' she said.

'Christmas lunch.'

'Really?' May looked pleased all over again.

Rosie walked May into the dining room. One of the male staff, dressed as Santa, sat at a keyboard playing 'Merry Xmas Everybody' while a plump carer, wearing furry reindeer antlers on a hairband, handed out thimble-sized glasses of sherry. As Nurse Todd came bustling down the long table, seeing everyone to their seats, she spotted Rosie and noticed that the kids weren't with her. She made her way over. 'Are you able to join us?' she said. 'It's so nice if relatives can stay. The more the merrier.'

Rosie hesitated, not wanting to be in the way.

'To be honest, we could do with as many pairs of hands as we can get. You'd be doing us a favour if you could just keep an eye?'

'Thanks, I'd love to,' Rosie said. She was directed to sit between May and an old gentleman called Anthony, who tried to rise and pull out a chair for her but, overcome by his shakiness, subsided.

'Very nice to see a young face about the place,' he said. 'Are you married?'

'Um, not any more,' Rosie said.

May nudged her sharply in the ribs. 'He'll propose if you don't watch out. He asks everyone.' She rolled her eyes. 'He's asked me twice this week already.'

A carer came round with a box of Christmas crackers and

Rosie helped May and Anthony to pull one. Soon there was a barrage of reports as others did the same and a hubbub of chat as plastic trinkets were examined, jokes puzzled over and paper hats worn at crazy angles. Anthony's blue paper crown slipped down over one eye and Rosie straightened it up for him. A disagreement broke out between two ladies over who should have the key ring that had fallen from a cracker; Rosie settled it by offering one of them the string of beads that had been in her own. Feeling that the event had something of the Mad Hatter's tea party about it, Rosie began to enjoy herself a little.

The carers were finding it hard to be everywhere at once: taking plastic covers off the meals, escorting people to and from the loo and replacing dropped knives and forks. Rosie despatched her turkey breast slices, tough roasties and Bisto quickly and went to help. She served some dinners, managed to defuse an argument over who had more stuffing by finding second helpings and, when pudding came, got a conversation going at her end of the table about the thruppenny bit that always used to be hidden in it: reminiscence and a good old moan about health and safety seeming equally enjoyable.

Once lunch was over, everyone retired to the sunroom where the chairs had been arranged in a wide circle and all the tables had been removed. The keyboard was brought in and the player gave them a medley of carols and then moved into old dance numbers. Couples shuffled around the room to the music, some of the elderly ladies dancing together, which Rosie found touching. It brought home to her the sad disparity in numbers between the men and women and also reminded her somehow of childhood, primary school dancing lessons where the girls took it in turns to lead, the boys all having melted away to play football. She danced to 'A String of Pearls' with

Anthony; he clasped her hand tight, his head nodding to a rhythm of its own as they made a jerky circuit of the room. 'Will you marry me?' he said as the melody ended.

'I think it would disappoint too many other ladies,' Rosie said as she gave him an arm so that he could lower himself into his chair.

After the dancing, they played pass-the-parcel, Rosie and the others dodging quickly around to help strip away the layers of paper, tubes of sweets rolling into laps and on to the floor and crossword books fished out and compared with competitive fervour. Then a raffle was drawn. Rosie joined in to help those without their glasses check their tickets. When May's ticket was called, Rosie took her up to the table to choose between bath salts, a flower vase and a box of Milk Tray. 'Well, I can't think what you'll choose, May,' she said and everybody laughed as May gleefully picked up the chocolates and stowed them in her bag.

The residents were served a cup of tea from the trolley and Nurse Todd produced a bottle of sherry for the staff. As she thrust a large glass into Rosie's hand, she said, 'Thanks for all your help.'

Rosie, pleased, murmured, 'Not at all.'

Nurse Todd raised her glass. 'Another party managed without major mishap. Cheers!' They all touched glasses and drank.

Rosie, enjoying the feeling of bonhomie, stayed on to help wash up. When she went to say goodbye to May she found her asleep with the album beside her on the table. She tiptoed away feeling that the whole visit had been worthwhile.

It was dark by the time she got home. As she stepped into the hall, she had the strange impression that someone left it:

a movement, as of someone slipping quickly through the kitchen door. Heart thumping, she hesitated at the open front door, keeping her path clear for retreat. A shaft of light from a passing car travelled along the wall in the hallway and was gone. Of course, she told herself, that's all it was, a car passing as I opened the door. Nonetheless, she stood, listening, a moment longer, the cold wind from the street rushing in around her.

She busied about putting all the lights on downstairs and then turned on the radio in the kitchen and the TV in the living room, filling the house with human voices. She changed out of her good wool dress into jeans, cosy navy sweatshirt and grey canvas deck shoes, worn soft as slippers. Having made a coffee, she settled down to watch *Dancing on Ice* but it didn't hold her attention. She wondered what the children were doing now. It was probably bath time. She hoped it was Josh's mum, Sandra, who was bathing them and not Tania, who Sam said always got shampoo in Cara's eyes. Or maybe they were in their pyjamas already, curled up on the sofa, surrounded by the presents they'd probably opened at some ungodly hour. There would be a fantastic tree; Sandra had always been good at all that stuff, greenery festooning the mantelpiece above the wood burner and long red candles everywhere. She looked around at her own meagre efforts. She hadn't been able to run to a tree; the holly she'd tucked around the picture frames seemed scant and half-hearted and the kids' presents still sat in their plastic carrier bags, waiting to be wrapped. Above the fireplace filled with fir cones, only four cards stood on the mantelpiece: from Corinne and Luc, Tally and Rob, one that Sam had made at playschool – red card and a blobby snowman made of cotton wool – and one from Tom Marriott. That had been a surprise.

She had been in to the office a couple of times while the maintenance case was being prepared. The first time he had been just as when they'd met initially: very professional, distant even, when in his office, and then pleasant and friendly as he saw her out, asking after the children and how she was, telling her not to worry and that the practice had a watertight case. He had walked with her all the way to the car park and she'd had the distinct impression that he wanted to say something to her out of earshot of the receptionist, but when they'd reached the car he'd hesitated as she unlocked it, opened his mouth and then closed it again and finally shaken hands with her, returning to his formal manner.

The second time, they had gone through all the points of the case and then he'd dropped a bombshell. He was not going to be able to represent her after all but would leave her in the very capable hands of Mr Douglas. He had said that Mr Douglas was more experienced in family law, whereas his speciality was conveyancing, but he had blushed when he said it and Rosie felt somehow that it was personal, wondered what on earth she'd done, and was duly offended. She didn't want to have to get to know somebody new or have to go through the story of her break-up with Josh all over again. It had been Tom Marriott who had persuaded her to go back to the court in the first place and now he was bailing on her! She had maintained her own formal tone beyond the bounds of the office door and when he'd moved to walk her out, she had quickly said that she had shopping to do and left him looking rather nonplussed.

Now, here was this card. Another puzzle. It was a nice card, not a business one for clients with a boring picture of bells or robins and a pre-printed message. Instead it read: *To Rosie and family. Hope you and the children have a wonderful*

273

Christmas and that the New Year brings good things, Tom Marriott. Nice of him – thoughtful – but why sign it only with his name? What happened to his 'and family'? Was he making overtures again or was the card by way of an apology after letting her down? The man was a puzzle. Well, now that he wasn't taking the maintenance case, she probably wouldn't see him again until she came to sell the house: that was, assuming he *felt* like taking her back on. She felt irritated all over again.

Rosie got up to close the curtains against the winter evening. Outside, the street had become quiet, everyone home with their families. A thin coating of gritty snow lay on the ground and gleamed on the cars parked under the orange light of the streetlamps. Opposite, a few houses down, one window still had the curtains open, revealing the flickering chemical-blue glow of a TV screen in an otherwise darkened room. All the other windows were sealed off, curtains closed to keep in the warmth, showing just the tiniest chinks of light. Rosie pulled the drapes across, closing herself in.

She couldn't be bothered to do much for supper so she put some cheese and biscuits on a tray, poured a glass of wine and picked and sipped while she watched a quiz show. At least trying to answer the questions kept her from brooding, but as it ended, her thoughts returned like a compass needle to the children. She turned the TV off and decided that she would wrap their presents; it would make her feel better to be doing something for them.

She got sellotape and scissors from the bureau and unrolled the wrapping paper on the floor: kids' paper with comic Father Christmases tobogganing their way across snow-covered roofs. She wrapped Cara's present first but didn't bother with ribbon as she had for Tally; she knew that the kids would have the paper off in seconds.

She was particularly pleased with the present she'd picked up for Sam: a remote-controlled loader, its metal painted a bright yellow, with a wide bucket and 'JCB' stencilled on the cab just like the real thing. The controls moved it around and lifted the bucket to scoop or push earth along like a bulldozer. She took it out of the box to fit its batteries so that he would be able to use it straightaway. It would be brilliant if the snow got heavier, she thought; he'd love using it in the snow.

As she knelt on the rug beside the toy and fiddled to get the battery compartment on the remote open, something about the colour of the loader nagged at her – that particular shade of yellow . . . Yes, it was the same colour as the whizzing object she remembered from *that* day, that awful day at the beach. Faintly the whirring sound began and she shook her head to drive it away. She tried to block it out, concentrating instead on the good things that her visit to May had brought. She conjured up the new image that she had formed of herself and Lily: two babies on their very first birthday with gooey fingers grasping their puppets-on-sticks.

Two sticks.

One each.

Something was slotting into place.

A windy day. Sunlight and flashing yellow. Windmills! Two yellow plastic windmills on sticks that Maria had bought for them from one of those shops full of such glories: rubber rings and fishing nets, blow-up dolphins and bucket-and-spade sets. They had held the windmills up outside to get their folded plastic petals to catch the breeze, but in the shelter of the buildings they flicked and stopped, turned and then stood still. Maria had taken them out on to the jetty at the beach. Rosie closed her eyes tight, willing the pictures to keep on coming.

Steps up, one on either side of Maria, a matching pair. The

275

smell of salt and seaweed. Maria holding their hands tightly, keeping them away from the edge. Green-painted posts beside them and, underfoot, wooden boards with gaps where the sea moved and glittered beneath, great dizzying swells rising and falling away to gurgle and suck around the stilts of the jetty. Out further, out towards the end of the pier with the wind whipping their dresses and hair, Maria urging them to hold the windmills up to make them whizz round.

Mine was whirring now but Lily wasn't holding hers firmly enough. The blustery wind twisted it, turned it crooked in her hand, buffeted it first one way then the other. My words, taken by the wind, 'Not like that! Like this!' as I reached across in front of Maria and triumphantly thrust my windmill at Lily, knocking her hand. And in a split second, the wind had it, plucking it from her fingers. For a moment it flew, and then, with a scratching sound, went scudding along the boards towards the edge. Maria let go of Lily's hand and lunged to grab it and Lily, with a squeal of indignation, ran forward, stumbled and slipped . . .

Rosie sat back on her heels, the batteries rolling away across the floor.

There was screaming . . . her hand held in a grip as tight as a vice as she was dragged forward, her parents' voices shouting, desperate, the sound of strangers' feet running, pounding along the boards, and then nothing. Just the yellow petals flicking round between her and the brightness of the sun and the endless whirring blocking everything out.

Shakily, Rosie levered herself up to sit in the armchair. She sat still and closed her eyes, breathing heavily. *It was her fault.* If she hadn't *interfered* it would never have happened. She hadn't been trying to help, not really, she'd been doing what she always did with Lily, competing, trying to get attention, and showing off. Oh God! It was her fault. Poor, dear Lily.

276

When she opened her eyes it seemed unreal to see the room before her with its patterned rug and familiar red sofa, as if she expected the past to open up and swallow her back into it. The ordinary things in the room seemed distant and insubstantial, as if she might step on to the rug and feel her feet sink into sand or reach out to touch the table and find only the emptiness of air and salt spray.

She made herself pick up the glass of wine beside her and drink it to the dregs, hoping that it would warm the pit of her stomach where a cold block now sat. Had Maria told her parents how it had happened? Was that why all trace of Lily had been erased from her life – so that she, Rosie, wouldn't be brought face-to-face with what had taken place, so that she could forget? She had seen the way that her parents had kept Lily's existence a secret as incomprehensible, even callous; now it seemed, on the contrary, a huge sacrifice for *her*. They had given up the little they had left of their daughter: the photos and keepsakes, the exchanged 'do you remembers', the release of openly expressing their grief, so that she could be free and unburdened. They had hidden their memories deep inside in the black dark so that hers could be washed clean, so that even if their joy was lost forever she could start again afresh. Tears filled her eyes. She would never forgive herself. She curled up in the chair, her head resting on its arm, hands clasped around her knees, and sobbed.

A sharp sound woke her from an exhausted sleep. She sat up with a start as everything rushed back. The room felt cold; it must be getting late; the heating must have gone off. She was stiff all over. Frozen. What on earth could that noise have been? A faint mutter still came from the radio in the kitchen but it couldn't have been that – it had sounded more like breaking china. Blearily, she struggled to her feet, hobbling at first as pins and needles shot through one leg.

In the hall, her mother's china plate lay shattered on the tiles, pieces strewn around the wheels of the bike and spread as far as the kitchen. Her eyes travelled to the wall beside the cellar door, where a round grey patch marked in dust where it had hung and where the picture hook remained intact. How . . . ? It would have to be lifted half an inch into the air to come off the hook. Groggily, she picked her way between the broken shards to fetch a dustpan and brush. She turned the radio off to listen and felt silence flow back into the house, thick and pressing.

As she gathered the larger pieces together in the pan, the tiny sharp sounds as they chinked together broke against the uneasy quiet. Numbly, Rosie tried to reassemble the pieces, fitting together peony and butterfly; she mourned the loss of the keepsake of her mum. It was useless. Giving up, she swept up the smaller fragments and moved the bike so that she could get at the remaining shards. She turned them over and back in her hand. There had been no one there to knock it; how could it possibly have happened? It would take a minor earthquake. And here was another strange thing: the air didn't smell right; there was a trace of something burning. She sniffed – no, *burnt*; it smelt like soot.

She went back to the living room expecting to find that there had been a fall of old soot down the chimney, a mess on the carpet and black dust puffed out all over the room. Nothing. The pile of pine cones in the grate was clean and undisturbed. She went upstairs and checked the two bedrooms that had tiny fireplaces, although she knew the flues were boarded up. The grates were clean and when she bent and sniffed to see if a fall sat behind the boards, there was nothing

278

but a faint trace of damp. Yet the smell was getting stronger: as she came back downstairs it seemed to rise to meet her.

She stood again in the hall, staring at the mark where the plate had hung. She tried to think rationally. What could possibly connect the two things? With a flash of inspiration, she remembered the big crack in the cellar wall and her fear that there might be subsidence. Perhaps that was it: the building had moved; she remembered her dad telling her that the Georgians were jerry builders – beautiful proportions but all built on shallow rubble with no proper foundations. Maybe something had crumbled and shifted. That could have jarred the plate and loosened soot in the old stovepipe in the cellar. Oh God, if it was bad she'd have to have it underpinned or she'd never be able to sell the place. Another bloody financial disaster.

She wrenched open the door and a gust of freezing air, laden with the reek of soot, assailed her from the black belly of the cellar. She clicked the light switch and then remembered that she'd never got round to fixing it; she would need a torch. From the cupboard under the sink she pulled out bottles of Flash and Windolene, dusters, drain cleaner, scouring pads . . . What now! No torch! This bloody, bloody house, taking all her money, all her energies . . . a bottle of bleach went rolling across the floor.

She had a brainwave and went back to the hall to unbuckle the lamp from the bike. When she switched it on, it went on and off intermittently as if a connection were faulty. Stemming the urge to hurl the thing against the wall, she tapped it smartly on the base instead until she got a steady, if feeble, beam of yellowish light.

It cast a round disc on the steps as she went down past the turn in the stairway where she lost the light from the hall.

The lamplight glinted on moisture condensed on the cold stone. A cobweb touched her face and she brushed it away with a shudder. She lifted the lamp to look at the crack. It zigzagged down the wall like a slalom run, but was it wider? It was impossible to tell. She picked her way carefully down the slippery steps, following the feeble light. The stench was stronger, acrid; it caught in the back of her throat with a bitter taste of coal dust.

From somewhere in the darkness yawning before her came a soft sound, as though something shifted, and her skin prickled as its tiny hairs rose. She lifted the lamp to shine its dim tunnel of light into the dark, expecting to see a new fall of soot. The light played unsteadily over the stack of cast-off objects: bedstead, cupboard, boxes, mirror. As it passed over the frame of the mirror, she glimpsed a movement, something small and pale, and shakily swung the lamp back. Its reflection flashed in the glass and whatever had moved was gone.

She edged her way through the lumber, past the boxes of jam jars to the back of the cellar and shone the light at the foot of the old stove flue. There was nothing there. No soft pile of black dust, just an empty patch of bare floor. In disbelief, she thumped the pipe with the flat of her hand. The hollow metal clang shattered the silence; it reverberated against the brick walls as if the room were an echo chamber. From the flue, a thin trickle of grit and dust fell at her feet. In the silence that followed, Rosie stood staring at the little pile of detritus.

As though the sound disturbed something, the shifting noise came again. Rosie swung the light wildly around her and the shadows of the lumber danced, looming and shrinking against the walls. The sound stopped. She stood absolutely still, straining to listen, afraid to move.

The smell grew stronger. There was a tightness in Rosie's chest; she struggled for breath. Now, mixed with the soot was the smell of burning rotten flesh. Dizzy and sick, she was overtaken by a cold sweat. Rosie put her arm across her nose and mouth as waves of nausea hit. From all around her came the tiniest sound, a continuous soft rustle, like leaves stirred by a breeze. Something touched her face, something light as paper, grazing her cheek as it fell, and then another, tangling in her hair. She felt for it and her fingers met a fluttering shape that she knocked to the ground with a cry. She raised the lamp and looked above her.

The ceiling was covered in a thick creamy layer, in constant swarming motion, as thousands of moths crawled over one another. In places the blanket grew so thick that they hung down in pale stalactites until, grown too heavy, some would drop away and fall to the ground. Directly above her, a swag of soft insect bodies hung, shimmering, wings shivering as they crawled.

The lamp went out. In utter darkness, Rosie stood absolutely still, her heart pounding, not daring to even stir the air around her, terrified of hearing the soft collapse and slide of globs of teeming creatures. Beside her, low down, other noises began, human noises, short gasping breaths and a scratching around on the ground. Closer, so close that she could have reached down and touched them, someone was casting about, feeling across the floor, searching . . . a hand brushed her foot, clasped and then gripped her.

Rosie dropped the lamp and fled as the room filled with a child's sobbing and a desperate scrabbling sound. Arms outstretched, she groped wildly towards the stairs and knocked into the lumber, clattering the jam jars in their boxes. Stumbling up the steps on hands and feet, behind her a cry was abruptly cut off and something metal scraped against the brick. As she scrambled for the door, an icy blast hit her back, a freezing cold flowing around her as if the windows had been punched in.

Then she was up, pushing past the bike, not caring that the handlebar caught her hip a jarring blow. She pulled at the front door, crying out as the latch held fast, fumbled to release it and threw the door open, leaving it swinging. She banged with both fists on Tally's front door and a light came on inside. Tally came to the door, took one look at her face and opened her arms.

SIXTEEN

Rosie, sitting tensely on the edge of the sofa, warmed her hands round a mug of tea.

'Better?' Tally said, sitting down beside her.

'A bit.' She could still feel the icy chill inside her and when she took her hand away from the mug it trembled.

Rob came in from next door carrying a torch and bringing her handbag and keys. 'There's nothing – just a load of old tat down there.'

'Did you check the whole house over?' Tally said.

'Yes, and I locked up. Everything's secure.'

'There was something,' Rosie said. 'I know what I saw. I'm not mad, I . . .' Her eyes began to fill and Tally glanced at Rob with a meaningful look.

Rob, taking the hint, said, 'I'd better turn in then. I'm on duty tomorrow.' He gave Rosie's shoulder a pat as he passed.

'I think something awful happened in that house and it's . . . I don't know . . . somehow still there. Some people think that, don't they, that horrible events leave something behind, like an electrical charge – well, not electricity but some kind of force field that a susceptible person is able to pick up. I mean, we didn't know about magnetism or radio waves or bacteria or any of that stuff at one time but they were there waiting to be discovered . . .' She trailed off.

Tally squeezed her hand. 'I think something happened to disturb you down there and I think you're still a teeny bit in shock.'

'I think someone died in that house,' Rosie said stubbornly.

'Well, I suppose that's true of every house, isn't it?' Tally said mildly. 'Every house of any age, that is.'

'You think I'm losing the plot,' Rosie said miserably. 'That's exactly why I haven't told you about all this before. People will say I'm not coping – like before when I was depressed after having Cara. Josh'll say I'm just like my mum. He thinks I shouldn't have the kids.' She wiped her cheek with the heel of her hand and Tally put her arm around her.

'Shh, shh, no one's saying that. You're a great mum; don't think that way, not even for a minute.'

'I'm not losing it! What about the plate? That didn't just break itself, did it?'

'Look, you experienced something horrible, I'm not denying that, but there's got to be some rational explanation. What happened just before all of this started? Tell me what led up to it.'

Rosie looked down into her mug of tea and shrugged.

'Rosie? Was there something? Something that upset you?'

284

She hugged her tight. 'Come on, you've been sitting on this ghost thing for months and it's made you feel awful; if there's anything else, don't you think it would be a good idea to get it off your chest?'

Rosie let out a long wavering sigh before beginning to speak. The certificates in the bureau, the newspaper report, the memory of Lily's death and her part in the tragedy all came out.

'But it wasn't your fault! You were tiny!' Tally exclaimed. 'Come on, that sort of thing happens all the time between kids. Think of your two, or my girls, always vying for attention. All kids do it.'

'You really think so?'

'I know so.'

'But if I hadn't knocked her hand, if I hadn't been showing off . . .'

'You might just as well say if Maria hadn't bought you the toys, if she hadn't taken you on the jetty or if it had been less windy . . . on a different day . . . in a different year . . . It was an *accident*. Come on, you've got to stop blaming yourself, OK?' Tally took both of her hands and leant forward to look into her face.

At length, Rosie nodded. 'OK. But it doesn't really change anything. I can never get her back.'

There was a moment's silence.

'No,' Tally said softly. 'You'll never get her back. There's nothing anyone can do to change the past, but you *can* do plenty about the future.' She rubbed the knuckles of Rosie's clenched hand. 'What I think would do you the most good, now, would be to concentrate on your stake in the future. I think you need your kids with you.'

'What do you mean?' Rosie said dully. 'Josh has got them

until tomorrow night.' She seemed to shrink back into herself as she said it.

'Rosie?' Tally said. 'How do you feel about that? Honestly?'

Rosie thought about it. 'Bitter.'

'Then you shouldn't put up with it. Go down there! Fetch them back!' Tally said, desperate to put some fire back in Rosie's belly.

A glow of colour rose to Rosie's cheeks and her shoulders straightened. 'Right, right! I'll go now.' She started unwinding herself from the duvet. 'Josh pulled the "weekend" card on me – well, he's had his weekend.'

Tally, alarmed at the thought of her striding into her in-laws' house like a madwoman, said, 'Hang on a mo. It's still the middle of the night. Maybe better wait until the morning?'

'Is it? Oh, yeah, of course it is.' Rosie pushed her hand through her hair. 'I'll go first thing tomorrow.' She rooted through her bag for her phone and set an alarm.

Tally went to find her some pyjamas, a towel and a toothbrush. When she came back, she said, 'Would you like me to come with you?'

Rosie hesitated. She couldn't really believe what she was planning to do. 'No,' she said. 'Thanks, but this is between me and Josh. I think I have to do it on my own.'

Rosie got up while it was still dark. She pulled on her jeans, sweatshirt, and the old grey canvas shoes, had a quick chat with Rob as he left for his shift, and then left a note for Tally, who was still sleeping. Outside, the streetlamps showed a world transformed by a fresh snowfall. The snow stood inches thick like a cap on cars and fence posts and muffled hedges and shrubs, rounding sharp angles to indistinct softness. Her house was in darkness, lights off and the curtains all closed, its expression blank and secret. Rosie shivered as she passed the front door and went straight to the car.

She edged tentatively backwards and forwards to get out of the tight parking space and crawled along the snowy street. Once she was out of the village and on to A roads and then motorway, the journey to Hertfordshire was straightforward; the roads had been gritted overnight, but as she returned to countryside at the other end of the journey the lanes were treacherous and she was glad it was now light, the trees casting long blue shadows over the fields. She passed the little station where her father-in-law, Gareth, caught the commuter train to his job as an actuary in the City; it was closed and deserted, the empty car park a carpet of white.

Sandra and Gareth lived a mile outside the village and as she turned along the sunken track that led down to their barn conversion, the back wheels of her little Fiat slewed to the right and almost put her in the ditch. Carefully, she pulled off again, straightening up, and made slippery progress in the wide tyre tracks of more practical vehicles that had compacted and printed the snow. Gareth's four-by-four no doubt made light work of this weather. She emerged into open fields and ahead of her the huge windows that had replaced the original barn doors flashed out, catching the sun and making her blink. She'd not been here for a couple of years and had forgotten quite how spectacular it was, the original building gutted and re-formed with cantilevered ceilings and green glass stairs up to mezzanine floors.

She swung the car round on a sweep of gravel. As she pulled up beside the garage block she saw that the house had been extended still further. From a long, low building, a vent exhaled a steady stream of steam. A pool-house, she thought, Gareth must still be doing well for himself. Then, almost immediately: Had the children been in the pool? Sam had never mentioned it.

In the garden stood the broad tubular structure of the new trampoline, its blue netting showing through the snow, and beyond it, the humped shapes of a slide and a climbing frame with a pirate deck. There are whole worlds in my kids' lives that I know nothing about, she thought. She sat for a moment with her hand on the ignition, then took a deep breath and got out, the snow soaking instantly through her canvas shoes.

Josh answered the door. He was dressed in a white cotton shirt, navy chinos and leather flip-flops. He had a piece of toast in his hand and he looked a bit the worse for wear. 'What the fuck!' he said when he saw her.

'Happy Christmas to you too,' Rosie said.

'What're you doing here?'

'I've come to fetch the kids home.'

He ignored that and said, as if she were a tradesman who had turned up at an inconvenient moment, 'It's a bit early, isn't it? For dropping in out of the blue?'

'It's after nine, Josh. It's hardly the crack of dawn.'

Josh glanced behind him down the hallway towards the kitchen door, as if checking whether anyone could hear. Rosie had the distinct impression that what he'd really like to do was to shut the door on her. 'Look,' he said, as though he was reasoning with an idiot, 'I said I'd bring them back tonight. This isn't what we arranged.' He glared at her.

'I can save you the trouble,' Rosie said stolidly.

Gareth came out of the kitchen, saying, 'What is it? You're letting in an awful draught . . .' Then: 'Rosie! What a nice surprise!' In the same old corduroy trousers and baggy oatmeal sweater that Rosie remembered him jokingly calling his 'leisurewear', he slopped along the hallway in his slippers towards her and Josh had to step aside. Gareth enfolded her in a bear hug and rocked her to and fro, his stubbly chin rasping against her face. 'Come on in, come on in!' He led the way to the kitchen where, over his shoulder, Sandra and Tania were sitting at a round oak table. The two chairs that Josh and Gareth had left vacant sat in front of plates full of congealing fried breakfasts. Tania, dressed in taupe trousers and a matching cobweb knit jumper, was leafing through a glossy magazine with nothing in front of her but black coffee. Sandra was in the middle of helping herself to scrambled eggs and muffins, her grey bobbed hair with its stylish streak of white at the front tucked back behind her ears.

Gareth took her hand and drew her into the room. She felt everyone's eyes on her and was acutely conscious of the snow she had tramped in with her, melting in little pools around her feet, and the dark water-stained canvas of her cheap pumps. Their relaxed demeanour in their casually expensive clothes, clearly at home in the designer kitchen with its range of fancy appliances, breathed entitlement. In her baggy sweatshirt with its dangling toggles and drooping hood, her usual wisps of hair escaping from its scrunchy, she felt faded, threadbare, a person with no definite outline.

'We've missed you,' Gareth was saying. 'Why don't you come and see us? Bring the kids?'

Tania visibly winced. She glanced at Josh accusingly.

'Rosie and I seem to have got our wires crossed,' Josh said disingenuously. 'I've been telling her that we've got all the cousins coming back for lunch today so the kids won't want to go yet. I'm sure she understands.'

Rosie opened her mouth to disagree but Sandra, seeing Rosie's tense, white face and sensing that all her preparations for a perfect Christmas might be about to go up in smoke, said smoothly, 'Perhaps Rosie would like to stay and join us for lunch?'

There was a silence while everyone considered the prospect of awful awkwardness *that* would entail.

'Thank you, but no. We need to be getting back,' Rosie said, mustering her reserves of politeness.

'It's out of the question,' Josh said. 'We had an arrangement.'

Sandra and Gareth exchanged a glance. 'The children would be very disappointed,' Sandra said. 'They've all been getting on *so* well. Let me pour you a coffee while you think about it.' She reached for the pot and then let her hand fall as they all realised that there was nowhere for Rosie to sit.

Gareth said, 'Well, never mind all this tea and coffee lark. I think it's time for a real drink. Rosie? Sherry with your old dad-in-law?' He held the kitchen door open for her to pass through. Before it swung shut behind her, she distinctly heard Tania saying, 'If you start giving in to her now, she'll take you to the cleaners when we get to court.'

Gareth led her into the lounge opposite, with its massive windows extending the whole height of the building. A fire roared in a wood-burning stove and a huge Christmas tree stood decked with white fairy lights and shiny white ceramic hearts and icicles. 'Do you like the tree?' he asked mildly. 'Sandra's idea: to use the height we've got here. You can't get one that size in most houses. You know Sandra, she goes in for Christmas in a big way.' He sighed.

Rosie nodded. 'I bet the kids really loved it. Where are they, by the way?' She tried to sound casual although all she really wanted to do was to tuck them one under each arm and run.

Gareth put a glass of sherry into her hand and beckoned her to follow him. He pushed open the door of the snug where

290

Sam and Cara were both fast asleep on the sofa in front of the TV, a cartoon running with the sound turned right down. They withdrew, Gareth saying, 'We let them come to midnight mass on Christmas Eve and then they were up at six on Christmas morning. I think it's finally caught up with them.'

They sat down on sofas opposite each other.

Gareth looked awkward. 'The thing is, Rosie, love, Sandra's gone to a lot of trouble. She wanted to get everyone together.'

'Not quite everyone,' Rosie said drily.

'And she was trying to do you a favour, really . . .'

'Sorry?'

'As you weren't feeling well. She thought it would give you a break.'

'Who said I was ill!'

'Well – Josh.'

'Because, as you can see, I'm not.'

He rubbed his head, appearing to digest this, and then shrugged. 'This family stuff's really Sandra's area. I try to stay out of it.' He took a drink. 'I just bring home the bacon.'

'Look, I didn't come to make a scene. It's not unreasonable to want a share of my own kids' time at Christmas. Josh hasn't been playing fair.'

'Couldn't you just stay for lunch? I'll get it in the neck if I don't persuade you.'

Rosie snorted. She was pretty sure Sandra had been bluffing with her invitation, simply intending to embarrass her into giving in and going away. 'I don't think anyone really wants me to stay. I'd be like Banquo's ghost.'

The door from the snug opened and Sam came in, his hair tousled and his shirt done up on the wrong buttons. Still half asleep, he wandered over to Rosie and climbed on her lap, snuggling in. Rosie hugged him. 'Time to go home, soldier,' she said. 'Can you show me where your bag is and help me pack up your things? And Cara's things too?'

'Rosie . . .' Gareth remonstrated, raising his hands in a helpless gesture.

She lifted Sam down off her lap and they went upstairs together.

When they returned, Josh, Tania and Sandra had joined Gareth in the lounge. Sandra had a sleepy Cara in her arms and Tania stood at Josh's elbow as if ready to give him a nudge. Josh said, 'What's this, Sammy? I thought I was going to teach you how to hit a snooker ball today? You're not going already, are you?'

Sam stood in the middle of the room looking uncertainly from his mum to his dad. Rosie began to feel angry. How could Josh play on Sam's feelings like that? It was a low trick, dragging him into it, putting emotional pressure on him. Keeping her voice even, she said. 'Go and pick up your Lego, Sam, and put the box in your bag, please.' Sam trailed over to the tree and began dropping pieces of Lego one by one into the box.

Rosie walked over to Sandra to take Cara from her but Cara let out a wail and turned away, burying her face in Sandra's shoulder. Rosie stopped as if someone had slapped her, even though she knew that Cara did this every time at nursery when she picked her up: a toddler's protest at having been left by her mum.

Josh pounced on it. 'Look, this isn't going to work. It's just confusing them. Why don't you go home and I'll bring them back later as I told you in the first place.'

From the corner of her eye she saw Tania give a tiny smile.

'Perhaps that would be best,' Sandra said. 'If that was the agreement.'

She looked to Gareth for support. He took another drink and said nothing.

Suddenly, she felt Sam's hand slip into her own. She squeezed it tight and took a deep breath. 'Right then, let's talk about agreements,' she said to the adults. 'The bald fact is, Josh's access agreement is every other weekend, as he very well knows. Today it's not a weekend and he hasn't any right to have the kids. I think things'll go a whole lot more smoothly if Josh respects that in future.' She put the kids' bags over one shoulder and then firmly took Cara from Sandra, hefting her on to her hip.

She got as far as the door and then stopped. 'What do you say, Sam?'

'Thank you for having me.'

'Good boy. Now go and give everyone a kiss and then we're going home.' Even Josh had the grace to look a little shamefaced as he bent to be hugged and kissed on the cheek.

Rosie drove back towards the motorway while next to her Sam played a game on her phone and Cara dozed in the back. She tried to calm herself. The mixture of anxiety over taking on Josh and elation at her success had left her feeling strung out, every nerve overstretched and humming. She had won the battle; she was taking the kids home, but when she thought of going back into the house she found herself taking in a deep breath and holding it. She let it out slowly through her mouth in a long, blown-out sigh. Last night, in the warmth of Tally's home, safe among friends, she had almost managed to believe that she'd imagined it all, that the long-term strain she'd been under and the distress of remembering how Lily died could have flipped her mind in some peculiar way: the broken plate a mere accident; the whole experience in the cellar the hallucination of a troubled mind, brought on by a mix of drugs and wine she knew perfectly well she should avoid.

Now, alone, and with time to think more clearly, she could

see the way this rational explanation held together but try as she might she couldn't *feel* it. How could an imagined experience be so complete: smells, sounds, even touch?

And now she had to go back. The thought of returning to the scene of last night's nightmare filled her with dread. She drove on through the snowy fields slowly, although the roads were clear, almost everyone tucked up indoors for the holiday. Longingly, she thought of last Christmas, at the flat, when she and Mum had cooked dinner and got tipsy together in the process.

Soon she would reach the motorway. She could turn right for the Midlands or left for London. She didn't have to go back; she had a choice. A picture of the flat as she'd left it came into her mind, the living room small and shabby but full of familiar, comforting things: her books, the battered leather sofa, a litter of the kids' toys. And her bedroom . . . the light through the branches of the plane tree in the street, the quilt Mum had made for her, spread smooth on the bed.

They passed the first sign for the motorway junction. Was it a good idea? Once she was back at the flat, it would get harder and harder to return to the house, and there were things she had to do to be able to move forward: sort out all the contents, get it ready for sale; no one was going to buy it with that ancient wiring and the garden like a jungle. She should really just grit her teeth and get on with it. Nonetheless, she imagined the padded texture of the quilt under her cheek, lying down, forgetting everything, feeling safe. Where was the harm? Just for a few days, to get her head back together?

They would soon be at the roundabout. She glanced at Sam, still deep in his game. 'I've been thinking, do you want to go home, chump-chop? What do you say?'

'Of course.' He looked up. 'Can Nicky and Amy come round to play?'

Rosie paused, amazed at how quickly Sam had laid aside his old home.

'They've gone to relatives today,' she said automatically. 'They're seeing their family.'

'But they *are* their family,' Sam said logically.

'No, I mean aunties and uncles and their granddad and . . . and their granny.'

'Oh.' Sam went quiet.

Rosie glanced at him. His head was bent over the phone as if he was playing, but the screen was blank.

'I know you miss your granny; I miss her too,' she said gently. 'She wouldn't want you to feel sad though, not at Christmas.' She reached over and touched his cheek. 'Tell me what you'd most like to do today.'

'Can I open my presents? Can I show Amy tomorrow?'

Rosie signalled right, got into lane, took the Midlands exit.

Leaving the kids asleep in the car, Rosie braced herself and let herself into the curtained house. The dim hall was warm and quiet, the only sounds the familiar whoosh of the boiler and the trickle of water in the radiators. She snapped on the hall light. A yellow glow shone on the bike, knocked askew by her frantic flight, and on the cellar door, which she saw Rob had bolted: a protective gesture that Rosie found touching. She straightened the bike's handlebars, wheeled it forward and leant it against the door as if to barricade it. She stood and listened, as she had last night, down there in the dark. It was quiet and calm now, yet she felt weak at the memory of her fear. It hadn't been all in her mind; she was sure of it. There had been something outside her self: a presence. You knew it in the same way that you sensed a spider's eyes on you or smelt rain before it came. Instinctive.

The child had been there, right beside her. She looked at her makeshift barricade and knew that if the girl were to come again, neither the bolt nor this mechanical barrier would be any use whatsoever.

Without allowing her eyes to wander to the shadows at the kitchen door or at the turn of the stairs, she hurried into the living room and swept the curtains back. She found the batteries that had rolled under the bureau the night before, fitted them, wrapped the presents quickly and put them on the hearth. It's no good averting your eyes, she told herself strictly; you're going to have to look before you can bring the kids in. Forcing herself to be thorough, she checked all of the rooms. Taking a deep breath she walked into the centre of each and turned slowly all the way round. Only when she'd scanned every corner, and sensed in every room an ordinary everyday emptiness, did she go to fetch the children in.

Carrying Cara and leading Sam by the hand, she brought them into the living room and said brightly, 'Oh look! Santa's been while you were away!' The wrapping paper was off in seconds and Sam danced about, desperate to get outside and try the loader in the snow.

An hour later, after Sam had scooped and bulldozed a veritable fort and Rosie had made a stumpy snowman with Cara, they peeled off their wet coats and Rosie warmed up soup and made toast. She brought down a pile of kids' books and a duvet and tucked them up all together on the sofa.

'Isn't Cara going for a sleep upstairs?' Sam asked, wanting their usual storytime to himself.

'Not today,' Rosie said. 'We'll make our camp here and Cara can curl up and drop off when she wants.' They sipped their soup and she read to them for a while until Cara fell asleep and Sam asked to watch *The Snow Queen*.

Once she was sure he was engrossed, Rosie got out her laptop and searched 'ghosts'. Scrolling through links to movies and sites featuring supposed ghostly images, she found a research site and a heading caught her eye: 'Residual ghosts: the Stone Tape theory'. She read:

The **Stone Tape theory** is the speculation that ghosts and hauntings are analogous to tape recordings, and that emotional or traumatic events can somehow be 'stored' in rock or the natural environment, and 'replayed' under certain conditions. The idea was first proposed by British archaeologist turned parapsychologist Thomas Charles Lethbridge, in 1961.

Many serious paranormal researchers accept that some ghosts behave like recordings. They show no knowledge of their surroundings and repeat the same actions whenever seen. They even sometimes appear to follow different room layouts from the existing ones. Such residual hauntings can be prompted by a range of events, from traumatic events such as a murder, rape or suicide to high-energy events such as a ball or celebration, when music, singing, dancing and conversation may be heard.

The most impressive evidence on which the case for a recording theory rests is the idea that apparitions repeat themselves. In classic cases, as well as in fiction, the ghost is often said to be re-enacting some tragic part of their lives or trying to right some wrong done to them. When a residual haunting appears, the percipient is essentially witnessing or hearing an event in time being replayed over and over again.

Rosie paused. The article said that an event could be replayed 'under certain conditions' but didn't specify what these might be. She searched again, typing in, 'When do people see ghosts?' and found some research that simply sought to gather experiences of sightings and compare them to classify them and produce a taxonomy. Here she found a great deal that matched her own experiences: apparitions tended to be reported as solid rather than transparent and were often said to be so realistic that the subject only doubted their reality after the event; they generally did not interact verbally and events tended to happen in everyday surroundings such as the subject's own home and most often when the environment was secluded, dark and quiet.

Reading on, a point caught her eye: *Those who had seen ghosts also reported being anxious or distressed at the time.*

Sam pulled on her sleeve. 'Why aren't you watching it with me, Mum? Cara's gone to sleep.'

'I am watching,' Rosie said, laying the laptop aside and putting her arm around him as he wriggled closer.

. . . *being anxious or distressed at the time.* This struck a chord. She began to go through the times she'd seen the weird things she couldn't explain, thinking about how she'd been feeling each time. The girl had appeared in the garden on their first day at the house and then again in the weeds under the mulberry tree. Newly arrived at a house packed with her mum's things, both times she had been feeling the loss of her mother sharply. When she'd caught the strange moth: that had been just as she was about to go through difficult personal things in the bureau. And then on top of mourning Mum, she'd found out about Lily. She remembered the feeling of terrible sadness as she sat in the darkening garden thinking of hiding long ago with Lily and Maria under the mulberry tree and how it had seemed to conjure in answer another presence in its shade. And, yes, it had been later that night that she'd seen the child bending over Cara, as the silk fell around them. Then, last night, the worst experience of all, hard on the heels of her remembering how Lily died.

Tally would say this was all evidence that her imagination was affected as a result of strong emotions, that at moments of grief and stress her mind was creating strange perceptions – things that weren't real – but what if it was the other way round? What if the apparitions she saw *were* real but she was only able to see them when her own emotions were running high? A sighting would only happen when a person became susceptible through being vulnerable themselves, in a heightened state of sensitivity. Something could have happened in the house to people long ago that somehow struck a chord with her own situation, like two tuning forks vibrating at the same frequency, a kind of emotional resonance. Perhaps there was some kind of link – some common experience or loss? She was grieving for Lily, who had died as a child . . . More than once the girl had appeared close to Cara, seemed drawn to her . . . She gave up her guessing game. The only thing she was sure of was that the girl – her imprint, ghost, spirit, whatever you cared to call it – did exist. She knew it. Something awful had taken place here. She remembered the struggling noises as she'd escaped from the cellar, the scrabbling and the scrape of metal, and the clinging smell of something bloody burning.

She shook her shoulders and turned the memory away; she must think logically and think hard. If the visitations happened when she became distressed, *because* she was distressed, then allowing herself to become disturbed was like opening a door to let the girl in. It was what mediums claimed to do when they contacted the spirits of the dead. What was the word? . . . Channelling. She had been opening a channel for something

299

other, someone else's loss or trauma, to move through, creating a space in which it could exist. She mustn't let the channel open. She must take control of her feelings and shut the girl out. She told herself that as long as she didn't buckle under her emotions, didn't let the channel open, then nothing could happen.

If sadness over Mum or Lily were to assail her she would have to block it out, force her thoughts towards the future, make plans in her head, anything to keep herself calm and focused. Oh God, even this passing thought of Mum and Lily made her feel weepy. How on earth was she going to cope? She just had to, for the kids' sake, that was all. She hugged Sam harder and put her other arm around Cara, gathering them in. Come on, think of something else, make a list in your head. *Get an electrician in to rewire upstairs, then a plasterer, then I can decorate,* she rehearsed. Her jaw felt tight from trying not to cry. *Get the cellar cleared out,* she thought grimly, *that's top priority, then tackle the garden. Press on regardless. Finish what you've started.* That's how Mum would have acted: got on with it, had the strength of character to endure in silence and shut her feelings away. Wasn't that what Mum had done about Lily, for her sake? She'd kept silence about her lost child, carried the weight of her grief inside, so that Rosie could have a childhood: tranquil, innocent, protected. Her heart went out to her mother. How her memories must have risen up and followed her, a child trailing behind her reaching out to take her hand. She thought: Everyone who's ever lost someone is haunted.

SEVENTEEN

1812

Effie lay sleeping on a low wooden bed with a thin rag mattress, one of a row of such beds that lined the walls of a long, white-washed room. The windows, low under sloping eaves, spilled bright unforgiving light across the bare boards, and the heat, trapped in the attic room beneath the thick thatched roof, was oppressive.

An old woman in a brown grogram dress and a plain mob cap, sat beside the bed. At her elbow a table was strewn with the accoutrements of the sick room: a bowl of water with a cloth for cooling a fever, a cracked china cup with the dregs of an infusion of yarrow which gave off a musty sickly smell, and a basin and blade for bloodletting. The woman's eyes seemed to droop in sleep but her hand moved idly every now and then to flap away a bluebottle, its buzzing loud and irritating in the quiet room.

Effie stirred and opened her eyes, at first following the random movements of the fly and then taking in the bed, the room and the woman beside her. 'What is this place?' she said slowly, her tongue thick in her mouth and her throat dry.

'Why, 'tis the parish workhouse where you've been these past three days with childbed fever. But now it has passed, praise the Lord,' the old woman said with equanimity.

Effie sucked in her breath as her loss came back to her, a longing that was a physical ache at her core. At the thought of her baby, her body responded and her breasts began to leak milk. The memory of how she had come here returned: her after-pains as she lay amongst the bundles of kindling in the bumping cart; her error in foolishly showing the carter her purse without thinking, so that he took all her money; sitting, bent double, in the porch of the workhouse while the gatekeeper went for a girl to help her inside. The women's overseer, Mrs Smedley, an exceedingly plain, buxom woman in a stiffly starched dress, had asked her questions and written her answers in a book. Surely she had told her nothing of the baby; she'd simply said that she couldn't pay her rent, hadn't she? She had said that she'd been evicted and had nowhere else to go and remembered watching with relief as the woman had written under Cause of Admission *Vagrancy,* rather than *Disgraced Woman.*

She placed her hand upon her belly, wincing at its tenderness. It was soft now, the flesh loose, but it was still big, still rounded. This woman had cared for her and had dressed her in this rough nightgown; of course, she would know the truth. 'Did the doctor have to come? Does anyone else beside yourself know?' she asked anxiously.

302

'In your fever you drew close to your Maker. 'Twas a near thing. The doctor promised he would say nothing unless you passed over, when he would have to record the death as puerperal fever,' she said, her expression sombre. ''Twas not the doctor that exposed you but one of the Board of Guardians, the farmers and businessmen who oversee us here.'

Effie groaned. She had hoped that Hob's anger would play itself out; instead it had found vent in malice. Now she would be marked and Beulah along with her. 'Where's Beulah? Can she be brought to me?' She had heard that families were separated here, men and women segregated, husband from wife, children afforded only an 'interview' of a few minutes each day with their mothers. Who knew whether sisters were allowed to be together?

'There's no Beulah here.'

'You must be mistaken. My sister – Beulah? She's nine years old. She would have come later in the day.'

The old woman said again, 'No girl called Beulah. There are no more'n thirty of us here and I know every one.'

Effie struggled to sit up, her muscles weak as water. She had asked Alice to tell Beulah to come to the workhouse in Newnham village as soon as she finished her shift and impressed on her the need to reassure Beulah that she would be waiting for her there. Had she failed to keep her promise? What if Alice hadn't told Beulah where to come? A cold dread seized her. Beulah would have gone home to find it boarded up and deserted and her Effie gone! Where would she have gone for help: a child, afraid of Hob Talbot, afraid of Fowler, with no adult she trusted and no one to ask for help? She grasped the old woman's wrist. 'How long did you say I've passed in fever?'

'This last three days. You kept calling out for someone called Jack – your young man, I take it. Then yesterday, after the crisis, you fell into a deathly slumber and couldn't be roused. Last night there was a terrible storm but you slept on and heard not a thing.'

Effie pushed back the bedclothes and with wobbly legs set her bare feet on the floor. 'I have to find her.' She struggled to her feet and the woman jumped up, her chair grating on the boards, and took her arm to steady her as she swayed.

'You're not strong enough. You're half-starved.'

With a moan, Effie put her hand on to the bed and allowed herself to be slowly lowered down.

The woman said, 'Wait. Rest. I'll find out if anyone has been turned away. I'll return soon.'

Effie slumped back against the pillows. The trapped fly buzzed in the pane beside her. She tried to think as Beulah would. Perhaps she would be too afraid to go far from home. Perhaps she would have slept in the derelict cottage adjoining their own, or maybe the hen house. Could she send someone to see?

The old woman returned with a cup of small ale and a bowl of milk potage. She put them down on the table as Effie gabbled her request.

'I fear I cannot,' she said. 'Nor the others neither, for if you leave without permission you risk losing your place and may not be readmitted. You have to ask well in advance and are rarely granted permission unless 'tis to look for work.'

Effie took the cup from her and drank deeply. The woman put her hand on her arm. 'Slower. Your stomach has been empty too long. Drink and eat slowly or you'll vomit and lose all.' She took up the bowl of sops and began to feed Effie small spoonfuls. 'Like this,' she said. 'You should rest awhile and I will think if anything can be done.'

'What are you called?' Effie asked. 'I don't know you from hereabouts.'

'Mary-Anne Ryland is my name. You wouldn't know me, for it would have been before you were born when I came here and I've been here ever since.'

'Thank you for your kindness, Mary-Anne,' Effie said gravely. The thought that some were inmates at the workhouse for twenty years and more scared her but she kept it hid.

When Mary-Anne took the dishes away, Effie, moving slowly and carefully, looked for her clothes. They were neither at the end of the bed nor under it. Nor were there any garments in the room other than calico nightgowns like hers, each neatly folded on the pillows of the other beds.

Feeling a little stronger for the food and with heart put into her by the ale, she knelt down at one of the windows and looked out over the yard at the rear of the building. It was divided down the middle by a high brick wall. On one side, the men, stripped to the waist, were crushing gypsum for plaster-making. Their skin and hair were powdered white but she recognised one of them as the blacksmith who had lost his business when a shard of metal had lodged in his eye. He had been a strong wiry man but now his sloping shoulders and stooping gait spoke of frailty beyond his years. Another, she saw, was old George Turnbull, who'd lived in a shack in the woods and was reputed to have drunk himself into insensibility so many times that his brain had become dulled. The master, Mr Smedley, stood off a little way, barking instructions, at a distance sufficient to protect his dark jacket from the dust.

On the other side of the wall the women, dressed in the same uniform brown as Mary-Anne, sat on low stools bent over some close work that Effie could not make out, surrounded by baskets and hanks of rope. She recognised several: Agnes Barnwell, whose sailor husband had never returned, Sarah Nevin who had been gaoled more than once for drunkenness and the simpleton Mariah Slade with her wide, flat face and narrow eyes. Across the far end of both halves of the yard lay a hedge, beyond which a group of children were hoeing a vegetable garden. Two ancient women sat in the scant shade of an elder bush, keeping an eye on the children while knitting stockings. Behind the ordered rows of the kitchen garden lay an orchard of apple and pear trees, heavy with fruit.

Mary-Anne returned carrying a pair of heavy work boots in her hand and over her arm a coarse-spun petticoat, a plain grey shawl and a dress that had yellow and black stripes sewn upon the bodice. Effie eyed the waspish garment with apprehension. 'Why is it different from the other women's dress?' she asked, although in her heart she already knew the answer.

'I'm sorry to say it but 'tis to mark you out as fallen,' Mary-Anne said. ''Tis meant to shame you, and warn others against you so that they will avoid you to keep their own reputations.'

'Will no one even speak to me then?'

''Tis not such a loss,' she said gently. 'We work and eat in silence in any case. 'Tis only in the evenings there's any chance to converse.' She helped Effie out of the nightgown and into the ill-fitting clothes.

'You will still speak to me, won't you?' Effie said.

'Aye,' Mary-Anne said, doing up the buttons at Effie's cuffs. 'I've nursed you from death's door; I'll not abandon you now.' She gave a tiny smile. 'Besides, I'm beyond worrying about my reputation.' She turned Effie towards her by the shoulders and looked at the effect of the garish dress. 'You must cover yourself with the shawl, in spite of the heat, or all will know you come from the workhouse. There's a back way out I can show you,' she continued. 'If asked, I shall say you are still recovering and need rest. No one is allowed in the sleeping quarters until after evening prayers so they'll not know any different. You must be back by eight o'clock though, mind.'

Effie squeezed her hand in gratitude. She quickly put on the boots and followed Mary-Anne, wrapping the shawl around her.

The cottage already had the sad air of desertion. Rough boards were nailed across the window and the door, so that the expression of the house was hidden, like eyes closed in sleep. After the storm, the air was humid and a vegetable smell rose from the garden. Clothes still hung from the line, wet and draggled, and the wind had loosened the corner of a sheet from its peg so that it lay half upon the ground. The hen house was empty: the hens and even the remains of their grain had been taken. Inside the neighbouring cottage there was no tell-tale gathering of bracken for a bed nor remains of food, only shards of broken glass and pigeon droppings spattering the ground and clumps of weeds that had taken root in the earth floor. No sign of Beulah anywhere.

Her alarm growing, Effie picked up one of the pieces of glass and returned to the front door of their old cottage. On the boards she scratched out a message in angular, capital letters.

FIND ME AT THE WORKHOUSE, E

She went to the well and drew up a bucket from which she drank and then washed her face and hands until she felt cooler. Now she would need to walk to Weedon Royal and make enquiries there. The weight in her heart dragged upon her as she thought of what had happened there and her lost baby. Beulah was too young to have witnessed a birth, far less dealt with a stillborn infant; she must have been terrified by the

307

glimpse into such an adult world. Perhaps she had gone home at the end of the day with one of the other children, maybe Biddy? Even if Alice had told her to go to the workhouse, Effie knew that she would have been afraid. God knows she had dinned it into both Beulah and Tobias that it was to be avoided at all costs, that it was viewed by all as a place of shame, even though its punishment was for the guiltless crime of simply being poor.

Effie reached the silk factory as the afternoon drew to a close. Overawed by the shiny black paint and brass knocker of the main entrance, she loitered in the street, further down, waiting for someone to come out. At length, Mrs Gundy came round the corner from the back, bearing the basket of eggs to take to the cook at the High House, and Effie stopped her. Mrs Gundy told her that Beulah had not been seen for three days and that as a result she had been caused great inconvenience by the lack of a scullery maid. Effie, her misgivings multiplying, asked her to fetch Biddy out to see her.

'I cannot do that! The master wouldn't allow it,' she said brusquely. 'And I can tell you now that she'd say no different. Beulah hasn't been seen here since Friday afternoon. Not by anyone.' She pushed past and hurried on with Effie dogging her footsteps.

'Can you tell her, if she comes back, to come to the workhouse in Newnham?' They reached the door of the High House. 'Tell her that her sister has been looking for her and she mustn't be afraid to come. Tell her all will be well . . .' Mrs Gundy closed the door firmly in her face.

Effie stood in the street for a moment, wondering where else she could look. Three days! Anything could have happened. She paced up and down and asked the first passer-by to direct her to the constable. She would lay the facts before him and ask for his assistance in making enquiries. Then she must get back to Newnham before the workhouse closed its doors. She must be there in case Beulah came.

Later that day, Mr Boddington sat in Mr Fowler's office waiting for the silk master to be informed of his visit. He studied the rolls of ribbon and bolts of patterned silk stacked on one side of the wide desk, their sumptuous colours and luxurious sheen reflected in the polished mahogany surface. A huge clock ticked above him and the brass weights on a set of scales gleamed. All was measure and order. And yet . . . Boddington could not forget Fowler's bullying of the Fiddement child. Surely it had been this very chair, on which he now sat, that the man had forced her to stand upon. Boddington thought of the grave young woman who had visited him and expressed her concern. He had an uneasy feeling in his gut about this matter. Fowler was known throughout the village as a harsh taskmaster; perhaps this time he had gone too far.

Fowler breezed into the room. 'To what do I owe this pleasure?' he asked, smiling, straightaway making for a corner cupboard where he kept glasses and a bottle of port wine. 'It's very timely to see you, Mr Boddington, very timely indeed, as I'd like to discuss my apprentice scheme for paupers a little further with you. My detailed plans have been submitted to the parish vestry now and are to be considered next month.' He handed Boddington a glass and settled himself in the club chair on the other side of the desk.

Boddington put the glass down upon the desk without drinking from it, and cleared his throat deliberately. 'That will have to wait until another time,' he said. 'I'm here to enquire after the Fiddement girl, whom I understand has disappeared.'

Fowler's eyes slid away momentarily. 'Indeed she has, and I suspect it is connected with another disappearance – that of a piece of yellow figured silk.' He tapped his fingertips together as if considering a weighty matter.

'Why have you not reported this?'

'I discovered it missing only this morning, through checking an inventory. Prior to that I had assumed that the child must be sick. I should have known there would be some dishonest business afoot, after the roguery of her brother.'

'But you have no actual evidence to suggest the child is a thief other than coincidental circumstance?'

Fowler looked annoyed. 'It seems the most likely explanation. The whole family is nothing but trouble.'

Boddington rose, leaving his glass untouched. 'I shall interview your workers, starting with the children.' He held out his hand to stop Fowler from following him. 'No need to accompany me.'

Fowler shrugged, affecting nonchalance. 'As you wish.'

Boddington climbed to the top floor. The heat was intense; the stink of sweat and the never-ending clatter of the looms were oppressive. He called the children from their work, one by one, and questioned them outside the workshop at the turn of the stairs where it was a little quieter. No one knew much beyond the fact that Beulah had been moved to work 'below stairs' and that Alice had been in charge of her, until he came to Biddy.

When he asked if she had seen Beulah on Friday, she said, 'At lunchtime she were well. I gave her some bread when she were fetching and carrying to the table.'

Boddington considered her answer. 'But you think that after lunch she may *not* have been well, Biddy?'

The child gazed at her feet.

Boddington tried again. 'Did you see her after lunch?'

'No, nor since.'

'But you saw something. Something or someone has made you concerned.'

Biddy glanced up at him. 'You won't say I said? Not to anybody?'

'No one will know who has told me anything. I can assure you of that.'

'The master chided me for falling to sleep. He pulled me by the arm to wake me and I saw . . .'

Boddington raised his eyebrows in enquiry.

'There were blood on his sleeve.'

'I see,' he said thoughtfully. 'Which side?'

Biddy screwed up her eyes. 'The left.'

'Thank you, Biddy. You've done well, never fear. Now you can return to your duties.'

He spoke to the rest of the children and then moved along the line of weavers, calling them out, noting the concern that crept into the eyes of Jervis, Ellis and some of the others as they realised that Beulah had not been home. None had any idea of her whereabouts. The workers on the first floor were no help either, as they had little to do with the top floor workshop and some even seemed unsure which girl was Beulah.

He went down to the kitchen and saw Mrs Gundy, who told him of seeing Effie in the street that afternoon. She told him of Beulah's work feeding the worms and showed him the cellar where they had been kept. The room was now completely cleared: the worm beds and floor scrubbed, the stove cleaned out and the windows left open to ventilate the place. 'Disease,' she explained. 'Nasty, horrible things, those worms. Should never have been anywhere near my kitchen.'

He returned to the office where he found Fowler at his desk, his head bent over a pile of bills. 'There was blood on your clothes on Friday afternoon,' he said abruptly and watched Fowler's head jerk up from his work.

'On my . . . Oh yes, I caught my arm on a hook when mending one of the throwing machines,' he said smoothly. 'It was nothing. A mere scratch.'

'May I see?'

Fowler's face coloured crimson at this physical infringement but, nonetheless, he slowly rolled up his shirtsleeve to reveal a small, deep wound, just beginning to scab over.

'More of an incision than a scratch,' Boddington said. He had thought to see scratches that could have been made by a child's nails.

'A figure of speech. As I said, a metal hook did the damage.'

Boddington nodded. 'I've not yet seen Alice Brooks. Could you send for her please?'

Fowler went out and returned with her a moment later. Boddington gestured that she should sit. 'Now, Alice, you were overseeing Beulah's work, weren't you?'

'Yes, sir.' She glanced at Fowler as if asking his permission to speak.

'When was the last time you saw her?'

'I saw her on Friday afternoon, running from the factory along the Farthingstone road.'

'And where were you?'

'I was out the front, in the street. I'd been talking to the carter. I was just setting him on his way,' she said defensively.

Boddington looked thoughtful. 'And was she carrying anything?'

She glanced at Fowler again. 'Well – yes – I think she was . . . a . . . a bundle.'

Fowler broke in triumphantly. 'You see! I told you! There is a length of cloth missing and the girl has stolen it.'

'What kind of bundle?' Boddington said, scowling at Fowler.

'A roll . . . it could have been a roll of cloth.'

'She will have gone to join her brother, no doubt,' Fowler said. 'Find one and you will find both.'

Boddington ignored him and fixed Alice with a keen stare. 'Alice, now this is important. If you were in front of a justice, could you honestly swear, on the Bible, that you saw Beulah Fiddement, alive and well, absenting herself from the factory on Friday afternoon? Think carefully before you answer.'

'I could and I would,' Alice said firmly. 'I swear I saw her running up that road as if all Hell were after her and now I understand why.'

Boddington let out a long sigh. 'Then I must inform all the toll keepers on the turnpike roads to look out for her, and the constables in other parishes too.'

Fowler sent Alice away, barely able to keep the smile from his face. He poured himself another measure of port. 'Come now, Boddington, do join me,' he said, indicating the glass that still stood on the desk. He leant back in his seat and rested his elbows comfortably on the arms of the chair. 'About the meeting next week, I believe I have the good offices of Hinchin and two others but I must have a majority if I'm to carry it. I trust I can rely on your support?'

Boddington ignored the proffered glass. He thought such schemes simply a way of exporting pauper children from work-houses to become unpaid drudges. 'You trespass too far on my goodwill, sir,' he said. 'These schemes are nothing more nor less than farming the poor.'

Fowler's expression changed to one of open dislike. 'You spoke of taking this case of the Fiddement girl to the justice,' he said coldly. 'You may not be aware that I had dealings with him over the frame breaking earlier in the year. We share similar

313

views; indeed I consider him a personal friend. He was singularly unimpressed at the handling of that affair and I fear may look equally unkindly on your handling of this afternoon's matter.'

Boddington stared back. 'Have a care. You overreach yourself, Fowler.' He rose and strode to the door. 'I give you good day.'

The following day, in the yard at the back of the workhouse, the women sat in rows, oakum picking. Effie's stool was set apart from the rest, at the front, under Mrs Smedley's eye. Effie pulled out another hank of tarry rope from the heap in front of her. She started to tease out the threads of the old hemp into fibres that would be sold for the making of string or the caulking of ship's timbers. Unused to the work, her fingers bled where the nails had pulled away from their beds. She dared not stop, not even to suck her fingertips for she had been too late in her return to the workhouse yesterday and had been caught.

Almost fainting with exhaustion, she had stood before Mrs Smedley in her dingy office.

'This is not a boarding house,' the matron said. 'It is a place of relief for the infirm and of punishment for the idle, refractory and profligate! You are not a guest, to come and go as you please, but a pauper, dependent on the charity of the parish and the rules of this house. Do you understand?'

With lowered eyes, Effie said that she did.

'Louder!'

'I understand.'

'Do you have anywhere else to go?

'No.'

'No,' Mrs Smedley repeated with satisfaction. 'Precisely.' She took up a tiny pair of pince-nez spectacles and, peering through them, wrote slowly and painstakingly in the record book. Effie watched, all the while terrified that she would be turned out. Finally, Mrs Smedley looked up and laid down her pen. 'If you decamp again,' she said flatly, 'you will not only lose your place but will be charged with stealing workhouse property – that is, your clothes – and sent to the House of Correction, which you will find considerably less amenable, I can assure you.'

Afterwards, Effie had been made to stand while the other women knelt for evening prayers and then held up as an example of shameless waywardness. The women filed past her, averting their eyes. In the sleeping quarters she had found her bed moved into a little alcove away from the others and had lain with her face to the wall, listening to the buzz of conversation behind her as the women at last had leisure and opportunity to talk. Only a cup placed beside the bed with a further dose of Mary-Anne's infusion of herbs gave her any cheer: the act of kindness lending sweetness to the bitter brew.

Today, once more she was set apart. As she worked in solitude, shredding the old rope, she reflected on her new life and it seemed to her that the workhouse, far from being a place of succour for the needy, was little better than a prison. Each day was a round of hard labour, tract-reading and chapel. They were encouraged to reflect on their sins and kept in silence to make them look inwards. But there she found only pain and loss: of her kin, of Jack, of her infant child. She couldn't see how she was to bear it.

Her reverie was broken as Mr Smedley approached his wife. 'The *constable* is here to see Euphemia Fiddement,' he said with heavy emphasis. Effie's heart beat fast as she followed him. Until now, she had hidden from the worst fear of all. Now, Boddington's visit filled her mind with horrible possibilities: Beulah fallen in a quarry, drownded in a pool, beaten and left in a ditch . . . When she saw Boddington, she caught at his sleeve. 'Have you found her? Please . . . tell me!'

He shook his head and led her into the empty dining hall. He handed her a broadsheet, folded up to show a column of print.

WHEREAS Beulah Fiddement, bobbin winder and late servant to Mr Septimus Fowler, Silk Master of Weedon Royal, ABSCONDED FROM HIS SERVICE on Friday 31st July, stealing a piece of yellow silk figured with sundry birds and flowers, whoever will give Information of the Offender, so that she may be brought to Justice, shall, upon her conviction, receive TEN POUNDS for a Reward.
    SEPTIMUS FOWLER

Effie read it and was filled with indignation. 'Beulah would never do such a thing! She's no thief – I've brought her up a good girl!'

Boddington held up his hands. 'Mr Fowler maintains the silk is missing and Alice Brooks swears she saw Beulah running up towards Farthingstone carrying a bundle.'

Effie blanched at the mention of a bundle.

He added quickly, 'However, this in itself is insufficient as evidence.'

Effie recovered herself. 'Why, 'tis ridiculous! Where would she sell such a thing? It would be apparent that it had not been come by honestly. Who would buy it from her – a child with a piece of expensive cloth? This is a charge trumped up by the master out of spite. He has been venting his anger on Beulah ever since Tobias left.'

Boddington, who feared Fowler's motives for the accusation might be even worse, but who had no evidence to set against

Alice's testimony, kept his thoughts to himself, not wishing to fuel the fire of the young woman's alarm. Fowler's violent reputation and ungovernable temper were well known and rumours had already spread from the manufactory to the village, growing and exaggerating with every telling of the tale: he had beaten the girl before; he punished her by keeping her locked in a cellar; he had been seen by Biddy Tranter with blood on his hands . . . In the bakehouse and over garden walls, at the public houses and on street corners, the story rumbled like distant thunder, ebbing only to return in another quarter.

Effie began to pace the room, up and down the corridor between the rows of tables and bench seats, wringing her hands as she went.

'Please, Miss Fiddement, do not upset yourself so. I've informed the turnpike keepers and constabulary hereabouts and when she's found we shall establish the truth of the matter and all will be put to rights.'

'But if it is not?' Effie stopped and faced him. 'If she were found guilty she could be transported, or worse? Folk have hanged for sheep stealing, even poaching rabbits! A piece of silk – that is a valuable item . . .'

Boddington, seeing the paleness of her face and concerned by her distracted air, spoke firmly. 'There is no point in such dire speculations. Instead we should bend all our efforts to finding her.' He took her arm and led her to a bench. Effie sat and began rocking herself back and forth. He said, 'Now, is there any other place, anywhere at all, that you think your sister might have gone?'

Effie considered. 'No,' she said at last. 'I can think of nowhere but home and she has not been there.'

He sighed. 'Well, if you recollect anywhere you should ask Mrs Smedley to inform the Newnham constable and he will let me know. Of course, I shall inform you if she's found meanwhile.'

Effie nodded mutely. Ever since her discovery that Beulah was missing she had been praying that someone would find her. Now, as with Tobias, she must hope that they would not. The thought broke her heart.

Boddington saw black despair in the girl's eyes. He laid his hand briefly on her shoulder, unable to think of any words of comfort.

As he left, he passed the open door of a room where children were being taught their catechism. They sat in a row with slates upon the bench in front of them, fidgeting, gazing out of the window or watching the clock: longing for the lesson to be over. Full of restless energy. Full of life.

EIGHTEEN

By the time a month had passed at the workhouse, Effie felt blurred at the edges, as though her sense of her self, her way of *being* and responding to the world, was fading, eroded by the demand to constantly conform. You could eat and drink but must neither leave a crumb (that would be wasteful) nor ask for more (that would show ingratitude). You could go somewhere else in your head but could not lose yourself completely, as even when daydreaming your hands must never be still but always occupied and busy at work. You must not whisper or smile or laugh together, as levity showed a lack of awareness of the seriousness of your position, nor was it possible to speak one's mind as certain of the women would report such dissidence to Mrs Smedley, hoping to gain favour.

Small luxuries such as meat or tea were given or withdrawn, much in the manner with which one might train a dog.

In desperation, Effie attempted to convince Mrs Smedley of her skill with letters, in the hope that she might be afforded work in the classroom. She was told roundly that she was unfit and was not to be allowed to exert any influence on young, unformed minds. To punish her presumption she was separated entirely from the rest and set to work on her own, the better to dwell on her shortcomings and repent her loose ways. Sometimes she was sent to work in the garden, doing hard, manual jobs, sometimes she was confined to a room off the kitchen that had once been a storeroom and struck chill even in the warmest of weather. Here she spun lint or tow for the use of the house, her wheel beneath the high window repositioned often during the day to follow the small patch of light as the sun moved round. The repetitive work allowed her mind to wander and it followed those she loved along their strange and distant pathways: Jack marching away over some foreign field; Tobias tramping a towpath through some unknown city; Beulah carrying the baby to some dark place where Effie could not follow. All gone. All out of reach. The thoughts returned and returned, regular as the click of the wheel as it spun. *No one will come back. No one will come back,* the treadle sang to her. In her blackest moments she thought: I will be like Mary-Anne, living out the rest of my days here without kin, without husband or child. I will moulder here.

On a day early in September, Effie was set to work in the kitchen garden to lift the crop of beetroot. The afternoon was hot and she rolled up her sleeves and tied her hair back with a string of oakum to keep it off her face, though she dare not hitch up her skirts for fear of being seen and reported as immodest. As she knelt and dug the dry ground with her trowel, pulled on the leafy tops and shook off the soil clinging to the roots, her bones ached and the sun beat down on her back.

From the yard beyond the hedge, she heard voices coming towards her: Mrs Smedley sounding unctuously polite and a man – a man whom she dare not think familiar. It couldn't be! The sun must be addling her brain.

'I shall take you to her directly,' Mrs Smedley was saying.

'If you would be so kind,' said Jack's voice.

As Jack rounded the hedge, he caught sight of her bending to the earth, as she had been the first time he'd seen her picking snowdrops. Something inside him twisted unbearably. She was so changed: half wasted away, thin arms protruding from her sleeves, her delicate skin browned by the sun and smeared with dirt. His darling Effie! 'Please leave us,' he said in a tone that sent Mrs Smedley scuttling for the house.

Effie, on her knees in the dirt, dropped what she was holding and stumbled to her feet. She ran to him; Jack folded her into his embrace and they clung together, kissed and clung again. 'Thank God! Thank God you're safe!' Effie said. Hardly believing this was real, she rested her cheek against his tunic, feeling the warmth, the solidity of him.

Jack held her close. He could feel her shoulder blades, sharp and bony through her dress. She felt so slight! As though a high wind might carry her away.

A bell rang inside the workhouse and Effie jumped and stepped back from him as if she had been called to heel; then she checked herself and stayed where she was. He took her hand. 'Oh, Effie,' he said sorrowfully. 'How did this happen? When I came to the cottage and saw it deserted I thought that illness must have come. I thought the very worst . . . and then I saw your message and came on here.'

'We were turned out of the cottage,' Effie said. 'I had almost given you up.'

'*Why* did you not go to my parents as I said?'

Effie looked away from him. 'There are things I must tell you.' She took his hand and led him to a seat at the edge of the orchard. They sat beneath a medlar tree, Effie silent at first, watching the dark dots of wasps zigzagging along the ground at their feet and crawling in and out of the windfall fruit. Without looking up she said, 'When you were sent away, I was already with child.'

Jack's eyes brightened and then, seeing her face, his expression became uncertain.

'I didn't want to shame you by going to your family and I hoped the war would end and you would come back . . .' Her voice began to break. 'But then I lost the baby anyway. Oh Jack! Our baby, our boy . . .'

He put his arms around her as she cried, holding on to her as the pain hit him. A child, his child.

At last, he asked, 'Did you give our boy a name?'

'I called him Jack, after you.'

He swallowed hard. 'Where is he buried?' He knew that children born outside marriage weren't allowed to be buried within the bounds of the churchyard but were afforded only a lonely plot outwith the wall.

'Beulah took him.' Effie began to rock to and fro, her arms folded across her stomach as if remembering the carrying of her child. 'It was at the silk factory and Alice said . . . Alice said there was no life in him and Beulah took him away. But she didn't come back!'

'Shh, shh.' He put his arm around her and took her hand in his.

'We have nothing of him, not even a patch of earth to mourn beside,' she said, her eyes desolate.

He held her while she wept again, until at length she rubbed at her face, leaving streaks of dirt and tears. 'Look at me, Jack. What a state I'm in!' She held out her hands to take in her stick-thin figure in its ugly dress, her lifeless hair and her ruined hands. 'I'm not the woman you fell in love with.'

'Yes, yes you are and always will be!' He traced her cheek with his fingertips. 'I'm taking you away from this place today; you'll not stay here another minute. We'll find you board and lodging at Weedon Royal until we can be married and then I'll try again for married quarters at the barracks.'

Effie looked at him searchingly. 'You know that people will talk? They'll say you're marrying into a family whose name is disgraced.'

'There is no fault for you to answer; it's I who have brought you to this,' Jack said gravely. 'You must let me make it right.'

She frowned. 'But it is not just . . . duty?'

'How can you say that!' His eyes filled and he took her in his arms and kissed her.

Afterwards, as she sat with his arm around her, she asked, 'What of your family, Jack? You wanted to ask your father's blessing and do all in proper order.'

'Desperate times demand desperate remedies, so we will not delay the marriage and will go to them afterwards. I shall go first and explain.'

'Not about the baby!'

'No,' Jack said thoughtfully. 'That's our private sorrow and no one's concern but ours. I shall say only that in my absence you fell prey to an unscrupulous landlord and, being from a respectable family and too proud to apply to them for help, fell into such want that I decided to act straightaway, as I know they would have wished me to, in order to relieve it.'

323

Effie nodded slowly, considering. 'And you believe they will forgive me for entering your family so abruptly?'

He touched his forefinger gently against her lips to stop her doubts. 'They want only my good and when they see how I love you, dearest Effie, they will know that you are where that good lies.'

Effie rested her head against his shoulder, letting relief wash over her, at last laying this burden down. She asked him about his foreign service and he told her how they had taken Badajoz but he had been caught by a shot from a window and forced to take cover in an alleyway. 'I lay there wondering if I should ever see you again,' he said. 'Such a deep sadness came over me at the thought that we might be separated until the far side of the grave. I can't express how much it grieved me, and how I longed to see your face. All around me was the clamour of plunder: muskets shot through keyholes and wine barrels rolled out, their heads tapped in to run wine and liquor into the streets so that men lay down and drank from the gutters! The drunken rabble ransacked houses, destroying what could not be taken and I thought that if it were my fate to die, I would not die in this very Hell.'

'How did you escape?'

'I hauled myself up using the wall as my support and ventured out. I had the good fortune to meet with a fellow officer who was trying to keep order.' Jack attempted a smile. 'I think he was as glad to meet with me and escape this obligation as I was to meet with him and have his help.' He told her of his time in the hospital, the fever and his slow painful recovery, and then the unexpected joyful news that he had been recalled to his old station.

He asked her to tell him more of Beulah's disappearance. He looked grave at her answer and when she told him of Fowler's accusation he looked graver still.

'We will mount our own search,' he said determinedly, although, with a month gone by, he feared the trail would be cold.

He stood and offered her his hand. 'Your old friend, Maisie, is tethered outside,' he said. 'I shall walk and you shall ride. We'll be in Weedon Royal within the hour, have you lodged safely by sundown and be married in a month, once the banns are read. How does that sound?'

For answer, Effie took his hand and they made their way together.

On Sunday, at Weedon Royal church, the Fowler family sat at the inside end of the row directly behind the gentry. The surveyor, Marshall, and his family were next to them, then the doctor and the constable, the whip maker and his family. The smaller farmers, landlords and other businessmen with their families filled the rest of this rank: the men in dark jackets, holding tall hats upon their knees, the women in pastel, high-waisted dresses and their best hats or bonnets. Behind them, the mass of common folk – the servants, manufacturing hands and farm labourers – sat or stood at the back. The hierarchy arranged itself from wealth to poverty, mighty to lowly. The weavers and their families were scattered among the latter. Ellis Coulishaw had picked a place at the end of a row, the better to stretch out his injured leg that stiffened with inactivity and the damp chill of the church; his wife and gaggle of children took up the whole pew. Old Griffith Hood and Jim Baggott sat together near the open door to catch a little of the warmth and freshness from outside. Jervis sat with his family, his head already bowed in thought, if not in prayer. The east window, one of fine stained glass, was afire in red and yellow and the sun that streamed through it, cutting a path of light to the back of the nave, shone indiscriminately on every man, woman and child.

Septimus Fowler, in black tailcoat and high collar, with a grey silk cravat wrapped up to the chin, sat staring into space, his mind elsewhere. He had been too busy to attend church for the last few weeks: writing letters to canvass for larger orders from his existing customers, placing advertisements to bring in new orders, calculating break-even points assuming lower labour costs. Losing the Jacquard looms had hit his pocket hard and there had also been a falling-off of trade. His credit with the bank was used up and he could not put up prices; the market wouldn't stand it. He needed to raise productivity, increase orders but also cut costs, get more work done for less outlay. The truth was, he was running out of cash. Unless he took prompt action, the whole manufactory, everything he had slaved over, could go to the wall.

The bells were yet pealing out, calling all to service, and the church was still abuzz with conversation. Fowler tapped his fingernails on his prayer book in irritation. Church was all very well but he wished they could get on with the proceedings. The real business of the morning would be to buttonhole the members of the vestry afterwards to make sure of those he had already secured as supporters for his scheme to employ paupers, and to persuade those he had not. The matter was to be discussed the next day and he *must* make sure of it. In preparation, he leant forward to look past Marshall and his fidgeting children to try to catch the eye of Hinchin, who sat further along, across the aisle. Hinchin, however, did not look his way and seemed engrossed in reading the numbers of the hymns and lessons that hung above the pulpit and marking them in his book. Fowler half rose and raised his hand but still Hinchin did not turn his way. At his rising, he sensed a change in the

326

level of the noise of conversation behind him, a sudden dip as if many individual voices had broken off, their interest caught. As he sank back into his seat he was aware of shuffling and nudging going on behind him and when the congregation began to converse again it was at a muted rather than a cheerful pitch and filled with mutterings and whispers. He strained to hear and thought he caught a snatch or two: *'Tis a disgrace . . . Still never been found.* Uneasily, he glanced at Tabitha and Hebe, who sat between him and the wall, to see if they had marked the change. Hebe, looking delicately pretty in a white dress and short powder-blue jacket, was fiddling self-consciously with the buttons of her gloves, while Tabitha, looking lumpy in dark bombazine, fished around in her reticule to check, for the umpteenth time, that she had the collection for the plate. Neither seemed to have noticed anything untoward and he let his shoulders drop and, with fingers and thumb, smoothed his whiskers.

The pealing bells stopped and then began a mournful tolling as a last warning that the service was about to begin. Did he imagine that as the final note faded away he heard the name *Fiddement* just as a hush fell on the congregation? The music of hautboy and viol began from the balcony at the back as Parson Hawkins, a gaunt-looking middle-aged man with his hair cut in the Brutus style, led the choir forward to the chancel. They filed in to the choir stalls and the parson climbed the creaking steps to the pulpit. As he gave the bidding prayer, his hooded eyes scanned the kneeling congregation, as if to draw them all in, commanding them through his sombre expression to leave their everyday thoughts behind and concentrate on the state of their souls. Those who had not already bowed their heads hurried to do so, but Fowler, still thinking of the mutterings of the village, was caught unawares as the parson's sweeping gaze snagged on him. For a moment the parson turned a piercing look upon him and then passed on.

After the prayer, they sat once more, Tabitha surreptitiously rubbing from her knees the ache from the hard, chill floor.

'Here beginneth the first lesson,' the parson intoned, 'from psalm sixty-eight.' His deep voice boomed out into the high spaces of the nave:

'As smoke is driven away so drive them away: as wax melteth before the fire, so let the wicked perish at the presence of God.

But let the righteous be glad; let them rejoice before God: yea, let them exceedingly rejoice.

Sing unto God, sing praises to his name: extol him that rideth upon the heavens by his name JAH, and rejoice before him.

A father of the fatherless, and a judge of the widows, is God in his holy habitation . . .'

Fowler, who paid no attention to the lesson, excising it from his consciousness, as was his habit, was thinking instead that if he were able to reach Hinchin quickly after the service he might be able to draw him over to speak with the doctor, who still remained sceptical about his scheme. He would explain to him the figures he had calculated for the likely savings in parish relief currently paid to paupers. Hinchin's presence would help to imply that there was general agreement to the scheme and that the doctor would be out on a limb if he should stand against it. He felt sure that he could win him over.

As the parson announced, 'Amen. Here endeth the first lesson,' Fowler came back to himself and found Hawkins's eyes once again directly upon him. He shifted uncomfortably in his seat. What was the matter with the man?

It had been apparent from the inception of his plan that the parson was not going to support it. Fowler could see that he was a reformer type who refused to keep his religion where it belonged, within the walls of the church, and let it spill into every day of the week and matters in which it had no place. Why, earlier in the year when the parson had overheard him talking after church of the new Frame Breaking Bill, with Hinchin and some other men of business, Hawkins had had the brass neck to interfere, pushing himself into the conversation. Just as he had been telling Hinchin that the new measures would prove an excellent deterrent, Hawkins had said, 'Can you commit a whole country to their own prisons? Will you erect a gibbet in every field, and hang up men like scarecrows?' He had rejoined that this was a gross exaggeration. Parson Hawkins, with an unaccustomed twinkle in his eye, had said drily that, in that case, Fowler disagreed with Lord Byron, for it was he who had expressed these sentiments in his maiden speech on the Bill to the House. This had left Fowler feeling foolish in front of the other men, and he had at once categorised Hawkins as foe not friend in this matter. He had turned his attention to other vestry members with minds more open to progressive ideas and their own advantage, those where he judged he would be pushing on an open door.

The service rumbled on with the repeating of the creed and the singing of a hymn, ''Tis by Thy Strength the Mountains Stand'. Fowler was aware of Hebe's high clear voice beside him, and he sang out in his own rich bass so that between them they should drown out Tabitha's wavering alto. He had told her before that she should mime the words and her flouting of his wishes tested his patience.

329

For his sermon, the parson took as his text 'The Fatherless Child'. First he expounded upon the idea that without faith all should be 'fatherless children', as each one would be cut off from the bounty and grace of the Lord. Then he spoke of the responsibility to emulate the Father in caring for widows and orphans, drawing on the psalms, and Fowler began to take notice.

'*Defend the poor and fatherless: do justice to the afflicted and needy . . . rid them out of the hands of the wicked.*' Hawkins's deep voice rolled out over the congregation as he turned first to one side and then the other. Was he imagining it or did the parson look with special meaning at the doctor, at the constable, at the members of the parish vestry, even at his own man, Hinchin? How dare he! How dare he use his position and the platform of the pulpit to prick their consciences about the paupers of the parish and try to influence a decision on a secular matter! Fowler's brow drew into a deep scowl.

The parson expanded on his theme of responsibility, speaking of the giving of alms, of Charity beginning in one's own parish, of being your brother's keeper. At this, Fowler's temper rose further. He crossed his arms in front of him and secretly clenched and unclenched his fists, unable to find vent for his spleen. Tabitha glanced sideways at him and began to fidget anxiously and Hebe, sinking down in her seat, started to plait and unplait the silk-ribbon place marker she used for her Bible.

The parson's voice rose as he shifted his ground to justice for the poor and oppressed and for all those made vulnerable by misfortunes not of their own making. 'I shall finish with a second lesson,' he announced, 'and exhort you to examine your consciences and repent any actions that exploit your fellow man or take advantage of their poverty or weakness.' In a sonorous voice that rang in the rafters, he spoke out with a passion:

'Lord, how long shall the wicked, shall the wicked triumph?
How long shall they utter and speak hard things? and all
  the workers of iniquity boast themselves?
They break in pieces thy people, O Lord, and afflict thine
  heritage.
They slay the widow and the stranger and murder the
  fatherless.'

At this, there was a stir in the congregation. Fowler turned round sharply and saw it run like a ripple to the very back of the church. A hundred pairs of eyes seemed to fix upon him and he quickly sat back, stiff and upright in his seat.

The parson continued, his voice gradually rising, swelling with passion at the stirring words:

'Yet they say, The Lord shall not see, neither shall the God
  of Jacob regard it.
Understand, ye brutish among the people: and ye fools,
  when will ye be wise?
He that planted the ear, shall he not hear? he that formed
  the eye, shall he not see?
He that chastiseth the heathen, shall he not correct? he
  that teacheth man knowledge, shall he not know?'

The last words resounded in the lofty building and many cast their eyes heavenwards as if believing that the roof might suddenly open and the judgement of the Lord manifest itself. As the parson smoothed the page and shut his Bible, the stir became a mutter and the mutter a hubbub. The parson, above them in the pulpit, held out his hands, pressing them down through the air to quell the sound. Voices died away.

A pregnant silence hung in the church. He gave the blessing and then climbed heavily down to lead the way from the church. The choir filed from their stalls behind him and, once they had turned aside to disrobe, the gentry began to vacate their pews, the ladies showily gathering up fans, gloves and parasols. The congregation respectfully let them pass before starting their own orderly exodus following one pew at a time from the front. When it came to the turn of his row to empty, Fowler, still filled with rage, picked up his cane in one hand and his hat in the other and moved slowly forward along the pew. The clamour of voices began to rise again and from the corner of his eye he was aware of the faces in the pew behind, all staring at him with expressions ranging from naked curiosity to outright distaste. Beyond them, fingers were raised to point and there was nudging and shuffling, as though some were pushing forward before their turn.

'Come along, Tabitha, Hebe.' He stared fixedly ahead as they moved along behind the others towards the aisle. As they reached the end, the Marshall family stepped out from the pew and moved away but before he had a chance to follow, those in the pews behind pressed forward as one, crowding in front of him, trapping him where he stood.

'Why are they not waiting for us?' Tabitha asked indignantly. 'Why do they not hold back?'

Hebe's face was flaming with mortification.

The hoi polloi poured into the aisle before him. Faces turned back to stare, some with quick glances of derision, some blank and dumb, some openly sneering. Fowler stood impotently gripping his cane as the whole church emptied through the bottleneck of the main door, slow as an hourglass.

When the lowliest labourers and their families filed out from the back, he stepped out into the aisle but made no move to go further.

'I want to go home,' Hebe said, her voice trembling.

'Septimus, can we not go?' Tabitha agreed.

'Be quiet!' Fowler snapped. 'I will not follow directly behind a row of crossing sweepers and snotty-nosed ploughboys!'

After the last person had passed into the porch, he waited a little longer, calculating that the congregation would by then have bade farewell to the parson, who always shook their hands at the door, and dispersed through the churchyard and into the lane outside to stand around in knots and exchange pleasantries.

'Very well,' he said, at length. 'Tabitha, take Hebe's arm. Hebe, hold your head up; you're not a child!' He marched down the aisle, the metal tip of his cane tapping out his steps.

As they emerged into the light, he saw that the parson was still waiting at the door. Beyond him, the whole congregation stood around in groups: some obstructing the path to the lychgate, stiff, black-coated figures in their tall black hats; some up on the banks either side, finding room among the gravestones, men in flat caps with their dowdy wives and clinging children, Jervis and others of the weavers among them. All, it seemed, had stayed behind to see him leave. A silence fell.

The parson stepped forward and with an inscrutable expression proffered his hand. Fowler took it so briefly that it appeared ill-mannered and muttered, 'Good day, sir,' with bad grace.

In a clear voice the parson said, 'Good day, Mr Fowler. Thank you for visiting us today. I shall return the courtesy and visit your manufactory very soon.' He pressed the hands of Tabitha and Hebe with more warmth and a look almost of pity came into his eyes.

Fowler walked away and the women followed. The groups on the banks above them, among the graves, drew nearer to the path, filling in the gaps until it seemed they walked along a deep passageway made of people looking down upon them. At the far end, by the gate, a group of men had gathered, Hinchin one of them. Fowler strode on ahead of Tabitha and Hebe, brazening it out. 'Ah! Hinchin!' he exclaimed, this time so loudly that he could not be missed. The whole group of men looked towards him and Fowler paused, his cane half-raised in greeting. Hinchin would not fully meet his eyes; he cut him, turning back to his companions as if Fowler had never spoken. Fowler hurried on through the shadow of the lychgate, Tabitha and Hebe close behind. He cursed Hinchin. He cursed them all. He would see them all in Hell.

He strode away, tapping his cane on the road so smartly that sparks flew from its metal ferrule. As they reached the centre of the village, Tabitha called out breathlessly, 'Septimus! Need we be in such awful haste? Can you not pause and explain? Why did everyone snub us so? What have you been *doing?*'

He rounded on her. 'It is not my place to explain to *you*,' he said viciously. 'Rather you should explain to me your failure with Hinchin's wife! You should have made sure of her – found some way of putting her under an obligation.'

Tabitha, shocked at his vehemence, put her hand to her throat. 'I visited and befriended her. I did all that I could.'

''Tis true,' Hebe ventured. 'I went with Mama to the house on several occasions.'

'Hold your tongue, Hebe; this is no business of yours – and don't conjure up the tears!'

Tabitha, seeing that Hebe was indeed on the verge of tears, tried a more placatory tack. 'Septimus, luncheon will be waiting.

Perhaps we should talk after our meal when all are in a better humour?'

Ignoring her, he marched on again and when they followed, he turned with a face full of fury. 'Go home!' he shouted. 'Do you think I want you women at my heels like trotting dogs?'

Tabitha and Hebe stood together uncertainly as he set off down an alleyway towards the factory. Tabitha set her jaw and handed Hebe her handkerchief. 'Let him rant. We'll go home. There's no point letting a good dinner go to waste.'

Fowler let himself into his office. He threw his hat and cane down on to a chair and stood for a moment in the centre of the room. Sunday silence filled the factory: the looms all still, the workers all gone. The only sounds were the ticking of the great clock and the thrumming of his blood in his ears. The deadness of the silence seemed to press down on him from the floors above as if it had a weight of its own. He stepped forward to the desk and with a strangled cry swept cloth, scales, weights and all to the floor with a mighty thump. Silk crumpled and rolled on the dusty boards: pinks, yellows and blues, patterns of roses and ogees, cherubs and vines; pan, scales and weights scattered over them.

Breathing heavily, he walked round the mess to his seat behind the desk. He took off his uncomfortable jacket, yanked open a drawer and pulled out the ledgers, a quarto notebook, pen and ink. There must be some way to recover from this! He ran his eye down the columns of figures but could not take in their meaning. In his head, he cursed the vestry roundly. Who did they think they were, to scorn him in this way: a gaggle of jumped-up, inky-fingered clerks! Hawkins might think himself the Voice of God but he was nothing but a common country parson, and as for Hinchin, the man had the initiative of a rocking-horse. Yet they had treated *him* as some kind of pariah! He saw again the staring eyes and pointing fingers, people pressing in upon him, crowding him in the church, lining the churchyard path, making a dark passageway through which he had to pass . . . Hinchin turning away . . . He might as well have been clothed in workhouse weeds or swinging a leper's bell.

He thought of all the labour he'd put in to grease the wheels of his business through ingratiating the family into the social round of the village, all the dinners and card parties for which he had inveigled invitations. After today's humiliation, every such invitation would cease and, in his absence, lurid rumours would thrive and spread, harming him and his business further. His contact with village society would be limited to creeping in and out of church on Sundays with his tail between his legs, for if he stayed away, all would say it was an admission of guilt. Yet with Tabitha and Hebe trailing behind him with whey-faces and downcast eyes, how was he to hold his head high and brazen it out?

Those damnable Fiddement children! To think that such a worthless chit of a girl could have brought him such trouble! His workers had witnessed his public disgrace in front of the whole village today. Now, even in his own factory he would be forever conscious of sneers behind his back and snide remarks muttered just out of earshot. It was insupportable! Was he to suffer the opprobrium of drawboys and bobbin winders? With every attempt he made to exert discipline he'd be aware of the rumbling growl of dissent, his workforce like a dog sleeping with one eye open, ready to spring. For God's sake, Jervis would be after him, like a hound scenting a weakness in its prey, demanding better wages, shorter hours. And soon Hawkins would be visiting, poking his long nose in. He threw down his pen. Was he to have his business inspected by a *parson* who knew nothing of Industry, of the vicissitudes of the Market, the responsibilities of a Master? The man was capable only of the most myopic, narrow view. He would nose around his factory seeing only the superficialities. He could hear him now, bleating on about the cramped conditions, the sweat and smell, the air too thick to breathe. He would moan that the children looked thin and exhausted and that veterans who had already fought for their country shouldn't be adding bent backs and ruined eyes to their injuries. He wouldn't see the Planning, the Vision and the Creation of Wealth for the Nation. Hawkins would spout reforming nonsense at him and using the power of the vestry; he would force yet more expense upon him, demand more space, better ventilation, a living wage, potatoes, meat, eggs: good vittles wasted on dross. Ah yes, Jervis and the parson would have him in their pincers.

The harsh fact of the matter was that without the paupers as cheap labour he would be unable to squeeze out sufficient profit. He would find it hard to tread water, never mind forge ahead. He pushed away the thought of his losses in Spitalfields long ago and his ignominious flight from his creditors. Could he sell his properties to tide the business over? 'Twould not be sound business sense; they brought in regular rents, a reliable income, unlike the swings in fortune attendant on the market for silk. In any case, it would be the talk of the parish if he sold property. Everyone would know that he was in difficulties. Viciousness would spread the fact further abroad, along with all the other rumours, and would turn yet more business away. If his suppliers withdrew credit he would be done for . . . Behind the regular beat of the great clock, he heard voices, the babble of gossip and spite dispersing from the village like a contagion amongst his creditors, amongst his customers: *financial difficulties, a cruel taskmaster, trouble with the Law.* He saw it spreading, like a dirty smear across his silks.

No, he could not sell the properties, but without the money neither could he modernise. Instead, he would be stuck with old machines and costly labour and all his great plans would come to naught. Rather than priming the bellows with cash to pump new life into his venture, he would be presiding over its slow death.

He stared, unseeing, at the open ledger. Above him, the clock ticked on in the cavernous silence.

NINETEEN

Effie sat at the window of her room at the Wheat Sheaf Inn, in the part of the village known as 'Weedon-in-the-Street'. The turnpike road below was busy with carts and carriages, mail and passenger coaches. Traffic was always passing, for this road, which passed east to west between Northampton and Coventry, was crossed here by the Watling Street, the Great Road that ran south, all the way to London and beyond.

Effie was sewing her wedding dress. A bright square of sunlight fell on her lap where the pale, slippery silk of the bodice lay. She paused now and then in her stitching, welcoming the distraction of the shouts of the carriers or the hauling of portmanteaux on to the top of coaches. Preparing for her marriage was a reason for joy and every day she thought of the blessing that Jack had been safely returned to her, but she worried for Beulah and could not rest. As she stitched, her mind picked over and over all she had heard. It seesawed between Alice's adamant testimony to the justice that Beulah had absconded, now also corroborated by one of the bobbin winders, Thomasin Parks, and the rumours that had reached her from the bar of the inn that Beulah had come to harm at Fowler's hands.

Although there was no proof against him and she knew that one should hold a man innocent until proven otherwise, news of his shaming at the church had filled her with a fierce, vengeful satisfaction. Yet at night she dreamt of Beulah hiding some-where, in a barn or a hedge-bottom, scared and alone. In these dreams, she clasped her in her arms and told her, 'Effie's here – you're safe – Effie's here,' but she woke to an empty room and the clatter of the night coaches passing.

Assuming that Alice and Thomasin were telling the truth, where could Beulah be now? Time and again she berated herself for having left Alice to pass on her message to Beulah to come to the workhouse. If only she hadn't relied on the woman! If only she hadn't let Alice hurry her away. If she'd had the chance to comfort Beulah after the shock of the stillbirth she felt certain she could have reassured her. They had asked too much of her. Beulah was too young to cope with it alone.

As the days had gone by, Mr Boddington's assurances that Beulah would be found had sounded hollow to her ear. She and Jack had walked out along the Farthingstone road, where Alice said she last saw Beulah, and then cut across the fields all the way back to the cottage at Newnham hoping to find some sign of her by retracing her most likely route home. Jack had ridden out to the toll gates and given a description to the keepers, handing them small coin to ensure discretion and promising more for any information that might lead to the recovery of the child. All had drawn a blank and as time slipped on it seemed less and less likely that she would be found.

There was a tap on the door and she put her sewing aside to answer it. Hannah, the maid-of-all-work, bobbed a curtsey and said, 'Lieutenant Stamford, ma'am – in the parlour.' Effie caught up her shawl and followed her downstairs.

As Effie entered the tiny parlour, Jack thought with satisfaction how proper rest and decent food were doing her good. She was beginning to fill out once more and her complexion was regaining its colour. She looked stronger. 'Shall we walk?' Jack asked. 'It's a fine evening.'

They set off, arm in arm, first along the London road and then, turning aside to enter the village, they passed the long wall of the arsenal and crossed first the swing bridge over the canal and then the brick bridge over the river. As they went, Jack told her of his day, of the improvements he had made in the drill of the artillerymen and, hoping to amuse her, of the new bugler who had played reveille out of key. When they reached the crossroads at the Plume of Feathers, he steered her away from New Street and towards West Street, thinking to avoid passing the silk manufactory and save her pain.

Effie resisted the pressure of his hand upon her arm. 'I'm sorry, Jack, but can we walk up towards Farthingstone again?'

Jack sighed. 'It does you no good, Effie. It'll only upset you.'

'Please?'

Jack feared it was hopeless but nonetheless humoured her. They walked on, crossing to the far side of the street when they reached the factory and then ascending the hill that led out of the village. Jack asked questions about the landlord's family at the inn, with whom Effie, as a long-term guest, was now on friendly terms. He tried to distract her and draw her into conversation but he saw how her eyes strayed always fearfully to the ditches. At length, he gave up all pretence that they were walking out together exchanging trivialities like a normal courting couple and fell silent. They walked along the ridge, out beyond the village, until there was only open farmland on either side: on the right fields full of sheep dotted with crows, and on the left a pattern of wheat fields and pasture sweeping down and then up again to a skyline pieced with woods, like uneven clumps of bristles in a brush.

Jack began to speak, instead, of more troubling matters, closer to their hearts. He pointed to the nearest field on their left saying, 'Do you see that elm tree? That's where Tobias was hiding. Thank God it was I and not Clay who found him and that he was able to reach the woods.'

Effie squeezed his arm. 'He was always a good woodsman. He said you needed silent feet and wide eyes for rabbiting.' She gave a sad smile as they walked on.

'Effie,' Jack said thoughtfully, 'did Beulah know much about Tobias's escape?'

'She knew that his escape was through these woods, though not your part in it.'

They looked at each other, both thinking the same thought.

'So,' Jack said, 'if Alice's story is true and Beulah fled along this road, might she not have remembered and sought the same secretive route as her brother?'

They bent their steps towards the nearest wood, Castle Dykes, a dark ring of trees on the horizon.

They found a narrow, overgrown track leading from the road. It ran between pasture on one side and a cornfield splashed with poppies on the other, and passed into the trees through a cleft in a deep ditch and steep bank. An ancient fortification, it would once have been clear of trees and afforded, for its Iron Age tribe, a view of twenty miles over the surrounding countryside. The bank, once topped by palisades, was over-grown with trees, the ditch half-filled with fallen branches and a litter of weeds, knee-deep in leaf mould.

The trees enclosed a large central clearing, sunlit, scattered with stumps and swathes of bracken but largely covered by tough, dense grass, criss-crossed by earth paths. To one side, the remains of a campfire showed: a large patch of scathed turf scattered with charred wood, ashes leached and spread by rain. Upended logs were placed around it, a couple fallen over on their sides. Nearby, large patches of grass were yellow and dead as if something had stood there, and in other places there were holes in the ground as if pegs had been driven in as tethers.

At the back of the clearing, a low shelter had been made, a limb pulled down from a young sycamore and pinned to the earth with cut branches and bracken piled against it on either side to form a rough tent of wood and leaves. Seeing it, Effie ran over, calling out, 'Beulah! Beulah!' a wild hope rising in her.

Jack joined her where she stood disconsolate beside the empty shelter. 'Whoever was here has long departed,' he said. 'The campfire is old – and look, here' – he put his hand on the brown fronds and fragments came away at his touch – 'the bracken is all but shrivelled away.'

Effie, still breathing hard, rubbed her hand across her brow. 'I thought . . . just for a moment . . .'

'We can try the woods further along, work through Everdon Stubbs,' Jack said in the most encouraging voice he could muster. 'We can come back another day or even carry on now, if you feel strong enough?'

Effie wasn't listening. She was staring at something hanging above the shelter, a patch of red in a mass of green. As if in a dream she pulled a branch away to reveal it. Dangling from a twig, knotted at one corner, as if hung out to dry on any homely clothes line, was a red flannel kerchief. She reached out and felt it between her finger and thumb.

Jack came and looked over her shoulder. 'Gypsies' washing left out by accident?'

Effie unknotted the cloth and turned it over, running her thumb along the hem. She turned to him, her eyes shining. 'Beulah's!' she said.

'Wait, Effie; how can you know that? Red flannel kerchiefs are ten-a-penny. Even if Beulah had one it doesn't necessarily follow . . .'

''Tis a message! To say that she's been here, with the gypsies! 'Tis a message for me, to let me know she's safe!'

Jack, torn between wanting to believe it so that she might have some peace of mind and feeling that this false hope would hurt all the more when logic dashed it, hesitated, undecided.

'Look – look here,' Effie said, folding the cloth so that the hem showed. 'Do you think I don't know my own stitching?' Clutching the kerchief to her breast, Effie went and sat down heavily on one of the logs and Jack rolled another over and sat beside her.

'Even if it is the case, you realise that there's little chance of finding her. They could be anywhere by now,' he said gently. 'The gypsies wander the whole country without rhyme or reason. There's no pattern to their travels; they stay somewhere until they're on the brink of getting caught at some mischief and then move on.'

'But she's alive! She's alive!' Tears of relief stood in her eyes. 'And they may come back.'

Jack nodded a tentative assent. 'If you really believe it, we should speak to the constable. We should tell him what we've found – present it as evidence. It does support Alice's testimony.'

Effie looked up sharply. 'What! So that monster, Fowler, can send the law after her? No. He's made others suffer long enough. 'Tis time he suffered himself and I'll do nothing to clear his name.' She folded the cloth and hid it away in her pocket.

Jack rubbed his chin but argued no further.

Effie looked around, her eyes lighting on every patch of disturbed ground.

'What are you thinking?' Jack asked softly. 'It must be a small band of gypsies. See' – he pointed to the rectangular patches of yellowed grass – 'just three carts, I think.'

Effie shook her head. In a low voice she said, 'I was thinking that perhaps our baby is buried somewhere in this place but I shall never know where.' She leant forward and rested her elbows on her knees, putting her head in her hands.

Jack put his arm around her, pulling her close. 'Darling Effie, I know it's hard to believe it now but one day you will be happy again. *We* will be happy, together. I shall make it so, in time.'

In a muffled voice, Effie said, 'Tell me the story. Tell me again about the house where we're going to live.'

In the warm clearing all was silent save for the chirrup of grasshoppers in the bracken and a woodpecker far away drumming for its mate.

'The house that Mr and Mrs Stamford will live in is a small house in Ordnance Row,' Jack began, 'but solid, in a terrace of four, all junior officers' houses. There's a little garden to plant with all your favourites: sweet peas and roses and gillyflowers.' He paused to kiss her forehead. Her eyes were shut tight as if she were watching on the back of her eyelids the scenes he painted.

'At the far end of the gardens is a washing yard where the

wives gather and gossip and swap receipts for their best dishes, while they're pegging out the sheets. The house itself has a sunny parlour where the Stamfords will sit and talk together or entertain their neighbours, and in the winter we shall be snug either side of a good fire.'

''Tis make-believe,' Effie said.

He turned her face towards him and kissed her cheek. 'There are two good bedchambers,' he said. 'In the large one we shall have a feather mattress as deep as a hayrick and twice as soft.' He leant his forehead against hers. 'The other room is tiny but there is space for a cradle and a truckle bed too, one day, when we are blessed again . . .'

''Tis just a fairy tale,' Effie whispered, a catch in her voice.

'Trust me.' He kissed her softly on the lips. 'We will make it true.'

Three weeks later, dressed in silk and with fine lace at sleeves and throat, Effie stood waiting anxiously in the church porch with her matrons of honour, Ann and Sarah, Jack's sisters-in-law. Two of his little nieces sat upon a wooden bench seat, fidgeting and swinging their feet.

From outside in the lane, deep male voices drifted. Jack had arranged that, after the wedding, the path to the lychgate was to be lined with redcoats standing to attention, and that they were to pass under the crossed swords held aloft in their honour. The men's jovial conversation was punctuated by the higher voices and laughter of the children who were gathering, ready for the thrill of climbing on to the churchyard wall with their handfuls of wild flowers, to shower them with petals. Effie tugged at her sleeves in nervous excitement, thinking of all the villagers who would turn out for the spectacle.

The heavy studded doors of the church were open a crack

and Effie peeped through. Jack's family filled most of the pews. His father and brothers were dressed in sober clerical grey; the wives' bonnets nodded as they talked; children squirmed round to talk to others behind them and babies were handed from lap to lap. Effie's side was woefully thin, just one pew lined with the women with whom she used to pick snowdrops, the younger ones bright with ribbons, giggling and nudging each other.

The curate was to come and fetch her, there being no kin to walk her down the aisle, and Effie watched anxiously for his appearance. She was grateful, of course, for Parson Hawkins's sensitive suggestion, but could not help but be a little tearful when she imagined how proudly her father would have led her in, or with what solemn care Tobias, gangly in his Sunday best, would have discharged the duty. She did not know Parson Hawkins or the curate and, for all their kindness, neither did they know her. She was to be given away by a stranger.

She pushed the door open a little further and a shaft of light fell upon the stone flags. Jack and his elder brother took their places beneath the pulpit, backs stiff and straight, Jack's red coat neat and spruce, belt and boots polished to a deep shine. Effie wished that he would turn round, if only for a moment. She longed for his reassuring look. He would not turn. It was not the custom. She must wait until the curate came and flute and viol started to play as they made their entrance, before she could look on his face.

Ann touched her arm gently. 'Your veil . . . I fear it may be coming loose?' she said shyly, for they were still new to each other, although they were to be sisters.

Effie's hands flew to her head.

'May I?' Ann asked. She fastened the veil of net lace more firmly above the coil of Effie's hair. Effie thought of Beulah and how much she would have loved to be her maid. She blinked hard.

The lychgate creaked open and they all turned to see what late guest was arriving. An old bent figure, dressed in a threadbare coat and waistcoat, and old-fashioned gaiters, made his way slowly up the path.

'Why 'tis old Martin the shepherd – Mr Eben!' Effie said. 'However have you come all this way?'

'An early start and Shanks's pony, m'dear,' Martin said, smiling broadly at the assembled company. 'Ladies.' He bowed, sweeping off his battered hat, and then clapped it on to the head of the smallest bridesmaid, making her laugh and wriggle.

'I'm so glad to see you.' Effie held out her hand and he enclosed it within his own, the knuckles red, the palms deeply seamed.

'Well, it crossed my mind that you might need an arm to lean on, your father being gone. And though mine might not be the sturdiest, 'tis nonetheless willing, like, should you need it.'

Effie squeezed his hand tight and her thank you came out in a whisper.

'Well, who'd miss such a chance? A wedding breakfast with much drinking-of-healths and speechifying! Why, 'tis only right to come along to touch glasses and wish you both luck.'

The curate arrived and, taking in the scene, smiled and shook hands with Martin. At a nod from Effie, Ann reached behind her, lifted the edge of her veil and brought it down over her face. Closed in, behind its gauzy folds, everything around her was softened, as if she looked through a fine mist. Martin held out his arm and she took it; then they were walking in procession behind the curate as flute and fiddle struck up and filled the high space with cheerful sound. Faces looked towards her, all of them smiling, and she, looking only for one face, one smile, saw Jack turn, his eyes soft and full of expectation.

The parson stood at the altar, beaming. He spoke of marriage being ordained for the mutual society, help and comfort that the one ought to have of the other, and for the procreation of children, and then they made their vows. 'Who giveth this woman to be joined to this man?' he asked and Martin spoke out and handed her forward. As her eyes met Jack's, her heart filled with a joy louder than any music, higher than the lofty space around her, and she took her place at his side.

TWENTY

In the middle of January, Rosie received two letters that filled her with new hope and energy.

The first was from Mr Douglas, the solicitor, informing her that her case had been successful and that an increase to her maintenance payments had been awarded. Rosie, reading the letter in the hall, where she'd swooped on it as soon as she saw the solicitors' logo on the envelope, let out a huge sigh of relief. The little bit extra each week would let her finish readying the house for sale. It struck her that once she would have felt fearful of Josh's response, the snide comments and petty revenges he indulged in whenever he didn't get his own way, but since their confrontation at Christmas she felt that something in their relationship had shifted. She thought he was now less likely to take her on, and, perhaps even more importantly, she felt less vulnerable to his criticism. She had stopped worrying what he thought about her; *she didn't care.*

She hired a skip and Rob and Tally joined her to clear out the cellar. Together they hauled out all the rubbish and dumped it in the big yellow container in the road, turning the cellar into an empty echoey space. In daylight and fresh air, the bedstead, cupboard, boxes and mirror lay higgledy-piggledy in the bottom of the skip with the pitiful look of any unwanted, everyday objects.

'Better?' Tally said.

'Much,' Rosie replied.

Once the cellar was clear, Rob got a mate who was a builder to check the crack in the wall and confirm that the structure was sound and Rosie was extremely grateful to have no further reason to go down there. Feeling that a weight had been lifted from her shoulders, she pressed on and did most of the decorating and was ready to tackle the garden.

Her plan was to have the house ready for sale by the spring. They would stay until it sold, so that she could show prospective buyers around a house that seemed warm and lived-in. Then, in the longer term, once they were back in London, Sam would start school and she would find a nursery place for Cara. She would make an appointment at the teaching agency and say that she was keen to take on supply work again. She felt sure that once she could guarantee that she was reliably free she would pick up work easily; it was all about being around and available.

The second letter came a few days later and was postmarked Oxford. As she eased the sheet of paper from the brown envelope, she saw the letterhead of a small indie publisher to whom she'd sent print samples. She expected the same polite rejection that she'd received from others at intervals over the past few months. Her eyes scanned the letter: *We are pleased to tell you . . . impressed by your portfolio . . . unique style . . . a children's book . . .* She let out a yelp of surprise and delight. If she was agreeable in principle, they would like to send her the full manuscript and then fix a date to discuss her ideas with the art director. She sat on the bottom step of the stairs and read the synopsis that was attached; it was a story set in Tibet about a boy called Tashi and his adventures in the mountains. At once she was picturing spinning prayer wheels, cross-legged statues of Buddha and horned yak with woven woollen saddles. She wrote back that evening to say that she agreed and would love to meet up. The payment offered was modest and the publisher small but it could be the start of something that might grow. For a moment she dreamt of being able to make a living as an illustrator – what bliss to be free to work away in the quiet, light-filled room upstairs on projects that would fill her with enthusiasm and ignite her imagination! If only she could get regular commissions they could afford to stay here, amongst friends, instead of going back to the poky flat. The rent agreement was due for renewal in February. What if she didn't renew, tried to sell her own work instead of going back to teaching, moved up here wholesale? It was an idea, and sometimes you had to make a leap of faith . . . She reined herself in. The thought of going entirely freelance scared her. She hadn't got the nerve to take the risk.

Still, the letter was wonderful news. She hadn't touched pen and ink for months, hadn't even felt the urge to sketch. This would make her pick up a pen again and she was thrilled to have the chance of a proper commission.

There was one last snowfall that remained for a week and then a thaw that left the world rinsed clean and returned to colour once again. In the garden, beneath a cold, clear sky, the red stems of dogwood glowed against the fence and yellow algae painted the bark of the trees.

While Cara was at playgroup one afternoon, Rosie and Sam, wrapped up round and fat in layers of clothing, wearing scarves, gloves and beanie hats, had come outside and were making a start on clearing the undergrowth. Rosie was chopping with secateurs through the woody stems of brambles and dragging them out. Some were yards long and she made Sam laugh when she pulled them and the undergrowth twitched and shivered at the very end of the garden; they had bets on which would prove to be the longest.

Each time she cleared a patch, pulling out nettles and docks once the briars were out, Sam's job was to fill up his little blue wheelbarrow with the old bricks and bits of mortar beneath and trundle them over to the sacks which Rosie planned to add to the skip. He was in his element, doing the job of a loader for real, and Rosie felt quietly companionable as they worked alongside each other, Sam puffing back and forth with cheeks pinched pink by the cold air.

Rosie paused to stretch her back and Sam parked his wheelbarrow beside her. 'It'll look so much better when we get rid of all this mess,' Rosie said, thinking aloud. 'It'll double the useable space and we'll get the path back again, maybe even open the door up at the bottom so we can get out the back way.'

'Can we have grass? For football?' Sam said.

'Mmm, it's a thought. Maybe I'll turf it to make it look tidy to help sell the house.'

'Can I have goal posts?'

'Well, I'm not sure it'll be worth it. There's no garden to put them in back at the flat, is there?'

353

Sam looked grumpy. He picked up the handlebars of the empty barrow and began running it at the pile of weeds and rubble, banging it against it with a clang.

'Don't do that, Sam. You'll chip the paint off it and then it'll get rusty.'

Sam carried on.

'Sam!'

He stopped.

'Maybe when we're back in London we can find a football scheme for you to join. Would you like that?'

Sam shrugged, picked up a stick and dropped it into the barrow.

'Or when we move back and you start school in September, perhaps they'll play football in the games lessons. That would be good, wouldn't it?'

'I don't want to go to school,' Sam muttered.

Rosie squatted beside him, getting down to his level. They had had this conversation before.

'Why not?'

He clamped his mouth shut, pushing forward his lower lip.

'You'll have to go to school sometime this year, love. You'll soon be five. Everyone has to go before they're five, you know.'

Silence. She put her hand, huge in its leather gardening glove, on his arm.

'Do you feel a bit nervous about it? Everybody feels nervous on the first day but they soon make friends.'

'I'm not going there.' Sam pulled away. He tipped the barrow so that it lay face down on the pile. 'I'm going in to watch telly.' He mooched off and Rosie left him to himself. He would feel better when he'd warmed up indoors and forget all about his mood once he was engrossed in a programme. She would leave tackling the question of school for the moment.

She turned back to the task in hand, pulling out handfuls of sticky weed before starting once more to cut back brambles and shift the rubble beneath to a pile behind her, beside the fence. She had cleared a good area this afternoon and had reached as far as the mulberry tree. She hesitated and stood back, considering it. Its boughs drooped to the ground in places, its knuckles in the earth like a gigantic malformed hand. The wintry sun hung low in the sky and the gnarled growth threw long twisted shadows across the undergrowth within its cage.

Steeling herself, she began to work her way in between two branches. She pulled out and cut the tough brambles, tightly wound with crisp, dry twists of old bindweed. Then she chopped nettles back with shears and dragged out the soggy mops of old bluebell plants beneath, their leaves pale yellow and slimy. Clearing the mound of plants from under one of the branches, bowed low to the ground by its own ancient weight, she found a rusty iron stake supporting it.

It reminded her of the old iron stove flue in the cellar and she shuddered. It's only a piece of metal, she told herself: a gardener's prop. She must get a hold of herself before she started letting in black thoughts. Yet as she moved past it, stooping to enter the cave of branches, the cold seemed to seep into her, rising from the very earth.

In here, Rosie! Quick! Get under!

Maria's voice called to her as the years fled away, drawing her into the hiding place under the boughs and gathering her and Lily close, so close that she could smell sherbert on Lily's breath and feel the warmth of her against her side. She remembered, clear and strong, her mother's voice, *Coming . . . ready or not . . .* and the delicious terror of being found, the fearful anticipation, their hearts beating fast together, she and Lily pressed against each other tight as pigeons in a basket. The sense of loss was a physical ache, in her chest, in her belly. Oh, where were they now – Lily, Mum? There was no one to find her, however much she longed to be found. She leant against a branch for a moment, feeling empty and desolate.

Around the trunk of the tree, thick as mistletoe, ivy grew in a great tangled mess, choking it. She bent over it, cutting as low as she could and pulling lengths of trailing growth away, the shadow of the branches above casting their own tangled bars across her back. These bleak thoughts were dangerous. She tried to shut them out, concentrate only on what needed to be done, drown out her feelings through physical movement, but still her sadness deepened, as if in cutting her way to the centre of this neglected ground she had disturbed something that brooded there, the deep melancholy that she had sensed before answering her own.

Gradually, as she worked, she became aware of faint sounds behind her. In her ear was a child's fast breath, panting, gasping with effort, and then, stronger, a strange, repeated scrape and slide that seemed to echo above it.

Rosie's fingers stilled. She stood with her hands hovering above glossy ivy leaves, the tough stems a mat surrounding the trunk, squeezing the life out of it. She wanted to clear space and to let in the light but she had begun to tire. It was impossible, the task too big, her will too weak; she was clearing not just stems and shoots but something else, something strong that reached out with grasping tendrils, entwining, covering, burying. *I won't let her come, I won't let her come,* she repeated to herself. This time she wouldn't be cowed and she would not run. She worked on, ignoring the sounds behind her, labouring breaths with a sob caught in the throat, the scraping sound faster and more desperate. Rosie grasped the roots and pulled upwards, stripping the tough ivy shoots from the bark. They came away, leaving a network of smaller threads and tiny suckers, pale brown needles prickling from the wood. She tore at it with both hands and didn't stop until she'd pulled the last tangle away and the tree was free of its girdle of green. Sweating and exhausted, she leant her head on her hands against the trunk's grey bark. Behind her, there was a sound of something heavy thrown down and then nothing more.

Heart hammering, she forced herself to look back over her shoulder. There was nothing but the tangled mass of briar and rubble surrounding her and her own small path cutting through it: no pale face with its expression of appeal, no crouched body barring her way, just silence now and a sense of sadness so intense that it almost overwhelmed her.

Bent double, she came out from under the branches and stood back, panting and drained. She'd had enough. The tree's broad girth stood naked and open to the air but it still stood knee-deep in weeds on three sides. Still the sadness hung there, dark and chill, like the exhalation from an old vault that has seen no sun for centuries when a slab is pulled away. She picked up her tools and trudged back to the house.

That evening, after she'd put Cara to bed, Rosie went to tuck Sam in. She sat down beside him and read him a chapter of *Moominland Midwinter*. 'I'm glad we don't have to hibernate when it snows, aren't you?' she said. 'It would be very boring with no one to play with.'

'I s'pose,' Sam said, still turning the pages and looking ahead at the pictures.

'The thing is,' Rosie ventured, 'I think that now you're getting such a big boy, you need plenty of friends to play with, and when everyone else goes off to school you would get bored at home.'

'I don't want to stay at home,' Sam said, scowling.

'But you told me you don't want to go to school either?'

'I don't want to go to *that* school.'

Rosie was so surprised that all she could say was 'Oh'. They hadn't even been to see the school in Streatham yet; how on earth could Sam have got it into his head that he wouldn't like it? 'Where do you want to go then?'

'I want to go to school with Amy.'

'Aah. I see,' Rosie said, relieved on one count, for school did seem to hold some attraction, and worried on another, as separating Sam and Amy when they moved was obviously going to be an issue.

Her phone rang downstairs and she said, 'OK, we'll talk some more about this another day. Night night, chump-chop.' She kissed him and tucked the duvet up to his chin before running downstairs.

She caught her breath and fished her phone out of her bag but she was just too late. Looking at the number, she didn't recognise it. She put the phone down and started to stack up the plates from teatime and take them over to the sink. A minute later the phone rang again. She dumped the plates with a clatter, wiped her hands on her jeans and took the call.

'Hello, yes?'

'It's Tom Marriott here. I wondered if you got the letter about your settlement all right?' he said in a cheery voice.

Rosie was puzzled, wondering why he was ringing out of working hours and, more to the point, when he had handed the case over to someone else. 'Yes, thanks. I did ring and thank Mr Douglas, actually,' she said rather stiffly.

'Oh, right,' he said. He recovered his stride. 'Well, I was just ringing to see if I could take you out to lunch to celebrate, maybe some time next week?'

Rosie thought this rather cheeky considering he'd dropped the case. Surely if she celebrated with anyone it should be with the man who'd done the work, although the thought of having lunch with the ancient Mr Douglas with his droopy moustache and clipped manner seemed unappealing, and also very odd. 'Do you do this for all your clients?'

'Well, no . . .' He sounded amused.

'Well then.'

'You're a hard woman, Rosie Milford! If you don't want to celebrate your good news, how about joining me to celebrate mine? I've finally got my own flat again so I'm out of my mum's and Viv's hair at last.'

Rosie was puzzled.

He went on, 'I'm not sure how much help I was there, really; I'm all fingers and thumbs with babies. David's back now anyhow.'

'Who's David?' she said in confusion.

'Oh, sorry, he's my brother-in-law. He works overseas; that's why my sister was staying at Mum's for a while to get a bit of help from us with the baby.'

Sister! Rosie did a mental double-take. So the baby stuff he'd bought at the supermarket had been for his niece, not his daughter, and the Christmas card . . . well *of course* that was only from him – he wasn't married. *He wasn't married.* A sudden burst of excitement at the possibilities warred with crushing embarrassment at the way she'd behaved. Whatever must he have thought about her frostiness?

Her silence had lasted so long that he began again. 'Look, I know you probably felt let down when I transferred the case. The truth is I wanted to ask you to have lunch with me but I didn't feel I could while I was acting for you – you know, fraternising with a client, ethics and all that – and then when

I told you Mr Douglas was taking over and I walked you to your car, you seemed so cross I couldn't get out what I wanted to say so I just stood there like an idiot and watched you drive away.' He paused. 'Are you still angry?'

Rosie, who found she was holding her breath, gasped, 'No.'

There was a moment's silence in which Rosie felt he might be smiling. 'So, will you have lunch with me to celebrate my new flat?'

'Like a date . . .'

'Yes.' He was definitely smiling. 'So like a date, in fact, that it'll be exactly that.'

'Sorry, I'm a bit out of practice.' Why on earth had she said 'like a date'? She sounded about fourteen. She felt about fourteen, she thought ruefully. 'Um, where did you have in mind?'

'Say, La Pergola, on Friday? One o'clock?'

'That would be lovely,' she said, slipping back into adult politeness. They said their goodbyes and she hung up.

Blimey. A date. With Tom Marriott of the crinkly eyes and the gallant manners. She sat down on a kitchen chair and ran through her itinerary for the week ahead. Could she get into town to get a new top, or maybe a dress? And perhaps get her hair cut – it was a bit dry and frazzled-looking at the ends. Maybe there was a good side to feeling like a teenager; she hadn't felt this bubbling, lifted feeling, this fizzing excitement, for years. It was nice. Even if it came to nothing, it felt good.

TWENTY-ONE

1822

A young woman stands at a gate on the ridge, looking out over the village of Weedon Royal. Her skin is as brown as a cobnut and she is dressed in the gypsy fashion: her skirt above the ankles and her boots laced tight, the better for running when there's the need. Her clothes are ragged at wrists and hem and a triangle of blue cloth is tied over her hair, which is braided and hangs down her back.

On the other side of the valley, the barracks and arsenal rise from the water meadows in redbrick, foursquare solidity: angular blocks at odds with the soft rounds of trees on the slope below. They impose upon the landscape, a physical expression of power: storehouses of potential destruction filled with soldier after soldier, thousands of muskets, and barrel after barrel of powder.

Below them, the village lies in a pool of early-morning mist. The slate roofs of the taller buildings float above it like open books laid face down and the church tower is truncated to a dumpy lookout post.

The young woman, Beulah, is searching for one roof, one particular building. The mist changes the topography; the houses no longer huddled and crowded together. There is white space between the occasional buildings that rear through it, so that bearings are lost. Nonetheless, despite this and the lapse of years, once she finds the long straight run of the roof of a three-storey building she instantly knows it for the silk factory. She leans her elbows on the bar of the gate, which is coarse-grained with pale green lichen, and looks out over the place that haunts her, remembering . . .

She can hear the clack and clatter of the looms that seemed to vibrate the very bricks and timbers of the place. The smell of the cellar, the sweet, musty scent of herbs barely overlaying the odour of rot, is in her nostrils, and the feel of Fowler's grip as he shoved her against the wall is on her flesh. Sliding to the ground, she had cowered down; her hands travelling over the brick floor, feeling for the metallic scrape of the scissors and then grasping them. In terror, she saw the Master's intention in his eyes as he turned the whip around and knew she had but a moment to act.

As he covered her mouth she brought the scissors down upon his forearm with all her force. He cried out and let his hand drop. In the second that he stood staring at his arm in stupefaction, she scrambled away from him and was at the cellar steps before he had dashed the scissors to the ground, and up them before he had roared after her, clutching his wound and bellowing like the very devil. Then she was out, out into the bright sunlight and running for her life, past the carpenter's shed, past the end of the building, round the corner to the street where a cart was pulling away, and on, to the road out of the village.

She ran uphill until her mouth tasted full of salt and she felt her chest would burst. She crouched over with her hands on her knees, gasping until she got back her breath, and then slipped through a field gate and ran again, heading across country to home and to Effie, who would know what to do.

There were men at the cottage. She hid in the hedge at the back of the house, watching one hammering boards across the windows and another catching the hens. When he caught one, he held it upside down by the feet. The man examined each bird, pulling its wings wide and prodding its breast. He shoved some, squawking, into a crate and pulled the necks of others with a sharp twist and a snap and then dropped them, limp, into a sack. She thought of Alice holding up the baby and saying, 'There's no life in it,' and felt sick.

She stayed under the hedge, curled up tight with her arms around her knees. She was afraid of what might happen, with the men there, if Effie came back. She wondered if Effie had already returned and was hiding in the house and would be trapped there. At last, the other man stopped hammering and put his tools into his belt. The two of them went off together, one carrying the crate and the other with the sack over his shoulder, chatting amicably as if this ruin of her home, her life, was all in a day's work. Their voices faded away down the lane. She waited, shivering, until it was utterly silent and then a little longer until the sounds of the songbirds returned, before coming out.

As she crept down the path alongside the washing that hung all haphazardly from the line, her steps raised tiny white feathers from the ground. They floated around her and fell again to catch in the glistening grass. She went to every boarded window, tapping and calling, 'Effie! Effie! It's only me, Beulah,' but there was no answer. She called louder through a crack in the planks across the door, 'Are you in there? It's safe now – they've gone!' The evening settled back to stillness, the peaceful murmuring of the doves in the hawthorn thicket at odds with the scene of desolation.

She sat on the doorstep and, after a while, played a game, idly throwing pebbles at a gap between the slats of the gate. She waited and waited. The air began to cool and she started to be afraid of night coming. She got to thinking that Effie must have been caught. She knew that having a baby without being wed could mean you were sent to gaol. The thought of being locked up made her mortal afeared. What if they were to come for her too? She didn't want to stay there, with the bats flitting around the eaves and an owl calling from the thicket, wondering all night if every squeak or crackle was the creak of a horse's harness or the rustle of a man's coat. There was no one to go to. Tobias was lost to her and she could go to no one at the factory for fear that the master would hear of it and find her; in any case, Biddy would have less idea what to do than she did. But soon she would lose the light . . . She hesitated and then decided. She would go to find Hanzi at Castle Dykes.

She shakes herself and narrows her eyes against the eastern sun, focusing on the long roof, glistening with dew, filling in from her memory the tall walls and rows of windows below, the scullery door and the pigsty beyond.

Beneath the mist, somewhere in the rows of trees behind the building, is a tree with a baby in its roots. In her dreams, the cage of its ribs is laced with curled taproots like two clenched hands. Its skull is a hollow cup, small as a bird's nest, and its finger bones are tiny sticks adrift in a sea of earth. Always it calls to her: from the ashes of campfires, from the gnat-filled shade beneath the trees where the horses are tethered, from the empty moors with their desolate spaces; and in the small hours its crying rouses her so that she thinks her own children have woken.

None of the others wanted to come back here. Over the last ten years, every time their meandering route has passed within fifty miles of this place she has asked Hanzi to help her persuade them to make camp at Castle Dykes. *Just once, just to let me search for my sister,* she has said every time: *please, Hanzi . . . I can't rest . . . if you love me . . .* She has worn him down. Despite his concern that only bad will come of it, this time he stood beside her while she told the others that she must go back. He bore witness to the nightmares that afflict her and the sadness that sometimes fills her until she feels she is drowning in it. He can see that she has no peace.

Yesterday, when they pulled into the clearing, the sign she had left for Effie was gone – but then so was the wood store, tumbled and rotted by wind and weather. She had hurried back to the cottage, in the forlorn hope that there might be some message, some indication that Effie had been back there, but she found the place derelict. The boards had been stripped from it, the planks jemmied off and even the door wrenched from its hinges, all taken for firewood. The windows were smashed and the rooms full of damp and beetles. The roof of the neighbouring cottage was completely fallen in, the gable end pointing emptily at the sky.

On the road to the village, a woman she didn't recognise came out from the farm, with two barking dogs on rope leashes. She took one look at her gypsy clothes and threatened to set the dogs on her. Beulah turned back and hurried away.

''Tis too dangerous,' Hanzi said. 'We leave tomorrow. Early.'

There is not much time. She has crept away from the camp, and come here at first light before even the ploughboys are up, to look over the valley and think of Effie and of the baby and be sorry.

Sometimes she imagines finding Effie again, how they would fall on each other's necks and weep with joy after all these years. Yet always in this daydream, as they step apart, Effie looks at her with a face turned to sorrow and asks her, 'Where is my baby?' And what can she say in reply? That she buried a living child deep in the ground and fled . . . That she was too afraid to save him? She has done a wickedness that cannot be undone.

'Where can I go to mourn?' Effie's sad face asks her and there is no cross or stone to show her. There is not even a small mound outside a churchyard wall to take her to, in the line where other infants lie, who died without a father's name or words said over them by priest or parson. There is no marker save a tree, the same as any other in the row. Now, she could not even tell which tree it was. So she has come to stand in this place despite the horror of the memories of the cellar, Fowler, her terrified flight – drawn back to gaze at the scene of her sin, a penitent who can find no rest.

Hanzi tries to help her. When she wakes from a bad dream, shaking and cold, he puts their youngest in her arms and tucks the blanket tight around them all. He doesn't understand that since she has had her own children it has brought home to her the enormity of what she did. Sometimes, in the evenings, while the others drink and sing, she can do nothing but stare into the flames of the fire. When she's asked why she's silent she says that she thinks of her family scattered to the four winds and a child who should never have been lost.

Hanzi says, 'We have our own family now.'

And she should listen, she knows. There are joys in this life: Hanzi, her children, the woods and moors and mountains she's seen, and familiar, known faces around a campfire in the midst of a wilderness. She knows that, alone, fending for herself, she would founder: soon taken into the House of Correction as a vagrant; but within her clan she's stronger. One man cannot arrest the whole band of them and, at the first sign of trouble, fleet and secret, they move on. She couldn't bear to live within four walls now; she'd find it stultifying, oppressive; she prefers the scatter of stars across the black triangle of the open tent flap, the smell of woodsmoke and the hiss of the fire.

It is a difficult life though, and she is often afraid. She is afraid when she goes out before dawn to milk a farmer's cow, creeping into the field, whispering to the beast and warming her hands on its flank. Each time they enter a new village she is afraid: of the barking dogs, of the taunts and jeers and of being spat upon and called pikey and rumney and gypsy's whore.

It *is* a hard life but she wouldn't change it. At least she can smell the clean air, feel the sun on her face and move through God's good earth. A gypsy's fears and hardships are transitory: thrown stones can be dodged, cold and hunger come and go with the seasons and can sometimes be cheated with guile and light fingers. It's not like the constant grinding hardship and fear of the factory worker, where every slip may bring a blow,

367

and a word spoken out of turn may mean dismissal and the workhouse.

She knows that masters such as Fowler exist in almost every mill and workshop. She's heard of children found hiding in the stores, too exhausted to go home, being whipped by the overseer where they lay, of beatings with a wetted strap and indecent liberties taken with the bigger girls. Stories are shared at Appleby, where the gypsies gather, offered up by other run-aways: masters who would take girls by the hair with one hand and slap them with the other – big or little, it made no difference; and boy apprentices hung by tied hands from a cross-beam, and left there.

When she thinks of the great body of humanity she knows that most of it is poor, starved, ragged and dirty, while the few live on their lifeblood as surely as ticks live on a sheep. To the masters, men are become only parts of their machines. They don't consider them human beings, but have shrunk them to merely 'hands'; they are reduced simply to their useful working parts. Her father used to tell her of the days of his childhood, when a man could live off the common land or ply his trade and be beholden to no one and independent in his views. Now men are no better than slaves: to an overseer, to the clock, to the moving parts of a machine. Never again will anyone have such power over her. Being an outcast is the price she has to pay for that freedom but she pays it gladly. She will never again call anyone master.

She gazes, snow-blind, at the fog that laps the roof of the silk factory. Somewhere beneath the mist, the dark wet trunks of the mulberry trees are pillars in the vapour; droplets form on leaves and twigs to gather and drip into the white silence. She knows that, forever, she will dream this place, her spirit drawn

368

to that of the buried child. She has no way of making amends and the past will never give her rest. This is her burden and she must bear it.

It is growing late but still she stands motionless, a dark silhouette high above the milky valley.

TWENTY-TWO

Rosie sits at the table in the room on the top floor, sketching out a mountain scene with Buddhist pilgrims climbing a winding road to a cloudy summit. She is happy, her consciousness hovering between the airy room, with its high ceiling and white walls, and the peaks and waterfalls forming in fluid lines of ink on the creamy cartridge paper. She is aware of both worlds, suspended between them in the half-trance state of creation. Something is forming in the back of her mind, something indeterminate between thought and feeling, so that she's not even sure if it relates to art or life.

She has heard a sculptor say that the figure he creates exists already within the block of stone and what he does is to find it: to chip away what is extraneous and liberate it. Her own work often feels like this, a search, through the movement of her hand, for the shape of an inner vision already complete, but the feeling she has today is more expansive; the joy she feels in painting is part of something bigger, more momentous.

A sparrow lands in a flutter on the windowsill in front of her and she looks up and is distracted. It's no good forcing such things, in any case; whatever the insight is, it will come in its own good time. The bird is a little ball, its feathers fluffed out against the cold. The breeze lifts and parts them. The sky is a bright, clear blue and the sun has melted the frost away in all but the shadiest corners. She rests her chin on her hands and looks down on the garden.

Where once there was waist-high undergrowth, there is now fresh, newly laid turf. She has cleared a path to the back gate, and the last of the brambles and bindweed is in the incinerator waiting to be burnt. She's worked hard, the last few days, and now the garden looks twice its old size. Sam loves to play in the sunny open patch at the bottom, where she's chalked a goalmouth on the fence. She's pleased with the result of her labours, only . . . Underneath the spreading arms of the mulberry tree, the shade is still gloomy and the grass looks bare and cheerless. She thinks, I could plant bulbs but they wouldn't flower until after we've gone back to London.

She wishes that her mother could have seen the garden cleared. It would have given her pleasure, perhaps reminded her of how it used to look when they first lived here. They could have replanted the borders together. Her eyes well up and she blinks and reaches to touch her mum's glasses, always kept on the desk in front of her, amongst her ink bottles. She runs her finger around their tortoiseshell rims, experiencing the familiar pain of loss.

371

As if her mother is answering a question she's not even aware she's framed, an idea comes. Snowdrops! Her mother always said that they do better if you plant them not as dry bulbs but 'in the green', as grown plants. She'd had clumps of them growing in the shade of the hedge at the cottage in Somerset; they were one of her favourite flowers. Rosie imagines how they would brighten the ground beneath the old mulberry tree. They would glimmer beautifully against the shaded grass and bring movement to its sombre stillness as the wind shook them.

The idea has hold of her now: she will plant them in memory of Mum, and Lily. A memorial garden. She screws on the lids of the inkpots and washes her brushes automatically, calculating how long she has before she needs to set off to pick up the children from Josh, how long it will take her to get to and from the garden centre and to do the planting, already knowing that she must do this, that it must be today, that it just feels *right*. She hurries downstairs to gather up her coat and keys.

One by one, she carries the trays of flowerpots from the car and places them in the half-shade at the edge of the mulberry tree. There's no breeze so before she starts she puts a match to the firelighters in the bottom of the incinerator, poking it through the hole in the side. There's a paraffin smell and flames lick up the sides of the white blocks, catch on dry grass and begin to sizzle through the bundled undergrowth. She stands watching for a while as the weeds curl and shrivel, spitting and crackling, but she doesn't hold her cold hands to the warmth. The fire is about ritual, not comfort. It is a cleansing, the burning away of old things, making way for the new. Yellow flames shoot from the funnel in the lid, flickering and hazing the air above it, the fence behind wavering out of true.

Rosie gathers her tools and a kneeling pad and stoops in under the low branches, pulling one of the trays in after her. She cuts a cross in the turf, peels it back and digs a hole three inches deep, then more holes, each a few inches apart. After sprinkling a little sharp sand into each, she tucks in small groups of plants, tenderly patting the turf up to the stems. She works methodically but to a carefully random pattern. Thinking of Lily, she doesn't want the drifts of flowers arranged in waves – she cannot have them foaming across the grass to break on the trunk of the tree. She aims instead for rounded shapes, tries to think of pillows, rest, peaceful sleep.

Sitting back on her heels, she touches a flower, lifting its drooping head with her forefinger. She remembers how her mother used to say that a snowdrop is like three drops of milk hanging from a stem and sees that this is true. Her mother's voice is in her head, 'Galanthus,' she says. 'It means milk-white flowers. My grandmother used to say that her great-great-grandmother was a snowdrop picker . . . that's not a job you hear of any more . . .'

Rosie wonders if this ancestor too came from these parts. How far back had the family lived around here? She thinks about the nuttery over at Newnham, where snowdrops used to be harvested right up to the 1920s. She's read about it somewhere. It stuck in her mind that the flowers were laid in boxes between layers of blue tissue paper and sent up to Covent Garden. Maybe, way back in the nineteenth century, that's where she'd worked as a picker. How strange to think of all those forebears living in one small corner of a county, generation after generation; perhaps she and her mother had even been the first to break away. Suddenly, she doesn't want

373

to think of going back to London or of someone else living here. The house and garden have come to mean something to her, to be part of her history – and May is here. The place and May are all she has left to connect her to her family origins, to give her a sense of belonging. 'My native place,' that's what Mum had called it, as though her life had grown from here and was rooted in its soil.

Belonging. After all the ache of loss, it is what she craves the most. It isn't only that she's found a close friend in Tally, or that she chats with people in the street, has joined a book group, talks to other mums outside playgroup, or even that she wants to know Tom Marriott better, although all these things are important. It's about having a place in the world that means something to her.

She returns to her digging, but slowly, thoughtfully.

Although she doesn't pray, she feels each plant that she sets in place is a kind of blessing. Mum, Lily, oh my lost ones, she thinks, how I love you and miss you. You are my family, my flesh and blood. She thinks of the strength of the tie of blood: the thread that still joins her to Lily and to their mother, the web stretching backwards to people unknown who yet form part of her, and forwards through Sam and Cara to those she will never know, yet of whom she will be a part. As she plants, the insight that she has felt just beyond her reach all day begins to crystallise: a slow, satisfying realisation. She is going to stay.

On her knees, she works on steadily, leaning forward under the low branches, reaching right under the branch with the rusty iron stake into all the darkest frost-dampened corners. Tiny pieces of bark catch in her hair.

As she reaches the trunk, about to continue around it and beyond, it is as if she's rolling back the shade. Behind her it is punctuated with glimmering, waxy-petalled light but before her the shadow seems deeper, as if something has been gathered in: an intensification of shade and stillness . . . and something else . . . a sense of someone waiting. She forces herself not to think about the girl, fights to block out the image of her crouching here, *right here*, elbow-deep in weeds as Rosie looked down, months ago, from the top-storey window and felt afraid.

Instead, she rehearses what she knows about snowdrops. 'Moly,' she says to herself sternly. 'The classical name for the snowdrop is moly. It was given to Odysseus to make him immune to the poisons of the witch, Circe.' It occurs to her that the witch's potion was to make captured sailors forget their homes and loved ones. *An antidote to forgetfulness. It's the perfect flower for a memorial.*

On her knees, Rosie cuts and digs. She sprinkles and plants. Behind her, something in the fire burns through and gives way, making her jump. The ashes settle with a sigh. After the sound, the stillness is heavy, the silence pregnant, as if she's being watched by someone who is waiting to speak. She carries on, pushing forward into the icy cold. She is going to do it, come what may. She is going to finish the job.

At the far edge of the tree's canopy she plants the last clumps of flowers in a broad swathe of white. She stumbles stiffly to her feet and steps back to look at her work. The fire has burned out and it is perfectly quiet. Beneath the tangled branches with their gnarled shapes and peeling bark, drifts of white flowers, each one new, smooth, perfect, reflect the light.

A breeze seems to pass through the garden, shaking the flowers, a shiver running through them, as if brushed by someone's skirt. The movement flows towards her yet Rosie feels no rushing draught upon her face or hands, only the slightest disturbance of the air, as if someone has passed her, close enough to touch.

The flowers are still again, each delicate head drooping, and yet the sense of stillness has subtly shifted. It is no longer expectant but peaceful. Rosie feels it in her bones: something has departed.

ACKNOWLEDGEMENTS

Together with a great deal of walking in and around the village of Weedon Bec, studying the following books and articles helped me to imagine the world of silk weavers, soldiers and snowdrop-pickers in 1812:

The White Slaves of England, compiled from Official Documents by John C. Cobden 1853

The Silk Industry by Sarah Bush (2009)

The Story of Silk by Dr. John Feltwell (1990)

The Silk Industry of the United Kingdom, its origin and development by Sir Frank Warner (1921)

The Luddite Rebellion by Brian Bailey (1998)

A Dorset Soldier - The Autobiography of Sgt William Lawrence 1790 -1869 Ed. Eileen Hathaway (1993)

A Postcard from Weedon Bec by Julia Johns, Weedon Bec History Society (2004)

Weedon Royal Ordnance Depot Revisited by J.E. King, Weedon Bec History Society (1996)

Storehouse Enclosure, royal Ordnance Depot, Weedon Bec, Conservation Plan Vol II Gazeteer by Liv Gibbs. The Historic Environment Consultancy Adopted 2005

The Inhuman Taskmaster - A story of Weedon Bec – an article by Victor A. Hatley.

Like Dew before the Sun - Life and Language in Northamptonshire by Dorothy A. Grimes (1991)

Workhouses of the Midlands by Peter Higginbotham (2007)

I am also indebted to the staff of The Silk Mill museum in Derby and Whitchurch Silk Mill in Hampshire, for their patience in answering my many questions and for showing me the operation of looms and other machines.

In researching the idea of residual haunting (the Stone Tape Theory) I was grateful for the following articles: www.parascience.org.uk/articles/musings.htm, wikipedia.org/wiki/Stone_Tape and wiki/Apparitional_experience, *Recording Ghosts* at assap.ac.uk/newsite/articles, forensic-architecture.org/lexicon/stone-tape-theory and *What kind of Person sees Ghosts?* at patheos.com/blogs/epiphenom.

In addition, heartfelt thanks are due to my editor, Katie Espiner, for her perceptive comments and suggestions, expert advice and invaluable support, to my agent, Laura Longrigg for her solid belief in my books and for all her efforts on my behalf, also Cassie Browne, Charlotte Cray, Richenda Todd, Linda Joyce, Charlotte Abrams-Simpson and Ann Bissell at HarperCollins, for helping to produce this beautiful book and bring it to its readers; Lucy Anderson and Pat Kent for their good company through many long days at the library; Janet Lambdon, Lynne Jennings, Katie Hill, Susan Foley, Diana Wingrove Owen and Susie Freer for cheering me on, and my family, near and far, for their unstinting encouragement, in particular my husband, Spencer, my son and daughter, James and Lottie, my sister Louise Gillard Owen, my father, Peter Gillard, and lastly, my mother, Isabel Gillard who, though sadly no longer with us, still buoys me up through the legacy of her faith in my writing.